All In

All In

The Clandestine
Book 1

Russell Isler

Best Wishes!

Russell Isler

BOTTLED
MONSTER
PRESS

ISBN 13: 9781961479005

Cover Design by Damonza.com

1st edition 2023

For Bella

Chapter One
Now

THE CLOCK STRUCK TWELVE, HIGH NOON, AND MY front door splintered as the hit team breached my home.

Okay, ya got me, I'm exaggerating. They used a stolen key card. Happy now?

Two of the operators flanked the door while the third planted himself directly between them, his back flat against the opposite wall. Each of the three hitters was decked to the nines in this season's best tactical gear: black cargo pants, plate carriers with those little straps for holding doodads, throat mikes, earpieces, and crazy night vision goggles. Don't forget the guns. Lots of guns.

They'd booked a room downstairs out of necessity— there was no way they'd be able to waltz through the lobby or the casino floor with all that on display. No sooner had they checked in than they'd come up via the stairwells, all loaded for bear.

The hit team had picked a good time to make their move. The only other suites on my floor (the top one, naturally) were owned by a sheik and some Hollywood guy. I'd never bothered to get either of their names. The sheik was only in his suite once a year, tops. Hollywood Guy was having a power brunch at the new buffet down the street with his wife-du-year. Meaning no one was around to hear any ruckus.

The oldest of the trio, judging by the amount of gray in his buzz cut, pulled back a flap on his wrist to check his watch. He took up a position beside my door, on the side with the card reader, while producing a gold-and-scarlet card from one of his many pockets. He eased the card into a slot in the door.

I mentally dubbed him "Team Leader" since it seemed like he was running the operation.

Number Two had a utility bag slung across one shoulder. In fact, he was the only one of them carrying anything other than guns. He pressed his back to the wall opposite and aimed an odd-looking assault rifle, boxy on top with a sinuous curve to the grip underneath, at gut height to anyone who might emerge from the room.

Number Three, the fella facing the door head on, raised the biggest goddamn shotgun I'd ever seen and sighted down its length.

The trio traded a round of nods, and in one smooth movement, Team Leader tugged the card from the lock and turned the handle with two fingers. Mr. Shotgun, in sync with his leader, booted the door open and charged into my home. His weapon tracked the swivel of his head as he swept the short entry hall. Number Two pivoted to keep station on Mr. Shotgun's left as Team Leader took his right. Team Leader's hand brushed past the sidearm holstered at his hip and instead raised a contraption that resembled a paintball gun, but with a barrel wide enough to shoot golf balls.

I'd left the lights on in my digs when I'd cleared out an hour earlier, which meant the fancy night vision goggles perched on the hit team's foreheads went unused.

In response to a series of hand gestures from Team Leader, Mr. Shotgun and Number Two began clearing the suite. Number Two cracked open the door to the coat room and eased inside. Since I wasn't huddling among the overcoats, Number Two emerged a moment later to clear the guest room.

Mr. Shotgun approached the windows that made up the entire west wall of my suite. I'd invested in some serious blackout curtains soon after moving in, and at the moment, they were all drawn. Mr. Shotgun pawed around in search of a pull cord. But because the curtains were motorized, there wasn't one for him to find, so he instead wound the cloth around his mitt and heaved a stretch of curtain free of the runners. As the heavy fabric pooled around Mr. Shotgun's boots, his mouth twisted. It was clear he'd been expecting to reveal my view of the Strip in all its daylight glory.

What he'd couldn't know was that the Golden Fortune had gotten a major overhaul a few years back, and I'd taken the opportunity to have some quality-of-life items added to my home. A set of lightproof shutters had been installed in the gap between the double-paned windows, and they'd locked into place as soon as the sun rose. Mr. Shotgun bobbled his noggin around in search of a button or switch that would open them.

I'd taken the window remote with me.

Team Leader's hand cut through the air. Once Mr. Shotgun's attention was on him, he jabbed a finger toward the wet bar.

Number Two, emerging from the guest room, tapped Team Leader on the shoulder and shook his head. Team Leader jerked a thumb toward the kitchenette. Number Two nodded as he hustled to search my pantry.

Team Leader, stepping with care, moved through the

3

carpeted conversation pit in the center of the room. His bizarre weapon swept the curved couch before pausing at the coffee table. He slid the stack of men's fashion magazines aside with the barrel of his weapon, causing them to spill onto the floor.

Rude.

One by one, they converged on the door to the one space they hadn't yet searched: my bedroom.

Number Two eased the door open a crack. He must have spotted the form hunched under the blankets because his clenched fist popped up at shoulder level, signaling the other two to freeze.

Beads of sweat squeezed from under Mr. Shotgun's headband, and his eyes scrunched in anticipation of the sting. Team Leader made another series of hand gestures that caused Mr. Shotgun to take a central position, aiming his weapon straight down the length of the bed. Number Two crouched low and crab-walked to one side.

Team Leader eased himself opposite and raised his weapon with one hand, three fingers raised on the other. One by one, they curled.

When the last finger curled, Mr. Shotgun's namesake roared, and my eight-hundred-thread-count silk sheets were ruined. Shreds of silk and stuffing leapt into the air as Number Two whipped what remained of the covers free. Mr. Shotgun racked his weapon and took aim again.

Of course, the only thing on the bed were some pillows and wadded-up towels. Shredded pillows and towels now. Housekeeping wouldn't come through until later, and they were going to just *love* cleaning up this mess. I'd better leave them a suitable tip.

Team Leader scowled and pointed to the gap under the bed. Mr. Shotgun, his weapon locked on that gap as he moved, lowered himself to one knee in order to peer underneath. "Clear," he whispered.

Number Two breezed into my walk-in closet, knocking coats and trousers from their hangers as he cleared the space. Tromping over the scattered suits on his way out, he shook his head.

The trio, in nearly perfect sync, turned their heads toward the door of the en suite bathroom, which was closed. It was clear what they were thinking. After all, it was the only place left for me to hide. They'd searched every other inch of the suite.

Number Two's hands picked up a minor tremble, and he squeezed the grips of his odd gun until they stopped. Mr. Shotgun's eyes scrunched tight. Team Leader just hunched his head down between his shoulders.

Team Leader eased the bathroom door open. The widening gap revealed only darkness. For once, I'd remembered to turn off the bathroom lights when I'd finished my shower. A quick nod of his head dropped his waiting night vision goggles into position as he used the barrel of his not-paintball gun to lever the door open.

"*FUCK!*" Team Leader flinched back as his gun fired with an odd *chuff*. A projectile, visible only as a silver-tipped blur, flew across the bathroom. It hit whatever Team Leader had aimed at with a *crack-THUD*.

Hand sweeping the wall beside him for a switch, Team Leader tossed his head to flip the goggles up and away from his eyes. "Dammit." He stomped across the bathroom to the far wall, where a foot or more of wooden dowel protruded from the tile, having torn through my hanging silk bathrobe on the way.

Nice shot, jagoff.

His mouth twisting like he was sucking a lemon, Team Leader drew another dowel from a sleeve on his thigh and racked it into his weapon. My robe and chunks of shattered tile tumbled to the floor when he yanked the other stake from the hole it had punched in the wall. He inspected the projectile, and light glinted across the silver point. The dowel's passage into the wall had dulled and bent the razor point. Team Leader's lip twisted as he jammed it into the empty loop on his thigh. "Scumbag's not here."

Scumbag? Screw you, buddy.

He turned to Number Two. "Secondary objective?"

Number Two shrugged. "It's a custom suite. Layout doesn't match any of the other rooms in the hotel. Safe wasn't in the closet—no room in the walls for it." He brushed past Mr. Shotgun and into the suite's main room. "Spotted this as we swept." He went straight to the wet bar that separated the "kitchen" from the rest of the main room. His finger rapped against a glass panel. "Too much cabinet in this liquor cabinet." Number Two swung the glass door wide and ran a hand over each bottle within. "A-ha." The dusty, unopened bottle of vermouth in the back didn't budge when he prodded. Twisting it instead caused the bottle to rotate. There was a sharp click, and the shelf of bottles, along with the mirrored backplate, slid down to reveal the dial of my personal, *private* safe. "Basic dial combo, no probs."

Number Two pulled an actual stethoscope from the tool bag slung at his hip and pressed it flat beside the dial. He busted my safe wide open in less than three minutes.

Kurt had been right. The safe needed an upgrade after all. Shame. I liked the old school Big Dial look. Classy, you know?

Number Two swung the safe door open with a little *ta-dah* flourish of his fingers. Team Leader shouldered by him to jam his mitts into my private stash. His search produced a bottle, which he unceremoniously tossed over his shoulder.

6

Number Two caught the tumbling booze and did an actual double take when he read the label. "Woah, do you know what this is?"

Team Leader, still rummaging in my safe, ignored him. Mr. Shotgun shrugged, raising an eyebrow.

"It's a Dalmore 64 Trinitas!" Number Two said. "This shit went for more than a hundred grand at auction."

That got Mr. Shotgun's attention. "No shit?"

Yes, no shit, I paid a hundred and fifty large for that bottle. That jagoff better not...

"I'm keepin' this shit, man." Number Two slid the bottle into his tool bag. "Bonus time."

Goddammit.

"It's not here. Motherfuck!" Team Leader yelled. "Mission's a bust. We're out of here." He turned and strode toward the door.

I got a laugh as Number Two and Mr. Shotgun nearly knocked their coconuts together in their haste to see what else was in my safe. Mr. Shotgun cleared his throat. "Cap, there's a shit ton of—"

"Whatever, ten seconds." Team Leader paused in the foyer and pointedly looked at his watch.

The only thing in the safe other than *my good scotch* was a stack of Credit Suisse ounce bars I'd stashed because, in my opinion, a safe just doesn't look like a safe if there's no glint of gold inside. Mr. Shotgun and Number Two scooped the lot up and into their pockets. They hustled, clanking slightly, over to Team Leader.

"We're gone. Exfil in ten."

They nodded, their weapons rising to ready positions. One by one, the team slid out my front door and down the hallway.

Once the stairwell door had clicked shut behind them, they were out of sight of the hidden cameras I'd had Kurt, my man in casino security, install in and around my suite. The team had spoofed the resort's camera network somehow, so that's where I lost sight of them. Definitely past time to have Kurt look into more upgrades.

Fifteen minutes later, they emerged from the casino-level elevators. The trio had traded in their Men's Tactical look for a more casual wardrobe of near-identical polo shirts and khakis. The team hustled through the casino, Team Leader somehow managing to rush without looking like he was in a hurry. Number Two leaned a shoulder into a squeaky-wheeled luggage cart piled high with suitcases and hockey bags. Mr. Shotgun nonchalantly kept an eye behind them as he strolled. Their path through the casino to the parking garage would take them right by the largest of the casino's lounges.

The Orchid Lounge boasted a glass tower of top-shelf liquor circled by a marble bar. A cluster of funky chairs sculpted to resemble the lounge's namesake flower were scattered in a loose orbit around the center. It was impossible to look good sprawled in those ugly things, so I'd taken up a spot on the far side of the bar.

I'd watched their little adventure through my home via a video feed Kurt had sent to my phone. Now I tucked the narrow slab of glass-fronted metal away in my coat pocket and leaned an elbow on the bar. I was waiting for them to notice me.

Team Leader passed the lounge, glanced my way once, and kept walking.

What the hell?

Not one of them showed any sign of recognition as they rushed by. A moment later, they were gone.

I didn't get it. They'd busted into my home gunning for me, assuming I'd be asleep after a night of partying, but they didn't know what I looked like? And what the hell were they looking for in my safe that was more important than money or top-shelf hooch?

Eh, whatever.

I had to deal with this type of vigilante shit every now and then. Usually, about once a decade, someone would get all high on Jesus or whatever and come to take a shot at me. Most times, we were talking about a preacher from the Deep South with a few gun-toting members of their flock or some "fearless hunters" from the "Old Country" where superstitions still got confused for facts.

Buncha fuckin' losers, if you asked me.

The way it usually went down was that either I saw these yahoos comin' a mile away or they were too incompetent to get the job done. In the early days, before I'd gotten set up at the Fortune, there'd been some close calls that had ended messily. In normal circumstances, I tried to avoid making a trip into the desert with a trunk full of bodies. Because, truth be told, most of the time these wanna-be vigilantes were no big deal. If I did get cornered by one of these yahoos, usually their moral outrage just wasn't as strong as their greed. You just handed them a bundle of cabbage and off they went. When that failed? Well, I still had a trick or two up my sleeve.

Today's pack were the first ones I'd seen with that level of training and gear. Lucky for me, I had a friend in the know as head of resort security. He'd sussed them out as they'd checked in. Takes a hitter to know a hitter, I guess.

I pulled out my phone and texted Kurt: *They're gone. Do me a favor and keep tabs on them, will ya? I wanna know if they drive or fly.*

Seriously, I love these little things. They beat all hell out of a party line. I ran an admiring finger across the three parallel gold lines of the logo on the phone's case before I signaled to the bartender. "Hit me with another two fingers of that George T. Stagg, will ya?"

"Yessir, Mr. Fry," Billy said as he reached for the top shelf.

I slapped the spin button on the screen built into the bar top, and Billy swapped out my empty glass for one with two fingers of a glorious amber liquid. The little ball in my video roulette game bleeped and blooped its way into the zero slot, and the five hundo I'd split between 19 and 15 vanished.

I nursed my drink and lost a few more rounds of video roulette until my pocket buzzed with Kurt's response. *They just pulled off Vegas Blvd into Sig. Looks like they got some serious backing, boss. They might come back for round two.*

I sent back, *Got it, good work. Remind me to give you a bigger Xmas bonus this year, brother.* I thought for a moment before sending Kurt one of those little pictures everyone used now, a thumbs-up.

Yeah yeah, Kurt shot back. *Headed upstairs, need to eyeball the damage.*

OMW. I knocked back the last of my bourbon, dropped a Benjamin on the bar for Billy, and headed for the elevators.

———

KURT HAD USED the master access card and was already in my suite by the time I popped out of the elevator on the thirtieth floor. His aging-wrestler build was hunched over my mattress, elbow deep into the hole left by Mr. Shotgun.

Once I saw the shredded sheets and exposed mattress coils for myself, I felt better about kicking... uh, what's-her-name out at dawn. Not that she hadn't been a real blast, but I wasn't looking for long-term commitments, you know?

10

And I wasn't that comfortable having anyone around while I slept the day away. I get antsy.

Kurt tugged his arm from the guts of the mattress, rattling a handful of whatever he'd found. "Pretty light for twelve gauge," he said, poking the tiny balls in his palm. He held his hand out for me to see.

"Not lead?" I asked.

"Not lead."

I counted five little balls and some fragments. I sniffed, my nose being better than average. "The broken-up ones, those are ash wood. The others are..."

"Silver?"

"Yup. Looks like they knew what they were doing."

Kurt nodded, and when he made to hand over the pellets, I yanked my hand back. "Keep 'em," I said. "Consider it a tip."

Kurt rolled his eyes but pocketed the pellets all the same. When his phone buzzed, he pulled it from the same pocket he'd dumped the shot into.

It was like he didn't even care about scratching the screen. Some people have no respect for nice things.

"They're gone," he said. "Private jet went wheels up five minutes ago."

"There goes my chance to get the Dalmore back from that rat fuck."

"Like you're not headed straight to the Florentine shops the instant the sun's down."

"You know me too well," I said over my shoulder as I strolled from the bedroom.

"Custom gear, silver shot, charter flights, not to mention they moved like the operators I knew back in the sandbox. You'll probably get that chance when they come back," Kurt called after me.

"They ain't comin' back."

11

Kurt followed me over to the bar. "Boss, you got lucky. These guys were the real deal, not some Bible-thumping hicks in over their head. They have real money backing them. They'll regroup, rearm, and come back for round two. With more bodies to throw at you, most likely."

I waved him off as I filled my glass. "If they do, we'll handle it. You line 'em up, I'll take 'em down. Just like usual."

"P90s and scatter-guns with silver shot, boss. That shit'll slow even you down." Kurt eyed the bottle I'd set on the bar top. The line between his brows, already knit in a frown, deepened, and he cleared his throat.

How rude of me. I poured a measure of the twenty-three-year-old bourbon and slid the glass over.

Kurt lifted the glass and, eventually, clinked it with mine.

"I'll cross that bridge when I come to it. Right now, what I need is some shut-eye," I said. "Been a long day, and I've got a long night ahead of me."

"You always have a long night ahead of you."

"Just living my best life, brother." I swished the glass under my nose. My eyelids drifted shut as a whirlwind of oak and rich tobacco, cherries, and vanilla danced into my nostrils. That earthy aroma—moss? I knew Pappy wasn't peated, but there was a hint of...

"Boss, hey!" Kurt was shaking my shoulder.

I'd gotten carried away with the sniffing again. "Yeah, thanks." When I opened my eyes, Kurt got a wild look and snapped his gaze away from mine. His arm came up to block the line of sight between us.

Shit. My eyes had changed on me while I was zoning out over the bourbon, hadn't they? "Sorry, sorry." I rubbed my eyes and thought about baby blue peepers until they felt normal again. "Better?"

"Uh, yeah, boss. Sure." Kurt didn't seem convinced.

As my inside guy at the casino, Kurt was the only one in the know. Still, when he was around, I tried not to be too flagrant with my... eccentricities. It made him cagey.

A shiver ran through Kurt's shoulders, and he drained his glass with a grimace. "Look, I have to get back down to the cage, do my rounds." He set the glass on the table on his way to the door. "I'll get maintenance up here to handle the mess ASAP."

"Go. I'll grab some shut-eye in my backup." I kept another room in the hotel set aside for my needs. Blacked-out windows, steel-cored door, all that jazz. I'd hang my hat there for a day or two, see how things shook out. "See you tomorrow, Kurt."

"Later, boss." He was already out the door, in a hurry to get away despite my sparkling personality. I'd known Kurt for, what, twenty years? The fella was a Desert Storm vet and a seasoned Vegas security professional, and the sight of my real eyes still threw him for a loop. Ah, well, he'd come around.

He always did.

Chapter Two

SIX FIFTY-THREE P.M. ON THE DOT. I WOKE THE SAME way I do every night, all at once. There's no slow period of transition, no foggy head, no lingering dream. I just pop awake, bright-eyed and bushy-tailed. Been that way ever since... well, ever since.

My "morning" routine is a lot less involved now that there's no reason for me to shave. No stubble darkens my chin when I wake. All I need is a quick shower to get the funk off.

My backup crash pad didn't have all the amenities I usually enjoyed in my home suite, so I had to make do with the merely luxurious shower in a standard Golden Fortune room instead of the six-nozzle, rain shower extravaganza I normally treated myself to. I had the same Turkish cotton towels down here, though.

Even if the repair crew had already cleared my suite, riding the elevator in my bathrobe was not the way I wanted to start my night. Which was why I maintained a well-stocked wardrobe down here. I went for a more casual look tonight, slipping into a navy blue Brioni suit paired with a set of slick Bemers. Since I was keeping it cool, I skipped the tie, tucking a Charvet pocket square into my coat to round out the look. It's impossible to wear a suit without a pocket square, anyway.

Vestis virum facit—that's what I've always said.

The elevator dumped me out into the surge of tourist families clogging the lobby of the Golden Fortune. I never understood folks who thought the best place to take their kids on a vacation was somewhere sporting the nickname "Sin City."

The instant I spotted a gap in the stroller parade, I dashed through, intent on reaching the Florentine shops before they closed up. Kurt wasn't wrong about how predictable my shopping urges were. Okay, I'll cop to it being a bad habit, but sometimes I feel like I'm making up for lost time.

"Mr. Fry! Excuse me, Mr. Fry!"

Visions of a new watch slipping beyond the evening's grasp, I turned, sighing, to wait as the resort manager—what was his name? Franklin?—Franklin excused his way past a particularly hefty example of Midwest suburbanite perched on one of those scooter things.

"What can I do for you, Franklin?"

"Mr. Fry, a moment, please?" Franklin led me away from the thick of the crowd. "I've been trying to reach your uncle..."

"Great-uncle."

"Great-uncle for over a week now. I have not been able to reach him or his assistant at all."

"That's it? You know Uncle Elwood—he's off getting his aura cleansed or whatever BS he's into this month." I'd been pretty thorough in establishing my "great-uncle," the owner of the Golden Fortune Resort Hotel and Casino – Center Strip, as a reclusive eccentric prone to extended stays at organic health retreats, mountaintop Buddhist monasteries, and whatever other excuse I could dream up to keep him on the other side of the world. This kept the old coot conveniently out of reach of the hotel staff. Why go to such lengths? Well, it was because "Elwood Friese" didn't exist.

Well, actually, because he was me.

See, a few years after my... ah, accident, Howard Hughes hit the local papers again. Seemed he'd purchased the Desert Inn in its entirety. He'd been on the verge of getting the boot, having overstayed his welcome in the penthouse, and that's how he'd settled his tab. I thought to myself, *Eddy, old boy, that right there's how you do it!* Sure, I wasn't a billionaire aviation mogul, but I didn't wear tissue boxes on my feet either. I set my eye on the Golden Fortune soon afterward. It was the top of my list of prospects, not just because of availability but the location. The immediate neighbor to the south happened to be my old stomping grounds, the Fabulous Flamingo.

It ended up taking me just over a decade longer than I wanted, and I almost lost the Fortune to one of the big bastards gobbling up the Strip, but in the end hard work, luck, and my special talents prevailed. I'd wasted no time building the Fortune's main tower up until it was exactly one floor taller than the Flamingo's. Ever since, the Golden Fortune had been home sweet home.

As I'd been legally dead, on paper at least, since the big accident, I ginned up "Elwood Friese" as the face of my enterprise. It worked great until folks started cottoning to the fact that I refused to age. Then it was "Elwood Friese, Junior's" time to shine.

By now, everyone who might have recognized me was either dead or in a nursing home, so I'd just gone back to being myself. "Great-Uncle Elwood" still owned the full kit and caboodle. I was the ne'er-do-well great-nephew mooching off his good graces.

Franklin, as resort manager, handled the day-to-day tasks that would otherwise tie Uncle Elwood (that is, me) down. All the piles of managerial paperwork, the routine hiring and firing, standing in for the big man at public events—those were all Franklin's responsibility. The only time I was hands-on anymore was when I wanted to be. That would be when the Golden Fortune needed renovation or (and this was my favorite part) when we were bringing in a new stage show. Or whatever issue this was that had sent Franklin to interrupt my evening.

"Yes, Mr. Fry." Franklin, looming like a scarecrow in a department store suit, did a passable job of keeping his opinion of me off of his face. "It's been some time since your great-uncle's been to his office, and he's not left any instructions as to where to courier these documents."

"Hold up, what documents?"

"Oh, nothing that you need be concerned about," Franklin said. "Merely some forms from the State Gaming Commission. There are new regulations concerning..."

My eyes glazed as Franklin went on about the one thing he truly loved: paperwork.

"Which is why it requires an authorized signature. As your unc... great-uncle is the chairman and sole owner of the—"

"I get it. Uncle Elwood is the only one who can sign this form," I said, cutting off Franklin. "You mind if I see for myself?"

Doubt creased Franklin's already well-lined forehead. "Well..."

"I might just be able to get Uncle Elwood to drop what he's doing and high-tail it back here. You know he always take my calls."

"Hmph. Very well, Mr. Fry. They're in your uncle's office." Franklin led the way across the lobby to a small door set between the VIP check-in and the concierge desk. He swiped his access card and led me into the private corridor. A few twists and turns led us to a cubicle farm, nearly empty at this hour. A few evening-shift office drones typed away, oblivious to our passing. On the far side of the cubicle maze, a private elevator waited for the two of us.

A couple floors of listening to a miserable Muzak cover of "My Way" later, the doors dinged open to reveal yet another hallway. Ahead lay a pair of tall wooden doors covered in carved Chinese dragons under a layer of red lacquer, fitting the casino's "Oriental" theme. Even the doorknobs were lucky pearls, each gripped in the claws of a dragon.

This portal led to my—or rather my Great-Uncle Elwood's—office. The heart of the Friese corporate empire, which consisted entirely of the Golden Fortune. Oh, and a beach house somewhere in Southeast Asia that I'd won in a poker game. Supposedly it had a great sunrise view across the Strait of Johor, but that wasn't my bag these days. I'd never seen it in person.

Producing an ornate brass key from one pocket, Franklin let us into the Friese inner sanctum. Shoulders hunched against the weight of my fictional relative's wrath, he tiptoed onto the thick shag carpet. "I left the forms on your great-uncle's desk last week." His voice was hardly more than a whisper as he gestured at the pile of papers stacked dead center on the blotter of the ornate mahogany desk.

I dropped myself into the high-backed leather chair and spun around once for good measure before inspecting the paperwork. Franklin wasn't kidding. That pile was hefty enough to crush a walnut. Honestly, I hated to deal with the boring parts of business. That's what I hired people like Franklin to do. Still, staying off the Gaming Commission's radar was top priority, so I grabbed a fat fountain pen from the brass holder and started flipping through the mountain of paper.

"Ahem. Mr. Fry. Those are for your uncle to sign." Franklin reached over the desk for the papers.

I rapped the fountain pen across his knuckles. "Hands off, Frankie."

"Ow! Sir, I have to insist that you give those forms to me right now. I know Mr. Friese gives you a lot of leeway around the casino, but you are very much overstepping the trust he placed in you." Franklin leaned forward, grabbed the stack of papers with both hands, and tugged.

"Frankie." I tugged back. This was getting old fast. "Franklin, look at me."

Looking up from our tug-of-war, Franklin met my eyes. His whole body shuddered once before going stiff as a board. "Mr. Fry, I, uh..." Franklin swallowed, his Adam's apple bobbing. "Uhh." His eyes lost their piercing focus, giving him a dazed expression.

I'd won the Golden Fortune and kept her all this time with hard work, luck, and my special skills. Situations like this were where the "special skills" came in. Eyes locked on Franklin's, I *pushed* at him with my thoughts. Something—I've never fully understood what it was—flowed through the connection between our peepers and into Franklin's head. I could feel him now, the shape of his thoughts, tumbling to a halt right there behind his eyes. "Franklin, listen to me. Are you listening?"

Franklin's mouth dropped open and, after a moment, he slurred, "Yesss?"

"Do you know who I am, Franklin?"

"Ummm." Franklin's eyebrows came together in a knot and went slack again. "Mr. Fry?"

"No, Franklin, it's Elwood. Elwood Friese. I'm here to

sign the papers from the Gaming Commission. The ones you called me about?"

"Ohh. Mr. Friese, sir. So glad to see you. It's been too long." His face stayed slack, but some personality crept into his voice. "Thank you for taking time away from your retreat to handle this personally." His eyes were still locked to mine as he spoke, his pupils dilated so wide the brown of his irises was all but gone.

"Thank you, Franklin. You've done a wonderful job in my absence. You'll keep everything up to par, I expect? I'll only be staying the one night. At dawn, I'm off to Tibet." It was best to keep it simple, let him fill in the blanks. I'd learned *that* the hard way.

"Thank you, sir. Yes, of course! I'm sorry to hear that you're leaving so soon. The rest of the team would have loved to see you again." Sweat had beaded up on the dome of his head and began running down to his face, which had gained an unhealthy pallor. I needed to wrap this up before he popped.

"That will be all for tonight, Franklin. My great-nephew Eddy will help me to my room once I've finished with this infernal paperwork. You can pick it up in the morning." I gave one last *push* with my thoughts. "You can go now." I let go of Franklin's gaze, and he loosened his death grip on the sheaf of papers.

His back ramrod straight, gazing beyond the walls of my office, Franklin turned to leave. Once he could no longer see me, he shook his head and let himself out. The giant doors *clump*ed shut behind him.

Easy as it was, I tried to not hit my people with the ol' hoodoo too often. Not only did it feel just a little unfair to use that particular "perk" my condition lent me, but I'd seen firsthand what happened if you messed with their heads too much. It wasn't pretty.

I flipped through the endless forms, scrawling "Elwood Friese, Senior" anyplace that looked like it needed it. Once I reached the final page, I tossed the papers on the desk for Franklin to deal with and dusted my hands together. Time to hit the Strip. After a hard day at the office, good ol' Eddy Fry deserved to blow off some steam.

Chapter Three
Then

"It's a sure thing, Eddy, I'm telling ya!" Bobby's voice crackled from the earpiece. "No way a thoroughbred loses a race like this, no way."

I leaned against the side table in Mrs. Dortmeyer's hallway while trying to focus on what Bobby was going on about. Mrs. D refused to spend any more than she had to, and as a result, the boarding house still had an old candlestick phone, which was sounding its age. The crackle on the line was thicker than a Du-Pars pancake. My fellow tenants and I had all complained about the party line phone, but Mrs. Dortmeyer was notoriously tight with a penny. I doubted we'd be getting a modern phone, or plumbing for that matter, any time soon. Meanwhile, Bobby was still going on about an off-season race this afternoon.

Bobby and I'd been from Ormoc Bay to Okinawa and beyond. Demobilization had hit after that, and the Army had cut the two of us loose. I'd gone home to LA, and since Bobby didn't have any family he cared to see, he'd tagged along.

"Besides, Eddy, I ain't been to the track in weeks! You

know it's no fun without someone to knock back a beer with," Bobby urged.

I gave it a thought. I hadn't seen Bobby since he'd gone and found himself a lady. Not to mention, I had the time to spare. My efforts to find a decent job had been coming up bupkis. In the months I'd been back in civvie life, I'd only managed a handful of days of work.

Sure, life had been good for those first few weeks, but I'd overestimated how far I could stretch my back pay. And it wasn't because of a lack of opportunities around Los Angeles. The papers were calling it a "boom," but so far nothing had landed in good old Eddy's lap.

Big deal. I didn't enjoy working an assembly line anyhow. If Bobby was right, and this was easy money, I'd be able to avoid getting the boot for at least another month.

I was sure it'd be fine. Bobby always knew what he was talking about when it came to track racing. "Okay, Bobby, you got yourself a deal. Let's go see some ponies."

"Great! I'll come get ya!" Bobby had spent *his* back pay on a brand-new car. Which, now that I thought about it, might have had something to do with how he'd landed himself a dame already.

I stuck the receiver back on the hook and tried to dodge Mrs. Dortmeyer. She'd been waiting, none too patiently, for me to wrap up my call. The instant the receiver left my ear, she came at me with a speed a woman of her age shouldn't be capable of. Watery green eyes glared at me over the rim of pince-nez lenses.

"Rent was due five days ago, young man!" Mrs. Dortmeyer said with a jab of her cane. She tugged her shawl back into place. "You know the rules. No rent? No bed, no breakfast."

I held up my hands. "Got me fair and square, Mrs. D. I

am *just* on my way out to get you your rent." I crossed my heart. "Honest in—"

"Hah! I've heard that before!" She poked me with the cane again. I didn't think she even needed that stick to walk; it was just for poking her tenants with. "You have one day, Edward Fry. One day." Her nose swung up with a sniff and she shuffled her way down the hall, "accidentally" jabbing her elbow in my side as she passed. Old biddy had an elbow like a bayonet.

I paused at the rack by the door, ultimately deciding against a hat today. It was August, and I'd had enough with hats in the Army. I turned back to the hallway. "It's just Eddy, Mrs. D. Just Eddy."

Another sniff was her only reply.

———

TRUE TO HIS WORD, in short order Bobby had rolled up outside Mrs. Dortmeyer's boarding house in Highland Park, sitting tall behind the wheel of his pride and joy, a 1947 Cadillac Series 62 Convertible with the glossiest sky-blue paint job I had ever seen. Bobby's ride sported whitewall tires, a chrome grill, and a leather everything interior. He'd spent every penny he had and then some on it. Now he drove everywhere he went instead of taking the Red Car like us mere mortals. He might have been my best friend, but every time I saw him in that big blue boat of a car, I hated him just a little.

"Get your ass in gear, Sergeant!" Bobby yelled, giving the horn a toot. Across the street, a mother covered her kid's ears and scowled.

I gave Bobby the side-eye as I sank into the wide leather bench seat. "Knock off all that sergeant shit, Mac. We're out, let it go."

Bobby grinned, chestnut hair flopping over his eyes. He flipped it up with the back of his hand. "Anything you say, Saaaaaaaargeant." Tapping the rabbit's foot hanging from the rearview for luck, he threw the Caddie in gear. His foot slammed down and the Cadillac's engine howled.

The *BAM* of a backfire had me gripping the door handle until my knuckles went white. It'd been well over a year since the last time I'd heard gunfire, but in moments like these, I still found myself looking for incoming. I glanced over, but Bobby only had eyes for the road, driving like the devil himself was snapping at our heels.

Bobby and I had met when he'd transferred to my squad after the Battle of Guam. At nineteen years, Private Robert Graves had been so green I wouldn't have trusted him to know which end of his M-1 the bullets came out of. I'd taken him under my wing, at first just for self-preservation. He'd been so rarin' to get some payback for Pearl Harbor that he was apt to run ahead and get us all shot. Two islands and two and a half years later, we'd saved each other's bacon so many times we'd lost count. By the end of the war, we were almost having fun.

As we shot through the Figueroa tunnels, Bobby held his breath for good luck. On the radio, Tex Williams was not quite singing about his frustration with nicotine addicts. When sunlight hit his face on the far side of the tunnels, Bobby returned to the subject at hand. "Oooookay, Eddy," he exhaled, "about Fair Truckle."

Here we go. Horse talk. Bobby, having been born and raised in a Kentucky barn, loved horses. I was pretty sure that in the race for what Bobby loved most, between his girl and horses, it was a photo finish. Okay, his convertible. Three-way photo finish. "Sure, Bobby." I had to yell to be heard over the wind. "Lay out this 'sure thing' for me, why doncha?"

"Okay, you remember Seabiscuit?"

"Who doesn't?"

"Right. Right. Okay. Okay. Seabiscuit's owner, guy named Charles S. Howard. The man knows from thoroughbreds, believe you me, Eddy." Bobby emphasized each point with a swerve from lane to lane, weaving his way south. Downtown Los Angeles slipped behind us, and we passed rows of new housing built to contain the population surge the war effort had caused. "Howard has thoroughbreds the way a dog has fleas. Each one a winner." He looked over to make sure I was paying attention. Eyes on the road, Bobby! "But this one, Eddy, this Fair Truckle is special. Howard went all the way over to Ireland to snatch her up. He's had her running all up and down California the last few months, and she's not lost a single race. Not one. You wanna know what her time is, Eddy?" Bobby glanced over at me, his eyes flashing.

"Shoot." The Horse Fever had Bobby. There was no stopping him now.

"Not a bit. Not. A. Bit over two point four. That horse is faster than Edna here, I am telling you." Bobby patted the dash. "Sorry, girl."

"All right, the horse is fast. It's a fast horse." I held on to the door to avoid being flung into Bobby as he spun the wheel to send us careening westward onto Manchester. Horns blared in our wake, and a nice old lady gave us a very un-nice-old-ladylike finger as she leapt back onto the sidewalk. "Who's she racing? What the big deal?"

"That's the *best part*, Eddy!" Bobby gunned the engine in time with his words. "It's a *quarter horse!*" Bobby cackled. "Some farm horse fit for the glue factory. Barbara something, who cares." Bobby downshifted and wedged us between two slow delivery trucks before they could line up to block traffic.

"Wait," I said. "Aren't those both racehorses?"

"Oh sure, if you want to be *technical* about it." Bobby's lip curled. "A quarter horse is a sprinter. Quarter mile, okay?"

I nodded.

"They can't keep up the pace like a thoroughbred can. No way can Barbara go the distance. Fair Truckle is gonna run her into the dirt." Bobby slapped the steering wheel. "This whole race is just a wager, okay? Howard bet some Texas horse-shit-for-brains cowpoke that Fair Truckle could beat his nag. I guess the cowpoke mouthed off one time too many, and Howard's decided to show him what racing is."

The Art Deco filmstrip of the Academy Theater flew by, the marquee displaying *The Hucksters*. Speaking of, I wasn't sure if that Howard was the huckster in this race, or if the cowboy from Texas was. "So it's a real race then, Bobby? Truckle's gonna tire out this quarter horse on a real mile track?"

"Absolutely, Eddy." Bobby nodded and hauled the wheel over. Edna's tires screeched us to a halt behind the line of cars leading into the Hollywood Park racetrack. "Trust me."

Chapter Four
Now

I ambled along the wide avenue between the pit games and the slots, hands tucked in my pockets. The slot machines sang their electronic siren song to the passing vacationers. The croupiers made their final call for bets. Winners and losers were announced. In the Lotus Lounge, a band was belting out a rock cover of "The Lady Is a Tramp." I veered hard away from that bit of musical malpractice. Orchid Lounge, it was!

The crowd was thin, but it was still early. In another hour, the tourists would wrap up at the buffets, and the casino floor would fill right up. This was Vegas, so even a thin crowd was still a crowd. More than half the tables in the pit sported two or more hopefuls hoping to lose as slowly as possible. One of the army of cocktail waitresses working the crowd strutted by, tray full, and I gave her the once-over. The Golden Fortune's "uniform" for the cocktail waitresses had the ladies in those high-collared Chinese dresses, an embroidered dragon curling down one side. The dresses were color coded for the different zones: red for table games, blue for the sports book, you get the idea. The Fortune's uniforms were designed with a split up high on

28

the left hip and something like a—how shall I describe it politely—"cleavage window" up top.

Hey, don't blame me. This is Vegas! There's an expectation of low-key sleaze to maintain in this town. The fact that I enjoyed the view had nothing *at all* to do with the design.

Besides, as a rule, I limited myself to merely enjoying the scenery around employees of the Golden Fortune. As tempting as it could be, they were strictly off limits when it came to a roll in the hay... and other things.

Okay, other than the bit of hoodoo required to keep all the plates spinning on my cover story. That didn't count.

Back in the old days, I'd learned from someone I respected: "You don't shit where you eat." Little Mickey had pounded that into my head right away.

Sliding into my favorite seat at the Orchid Lounge, I passed on the video roulette in favor of people-watching. The Vegas crowds never failed to be entertaining.

"Hey, Mr. Fry, get you anything?" Billy, the bartender, called out.

"Give me a shot of the Pappy, Billy. Neat."

He nodded on his way to the far side of the crystal booze pillar to find the bottle.

Kurt had been on my case to keep my wits about me after that raid on my quarters the other day. I'd told him it was no sweat. I'd let them abscond with the moolah I'd left in the safe—I was miffed about the Dalmore, though—so they'd feel like they'd got one over on me. Now that they were flush with my cash, I didn't think they'd be back.

If they did come back, that's what I paid Kurt for.

Billy slid a short glass across the marble to me. The gleaming crystal was half-full of swirling amber heaven. "Two fingers, just for you, Mr. Fry." Billy winked.

"Thanks, pal. What's new under the sun?"

"Nothing I've heard, Mr. Fry. Although, now that you

mention it, Monica over at the Lotus Lounge tore that barback a new one this morning."

I nodded along as the torrent of gossip began. Nice guy, Billy. Fella had friends in every station and section of both the casino and resort sides of the Golden Fortune. Through him I got the inside line on every argument, affair, and stubbed toe in the joint. Better than any quarterly action report, believe me.

While he talked, I brought the glass of quality bourbon up to my nose and gave it a gentle swirl. The aromas slithered into my nostrils, and my head filled with the memory of gingerbread. Butterscotch danced its way into my head, then tobacco. A rich note of burnt oak teased the very back of my sniffer.

While my condition might have a generous list of benefits, I'll cop that there might be a drawback or two. Food and booze, those're the big ones. I can still eat and drink if I want to, don't get me wrong. There's just no *point* to it anymore.

A gaggle of soccer moms piled into the lounge then, crowing over their penny slot victories. They called for "more cosmos!" and Billy cut short the gossip report in order to go shake cheap cranberry juice into cheap vodka.

While he satisfied their craving for cocktails, I turned to the casino and let my eyes wander. Good crowd for a Thursday night. There'd definitely be some prospects to be had.

Mouth open, I inhaled to let the air flow across the roof of my mouth. While I might use it mostly to pick up subtle notes in an excellent whiskey, my sense of smell was good for so much more. I couldn't tell you how it worked, but I could pick out each person around me by their scent alone.

The old me hadn't really spent a lot of time thinking about how folks smelled unless someone turned up extra ripe. Now, well, it's like how a kitchen used to smell. It smelled like lunch.

I could *taste* the excitement and crushing despair that rolled off the gamblers. The lust and the loneliness from the party crowd. It was all better than anything coming out of the Beverlywood Bakery ever was.

Except for Axe body spray. That shit could go to hell.

One thread of desire floating through the casino led my nose to the cluster of cosmo-sipping soccer moms. The third one over from the left, with the auburn bob cut and the sparkly low-scooped top, was definitely giving *me* the once-over. When I glanced over, Soccer Mom Number Three turned her head a bit too quickly to laugh at her friend's joke. Sat up straighter on her barstool. She slid her gaze my way again when I looked away.

I could work with that.

When I looked back at the group, what do you know? Of all the manicured fingers, *her* left hand was the only one without a ring. Just a pale band where one had been until recently.

I could *definitely* work with that.

I try to be strategic about who I make a move on and when. No married dames—keep your eye peeled for that ring! No gals who are already deep into another guy. That's just a dick move. The best places to look are the gaggles of honeys who are all there as a group. Bachelorette parties or whatever. The louder and rowdier, the better. Now, you'd think it'd be impossible to pull a gal from a crowd like that. Guess what? Those ladies are here to break rules, get crazy, and frankly, get laid like everybody else. You just have to show them a good time and not be a jagoff about it.

I knocked back the last drops of the Pappy. I hated to waste it. While "Great-Uncle Elwood" had left instructions that his great-nephew, yours truly, would enjoy all the fruits of the resort on his tab, Eddy Fry ain't no fink. I left a C-note folded neatly under the edge of the glass for Billy. I *may* have flashed my roll an itty bit more than necessary when grabbing the tip, but that's how the game's played.

Buttoning my coat as I slipped from the stool, I tried to double-check my appearance before remembering that I'd decreed there were to be no mirrors on the casino floor.

They annoy me.

Halfway around the bar, as I was intent on working my magic, my nose twitched. A new scent had wafted over from somewhere in the casino. This unfamiliar aroma seemed like it might come from a person, but there was an edge to it. Something spicy and distracting. Peppermint and cinnamon, but not quite.

I'd picked up something similar on other occasions, but not for a long time and never this strong.

My eyes lost focus as I reached for another talent that had surfaced after the accident. Around me, the air filled with swirls and ribbons of color that made the casino's own flashing lights and neon pale in comparison.

Hues and tints I couldn't name flowed around and through everyone and everything around me. Some of these Technicolor rivers twisted and branched into ever-finer strands, while others were thick around as tree trunks. Every person in the crowd now sported their own personal glow as well. I suppose you could call it a "halo." I didn't have a better name for it. But we're not talking simple gold circles floating over their heads, like something from a church window. No, this glow shone from their whole bodies, like everyone had swallowed a box of lightbulbs. Hell, *everything* had these auras.

And I was the only one who could see them.

Now that I was seeing the real crowd, so to speak, I tried to suss out where that scent was coming from. I wanted to use every tool in my toolbox to track down that amazing smell. My mouth was positively watering. It'd been at *least* twelve hours since my last meal.

Head swiveling until I felt I'd picked out the right direction, I shoved off from the marble bar top. The scent trail led me across the width of the Fortune's casino, past the table games and the poker room, to the depths of the endless slot machines. Pirates, astronauts, and safari animals all promised big winnings if you would just spin the digital wheels one more time.

I stumbled to a halt when the scent trail petered out. It hadn't faded so much as it had increased to where it positively surrounded me. Whoever the source was, they'd crisscrossed the clinking maze multiple times in the last hour.

This was where my special peepers came in handy. One row of progressive slots was backlit with a larger, more elaborate glow than the usual tourist produces. Assuming that was my goal, I sauntered in that direction.

As I got closer to the light show, I paused. I'd picked up this sort of scent once before, years ago. It had taken me nearly all night to track down the source and, like tonight, he'd had the same huge spiky aura.

I'd spent a couple night observing the fella, trying to figure out what made him so unique that his aura and smell were so different from everyone else's. Just as I'd worked up the nerve to go and ask him, he'd gone and got himself eaten by his own white tiger.

That was the end of that mystery. Until tonight.

I made my way around the row of slots, keeping it casual. I was half surprised to see that the "source" was a dame, and not a bad looking one at that, though she was more "punk" than I usually prefer. You could call me old-fashioned, but the green hair, shaved on one side, wasn't my bag.

Her outfit matched her hair. She'd propped one scuffed combat boot atop the console before her. Rainbow socks emerged from the boots, climbing her legs to peek through jeans so shredded it was a mystery how they held together. A black leather biker jacket, silvery studs punched into just about every inch, was slung across her narrow shoulders. Embroidered patches filled every gap in the metal, the largest of them dead center on her back. There, a skull sporting swirly blond ponytails grinned around a lollipop. "Fight like a girl!" was emblazoned on a ribbon winding around the bottom of the patch.

Normally, I'd be on my way back to Soccer Mom Number Three without a second thought. But that scent was *really* getting up in my nose. Call me a fish on a hook. Putting on my best "Eddy Fry" smile, I sauntered over beside her. "How's it going? Any of these machines paying out tonight?"

Punk Girl glanced away from the pennies dancing on her screen for a bare second before turning back to her game. Her unpainted lips twisted in a sneer.

Three seconds later, her back was stiff as a board, and the boot slipped from its perch on the console. Moving in staccato bursts, her head rotated until one hazel eye, white showing all around, slid into view. Sweat popped from her brow, and the heady musk of her fear added itself to the mix.

My head swam, and a fresh pang of hunger nudged at my gut. Now I *really* wanted to find out how that scent tasted.

Wait. Fear?

What the hell? Stark, raving terror was *not* the response I looked for when chatting up a skirt. I ran my tongue over my teeth to double-check. All normal. Same for my eyes; they hadn't changed. So why was she freaking out?

"Hey, sorry about that, sister. I didn't mean to sneak up on ya like that. Let me buy you a drink? I'm Edd—"

"I know what you are, bloodsucker!" she hissed, her voice low. "I am *not* on the fucking menu!" She swiveled in the chair to face me, shoulders hunching up around her ears. One hand crept toward her collar, while the other dipped into one of the leather jacket's many pockets. With a clatter of small knickknacks, she produced a small, metal-wrapped bottle. "Back off!" As she shoved the bottle at me, her thumb hooked under a clasp running down the bottle's side.

"Whoa, hey. It's cool. Don't splash me with perfume, okay? I like this coat. Besides, we're just off to a bad start."

Her thumb twitched, and the bottle's metal sheath hinged open like a little door. A thread of golden light, *actual* daylight, shot from that narrow gap. Every bit of my exposed skin stung like someone had splashed me with acid.

What the *fuck?*

Her fear was shading over into determination now, her scent changing again to reflect it. Her eyes narrowed, and I gaped as hair-thin rings of color, not that different that the light show around us, shimmered around the outside of each iris.

Could she see like I could? Is that how she knew what I was?

"Bottled sunlight, motherfucker. Fuck off somewhere else, or I'll melt you where you stand. I do *not* give a fuck about the cameras." Her free hand toyed with a metal tab riveted to the edge of the jacket's collar.

I put up my hands up in surrender. Every bit of exposed skin had begun to throb. "Sorry to bother ya." I shuffled away until I felt it was safe to turn my back on her and her damn bottle of daylight.

By the time I'd reached the end of the row, the stinging

on the back of my neck had stopped. Looking back, I saw that Punk Girl had hit the bricks without waiting for her payout. A strip of paper hung from the front of her machine. As I watched, one of the casino's degenerate regulars nabbed the slip and sashayed on without missing a beat.

Back in the Orchid Lounge, I slung myself onto my usual stool and told Billy to pour me another. It wouldn't get me drunk, but it would give me something else to think about.

Face it, Eddy, you're doll dizzy. One of these nights, I needed to quit hitting on every dame that caught my eye before I got into some serious trouble.

Across the bar, the crowd of soccer moms had moved to the next stop on their Vegas tour, with one exception. The lady who'd been sending me signals sat alone, tapping at the video poker screen in the bar top.

I waved to Billy, signaling for him to pour her another round, and slid from my seat. She looked up as the cocktail glass appeared by her hand. Billy tilted his head in my direction.

"Hi," I said, holding out my hand. "Eddy Fry."

The bridge of her nose crinkled as she smiled up at me. "Sharon."

One of these days, I'd quit. But not tonight.

Chapter Five
Then

"Fair Truckle," Bobby said, not having let up on the subject, "is fast. Damn fast. She's a fast starter. She'll be over that finish line before that farm horse can get up to a trot. Believe me."

I'd never been much for horse races, or any racing, really. Bobby, however, had been bending my ear about this race or that horse since the day we'd met. His horse tales had gone from an annoyance to a way to pass the time while we were stuck in our berths, waiting to be deployed. By now, I had to admit I had caught the fever myself. Long before we passed through the racetrack's side gate, I was ready to see some ponies run.

Bobby spat on the ground. "Look at all the damn cowboys! What a crowd! Hah, did you know that Mr. Howard tried to make this a private event? Fat chance of that!"

I took in the crowd milling about. Fat chance was right. There were so many Stetsons in the crowd that every farm from here to Houston must be wondering where their hands had got to.

"Okay, okay, Eddy. You know how you can tell these

are real cowboys?" He made a big show of sniffing the air. "You can smell the cow patties on their boots!" Bobby, being his own biggest fan, doubled over with laughter. A couple of the nearby cowpokes gave him the hairy eyeball, maybe looking to take offense at his joke. I stared them down until they went looking for greener pastures. I'd grown up getting into one scrap or another, but Bobby was a shooter, not a brawler.

The two of us elbowed our way through the mess in search of a good view. The front two bleacher sections were smack in the August sun. Bobby, pointing out a spot at the top of the stands, had the right idea. The upper deck had a roof that arched over the crowd, providing some relief from the growing heat.

"No better place to watch 'em run." Bobby flagged down a guy hawking cups of beer. I picked up the first round, despite my cash shortage, because dammit, I was gonna have a good time. "Only thing better would be a spot in Howard's own box seat," Bobby said between sips of the flat beer. "Howard owned Seabiscuit. Did I mention 'Biscuit comes from Phalaris's line? That was some fast fuckin' horseflesh, believe me."

"Only a thousand times, Bobby," I said and sampled the beer for myself. Exactly what you'd expect from a warm beer in a paper cup. I watched the crowd of nabobs, cowboys, and regular Joes like us churn while waiting for the big event to start. After a bit, I noticed that here and there a couple fellas, usually a cowpoke and a local, would hunch together, and money would trade hands. I downed the last of my beer. "Bobby, you got any money on this?"

"What? No, no, of course not, Eddy." A slow grin crept across his face. "'Cause we just got here!" He bought the next round, and we drank while he clued me in on the finer points of picking a winner. "None of that shit matters today, okay? It's just the two horses. If you can call that nag Barbara B a horse. Hey! Dom! Over here!" Bobby shouted over my head. "This is the guy I been waiting for. Dom, this is Eddy. Eddy, this is Dominic. Dom here handles all of my business," Bobby said, with a waggle of his eyebrows.

The fellow picking his way across the bleachers to us was on the shorter side. White-collared shirt, gray slacks, and a black-and-white striped tie that resembled the keys of a piano. He wore no hat, and there was enough grease in his hair to burn for a week if it caught a spark. Dom produced a pad and a stub of a pencil from his shirt pocket. Opening the pad with a flick of his wrist, he licked the tip of the pencil. "What'll it be, Bobby? You takin' the sure thing today? If not, I can give you good odds on Barbara B if ya want 'em."

Bobby elbowed me in the side and shot me a wink. "Oh no, it's the thoroughbred all the way, Dom." Bobby dug around in his pockets, pulling out a messy wad of bills. "Put me down for, ahh..." He flipped though his cash. "Hunnert 'n' twenty."

Dom shook his head. "No can do. Cheap seats filled up five minutes ago. I can't take any more small action on this one." With a flip of the notebook, Dom turned to go.

Bobby grabbed his arm, desperation scrawled on his face. Dom looked hard at the hand on his elbow before shaking it off. "Bobby..."

"Okay, okay, Dom, you gotta run a line on this for me. I can't miss out on this action!" Bobby said. "You know I've been good for it in the past, right?"

Just then, a cheer went up from the cowboys and cattlemen in the lower bleachers. A few Stetsons flew up in the air. A set of gates leading, I assumed, to wherever it was they stored the horses had swung open. Bobby's eyes went a little wild, and a hint of panic crept into his face.

Dom looked the two of us over. "I could run you a line, but you'll need at least two large for it to be worth my time. Think you can handle that action?"

Bobby swung around. "Look, Eddy, I can put my car up, but that's only gonna cover half."

Dom nodded at this.

"If you go in, c'mon, it's a sure thing! That's five hunnert apiece when Fair Truckle dances across that finish line!"

I knew it was a bad idea, but the beer and two hours of Bobby's never-ending horse chatter had worn me down. Not to mention that cash would sure come in handy. The 52/20 club had ended a while ago, and winning today meant I could put off finding a job for another month, easy. "You say it's a sure thing?"

Bobby's face lit up, and he put one hand over his heart. "Absolutely. One hundred percent! On my honor as a Kentucker. You in?"

What the hell. I nodded.

Bobby turned to Dom. "Okay, we're good. Two large on Fair Truckle to win."

Dom jotted a note down on his pad. Below us, the crowd started going crazy as they led Fair Truckle onto the track. Dom slid away, and I lost him in the sea of blue collars filling the stands.

Bobby jumped up again. "Holy shit, it's Johnny Longden! Eddy, do you see that?" he yelled straight into my goddamn ear. "That guy rode seventy-three wins this season alone! I *told* you this was a lock!" He slapped my back, and I let some of his excitement wash away the buyer's remorse that had hit me the instant Dom had turned his back.

It'll be fine. Sure thing.

The tone of the crowd turned ugly when the other horse, Barbara B, hit the track. The cowpokes went absolutely wild, but the locals in the crowd were booing, and more than one cup of beer got tossed in the quarter horse's direction.

I looked to Bobby for an explanation. Sure, Barbara B was the underdog, but that didn't explain the hissing from the crowd. Bobby clambered up onto his seat to get a better look.

"Goddamned jock's got spurs on!" Bobby said, his fist drumming my shoulder. "Jockey looks like it might be... Tony Licata. Yeah, that's him. That sonuvabitch's been banned from here to Greenland. Looks like Mr. Gill ain't above pulling some dirty tricks."

At my look, Bobby explained, "Roy Gill owns Barbara B. The fella that Mr. Howard set this whole wager up with. Now he turns up with a banned jockey *and* that sonofa's wearing spurs!" Bobby dropped back down into his seat. His brow furrowed as he slurped back the last of his beer. Eventually he nodded, the vigorous motion setting the lock of hair over his forehead a-flapping. "Looks like Mr. Gill might just be worried about his nag's speed! I mean, look how stringy that thing is! No chance she pulls a win out of this one." Bobby pounded me on the back and waved for more beer. "Nothing to worry about, Eddy. This is a lock."

———

"GodDAMNED Barbara B." Bobby buried his face in his hands, elbows propped on his knees.

I stared, numb, at the track where the horse in question was being pranced around by the spur-wearing bastard that had ridden her. Another round of Stetson hats went flying up into the air as the cowboys and chuck wagon folks whooped it up. I added my groan to Bobby's and sank to the bench beside him.

41

"My car, Eddy. I really love that car." Bobby's head tilted back, and he stared unseeing at the pigeons roosting above us in the rafters.

"Your car?" I said. "Your fucking car? Bobby, you jagoff! Thanks to you, I owe that Dom fella at least a grand. *A grand that I don't have!*" My voice climbed to a bellow. Heads swung around, looking over to see what the hubbub was. I tried to pull it together. "A lock, you said. A sure thing." My lip curled.

"Look, Eddy—" Bobby started.

"Don't you fucking 'Look, Eddy' me, you son of a bitch. I should break your neck for getting me into this."

We'd downed a couple beers apiece while waiting for the race to start. The jockeys had grandstanded, prancing their horses around before tucking them into the gate. When the starter pistol had gone off, Bobby and I had leaned forward to soak up every detail of Fair Truckle's inevitable victory. That five hundred bucks was as good as mine.

Barbara B had come out of the gate like she'd been fired out of a cannon.

"Shit." Bobby's voice was no more than a whisper. My mouth had gone dry.

Fair Truckle was fast enough but hung behind Barbara B by almost a full length. The two horses had pounded around the curve in near lock step. Every head in the stands turned in unison as we tracked the runners to the halfway mark. Bobby started punching my arm. Fair Truckle had put on a burst of speed to close the gap. "Here we go, Eddy! Here we go!"

Fair Truckle's forelock never passed Barbara B's shoulder. No sooner had the thoroughbred made her bid to pass than the cow pony had effortlessly stepped it up, pulling a full length ahead. Which was where she had stayed until

42

she crossed the finish line, a clear winner. It hadn't been anything close to a photo finish.

I stared at the track in horror. We'd lost.

"Bobby, my good friend," Dominic said as he slid up next to us. "I believe you owe me one fine Cadillac automobile." Dom raised an eyebrow. "That won't be a problem, will it?"

"No, no problem, Dom." Bobby fished around in his pockets until he found his rabbit's-foot fob. Fuck-all *that* had done for him. Or me, for that matter. "It's the blue Cadillac in the lot. Got the other half of this"—Bobby shook the rabbit's foot—"hanging from the mirror." Bobby's fingers lingered on the furry token as he handed the key to Dom.

"I know what your car looks like, Bobby. Always a pleasure doing business with you." A cheerful, neighborly smile had plastered itself across Dom's face as he dropped the keyring into one pocket and pulled the notepad from the other. He carefully ran a line through an entry at the bottom of the page. Then it was my turn. "Edward Fry, was it? Yes. I believe you owe one thousand dollars." The look on his face told me he knew I didn't have it.

"I might need a little time to get—"

Dom held up a hand. "I understand you don't have that kind of money on you today." With that, all friendliness drained from Dom's face like water down the toilet. "You will bring me my money in no less than two days. Two. Days. Otherwise, I will send some associates to collect. My hand to God, Eddy. You do not want that to happen." Dom's eyes never left mine.

"Uh, right. Yes. I can do that," I lied.

Dom's eyes bored into mine for a handful of seconds that felt more like a million years. Then he blinked, and the friendly neighbor was back. He pulled a card from the back of his notepad. "This is where you will bring my money.

Two days, Eddy. Don't forget." With a nod to Bobby, he swung on his heel and made his way down the stairs. "Lewis! You lucky so-and-so! Looks like you picked a winner, eh? How do you feel about Cadillacs?"

I hauled myself to my feet and looked down at the card in my hand. The address was a for a pawnshop in Hollywood, just off of Sunset. "Bobby."

"Yeah?" Bobby tore his eyes from where Dom had vanished into the crowd. He tried to meet my gaze and, unable to, stared at the ground instead. A lock of his stupid hair flopped forward to hide his eyes.

"Dominic's mobbed up, ain't he?" I showed him the address on the card.

"Um, yeah, Eddy. I thought you knew that," Bobby said, glancing up through his hair. He did a bad job of forcing a smile.

I nodded at him and tucked the card away. Then I punched Bobby in the fucking mouth. Down he went, landing on his ass between the bench seats. Blood leaked from his lip where I'd split it. He opened his mouth, and I just stared at him. Bobby's mouth closed with a snap as his arms flailed for something to haul himself up with. I thought about hitting him again. Hitting him a lot, actually. Watching him go down had made me feel better.

Rubbing my knuckles, I stepped over him. It was a long walk to the Red Line, and a longer ride home.

Chapter Six
Now

I JAMMED MY HIP INTO THE GAP TO CATCH MY DOOR and swung the soccer mom, Sharon, around as we staggered in. Giggles bubbled up, and she clung to me as I spun her around again, fast enough that her feet left the ground. A tiny squeak popped out of her, and it was my turn to laugh. I made *damn* sure the Do Not Disturb tag was in place as I shut the door.

"Nice place," Sharon said, as her gaze drifted around. "Faannncy." She stepped out of her heels on her way to the windows. At sundown, the shutters had retracted and now the full spectacle of the Las Vegas Strip was on display. I draped my coat over a chair and joined her as she pressed her nose to the glass. Even though I'd seen the view a million times, it never got old.

"Wow. You weren't kidding, Eddy. You *can* see everything." Sharon pressed against my side as she gazed over the fake Roman coliseum across the boulevard. "Too bad we missed the sunset. I bet it's *amazing*."

I'd never seen the sunset from up here, or the sunrise either. "Mm-hmm."

Sharon leaned into me while she dug her toes into the carpet. I slid my hands around her waist and just enjoyed the press of her body against mine for a while. The lovely arch of neck flexed as she turned her head to peek at me, her nose wrinkling again. I leaned in for a kiss, but she spun away, a trail of giggles in her wake.

I watched as she circled the cushioned conversation pit. "Ooh, retro. I like." Breezing past the bar counter, she paused. "What do we have here?" Her grin said she knew damn well where that door led. The lights from the Strip glinted from her sparkly top as she vanished into the darkness of my bedroom.

Well, it would be rude of me to keep a lady waiting.

The hotel maintenance crew had completely replaced the bed that Mr. Shotgun had ruined. My new bed was a long oval shape that filled the back half of the room. Burgundy leather padding covered the headboard. You know the type, with those little brass nails in a diamond pattern?

The door to the walk-in closet was ajar, and Sharon paused. With a sly look, she stuck her head in to snoop. Eyebrows raised, she turned to me. "Wow, Eddy, you might have more clothes than I do." Another glance at the racks. "And I have a *lot* of clothes."

I slid my arms around her. "Can't blame a fella for wanting to look good," I said, resting my chin on top of her head. "I have a taste for the finer things."

Sharon leaned her weight against me. "The finer things, eh?"

"Mm-hmm," I murmured into her hair. "Only the best."

She sighed, her head tilting, as I brushed my lips across her shoulder, making a trail of feather kisses to her neck, then blew on the trail.

She pressed her rear against me with a groan, her hands sliding back to pull on my hips. She ground herself into me and paused. "Nothing yet?" She glanced up.

"Don't you worry, it's a slow burn," I said into the curve of her jaw. I wasn't worried about that particular bit of anatomy. It would only get fired up once I'd had a good meal. Which was exactly where things were headed.

Sharon turned in my embrace, her arms sliding across my chest and around my neck. "Slow burn, eh?" Her dark eyes gazed into mine, searching. I gazed back. Nothing extra, just enjoying the sight of her.

I know what you're thinking. Time for the old eye hoodoo, like I did with Frankie. *Bzzzt!* Wrong answer! What's the fun in that? Turning your date into a limp noodle? Lady makes her mind known, you listen. Give me an enthusiastic partner any day.

Sharon lifted herself up on her toes, closing the gap to press her lips against mine. The length of her body leaned into me, and I ran my hands down her back. When they reached the edge of her short skirt, I curled my fingers under the stretchy fabric, and my fingertips found the line where her legs curved into her ass. Her arms tightened around my neck, dragging me closer as she opened her mouth against mine.

A satisfying interval later, she came up for air, pressing her hands flat to my chest. She pushed, and I let her, backing away until the edge of the bed caught my knees. With a wicked smile she shoved, and I fell back onto the silk sheets. Sharon followed, a knee coming to rest on either side of my thighs. The sparkly fabric of her top glinted in the glow from the other room as she peeled it over her head. Auburn hair spilled about her face as she leaned forward to run her hands up the cloth covering my stomach, halting when she reached my chest. Her hands twined themselves in the cotton of my shirt, and she yanked. Buttons flew, *tick*ing as they bounced off the walls. "I've always wanted to do that," she said, a grin lighting up her face. Her bare skin pressed into mine as our lips met again.

I rolled us over, holding the kiss, until I was on top. I kissed my way along her chin, to her jaw, to the curve where neck met her shoulder. Her breathing took on a new urgency as my teeth nipped at that junction. She hooked my neck with one hand, the other guiding mine to the edge of her skirt. My fingers slid across the softness of her belly and under the elastic band. Sharon leaned her head into the pillow as my hand reached her warmth.

Her breasts pressed against my chest and her breath grew ragged. "Don't stop." I nipped again at the curve of her neck, harder, my fingers increasing their tempo. Her arm crushed my face into her neck, and I could feel her heart thudding against my chest. Beating enough for the both of us. My fingers curled, and the groan in my ear was delicious.

I worked my jaw to flex and loosen the joint while behind my lips, my incisors twitched. They flowed like candle wax until hardening into inch-long needle points.

Mouth wide, I set the tip of one razor tooth atop the line of her pulse. My fingers speeding her along, I waited until she was right on the edge and then paused. Sharon growled and clenched her thighs together around my hand.

As soon as she gasped, my teeth slid through the skin of her neck. Fire splashed into my mouth, sweeter and richer than any food I'd known in my old life.

Crying out, not in pain but with pleasure, Sharon clenched her fingers in my hair, pressing my head against her neck. Her orgasm pulsed from my fingers along the taut arch of her spine and through the connection I'd made in her throat.

Sharing in her ecstasy, I gave it back, waves crashing back and forth between us. I knew that as long as I fed, as long as my teeth were in her neck, she would continue to orgasm. So would I.

That's where things got delicate. Neither of us wanted it to end, but it *would* end. One way or the other. Either I had the willpower to stop drinking, or she'd run out of blood and, well, that would be that.

I didn't need to take everything she could offer, all of her blood, her life. But I wanted it. Oh *God* how I wanted it. I wanted to drink and drink until there was no more. Until all of that heat, that life, was inside me. Filling me. *Why not?* said the little voice in the back of my head. *That's what she's for. That's what* all *of them are for.* But I only needed a fraction of what Sharon had to get by. With the endless party of Las Vegas all around, I would never run out.

Images, memories, flashes of Sharon's life flickered behind my eyes. Her kid, a towheaded little rug rat, running through the grass on a sunny summer day. A husband, a mortuary paint job coloring his cheeks, silk pillow behind his head.

Okay, that was my cue. Once I saw their memories, that meant I was close to the safe limit. It only got more dangerous from there.

It took all my will, but I slid my teeth free of her. Before she could lose any more through the nick I'd made, I ran my tongue over the pinpricks. There's something in my saliva that does the trick, makes it close right up. By morning, she'd have nothing more than a spectacular hickey.

A shudder ran the length of Sharon's body and, with something halfway between a gasp and a sigh, she collapsed into the sheets. The tension ran out of her like ice melting in the sun. As she worked to catch her breath, I listened intently to the beat of her heart. Still juddering from the wave of orgasms, her pulse was strong and clear. I'd stopped in time.

Her head rolled until she could see me, though her eyes were unfocused and slightly crossed. "Oh *God,* Eddy. What the fuck was that thing you did with your fingers?"

"Magic." I grinned once I was sure my canines were back to normal.

"What do we have here?" Sharon's hand ran down my chest to my trousers, where the latecomer to the party had finally arrived. Now that I was freshly fed, the life in her blood had recharged *every* part of me. She gave me another one of those nose-wrinkling grins and tugged at my belt buckle.

"I told you it was a slow burn."

A giggle bubbled from her lips and she pulled me on top. I laughed and let her.

MUCH LATER, we lay intertwined, the silk sheets tangled around us. Sharon had, enthusiastically, given back as good as I'd given her. Her head rested on my shoulder, and her quiet snores fluttered the hair around my ear.

Propped on a pile of pillows, I could see through the bedroom door to the gigantic windows lining the outer wall. The Spring Mountain range stretched off beyond the repli-caRoman palace across Las Vegas Boulevard from the Golden Fortune.

With a tiny *snerk,* Sharon woke. She smiled as she prized her arm from around my neck. "Thank you," she said, her voice still husky. Pressed her lips to mine gently.

"You—" I began, but she shushed me with a finger on

50

my lips. She shook her head as she slid from the sheets. Unselfconsciously, she dressed, slipping the sparkling top over her head. I felt more than a bit of satisfaction when she wobbled, her legs still weak, as she tugged her skirt into place.

I crossed my arms behind my head and let myself relax. Usually, the most troublesome part of picking up a dame was getting them out before dawn. It's not that I had a firm "hit it and quit it" policy. I just don't care for people I've just met hanging around when I go dead to the world. Literally. It freaks the gals out, and then Kurt gets involved. It ruins the memory.

With Sharon, well, it looked like she didn't want or need this to be more than it was.

Sharon stood, framed against the light from outside, and gazed back at me. A heartbeat later, she blew a kiss and turned away. The front door opened, and the sound of her heels clacking down the hallway faded. Sharon was gone, back to her life, wherever it might be.

I didn't need to breathe, not really, but I pulled a deep one in then. The scent of her, and our fun, filled my head. I let the memories replay as I tugged the sheets up to my chin. I like to be comfortable, even if it wouldn't matter once the sun came up. From the main room of my suite came a soft chime, a reminder.

With a muted whir, the window shutters lowered themselves in their recess between the glass panes. As the light from outside dimmed, the curtains swished to cover the windows, the blackout fabric a second layer of defense should the shutters fail. Darkness closed around me, although I could still see the doorway and the room beyond as if it were noon bright. A heavy, metallic *clunk* told me that the suite's door had secured itself.

A pressure in the back of my head had been building for

several minutes. Well fed, a good lay. I didn't fight it. I'd earned a good day's rest.

Somewhere far to the east, the sun peeked its first ray over the mountains.

Dawn.

I was gone.

Chapter Seven
Then

I TRIED TO KEEP MY SHOULDERS FROM HUNCHING AS I passed the pawnshop a fifth time.

More than two years in the Pacific, with that jagoff Bobby, and the thought of walking into that damn shop had me quaking in my Florsheims. Fuckin' pathetic, Eddy.

I kept the shop's sign in the corner of my eye as I strolled down Western with what I hoped was a casual stride.

I knew I didn't have the green to pay off Dominic, or Dominic's boss. What I had was a plan to keep my kneecaps and my thumbs unbroken. To be fair, it was more of an idea than a plan.

All right, it wasn't much of an idea.

I crossed over and, before I lost my nerve, grabbed for the pawnshop door handle. The door stuck a bit in the frame when I pulled, which was almost enough to send me around the block again. A little bell tinkled above my head as I stepped in.

"About goddamn time you came in," the old-timer behind the counter said. "Five times you walked by. I was starting to think you wanted an invitation." As he turned his head, wisps of a bad comb-over drifted above spotted skin. A strained pair of safety pins held together one of his suspender straps. The old fella leaned against the glass counter, pencil in hand, hovering above a copy of the *Los Angeles Times* and a sales book. Grime obscured most of the goods, jewelry and watches mostly, on display beneath his elbow. The rest of the store had been stocked—barely—with tools, small pieces of furniture, and musical instruments. Did a half-empty pawnshop mean it was doing well or not? Hell if I knew.

I tugged my hat from my head and hung it on the stand by the door; spying the pawn tag on the stand, I snatched my hat back. A glance around the shop didn't reveal any other place to hang my hat, so I shrugged and slung it back on the hook. "I guess I'm not the first fella to take his time coming in."

The old-timer pulled his little, round glasses from his nose and jabbed them in my direction. "You're one of Dominic's clients, ain'tcha?" He gestured with the glasses to a door behind him. "Dominic and the boys are in back." He slipped the glasses onto his crooked nose and heaved the counter leaf up to let me pass.

I squared up my shoulders and marched past the old man into the back room, offering him muttered thanks as I went.

The back room wasn't what I expected. Instead of shelves and cobwebs, the walls were covered with wood paneling. In the back was a dark wood desk, complete with a tall leather chair behind it. You know the type, has those little brass nails in a diamond pattern?

Not counting me, there were five men already in the room. Two of the men, real bruisers, filled the small couch side to side. Blond, with matching work shirts and matching bent noses. Brothers for sure. Across from them was a

54

padded chair with its own occupant. That fella was big, as big as the two on the couch put together. Tucked behind his newspaper as he was, all I could see was an outline and his wide hands gripping the paper. An enormous loafer rested on the opposite knee.

Dominic sat, one leg hitched up on a corner of the desk, conversing with the older man seated behind the desk. The older guy's flashy pinstripe suit looked like it was a custom job. He had dark, receding hair above a round face that featured a prominent, wide nose between deep-set eyes... that were aimed right at me.

"Edward. Eddy, right? Come on in. Meet the boys," Dominic said from his perch. He jerked his chin first to the big guy reading the paper. "That's Little Mickey, and those're the Grace brothers, Ronnie and Donnie."

Little Mickey lifted a hand in a lazy wave before licking his finger to turn a page. The brothers said nothing, not moving much. Twin sets of bloodshot eyes glared at me.

Friendly bunch.

"You're here a day early. That's good, Eddy. Real good," Dominic said. He pulled the little notebook from his coat. "Let me see, you're on the hook for a full G. You're actually on time, so what say we ixnay the interest?" At that last bit, Dominic glanced at the man behind the desk. The man, apparently Dominic's boss, inclined his head a fraction of an inch.

"I appreciate that, Dominic, really I do. But honestly, I'm here to talk to your boss. I'm assuming that's you, sir," I addressed the man behind the desk.

The smile vanished from Dominic's face like someone had wiped it off. "Oh, Eddy, that's a real disappointment. I thought you were going to be one of the good ones. I really did." Dominic gestured with his chin, and I heard the couch creak as the pair of goons came to their feet.

"Sir," I said, trying not to rush, "Dominic's right. I don't have the cash to settle my account. But I am here to... What I mean is I'd like to settle up in a way that benefits you and your organization." I glanced around. "Not to mention keeping my various parts where they belong," I added under my breath.

Dominic shook his head. "Eddy, it doesn't work like—" He paused as the man in the chair held up a hand.

"What did you have in mind, Eddy?" the man asked.

"Well, sir, I saw more than my share of rough business in the 77th fighting over on Leyte and Okinawa. I'm not afraid to get my hands dirty. I'm no dummy, but I don't have much schooling, and there's no job that is going to earn me the grand I need to pay off my debt by tomorrow." I took a breath. "So, what I'm proposing is that I work it off. The debt, I mean. Instead of getting *my* kneecaps broke, I can go break a grand's worth of someone else's. Or whatever else needs breaking that'll clear my ledger with you." I tried not to clench my hands while Dominic's boss stared at me. "Sir."

Dominic turned to the man. "Mr. Cohen, I'll have the boys take out this trash." The room grew tense, and I fought to keep the panic off of my face. Behind me, I heard the brothers step close, itching to be let off their leash. I told myself that I was only imagining their breath on the back of my neck.

Mr. Cohen turned to Dominic, expression mild. "Now hold on, Dominic. Eddy came here on his own. We didn't have to drag him in by his heels, or his friends and family, for that matter. That's worthy of a little respect, even if he is a deadbeat."

I winced.

The chair creaked as he leaned back. "Edward, your experience in the war doesn't mean shit." He gestured, one hand turning as he spoke. "While I am, of course, extremely grateful for your service in showing the Japs a thing or two, do you have any idea how many of your fellow veterans are in Dominic's little notebook?"

Dominic glanced at his notebook, as if to check.

"Under normal circumstances, I'd just turn the Grace brothers loose on you. Set an example." Mr. Cohen jabbed a finger down on the desk blotter. "Lucky for you, these are not normal circumstances."

The faintest ray of hope loosened the knot that passed for my stomach.

"I do, in fact, find myself somewhat short-staffed due to a recent unforeseen tragedy and am in need of extra hands. Hands that know how to follow orders *and* are willing to do what it takes." His gaze drifted past me. "Of course, before I can seriously consider your application, you'll need to go through the interview process."

My heartbeat, which had been pounding in my ears, went quiet. Just like it had back in the Pacific, when the LCA landing ramp dropped.

I ducked, the swinging arm of a Grace brother ruffling my hair, and sidestepped. Little Mickey threw himself out of the chair, moving fast for a big guy. I was ready for it. The big guys *always* moved faster than you expect. Newspaper swirled in his wake as he charged me.

I juked his swing and my left came up inside his reach to slam into his jaw. His teeth clacked shut, his flinch giving me the opening to sink a jab into his gut. Behind me, I heard movement. The brothers were going to flank while Little Mickey held my attention.

I picked the one on my right—I didn't know if it was Ronnie or Donnie—and went right at him. His scarred fist was winding back for a haymaker as I straight-armed him, my knuckles extended to bop him in the throat. White showed all around his eyes as I followed up with a left to his nose that sent him reeling back. Blood spilled from his rebroken nose as he tumbled to the cushions, gagging sounds coming from his throat.

The other brother was just about to lay hands on my shoulders, hoping to pull me into a bear hug, which Little Mickey would follow up on. I knew I was a goner if that happened, so I stomped on his forward foot and ground my heel in before snapping my head back, smashing *his* nose flat. Putting the lie to his name, the Grace brother dropped bonelessly to the floor at my feet, out cold. His nose would still match his brother's, at least. I turned to face Little Mickey.

The big man peered at me over raised fists, and his watering eyes narrowed. I stepped back and shook out my arms before raising them in a boxing stance. Little Mickey's eyes did a quick down-up, taking in my posture. Then he did the unexpected. He dropped his fists. "What do you think, Mr. Cohen?" he said over his shoulder.

Mr. Cohen, chin propped on one fist, nodded.

With that, Little Mickey clomped over to the couch, scooping up his paper in one hand and the snoring Grace brother in the other on the way. Dropping the goon onto the cushions, he pinched his wide fingers around the choking brother's throat. There was a faint *pop* and the goon began breathing normally, gasping the air into his lungs.

I glanced from the pair on the couch to Mr. Cohen and then to Little Mickey before lowering my own mitts. Dominic's eyebrows were trying to crawl into his hairline, while Mr. Cohen just looked amused. One corner of his mouth twitched back in what could be considered a smile.

I tugged my shirt straight. Ran my fingers through my hair.

"You throw a punch almost as well as I do, Eddy," Mr.

Cohen said, leaning forward to plant his elbows on his desk. He flipped open a carved wooden box and tilted it my way. "Cigar?"

I took one of the offered Cubans. It would've been rude to refuse.

Dominic held out a lighter for Mr. Cohen and after a moment shrugged and offered it to me as well.

I puffed up a good cherry and looked at Dominic through the smoke. "In Leyte, I led the team they sent to clear the pillboxes. I took out fifty Japs, maybe more, across two islands. Best damn time of my life." I took a pull from the Cuban, rolling the rich smoke around in my mouth. "Then they had to go and end the war."

Dominic opened his mouth to say something, and I blew my smoke in his face. Setting the stogie down in the wide marble ashtray on my new employer's desk, I turned to face Mr. Cohen. "Thank you for the opportunity to clear my ledger, Mr. Cohen. I won't let you down."

Mr. Cohen looked at Dominic, then back to me. He smirked. "I certainly hope not. If things go well, maybe..." He paused. "Let's not get ahead of ourselves. Maybe there's room in the organization, maybe not."

He wasn't asking, which was fine. This was the best offer I'd had since landing in San Diego.

I nodded and plucked the Cuban from the ashtray. "When do I start?"

Chapter Eight
Now

I popped awake, bright and cheerful. I'd had a good meal and a good lay last night, and now I was ready to do it all again.

One shower and a quick pass with the comb later, it was time to pick the evening's outfit. A Zegna, I thought, since it was Friday. I dropped the needle on some Nelson Riddle to set the mood while I got dressed.

Just as I fastened the oyster band of a Mariner around my wrist, my phone buzzed from the bar top. *Here*. Kurt. I let him in with the remote.

Kurt lumbered across the room, yet another Walmart suit hanging from his aging linebacker frame. Dammit, I paid him more than enough to afford something nice. You'd think as head of casino security he'd take his appearance seriously, *especially* since he was representing my fine establishment. I made a mental note to have a word with him about his attire later.

"Okay, boss," Kurt said, "bad news." He scratched the base of his crew cut, releasing a cloud of dandruff. "Those guys who came after you the other day. They flew out in a private jet, straight to St. Louis. There they refueled and departed, a flight plan filed for Stockholm. The trail went cold over the Atlantic. Not a trace once it went wheels up. I called some guys I know, and they called guys *they* know at STL, and those guys swear up and down that no one got off the jet while it was refueling. Says they probably switched transponder codes." He ticked up his fingers. "Plane landed, refueled, took off, vanished. Trail ends. The real bad news is that facial recognition search got us absolutely dick-all."

Kurt had spent hours trying to explain the casino's advanced face search system to me. We used it to track the movement of players on the floor, flagging cheats and high-lighting celebrities for the house to keep an eye on. All the casinos in town shared their info around, just like when Gus would have me run over to the Frontier to finger a card counter for them back in the old days. That part I got. *How* it worked was not something I understood, or wanted to.

"The fuck does that mean, Kurt?" I poured myself a drink, adding a glass for him as an afterthought.

"We got good coverage of the team coming and going. Checking in, going through the casino, good angles on all three."

I spun my fingers in a "go on" gesture. "So what's the big deal?" I said, sliding the glass to him.

"They weren't in our local database, which isn't anything unusual. It just means they'd never been to the Fortune before. At least not since VISAGE was installed." Kurt waved off the drink. "We sent the images around town, same deal. No match found." He scratched his head again. "This is where shit went south. I pushed the search out to VISAGE-NET, see if there'd be a hit from Atlantic City or the Native American casinos. Hell, even Macao."

"Lemme guess, bupkis."

"Worse than that." Worry creased Kurt's brow. "When I sent the query in, the face scans of that team vanished."

"So send 'em again." I poured Kurt's unwanted bourbon into my glass. "No big deal."

"No, I mean they *vanished,* Eddy. From our system, from the Florentine's, from every VISAGE terminal in town. When I sent it in, the system reached back and deleted every trace of them. Even the raw footage from the cameras on the server here had been purged."

"So we got hackered?"

Kurt rolled his eyes. "Hacked. Maybe. I have the IT guys looking at it. So far, they say there's no sign of malware or any other compromise to our network. John's saying that most likely their faces"—Kurt circled one blunt finger around his own mug—"were flagged at the system level. When their images hit the VISAGE-NET servers, it executed some hidden, admin-level command to purge everything with their faces in it."

"Wait," I said. "Admin? Speak English, Kurt." I was losing track.

"Yeah, the purge function would have to be built into the whole facial recognition network, right from the get-go. The whole thing is compromised," Kurt said. "Whoever those guys were, someone with their fingers in a multibillion-dollar multinational security firm is covering their tracks."

After he'd dropped that little bomb, I sent Kurt off to do... whatever it was Kurt did when he wasn't working. Miniature golf maybe. He'd protested, insisting that I needed to be more careful. That someone should be watching my back until this all blew over. Frankly, it sounded to me like he wanted to dog my heels. No-go, buddy. Eddy Fry flies solo. I didn't need his cheap suit scaring all the talent away.

Once he'd left, I put all the technical mumbo jumbo out

of my mind. The Mercato at the Florentine was calling my name.

In no time, I was down the elevator and halfway through the Fortune's lobby. The Florentine was a pleasant evening stroll up the Strip, and I was already mentally browsing. Passing through the big crossroad in the casino center, my eye snagged on an alluring set of curves.

This dish, hoo boy. My head turned so fast it almost snapped my neck. She was a bit of a short stack, sporting pinup curves. The black silk number draped about her form drank in the light and threw it back in pinpoint sparkles. Her hair was a mass of artfully pinned and sculpted waves in a color so dark it made her gown seem gray by comparison. A string of diamonds flashed at her neck, a matching bangle at one wrist. As she turned her head, Kewpie doll lips like a pair of rose petals in a snowbank came into view. One emerald eye flashed from beneath a wave of her raven hair and met mine across the width of the casino. Her eye—oh *fuck*. When I saw that eye, I did the only thing I could think to do.

I ran like hell.

———

I PANICKED, okay?

I'd been living in Las Vegas for... well, a *lot* of years. At least half of that had been in my current condition. In all of that time, I'd *never* met another like me. Well, except the fella who made me like this, and that didn't count because he was dead.

But the gal that had me beating feet? Once I saw her eyes, I just knew. Don't ask me how. I just did, and she knew what I was right back.

I pushed my way through the Friday night party crowd.

Trying to dodge drunks, degenerates, and parents who were attempting to usher their little darlings through Sin City without exposing them to too much sin.

Good luck with that. It's sin all the way down.

I elbowed past a particularly large gaggle emerging from the Cirque Diabolique Theater—good show, by the way, one of the better ones we've had here at the Fortune—and aimed myself at the rotating door to the outside. My plan, if you want to call it that: lose myself in the sidewalk crowd, hustle to the Florentine, grab a cab. After that, hell. Just get the cab and keep moving.

That plan went out the window when a brick wall wrapped in a Hugo Boss suit planted itself square in my path. A massive dome of a head, topped by a shock of thin blond hair, was attached to a torso so wide I could probably climb inside with room for a date. Nearly colorless blue eyes regarded me from either side of a ship's prow of a nose. When Hugo crossed his arms, his shirt buttons groaned.

Arms windmilling, I stopped short of barreling into that massive slab of muscle. As I patted the lines of my suit into place, I took a second to *really* look at the guy. He wasn't like me or the dame back there, but he wasn't human either. There was something off about him. He smelled wrong, like ice and saltwater. I thought about decking him, then reconsidered it. I might be stronger, a *lot* stronger, than I used to be, but Hugo obviously knew what I was and didn't seem to be the least bit impressed.

Besides, a fight in a casino is hard to cover up. I may own the cameras, but every tourist and gambler had a camera in their pocket, and all of it would end up on the tubes in about ten seconds. My goose would be cooked even if I won the scuffle with Hugo.

This mountain that walked like a man raised the tree

trunk passing for his arm to point back where I'd come from. I played along as if I had a choice, saying, "Lead on, Mac."

During my initial retreat, I'd crossed most of the Fortune's casino floor in what seemed like an instant. The walk back, in contrast, seemed to take forever. Every step of the way had Hugo beside me. Herding me without seeming to. Anyone watching would just see a handsome fella walking his pet polar bear.

The dame was exactly where I'd first laid eyes on her. She hadn't moved an inch, content to have her goon retrieve me. Once I thought about it, I realized Hugo hadn't been with her when I bolted, yet he'd been able to cut me off a minute later. Which just raised more questions about whatever the hell he was.

Hugo lumbered to a halt, offering the mystery dame only a nod. Here we were, the three of us, in the middle of the Golden Fortune's casino at peak party time, Friday night. And yet the crowd flowed around us like water around a rock. No one pushed between us in a hurry to get to the bar. No one spared us a second glance. Every head swiveled away as they passed by.

Neat trick.

The lady gave me a once-over with bored, half-lidded eyes. Although I had the advantage on her, height-wise, I felt like a child waiting for a grown-up's scolding. I fought the urge to fidget. Eddy Fry does not fidget.

Her doll-like lips bowed further in a hint of a smile. "You are quite unexpected, Mister...?"

"Fry. Eddy Fry," I said. "Call me Eddy."

She tilted her head as if she expected more. At last, she offered one delicate hand. Crimson nails, each manicured to razor points, because of course they were. "Rebecca Weir. House Harkness."

What's House Harkness? Her employer?

I took the offered hand. Her skin was warm and distractingly soft, but when I tried to take my hand back, her grip was iron. Her smile turned sweet. "Mr. Fry, would you be so kind as to accompany me? I have a delightful villa across the street. A much more appropriate venue for us to discuss terms than out here among"—the hint of smile became a hint of sneer—"the rabble." She held me fast as her free hand tucked a stray midnight curl behind her ear.

Terms? Maybe I'd misheard. No matter, I was feeling like a prize fool. Bolting the way I had wasn't a good look, and neither of these two had done anything I could actually call a threat. It was best to hear what the lady had to say. I'd just need to ignore my gut screaming at me: *Run! Fight!*

I put on my best Eddy Fry smile. "All right. Why not?" I offered her my arm. "Lead on."

Rebecca switched her grip to my arm and imperiously waved Hugo ahead of us. The weird bubble of people who aggressively failed to notice our passing continued all the way to the portico. There, a massive stretch limo waited in the center of the valet lanes, blocking traffic. As we emerged from the lobby, the valets practically came to blows over who would get to us, to *her*, first. Hugo tossed a tip at one lad without breaking stride and opened the rear door for us himself. Rebecca lowered her curved behind into the leather interior, maintaining a grip on my arm when I tried to sit across from her. Defeated, I took the empty spot beside her. When Hugo dropped his carcass into the driver's seat, the entire limo rocked on its springs. How much did that goon weigh?

———

Rebecca had said "across the street," which in Vegas involved a mile or more of driving. As Rebecca

66

seemed content to wait until we arrived at her villa to speak, I spent the time checking out her ride. The smoked glass of the window was dark enough that I might actually be safe in here during the day. Judging by the doors' deep *thump* when Hugo had slammed them, plus the way the limo was handling on turns, I was ready to believe the whole shebang was armored. A rolling fortress. The only thing missing was a turret and a cannon. Hugo probably filled that role himself.

Ten minutes and a Vegas U-turn later, we were strolling beneath gaudy glass flowers. Rebecca and I trailed in the wake Hugo cut through the weekend crowd, my arm still trapped in her grip.

Rather than heading to the elevators, Hugo led us to an alcove beside the hotel's Chinese restaurant. There he waved a card and an unobtrusive door swung open.

The Beau Rivage's Garden Villa was the largest and most luxurious of the resort's high-roller suites. If I remembered right, it went for something like ten grand a night. I wandered into the main room and glanced toward the massive pane of glass that dominated the far wall. The man-made lake and fountains, the signature feature of the Beau Rivage, filled the view. Across that lake ran Las Vegas Boulevard, and past that loomed the replica Big Ben of the London Las Vegas. Flaring orange neon to the left of the tower outlined the entrance to my old friend, the Flamingo. Beyond that lay the Golden Fortune. I tilted my head. Yep, a straight view to my penthouse.

Fabulous.

Hugo, practically a door himself, took up his station at the suite's entrance. Rebecca at last released my arm and swept across the deep shag to perch on the edge of one of a pair of designer chairs. "Please, Mr. Fry. You are my guest. Have a seat."

I'd wined and dined—and dined upon—more than my share of ladies over the years, and this was the first dame since I was in short pants to give me a case of the nerves. Something about her sent up all the warning flags. I wasn't sure if it was because she was the first I'd met who shared my condition, or if there was more to it.

As soon as Rebecca had perched her derrière on the sweeping curve of her chair, she'd stopped moving. Completely. If a lock of her hair hadn't fallen across one eye, I could have mistaken her for a statue carved from alabaster and ebony.

Needing a moment to think, I wandered to the wet bar. She'd said I was a guest, so I might as well make myself at home. I spied a nice bottle of Talisker right away. "You mind if I...?" I waggled the bottle in question.

Rebecca seemed taken aback and looked at me like I'd asked to lick the doorknobs. An instant later, the cool veneer had returned. "But of course, Mr. Fry, help yourself."

Glass in hand, I braced a hip against the bar. "You said something about terms, Miss Weir?" I brought the glass up for a sniff. A wave of tobacco and cut-grass aromas almost carried me away. *Bad time for distractions, Eddy.*

"Rebecca, please. Mr. Fry."

"It's Eddy. When someone calls me 'Mr. Fry,' it makes me look around for my Pop." I took a healthy swig of the scotch and let it roll over my tongue. Still no flavor, but I went through the motions anyway. Again she had that look, as if she couldn't believe what she was seeing. I swirled the amber around the glass while I waited.

"Very well. Eddy it is, then." Pale hands folded themselves across her knee. "I must confess, Eddy, finding you was quite the surprise. I had no idea that anyone of the Blood was in Las Vegas."

The Blood? Oh, she means that, yeah. Got it.

Rebecca went on. "Nonetheless, you are here." She lifted one shoulder in an elegant shrug. "Please be so kind as to grace me with the name of your Sire."

"You mean my Pop? Hell, he jumped out a window when I was..." I thought back a bit. "Fourteen, I think?" I said. "What's Pops got to do with the price of tea in China?"

Confusion beat out Rebecca's usual bland expression. "I believe you misunderstand, Mr. Fry. Your Sire, the one who turned you. The one who brought you into the fold."

I snapped my fingers. "Oh! I get what you're putting down. That guy. Yeah, got no idea."

Rebecca flowed to her feet, crossing the room in an eyeblink. Five-foot nothing but somehow we were eye-to-eye. I froze, the glass halfway to my mouth. Would she try her eye hoodoo on me? Would it work if she did? I just knew I wouldn't be the one who blinked first.

The whites of her eyes bled red and her pupils swallowed the emerald of her irises. Her eyes became twin seas of crimson, each with an island of pure midnight at the center.

So that's what I look like when that happens. No wonder Kurt nearly pissed himself.

One blink and those dazzling green eyes were back. "You honestly don't know, do you?" A slender finger tapped once on the curve of her chin. "Are you even sworn to a House, Eddy?" She swished back to her fancy chair and perched upon it again.

"Sure I am," I said. "Cute little bungalow on the edge of town. I'd invite you over for drinks, but these digs have it beat." I saluted her and the Garden Villa with my glass.

"No Sire, no House. Curiouser and curiouser." Her manicured fingers drummed the arm of the chair as she gazed out the wide window. "Why, after all this time, have you not claimed Las Vegas as your own?" She seemed to talk to herself, so I let her go on. She clapped her hands once, lightly. "Delightful. You won't be a problem after all."

Uh-oh.

Rebecca's expression lost all trace of its former congeniality. I quashed a chuckle when she actually stuck her nose in the air. *Hoity, meet toity.*

"I am here under the authority and order of my Sire, Antoine Innsbruck Piotr Harkness. *Paterfamilias* of House Harkness, Lord of the Atlantic Estates. I..." She paused. "My Master claims this city and all of its spoils and chattels as his own. As his Second, I will be his iron law in this territory."

I did *not* like where this was going.

Despite not knowing this Harkness character or what an Estate was, I knew exactly what she was saying. Her Outfit back east had sent a crew to muscle me out, take my turf. I knew damn well what happened to the locals when that went down. I'd done plenty of it myself back in the day. Another pour of the Talisker bought me a moment to think, to keep the fury seething in my guts from boiling over.

"You have no House to speak on your behalf, thus you cannot expect to be welcome within any Estate. Therefore your deception, concealing your existence in this pit of a city, is understandable. You may rejoice, for I am feeling generous this evening. My Master's new Estate shall need subordinates. Swear fealty to me, and I will grant you leave to remain." Rebecca leaned back until her posture made the leather chair a throne.

"It's him, Mistress," an unknown voice said, and I jumped near out of my skin. If I'd still had a heartbeat, it would've been pounding like a jackhammer.

The owner of the voice was a slick-looking fella, about my height and sporting one of those messy-on-purpose hairdos. His bespoke suit made my own duds look like I'd grabbed them off the rack. I almost asked him who his tailor was. The biggest difference with Slick was that unlike me, or Rebecca or Hugo for that matter, Slick was plain Jane human. A human who'd walked up right next to me without me copping to it. Creepy.

"Explain," Rebecca demanded.

"The owner of the Golden Fortune," Slick said.

Rebecca tilted her head. The movement was brief, staccato, like a bird of prey.

"The pieces fit," Slick went on, ticking off the points on one hand. "Outclan, unknown to any house. The Golden Fortune is solely owned by a mysterious and reclusive eccentric. One 'Elwood Friese.'" He pronounced it "freeze." Slick curled his lip as he glanced my way. "The mystery man Rutger's team failed to neutralize."

"Excellent work, Marcus," Rebecca purred. "You serve me well."

Marcus swelled with oily pride and bowed his head.

She turned her attention back to me. "This presents you with a wonderful opportunity, Mr. Fry."

"How do you figure?"

"Turn ownership of the Golden Fortune over to me, and I will guarantee your status, under me, as a scion of House W-Harkness."

I couldn't stop myself. I doubled over as laughter tore its way free. "Lady, I wouldn't take that deal if you tied me down and poured it over me." I got it together, brushed my coat into place. "The Fortune is *my* home. It's mine, and it's staying mine. I built that shit up from the ground. You want to call yourself the Queen of Vegas? You go right ahead, but I'm keeping my home."

Rebecca's glossy lower lip jutted out, just a bit. I didn't think she liked my answer.

Movement caught my eye: Hugo. He hadn't so much as

shifted a hair during the conversation. Now he was on the move. Marcus had backed off, his hand creeping under his coat.

Disappointed in myself, I realized that all three of them had clean lines on me. At least I had the bar at my back, but that gave me no place to retreat. I'm no slouch in a brawl, but then I'd never faced someone like me before. Not to mention whatever the hell Hugo was.

"That's simply out of the question, Edward," Rebecca said. "I believe it is long past the time for you to learn your place in the order of things."

"What are you going to do? Hiss dramatically? Drink my blood?" As I said it, I thought maybe I'd watched too many movies in the name of "research."

"Don't be a boor." Rebecca's rosebud lips twisted in disgust as gagging noises came from Marcus. Rebecca raised a single finger. "Felix."

Hugo, or I guess it was Felix, thumped across the carpet. I put up my dukes, figuring to get the first licks in. I wasn't planning on pulling my punch, either.

My teeth started chattering as Felix closed the distance. A chill, like I'd stepped out into a blizzard, cut straight through my summer-weight suit.

Which was weird. Neither the heat nor the cold had bothered me since the accident. But this... this was like I'd been gut-punched by Jack Frost himself.

As shivers began twitching the muscles in my arms, Felix's skin withered, going all gray and leathery until it looked like rawhide left out in the weather. His eyes were gone, two pissholes in a dirty snowbank, and a chip of icy blue shone in the depth of each empty socket. Frost scrawled across the top of the bar as he drew closer, feathering the dark marble in white.

I'd been waiting on him to close the distance and once

72

he did, I threw my right straight into his jaw. Except my arm wouldn't swing. There was no gas in the tank, I couldn't even keep my fists up. Why was it so goddamn *cold*? My head drooped on my neck, too heavy to keep upright. Swaying on my feet, I closed my eyes against the bitter sting of winter.

"You will remain my guest until Marcus has arranged the details of the transfer, every legal nicety. Then you will sign, Edward, and I will have everything I need from you." Rebecca's voice drifted to me from about a million miles away.

The roaring in my ears drowned out anything Rebecca said after that. I pried my eyelids apart, slivers of ice clinging to my lashes. Above me, Felix cocked his ham-sized fist.

This is going to hurt, isn't it?

An avalanche of frozen meat and bone slammed into my face, and everything went black.

———

I BLINKED icy slush from my eyes as I came to. What the hell hit me? Oh. Right. A Norse giant with an avalanche of a haymaker.

They'd dumped me in the suite's guest bedroom. I gave myself a pat-down. All my parts were still where they were supposed to be. Any dents in my coconut from Felix's ham fist had fixed themselves while I was still seeing stars. I'd had a good meal before racking out this morning, so it would take more than a bash to the noggin to cause any lasting damage.

My wallet and phone were gone. Of course.

I hopped off the bed, and the room promptly spun, hard and to the right. Okay, I wasn't one hundred percent just yet. A good meal would set me to rights. As soon as I beat feet out of here.

With my hearing, it was easy enough to pick up snores from the other side of the villa. More than one set of lumber was getting sawed. Which meant that my guess was right. There were more flunkies around, *and* I'd been out long enough for them to hit the sack.

I could bust this door down, no sweat. They had to know as well as I did that nothing as light as a hotel door was going to be a problem. But that wouldn't help me if Rebecca and her pet monster were lying in wait outside.

I gave the room the once-over. Bed, desk, TV, luxury bathroom, windows. No guest exit. That would have been too easy. I wasn't in the mood to run into Felix's knuckles again, so the windows were the obvious choice.

They'd had blackout curtains installed, so they expected me to stay put through the daytime. Not in the mood to oblige, I yanked them open. Time to get the lay of the land.

The Garden Villa's dominant feature was its overlook of the Beau Rivage's lake. I could handle the drop into the water, but I'd be wading to shore in front of all of Las Vegas Boulevard. Now wasn't the time to be drawing that kind of heat.

Beside the room's window lay the terrace for the resort's top-flight restaurant. Which, by my watch, should have closed hours ago. I snugged my cheek to the glass. The coast was clear.

The villa's windows, like those in every other room in town, didn't open past an inch. Rebecca surely knew that, like the door, a quarter-inch strip of metal and a short hop wouldn't slow me down. Either she'd expected me to be out longer, or she didn't care if I made my own exit. My head spun from following the trail of "did she know that I knew she knew" logic.

I'd have to chance it.

I snapped off the bit of metal in the track and slid the window wide. I scoped out the crowd across the lake. Minimal eyeballs. I wouldn't get a better chance for this.

There was a time when attempting this jump would have landed me in the drink. Now it was like hopping off the curb. The restaurant was clear. The cleaning crew had already gone home for the night. I wasted no time in getting the fuck out of there.

As soon as I was mixed in with the flood of late-night revelers, my neck crawled. I didn't think I'd really run into Rebecca or Felix out here, but why take chances? At least until I'd gathered my wits, it'd be best to get home toot suite. Head on a swivel, I beat feet. I kept my retreat casual, though. No one runs in a casino.

The crowd thinned by the time I reached the pedestrian bridge over the boulevard. At this time of night, most revelers would be winding it down or at the after parties. I still had to dodge the inevitable guy pushing CDs, hop over a couple kids out past their bedtime selling water by the bottle.

I was looking over my shoulder *way* too much. Too obvious. *You've gone soft, Eddy. Too many years of Easy Street. Just because you can't see a tail doesn't mean there isn't one.* Fine, if it were the cops or one of the old Vegas Outfits, I'd have no trouble shaking them. But Rebecca? Maybe one of her crew could turn invisible. Hell, I didn't know. Until tonight, I hadn't known anything like Felix existed.

That brought me up short. Yeah, I was completely out of my depth. Goons? Fine. Cops? No sweat. Feds? For breakfast. But this? For all my years spent living the high life, I'd been making it up as I went. *C'mon, Eddy, be honest with yourself for once.*

You don't know dick about being a vampire.

Chapter Nine
Then

THE BLAZING DESERT SUN POKED ME RIGHT IN THE EYES as I stepped off the City of Los Angeles train, making me stumble my first steps onto the streets of my new home. I slung the ruck containing the sum total of my worldly possessions over my shoulder and pushed past the mill of fellow travelers.

"The Streamlined City," as declared by the neon sign above the station gate, was not living up to the name. Damn near everybody who'd arrived with me seemed intent on jamming their suitcases, and elbows, directly into me. I beat someone's grandma into the last available phone booth in the row. I cut her sputtering protestations off by shutting the door in her face. Too slow, Granny.

I dialed up the number they'd given me with the train ticket. "Yeah?" The voice on the other end was bored with me already.

"It's Eddy. Eddy Fry? I was told to call this number when I got here—"

"Okay, corner of Fremont. Next to the Overland. Someone'll get ya." With a *click,* the call ended.

I surrendered the booth to Granny and made for the

station exit. As I rounded the corner, the sight of Fremont Street stopped me in my tracks.

Signs overloaded with neon, dim in the afternoon sun, towered over the street from every building. Straight in front of me, occupying the corner of Fremont and Main, sat the Hotel Sal Sagev. Beyond the oddly named hotel, the Monte Carlo competed with the Sal for my attention.

My destination lay on the opposite corner: the Overland Hotel. I aimed myself squarely at a welcoming "BAR" sign beside the entrance. Overhead, the Overland's signature neon train puffed out streamers of neon smoke. I hoped the beer was cold. Sweat was already soaking my back.

Before I could enter the waiting establishment, a big black Cadillac pulled up beside me, showing care for the well-being of neither vehicle nor pedestrian.

So much for my beer.

I assumed this was my ride, and what a ride it was! Chrome trim wrapped around a black mirror finish. Not a speck of dust or dirt to be found on a chassis with more curves than a pinup. Once I'd paid my debt, one of these babies was *definitely* on the menu. While I admired the car, the rear door in front of me swung open, revealing a familiar pinstripe-clad giant. The Caddy rocked on its springs as his weight came off the seat. The short, dark hair was slicked to one side, and thoughtful eyes blinked in the morning sun. "Eddy."

"Little Mickey, good to see you." Even though I'd only met him once before, it was still a relief to see a familiar face.

"Mm-hmm." Little Mickey hoisted the trunk open. No bodies lay stashed beside the spare tire. Only a car jack and now, my ruck. I wasn't sure if I was disappointed or not.

Hey, I'd heard the stories too.

Little Mickey pointed at the back seat, and I hopped in. When he slid his own mass beside me, I was shoved across the leather like a little kid. The driver pulled away, cutting into traffic. This resulted in a blare of horns, which he ignored.

"Eddy," Mickey said, "Mr. Cohen wants you set up at the Flamingo."

I nodded. From what Mr. Cohen had hinted at back in LA, this wasn't any surprise. The Flamingo and what had happened to Siegel had been the top headline for the last month.

Little Mickey went on, "Mr. Cohen gave you a break, a chance to work your debt off. That is not something that happens often, not in my experience." He tilted his head, eyes drilling into mine. "You will be working off your marker by collecting money owed by guys who weren't as lucky as you were. You got a problem with that, we can drop you off right now." The fingers of the massive hand closest to me slowly curled into a fist as he said that last bit.

"Ah, no. No problem," I said. In all honesty, I *didn't* have a problem with it. Like me, all those Joes knew exactly what they'd signed up for. Like Little Mickey said, I'd gotten lucky.

"You're on the hook for a solid grand, plus vig. So don't be making any long-term plans, got it?"

I nodded. "Got it. You know, I didn't expect you guys to go for it. And this?" I waved out the window as the car left the bustle of Fremont in the dust. "Las Vegas is a pretty big step up for a guy in my fix."

A chuckle. "You made a good impression on the boss. Most guys, as you'll see, come in on their knees. Begging, crying their eyes out to be let off the hook, for another chance. For one more day." Little Mickey was rock steady, hardly tilting as the car barreled around another corner.

"You had the Grace brothers laid out without breaking a sweat. Sure, Mr. Cohen could have stuck you in a dive somewhere in LA. You'd be working off your debt forever in that kind of joint. Fortunately, Mr. Cohen is expanding the organization." He pointed forward, past the driver. "This is where the future is, Eddy. Bugsy might've fucked up his shot at owning this town, but the boss doesn't miss."

I leaned over to see. The heart of Las Vegas, Fremont Street, was far behind us now. Bare desert stretched all around as we raced down Highway 91. Ahead, where Little Mickey's blunt finger was aimed, shone an oasis in the waste.

A towering sign proclaimed FLAMINGO in neon, topped with an image of the namesake bird. Below it, a handful of cars were lined up at the valet. The only green in sight was three or four palms poking up from the building's center, hinting at a garden within.

The driver, who clearly didn't believe in sharing the road, hauled on the wheel to send us careening into the parking lot. He took us straight past the waiting cars without slowing. I craned my neck, trying to see over into the horseshoe center of the joint as we rounded the corner, but we were past before I could make out if anything of interest was lounging at the pool.

Damn.

"Time to get to work." Little Mickey shoved the door open and levered himself into the sun.

"Already? It's barely lunch. On a Tuesday," I said. "Who's going to be gambling now?"

Little Mickey leaned back down to stare at me through the open door. "Eddy," he said, his tone betraying more than a little disappointment, "this is Las Vegas. Someone is *always* at the tables. Which means someone *always* owes us." He hooked a thumb toward the staff entrance behind him. "You can get lunch later."

Little Mickey led me through the maze of the resort's innards. The drab hallway reeked of fresh paint, and I was glad when we popped out a double door into the main part of the joint. I got the nickel tour. Check-in, guest rooms, and the lounge all shining in the light streaming from the massive floor-to-ceiling windows. Every inch was brand spankin' new, not a scuff or scratch to be seen. Not even a cigarette burn on the bar.

The casino proper was a sight. Six long rows of slot machines gleamed at the front of the house. The steel cases were spit-shined brighter than I'd ever gotten my shoes in the Army. Scattered around the one-armed bandits sat a gaggle of ladies who alternated drags between their smokes and the arm of the bandit they sat at. Each one waiting for the ring of that bell, the one that would signal a jackpot. Next to that racket was a row of tables, blackjack and craps. Those were less than half full of hopefuls trying in vain to beat the house.

Little Mickey took us past the cashier through a nondescript door in the back. Another drab hallway, this one bustling with cocktail girls and porters. Everyone made space for Little Mickey and me—okay, mostly for Little Mickey—as he led me to a dark wood door trimmed with brass. He knocked on the door, waiting a moment before letting us in.

"Boss," Little Mickey said, "this is Eddy. One of the guys Mr. Cohen sent over. The one with the extra arrangement." He waved me past, shutting the door once I was in.

The cigar smoke swirling around originated from an older fella who could only be my new boss. The man was nearly hidden behind the mountain of paperwork piled high on a desk that took up the back half of the office. As we entered, he was selecting a crystal decanter from a bar cart that carried more bottles than the desk had papers. Ignoring us, he loaded up his glass with a generous pour of something dark. The first sip he swished around in his mouth until he was almost gargling. When it met his approval, he knocked back the whole glass as if it were a shot and poured himself another. At no point did he stop puffing up a storm with the stogie clamped in his fingers. Fishing a dripping ice cube from the bucket on the cart, he dropped it in his glass, swirling it as he ran a hand over his hair to slick it across the thin spot on top. "Mickey tells me you actually held up against the Grace brothers." He blew smoke at me as he spoke.

"Uh, yes," I said, then remembered to add, "sir."

The lines about his mouth deepened in a grin, cigar clamped firmly in his teeth. "Eddy," he said, "no need to be formal! You're in Las Vegas now!" He waved his hand, liquor sloshing over the rim of his glass. "Okay, fine. Technically, we're outside city limits, but nobody gives a shit about that detail except lawyers and politicians." He jabbed his stogie at me. "Sit." He dropped into his own seat, causing one of the many stacks of paper crowding his desk to tumble to the floor, where he ignored. it

I searched for a safe place to put the folders that covered my chair. Since every surface was similarly burdened, I shrugged and just dropped the stack on the floor. The chair's cushion was so soft I sank until the armrests were in my pits, the edge of the desk nearly level with my eyes.

"Where was I? Right. You're the SOB Cohen's saddled me with, working a debt off." He leaned forward. "Don't you make the mistake of thinking you're getting off light." The friendly tone had vanished. "If you fuck up, if you try to find greener pastures someplace else, if Little Mickey even hints you ain't pulling your weight, well." He puffed a smoke ring and jabbed the cigar at me through it. "There's plenty of room out there in the desert." He knocked back a slug from his drink and pulled on his cigar. His ash was long, so long I was sure the paperwork on his desk was going to go up like so much kindling when it fell.

I nodded. "Yes, sir." I paused. "I mean, yes, Mister..."

He leaned back in his chair. "Greenbaum. But you can call me Gus, for now."

———

Gus LEFT the details of what he expected from me for Little Mickey to explain. There was more, it turned out, for cheap muscle to handle in a legal casino than I'd thought. For starters, officially I would work the casino floor under the pit bosses. Not as uniformed security and not for running the games, but helping them both and "other duties as needed."

I'd never been a gambling man. Sure, I'd played the odd card game or backroom craps table in my time. In LA, like most every city, gambling was illegal. The illicit card games and the bookies, like Dominic, were the Outfit's bread and butter.

Here in Las Vegas, at the Fabulous Flamingo, it was a different story. Slots, craps, blackjack, sports betting—all of that and more were perfectly legal. You'd think a legal casino would be a license to print money. And so it was, up to a limit. The tax man was never far away, ready to put a hand in the house's pocket.

The Flamingo, though, was a new bird. An experiment in excess by Bugsy Siegel, the previous owner. He'd borrowed money, a *lot* of money, from his fellow gangsters to build his pleasure palace in the desert. He'd spent too much time building, too much time planning more and bigger extensions to the design, and not enough time paying back what he owed. As a result, there had been a "hostile takeover." Gus and his partner had taken over the works three months ago. Little Mickey and I were part of a crew sent over by Mr. Cohen to ensure his investment in the property was looked after. It sounded as if the only reason I had gotten a break at all was because of a manpower shortage after this entirely legal establishment had changed hands.

Lucky me.

Anyway, unlike your more traditional Outfit gambling operation, a legitimate casino business such as the Flamingo needed to stay on the up-and-up. Every penny had to go on record, and the tax man was keeping count.

Or so *he* thought.

What actually happened was that Joe Schmoe would come in all fat and happy, ready to gamble legally. He'd blow his wad at twenty-one, and every one of those dollars would go straight into the counting room. There, each of those dollars would magically lose twenty-five to fifty percent of its weight before it ever saw ink on the page of the official ledger.

I wasn't close to what you'd call an accountant, so I didn't need to concern myself with any of that. My official job was to keep an eye on the marks on the casino floor, my peepers peeled for anything hinky. The way Little Mickey laid it out, there'd be no shortage of bums. Cheats who'd swap chips on the blackjack table. Cheats who would try to jimmy the one-armed bandits. Cheats who would mark the cards or count them. The list was longer than Little Mickey was tall.

He'd scared us up a couple sandwiches from the kitchen while he gave me the rundown. Someone who'd grown up in the life, as he had, would know this from the get-go, but to me it was all new. Wild, too. Like stepping into a Cagney film.

Only these stakes were real. No one was going to call "cut" if I fucked up.

Before we could finish our lunches, a reedy little guy in the house security uniform scuttled up to Little Mickey's side. Little Mickey's massive brow knotted as the guard muttered something into his ear. When he had delivered his message, the guard scuttled back the way he'd come. Little Mickey turned to me, a grin playing across his lips.

"Looks like you get to jump into the deep end on your first day, Eddy," he said. "We've got ourselves a live one."

———

"OH GOD, NO MORE! PLEASE," the man tied to the chair sobbed. "I'll sign, I'll sign." His chin slumped to his chest.

I looked from the poor SOB to my knuckles and back. The deadbeat had caved before I'd even gotten warmed up. My hand wasn't even sore.

The rope around his chest held the loser upright as he wept, his nose leaking blood and snot. At most, I'd given him a few love taps, and he was already pissing himself.

Literally.

I rolled my eyes. This fella had relaxed when I'd stepped into the room. Understandable, for compared to Little Mickey's size or the Grace brothers' muscles, I must have looked like a pushover who wouldn't throw a punch. Most folks guess wrong with that.

The room's only door opened, and Little Mickey stepped in. Deadbeat gasped, straining his neck to move his head as far as he could away from the giant of a man. Tears flowed down his cheeks, washing away some of the blood from his nose, and pale red spotted his shirt. I stepped aside as Little Mickey dragged a small table across the room, its metal feet squealing on the bare concrete. Slapping a sheaf of papers on the center of the table, he produced a pen from an inside pocket. The cap he carefully unscrewed from the pen's barrel, and the brass nib glinted in the light of the bare light-bulb overhead. Setting the pen on the papers, Little Mickey tapped a line halfway down the Transfer of Ownership form.

His hand trembling like an autumn leaf, Deadbeat reached for the pen until the rope tied across his chest pulled him up short. Once I cut him loose, he got down to business, scrawling his John Hancock everywhere Little Mickey pointed. His nose snuffled at each signature.

"W-what am I going to tell my wife?" Deadbeat asked with a moan. "She loves that house."

"Well," Little Mickey said as he slid the sheaf of papers to his side of the table, "you should have considered that before you gambled yourself into a hole. Show him the exit, Eddy."

I pulled the last of the ropes free and tossed Deadbeat his coat. Hand on his shoulder, I guided him to the hallway and the rear exit.

"Hold up, Eddy." Little Mickey raised a hand. "You're not in any shape to be representing this respectable establishment at the moment. I'll show him out."

I looked down. There was an arc of bright red spots across the left side of my chest. "This shirt cost me three dollars." I shook my fist at Deadbeat, who flinched.

Little Mickey chuckled. "Wash up, I'll be right back." He placed his dinner plate–sized hand in the center of Deadbeat's back, ushering him to the door. "Mr. Pearson, the Fabulous Flamingo Hotel and Casino hopes you enjoyed your stay in the lovely state of Nevada..."

I followed them out, turning right when they turned left, on my way to the men's washroom.

That had gone well, I supposed. Mr. Pearson, aka Deadbeat, had arrived at the Flamingo and right away he'd hit a run of beginner's luck at craps. He'd spent the next three days living it up with his wife, drinking champagne and throwing his winnings right back down the pass line. Not only had he lost everything he'd won, plus every cent he'd brought along, *plus* his wife's necklace, he'd ended up with a bigger marker than mine. His wife had gone home to Orange County the night before while Mr. Pearson played on, oblivious. This morning, when he'd discovered himself at the bottom of the hole he'd dug, he'd tried to pull a runner. Security had caught him before he made it three steps across the parking lot.

They'd had him tied to that chair for five hours, letting him sweat while waiting for the hammer to come down. Since it was my first day, Mr. Greenbaum—Gus—wanted me to handle the rough stuff. Just to prove I was up to the job. Made sense. If I couldn't deal with roughing up a weakling like Mr. Pearson, I wouldn't be able to pay off my debt to the organization *and* they'd have wasted a train ticket sending me here.

Mr. Pearson was given the option of paying off the fifteen grand he owed the Flamingo—meaning Gus—or he could take option "B." Which was a drive into the desert with a shovel.

He whined that he didn't have that kind of money, that he didn't have any family to lend it to him, that his job didn't pay him enough to advance him the dough. He'd spent two years' savings getting that room at the Flamingo for his wife, who'd gone all starry-eyed over photos of Bugsy in the papers—the before pictures, not the after—and he'd wanted it to be a surprise for their anniversary. A taste of

86

the glamorous movie mobster life. Instead, they were getting a taste of the real thing, and he wasn't liking the flavor at all.

The Flamingo's count room, being connected to the sort of financial resources legitimate and otherwise that the Outfit had access to, had scared up the one asset the Pearsons had to offer. Their house. Somehow that deadbeat owned it lock, stock, and barrel. He'd refused to sign it over, some drabble about it being his father's legacy or some horseshit. He wouldn't sign—where would they live?

That's where I came in.

———

I WAS STILL DABBING at the stains on my shirt when Little Mickey returned. "Don't worry about that, Eddy. It was an ugly shirt anyway."

I gave up and leaned against the counter. "I just realized that this job is going to run me a fortune in shirts."

His barking laugh reminded me of a giant harbor seal. "Eddy, Eddy. You can afford it now." He waved his hand around, encompassing the casino and the gambling town beyond. "No shortage of opportunities around here." He held up his hand to halt any commentary I had. "The terms Mr. Cohen laid out for you are, in a word, draconian."

I wasn't sure what his word meant, but I got the idea.

"You owe Mr. Cohen, which means you owe Gus, but as far as I'm concerned, you're part of my crew. Keep doing what you did today and everything will work out just fine."

I frowned. "I didn't do anything today, barely laid into that guy. A couple of taps and he rolled over."

Little Mickey went on. "You think Mr. Pearson caved because you hit him? Please, he would have held out a lot longer and wasted our whole day if it wasn't for one thing."

"What's that?"

"You, Eddy. I saw your face."

"Huh?"

"There's a look. Some guys got it, some guys don't. Mr. Pearson saw what I saw. It was in your eyes. He knew that if he didn't give up, you'd kill him and his wife." Little Mickey shrugged. "That's not your call to make, but he wouldn't know that. If he'd refused to sign, yeah, we'd have to make an example out of him. That's how business is done."

A shiver ran up my spine, cold and sharp, at the matter-of-fact way he said that. Part of it was fear of what I'd avoided, but the other part was anticipation.

Even though I'd barely thrown a punch at Pearson, there'd been a moment where things had all lined up. Like when the Grace brothers had come at me in Mr. Cohen's office. Like in Okinawa.

I'd had plenty of time for second thoughts on the train. Dishing out the hurt for Uncle Sam had made sense at the time. We were at war and besides, the Japs had asked for it by blitzing Pearl Harbor. I hadn't been at all sure I could do the same to some schmoe who owed a few bucks.

Today had answered that question.

From his pocket, Little Mickey produced a roll of bills as big as my fist. He peeled off a few, looked me over, and peeled off another. He held them out. "You're going to need new clothes. Something that fits the dress code."

I took the cash without counting it. "What about a place to lay my head?"

He hooked a thumb over his shoulder. "We have something worked out." He pulled the door open. "Let's get you a new suit. Then, I think a proper beverage is in order."

"A new suit?" The one I was wearing, minus the stained shirt, was less than a year old. I'd picked it up with my back pay after release from the Army.

"*Vestis virum facit*, Eddy."

I raised an eyebrow. What did that mean?

"Clothes make the man, my friend. You need to look respectable while you're working for Mr. Greenbaum. We like to present a certain air of... hmm, quality here at the Fabulous Flamingo." He grinned. "We're a legitimate and respectable business, after all." He tilted his head toward the open door, and I shoved off the counter.

"Eddy?" Little Mickey said.

"Yeah?"

"Welcome to Las Vegas."

Chapter Ten
Now

I WAS STUMPED.

Oh sure, I'd been living high on the vampire lifestyle for a few decades, and I'd enjoyed every minute. But that had all been by accident. Long story short, I got myself in a bind and woke up dead. Everything I knew about being a dead guy, I'd had to figure out on my own. Call it "dead reckoning," har-de-har.

Now it was all coming down around my ears. I didn't know if Rebecca was running a short crew, or if an army of bloodsuckers was on the march for good ol' Eddy Fry. Sure, I guess I figured there had to be more like me out there somewhere. I just hadn't bothered worrying about it. Now that brilliant use of my time was going to bite me in the ass.

Not to mention there was the iceberg-that-walked-like-a-man, Felix, whatever the fuck *he* was. Which just made me wonder: What else did I have to worry about? What other fairy-tale critters were actually real? The Wolfman? The Mummy? Actual fuckin' fairies?

I shook off the funk and checked my six. It looked clear, even in my "special" sight. I hoped anyone who wasn't a plain Jane or Joe human would show like a neon sign. So far, so good.

I needed a plan. I needed info. Fuck that, I needed an *education*. When I'd come to Las Vegas, I'd gotten some on-the-job training. Trouble was, even though I was clearly dealing with hoodoo shit, I didn't think I could go to the guy flashing a mitt full of playing cards on the video billboard above me. I'd have seen it with my own eyes if any of those shysters did real magic.

By the way, magic shows are a real letdown when your new eyes see exactly how the tricks are done.

Scratch the white-tigers-and-coin-trick crowd. I'd get no help from them. UNLV? I doubted there was a "Vamp 101" in the curriculum. My biggest problem was that anyone who knew what was going on was playing for the other team.

I halted in my tracks, a new thought tickling my brain. A frat boy, drunk of course, bounced off my motionless form and spilled his beer. His buddies lured him off with the promise of a refill while I chased my idea.

It was a long shot. It must've been a day, maybe more, but it was my best shot. My only shot, if I was being honest. I may not have known a wolfman, a mummy, or a fairy who could give me the straight dope on the woo-woo set, but I knew where I might find someone who could.

I legged it up the block to the Golden Fortune, making a beeline for the maze of slot machines. Somewhere in here was where I'd seen that hoodoo punk dame. Obviously, she wouldn't be obligingly working the same slot, especially after how she'd reacted to yours truly.

Which was another problem to deal with. First, I had to find her.

"Hot Hot Penny" was ablaze with animated flames and dancing gems. Unfortunately, the swivel chair was occupied by someone's chain-smoking grandma. Nothing for it; I needed to get close.

"Yer gonna hav' ta wait, buddy," Grandma coughed. "This one's ready to pop, an' it's all mine!" Granny shot me the hairy eyeball as she hunched over her game. Her bony finger never stopped stabbing the MAX BET button.

Here goes nothing. I took a cautious breath, drawing the air in through my nose and across the roof of my mouth.

Gag.

Granny must have absolutely bathed herself in White Diamonds. Luckily, before I could retch, I caught the trace I was searching for: the spice-and-sparkle of Hoodoo Girl's scent. When she'd run off, fear had been literally oozing from her pores. I'd felt a bit bad about spooking the gal, but now I was grateful I had. It made fixing on her scent that much easier.

"I think you're right. This one's gonna pop." My spirits were up now that I had a trail to follow. "If you win the jackpot, make sure you ask the floor manager for a buffet comp."

Granny, her eyes never leaving the dancing pennies on the screen, nodded in thanks.

Because my dinners were all donated by enthusiastic partners, I'd never really had to, you know, hunt. Not since those first few days, at least. In my old job, however, I'd had to track deadbeats all the time. Of course, that didn't mean I literally sniffed them out. Still, if my nose got me to the general location Hoodoo Girl had holed up, this'd be a cinch. I had a good, strong trail to follow now. Easy street.

That thought blew away the instant I was out the Fortune's door. Her trail was gone, right where it reached the sidewalk that connected all the casinos on this side of the boulevard. I suppose a million people tromping around on top of the scent trail doesn't exactly make for easy tracking. No matter how much I worked to find a hint, a trace, it was gone.

I wasn't *quite* desperate enough to get down on all fours and jam my schnoz into the pavement like a bloodhound. Time to get Kurt on the horn and on the case with me. I'd have him pull the feed from the night before and use that face-thingy to find out what other joints she'd been in. He'd be able to track her through every casino she'd so much as passed by.

First order of business, I needed some operating funds. Time to hit up the cage. I nearly entered through the staff door before I remembered that Rebecca had my wallet and my key card with it.

"Hey, darling, you mind pulling up my credit line?" I said when a teller in the VIP line—Janet, I think—waved me over. "My wallet got lifted. I need a refill. "

"Um. Yes? Mr. Fry." Janet's voice was wavering all over the place. "I, uh, sure. Let me see what I can do."

As she spoke, Janet helpfully slid open a cash drawer with one hand, while the other went under the counter. To the silent alarm.

What the fuck?

"You know what, on second thought, I'm going to call it a night." I stretched my arms and yawned in what I hoped was a convincing demonstration.

Before I'd gone two steps, the staff door spat out a small army of security. *My* security. The scrum of uniforms bristled with batons and stun guns at the ready. In the middle marched Leandro, Kurt's second-in-command.

"Mr. Fry," Leandro said as his squad took positions around me, "please come with me." His tone was neutral, nearly friendly, but his expression was an invitation. *Give me an excuse*, it said. Leandro didn't much care for the owner's freeloading nephew, I recalled.

"Leandro, what's with all the hubbub?" I gestured at the cage. "I was just telling Janet—"

"Jennifer." Her voice wafted from under the cage counter, where she'd hidden.

"Telling Jennifer that my wallet got lifted, and all I needed was a bit of cash. Uncle Elwood—"

"Sir, I am going to ask you one last time to come with us. Before things go badly for you," Leandro said, his hand moving to his holster. *His* sidearm wasn't a Taser.

"Okay, what the hell is going on here, Leandro? I'm, I mean, my great-uncle won't be happy when he hears about this."

"Who do you think gave the order to detain you, Mr. Fry?" Leandro's smile was wide with genuine glee. "He's back in town and would like to have a word with you concerning some irregularities in the books."

Okay, now I got it. Rebecca clearly had the same tricks I did, including the eye hoodoo I'd used to keep my secret under wraps. She, or maybe another vamp I hadn't seen yet, had used the time I was out cold to make some changes. Big changes. Hell, unless I got out in front of this, she wouldn't need me to sign over ownership. She'd have her own puppet installed, having made everyone think *he* was "Uncle Elwood."

"You know what, buddy? I think I'll take a rain check on that." I took a step back, stopping when the Tasers all came up. "Hey now."

"This way, Mr. Fry." Leandro swept one arm toward the staff door he'd come from.

I knew I could take a hit from a Taser, or a few bullets, without a problem. Leandro didn't have nearly enough men with him to slow me down. The *actual* problems were the casino cameras I no longer controlled and a circle of looky-loos clogging the surrounding aisle. Phones were out and aimed, ready for the free show if shit went down. My current plan did not include ending up in the interweb's hall of fame.

I could try to get in Leandro's head and undo what Rebecca had done, but doing that would raise some eyebrows for sure. I couldn't take the chance of a trigger-happy guard setting things off because their supervisor started drooling on the carpet. Unfortunately for me, I couldn't put the whammy on more than one person at a time. Trust me, I'd tried.

"Okay, you got me. Lead on, Leandro." I shrugged, hands visible, and allowed myself to be hustled through the staff door. Into the backrooms and hallways. Away from the public.

Perfect.

I played along until we'd passed the count room, heading deeper into the maze of support corridors. We were approaching a pair of "storage" rooms used to discourage card counters and the like from plying their trade in my establishment.

Hey, old habits die hard.

There weren't any cameras in or outside those rooms, by design.

Leandro held a door open and smirked. "After you, Mr. Fry."

"No, thanks." I said, giving him a measured shove into the room. I didn't want to break the guy. This wasn't his fault, not really. The other guards were reacting, their batons and guns coming up to deal with me, but my nitro-strength adrenaline was pumping. To me, they appeared to be moving like sleepwalkers. I bowled the nearest two aside, body-checking them into the walls. I heard at least one bone go snap, but those guys're tough. They'd live.

I wanted to be out of sight before Leandro pulled his

piece on me. The Golden Fortune was still mine, and I didn't want to chance any of my staff catching a bullet because of Rebecca's bullshit.

Two turns later, taking the corners by kicking off the walls, I had a straight shot out via a small loading dock. I wasn't worried about Leandro's team catching me now. It was the security office I was worried about. A lockdown would seal the exits, heavy-duty steel doors with magnetic locks. Those would stop me just like anyone else.

Also, I didn't know if Felix was in the vicinity. I *really* wanted to avoid that jagoff if I could.

A slap of the exit's release bar and I was clear of the building. Making sure I kept my pace to something a bit more relaxed, I hustled my way through the myriad parking lots and alleys that fed the service side of the resort. Once I reached Winnick, I hopped straight into the back of a waiting cab.

"Sorry, buddy, I'm off duty. You'll have to go to the stand out front for another cab," the driver told me around a mouthful of hoagie. He peeled the wrapper back on his foot-long in preparation for another bite.

"Hey." I tapped the plexiglass barrier. "Check this out."

"What?" The driver turned to look, and I had him.

Feeling only a little guilty, I flattened the driver's willpower with mine. "Just drive. Go, I dunno, head toward Henderson and let me think." I broke eye contact and dropped back against the seat's torn padding.

"Uh, yes. Okay. Hey, pal?" His voice slid up the scale from doped to normal. "I'm gonna take the scenic route. Just you sit back and enjoy." He dropped the hoagie on the seat beside him.

While he got busy putting distance between me and the Fortune, I tried to get it together. Goddammit, how the hell was I supposed to do this without a base of operations? I pinched the bridge of my nose. Okay, that could be handled. Thanks to the paranoia of my early days as a night-crawler, I had a couple of bolt-holes set up around town. I'd be safe when the sun came up. It was losing the resources of the Fortune that stung. It was like losing an arm.

My priority had to be convincing Hoodoo Girl to clue me in. But before that happened, I had to find her.

Okay, Eddy. Time to do this the old-fashioned way.

The trick to finding someone was to figure out why they'd come to Vegas. Get in their head. Figure out what kind of place they'd pick to rest their head, where they'd eat, that sort of jazz. I'd been pretty good at it once, and tourists ain't changed that much since then.

I drew up a mental list. Young, not a high roller, likely flying solo. She'd been cruising the Strip, but I'd bet a nickel she wasn't staying there. Her clothes had been worn in by time, not the fake wear of "distressed" fashion. That leather jacket had been lived in. Dollars to donuts her budget would land her in an off-Strip motel, not a casino hotel. Which was both good and bad. Good: I could avoid the cameras while searching. Bad: There were about a hundred times as many motels as casinos in this town.

But here's the thing. She'd been on the Strip, hitting the slots. She was here for fun. My guess is she wouldn't grab a motel all the way over in Summerlin, far from where the action was. No, she'd pick something cheap that was close to the party. That meant Strip-adjacent or Fremont Street.

"Hey." I rapped on the plexi. "Head to Fremont Street."

"Yup." The driver glided us into a smooth lane change.

I had the driver drop me a block away from the Palace. Without the scratch to settle up, I felt guilty for tearing him away from his hoagie. I told him to forget me, but I took his card. I'd settle up once the heat was off.

If I survived.

I burnt just over an hour hoofing it around the outskirts of Fremont Street. I wanted to avoid the casino cameras and prying eye of Johnny Law lest they tattle to Rebecca. I had no idea how long she'd been in town before cornering me. She could have her hooks in *anywhere*. For all I knew, she had a seat in the mayor's office.

Mind on the search, Eddy. Fremont didn't cover as much territory as I'd remembered. Funny, I'd thought there was more down here.

Okay, I could skip the blocks south of "the Experience." That area was all municipal-type establishments. No motels.

Instead, I stuck to the streets between Fremont and the highway, sniffing the air on each block. If she was staying anywhere close, she'd have to pass through here to get to Fremont. Even if she didn't hit up the old casinos, odds were in my favor. She'd head there for food or transportation. I was betting it all that I'd pick up her trail around here. If not, well, I'd always wanted to visit Iceland. Six months of long nights was starting to sound pretty good.

I was ready to throw in the towel when I hit the jackpot. She'd passed through here, on this street, less than an hour ago. At the same time, a glance at my Rolex confirmed the little voice in the back of my skull. I was cutting it close. Still, I had to do this now or risk Hoodoo Girl leaving town while I slept.

Her trail led me through four increasingly seedy blocks to the lot of a motel so beat up that its photo was no doubt in the dictionary under "fleabag." Finding her room was even easier. It had to be the door glowing neon when I looked at it with my Vamp-O-Vision.

What? I don't know what to call it. Second sight, I guess.

Someone had penned in the number eight, with a

marker, in the pale spot where the original plate had gone missing. I didn't need my special hearing to detect the snore from inside. Hoodoo Girl was sawing enough wood to build a cabin.

I raised a hand but hesitated. I'd never in my life had trouble approaching a dame, yet now my knees were almost knocking. For starters, her earlier reaction to me had been less than congenial. Then there was me, not knowing the first thing about hoodoo-slinging teenagers. I was out of my depth. I was overthinking it.

I knocked.

Ow!

I danced back from the door, hand stinging like I'd burnt it on the stove. Something had bit me when I'd knocked. I blew across my knuckles and inspected my hand. The skin was bright red from knuckles to wrist and beginning to swell like I'd stuck my hand into a boiling pot.

Oh. Right. Her door had been glowing when I'd used my second sight. I'd forgotten about it already. Good work, dummy. I checked the door again while I shook my aching hand. A network of hair-fine lines crisscrossed the thin wood, glowing in my other sight. Deep blue and amber threads wove in and out of the door. Definitely what had bit me. Okay, mental note, don't touch the glowing shit.

I was trying to decide if I could knock with my shoe when I caught up to the fact that the snoring had quit. The shuffle of feet crossing the floor reached my ears, and I did my best to look friendly. The curtain twitched and a bleary hazel eye peered through the narrow gap.

I waved. "Hey."

The curtain pinched shut. "Oh *shiiiiiiiiit.*" More shuffling, like she was pacing behind the curtain.

I tried again. "Look, I know you probably think this is

pretty messed up, what with me tracking you down like this. But I—"

"Go. Away." She wasn't yelling. Yet.

"Okay, I know you think I'm here for a late dinner. But it's not that at all—"

"Fuck off." Her voice was climbing. "Asshole." The curtain tugged open, closing again just as fast. "I'm not some blood junkie, you dick."

This wasn't the sort of neighborhood where yelling would attract attention. But then, I didn't want to risk some poor streetwalker getting caught up in the scuffle if the girl started throwing hoodoo around. Raising my hands, I tried to look harmless while I addressed the eye in the curtain's gap. "Listen, I know we didn't exactly get off to a great start back at the Fortune. However, I can point to the fact I haven't kicked the door down when we both know that flimsy sheet of plywood wouldn't stop a toddler. I am attempting to be, ah..." I searched for a word. "Diplomatic."

"Wards, motherfucker." A hint of pride joined the anger in her voice. Then, louder, "I told you back in the casino that I'd burn you if you tried any shit. You so much as touch this door and I'll torch you so fast—"

"Okay, I can see trust is going to be an issue here," I said before she could get any more graphic about murdering me. "I want to point out another detail that should help prove that I am not here to, erm, attack you."

The hazel eye narrowed. "What."

My fingernail ticked on the glass in front of her eye. "You didn't do the window."

A blink. "Fuck." The curtain jerked. The sound of her stomping across the floor reached my ears, followed by a muffled scream. Muffled as if with a dirty motel pillow. "*Ffffuuuuuuuuuuuuuuuck!*"

I waited for her to get it out of her system.

"Go away."

Great, we were back to that.

I checked the Rolex as a hint of warmth brushed the skin of my neck. Dammit, would you look at the time? "One sec." I held up a finger as I stepped away from Number Eight. Wandering around the motel's lot yielded me a battered metal chair, from the slab of cracked concrete serving as a patio next to an empty pool. I planted the chair, and my ass, directly in front of the window and its glaring eye. I noticed that while I'd been picking up the chair, she'd gone and—warded?—the window with more of those neon threads. Not as dense as the door, but enough to keep me from messing with it. "I think I'll just sit here until you hear me out. Don't worry. This won't take long. I'm sure you've got a good idea what'll happen when the sun comes up." I made a point of looking at my watch.

"The fuck are you doing?" she asked. The gap in the curtain widened to give her a clear view of where I sat. Green hair, tousled from sleep, tumbled over one eye and part of her face. It made her look young, much younger than I'd thought when I'd first laid eyes on her. Well, if I had any second thoughts about her know-how or experience, it was too late now. No way I could get to my hideaway before things got too bright. I was all in on this plan.

"Oh, I'm planning to sit here and enjoy the sunrise. It's been a bit since I've seen one."

"Why the fuck would you do that?" Worried now.

"I need your help." *Honesty time, Eddy.* My best smile felt fake, so I just watched her.

"*Buullll*-shit."

I shrugged and looked east, over the warehouse at the end of the block, toward the mountains in the distance beyond that. Not long now.

101

She bit her lip, working it like a chew toy. "Okay, fine. What kind of help?"

I checked my watch again. "I don't really want to air my dirty laundry for all the neighbors to hear. It's none of their damn business. Not to mention it's a long story, and it's getting cold out here." Actually, it was getting uncomfortably warm. The pre-dawn glow hit my skin with a nettle-like prickling.

While I'd been checking the horizon for signs of daylight, Hoodoo Girl had shut the curtains. Damn. Well, I'd had a good run, right? Maybe I could make it to that warehouse? Find a crate to hide in? Maybe I'd get shipped somewhere nice. I braced for a last-second dash.

A rattle of a chain brought my attention away from the east. Number Eight's door was open, the ward lines still in place like a glowing screen door. Hoodoo Girl glared at me from behind the screen. "Your word that you're not here for blood or..." She forced the words through gritted teeth.

"Sister, I have ladies lined up to donate. More than I can handle most nights. I mean, look at me. Do I look like I'm going hungry?" I said.

This was about as close to dawn as I'd gotten since the early days, and the prickling on my skin had turned to needles. I held up a hand and stared as it steamed in the rising light. Dawn was less than a minute away.

"What do you want, for real?" she asked. The door inched wider.

"Information. For real."

"From me?" Her brow furrowed. "Why?"

I talked fast. "You are the only person I'm aware of who *might* fill me in on all the shit I don't know about being a vampire." A blister formed on the back of my hand as I spoke, and I could feel more on my face.

Her eyes went wide and met my own, searching. I

didn't move a muscle. Glancing at the ceiling with a mouthed *What the hell am I doing?*, she pointed at me. "Your word."

I raised my blistered, steaming hand. "My word, no funny business." My voice caught in my throat, the rising light stinging the flesh in my open mouth.

Hoodoo Girl tugged one of the glowing threads of her ward, and it all unraveled into nothing. She backed away from the entrance, jerking a thumb over her shoulder. "In."

The sun crested the mountains as I dashed into room number eight.

Once I was out of the light of the dawning sun, the pressure was off, and I sagged in relief.

Kicking the door shut, I gave the curtains a grateful pat. They were thick enough to keep the sun out, an unusual feature in a motel at this price point, but I wasn't going to look that gift horse in the mouth.

Hoodoo Girl had retreated to the door of the bathroom; judging by how she gripped the knob, I assumed it had a window to let in the sun. She alternated between a cringe and a defiant glare while she waited to see if I would break my word.

I held up my hand, and the both of us watched as the blisters melted away. My skin resumed its normal fair tone, losing the sunburn. I shook my hands, getting the last of the sting out. "Oh, that's better."

When I glanced back to Hoodoo Girl, we both realized that the only thing she had on was a long T-shirt, the front emblazoned with a woman wearing a wide black hat and a red corset cinched over a black gown. When Hoodoo Girl bent to drag on a pair of ratty Levi's, I read the print on the rear of her T-shirt. "What the hell is a Sex Metal Barbie?" I asked no one in particular.

A hefty pile of keys, small toys, casino chips, and

random knickknacks littered the table beside her. Rummaging through the detritus, she produced a familiar pewter-sheathed bottle, the "bottled sunlight" from earlier. Still not ready to trust my word, clearly. With her back literally against the wall, sunlight in one hand, bathroom door handle in the other, she finally spoke. "Why me?"

I let my legs kick out as I slid to the floor and leaned my head against the thin wood door at my back. When I ran fingers through my hair, they came away littered with bits of skin. Ew. "I didn't have any other ideas. I couldn't think of anyone else to go to."

"Oh, come on. Fanghead living in Las Vegas? You must have a whole army of..." Her eyes narrowed. "Hold up." She crept away from the safety of the bathroom door, bottled sunlight extended ahead of her.

If I still breathed, I would have held my breath. Crouching just in front of me, her eyes narrowed as she scanned my face. When she leaned in, a chain spilled from the neck of her T-shirt. Two gold rings swung at the end of the cheap metal chain.

Hoodoo Girl's hand came up, and she paused, holding her own breath. Taking my chin, she tilted my head first one way, then the other. "Oh, no fucking way." She closed her eyes. "No. Fucking. Way." She glanced over her shoulder, addressing the room behind her. "Are you fucking kidding me right now?"

There was a fluttering, a sound in the air above us, and I froze. It was as if a bird had leapt into flight and was flapping its merry way around the room. As it faded, growing distant, there was laughter. A boy's voice, giggling.

"What the *hell* was that?" I asked.

"A pain in the ass, that's what that was." She brushed her palms across her thighs, tucking the chain and its rings away as she stood. "Yeah awright. Talk. What's so damn important you were willing to greet the dawn?" She dragged the room's one chair out from beside the bed and dropped into it. She still had the bottle in her hand, but it wasn't pointed at me anymore. I don't know who, or what, had vouched for me, but I wasn't going to question it. At least not right now.

"How many other folks do you know in the, hmm, nocturnal community?"

"Know? None. Seen and avoided like the plague they are? More than I care to." She thought about it. "No offense."

I waved it off. "Well, until tonight, I've never met anyone in my condition. Actually, I've never met anyone..."

"Supernatural?"

"That."

"Bullshit. What about the one who made you?" She leaned her elbows on her knees.

"Okay, yeah, him. But that was an accident. I didn't know the guy. We didn't exactly engage in conversation. I was too busy trying to stay alive. Which I failed miserably at." I laughed. "Guess I won by losing. Anyhow. I've been playing it by ear ever since."

"Until tonight?"

"Yeah." I nodded, patting my pockets. Shit, no wallet, I'd forgotten. I glanced at my wrist. What the hell. I popped the clasp on my Rolex and tossed it to her. Hoodoo Girl snatched it out of the air and held it up in the room's dim light.

"What's this?" she asked.

"A Rolex Submariner. Unlike department store junk, a Rolex appreciates in value. This one should go for, oh..." I did some math in my head. "Just over fourteen."

"Hundred?"

"Thousand."

Her eyebrows shot into her hairline. "You're trying to buy me? I told you," she said, her voice rising, "I am not—"

I held up my hands. "It's a retainer. I want to hire you, not buy you."

"Hire me?"

"As a consultant. Consider that"—I nodded at the watch in her hand—"a good faith guarantee toward compensation for services, which will *not* include feeding me, rendered."

She tapped the watch against her chin. "A consultant? What services?"

"Information. Vampire shit. Hoodoo shit. Whatever you think I need to know to get along out there. If you don't know something that I need to know, then help in locating someone who does. Let's say a week to start, longer if it works out." I crossed my arms over my bent knees and waited.

"How much are you offering? Other than the fancy watch, I mean." She clicked the oyster bracelet around her wrist, where it was only a bit loose.

"The green goes with your hair," I offered, getting a glare in return. "Okay, how about five a day?"

"Five hundred?" I shook my head and poked a finger upward. Her eyebrows went north again. "Five *thousand*?"

I nodded.

The tip of her tongue poked the corner of her mouth while she mulled it over. She punched her fist into the other hand and leveled a finger at me. "Make it ten. Ten grand a day, *plus* expenses. *And* a better place to stay, and meals."

I couldn't help it. She was already growing on me, but I made a show of thinking it over so I didn't seem too desperate. "Expenses, lodging and meals. Hmmmmm."

She raised the bottle of sunlight again.

"Okay, okay!" I hauled myself upright. "You got a deal, sister." I stuck out my hand. "Eddy Fry."

She sat there blinking, her jaw sagging open. Guess she hadn't expected me to agree to her terms. She stared at my hand. I waggled it. When she stood, her head was almost level with mine. Her hand came up. I waited. Her fingers brushed my palm, and I grabbed her hand, giving it a firm shake. "Done deal, Miss...?" I let the question hang.

She retrieved her hand, staring at it for several heartbeats. Shaking herself out of it, she said, "Call me Xenia. By the way, how are you awake still?"

"Oh, I've always been a morning person." Which deserved the eye-roll I got. I shrugged. "Fine. It's been ages since I've been forced to conk out at sunrise. Once I had a few years under my belt, I could stay up as late as I wanted. Don't get me wrong, I still have to sleep, eventually."

"Good to know." A yawn cut off whatever she was going to add, her jaw stretching wide enough for a bird to fly in. "Speaking of, I think I got like five whole minutes of sleep before you pounded my damn door down." She scooped up a pillow and a blanket from the bed. Okay, *I* wouldn't trust the linen here, but to each their own, I guess.

She paused at the bathroom door. "So, it's not like I don't trust you enough to sleep in the same room, but I don't." She popped open the bathroom door, and the daylight bouncing in through the dirty window was enough to make my skin steam. I skipped back away from the light and she added, "No offense, boss."

"I get that," I said to the closing door. "See you at sundown." I grabbed the only remaining do-not-steal-me motel coat hanger that hadn't been stolen yet and hung my coat. Nothing too disgusting presented itself when I eyeballed the floor between the bed and the wall, so I picked that as my resting spot for the day. Once I'd tucked myself into that narrow space, yanking the mattress sideways gave me a roof.

I'd told Xenia that I could stay awake long past sunrise if I wanted, but I'd left out a detail. It took effort. Every minute I kept myself awake used up a bit of my stamina, like keeping a muscle flexed. It was a muscle I could flex for quite a while, especially when well fed. I believe the longest I'd ever pulled it off was at a poker tournament, a couple of years back. I made it three days before bubbling out. Even though the pressure to sleep wasn't as strong now as it was then, today had been a hell of a night.

I stopped resisting, and I was out.

Chapter Eleven
Then

THE SUN BULL'S-EYED ME SQUARE IN THE EYE THROUGH a gap in the curtains, and I groaned awake. I considered jamming my face into the pillow to shut it all out, but my bladder chimed in with its two bits. I soldiered on, ignoring the impulse in the name of "just five more minutes."

When I couldn't hold it anymore, I hauled myself upright, or something like it. Shambled to the bathroom. Drained the lizard. Shaved. The razor had a mind of its own, and I had to stick a bit of TP to my chin to stop the bleeding.

Coffee, I needed coffee.

I've been hanging my hat at the Hotel Apache, but only until I could find my own digs. Because the boss's partner owned the joint downstairs, the Eldorado Club, I was getting a decent rate. For the room *and* the coffee.

I waved off the bartender's offer to "Irish up" my Joe. By my watch, it was almost ten, so I needed to hustle. I burnt my tongue gulping down the java and left two bits for the bartender.

You can always count on there being a line of taxis on every corner in this town. When I hit Fourth, there was no shortage of them clamoring for my attention. I dropped into the back seat of the lead cab and told the driver to head for the Flamingo. He took his sweet time checking the mirrors, looking in every direction, intent on doing anything *but* drive. I was ready to slap the back of the jagoff's head when he finally pulled, slowly, out into the morning traffic.

"Come on, step on it. Don't make me late."

"Yessir," the cabbie said, not stepping on it at all.

It was a four-mile drive to the Flamingo, so I had plenty of time to eyeball the new construction going in along Highway 91 while Grandpa puttered along. When we finally pulled into the Flamingo's lot, I saw that while I'd been sleeping late, they'd broken ground on the new wing of the casino. The crew was, of course, on break and nowhere to be seen. I knew Gus would see to it that despite the lazy workers, they would finish the new wing in no time.

The cabbie dropped me at the service entrance; following Little Mickey's advice, I tipped him well. I wasn't exactly rolling in dough, but he'd told me it helped to smooth things out. Never know when you'd need to get somewhere in a hurry.

Like *this* guy knew from hurry.

Little Mickey was nowhere to be seen. He normally lined me up with whatever job I was supposed to do when I arrived. Until I found him, I wasn't getting paid.

As I raised my hand to knock at Gus's door, the boss's office spat out the pin-striped form of Gus's partner. "Good morning, Mr. Sedway. How's the health today?" I asked the co-owner of the Flamingo.

He rubbed his crooked nose for a moment while taking stock of his ailments. "Stomach's acting up again on me, son." He shrugged. "I blame the rich living."

I laughed obediently. "I hear that, Mr. Sedway. Hope you feel better soon."

Mr. Sedway split his time between the Flamingo and his other property, the Eldorado Room, which meant I didn't see him as much I did Mr. Greenbaum. Not that I actually saw Gus that much anymore.

Little Mickey slapped me on the back, just about bouncing me into the wall. "Let's get to work."

———

OVER THE LAST COUPLE MONTHS, Little Mickey had been slotting me in with the floor crew. Contrary to my expectations, there wasn't a deadbeat to slap around every day, and if I had to rely on "collections" to work off my debt, I'd be old and gray before I'd paid off half. However, Little Mickey seemed to take pity on my financial bind with these assignments.

I didn't get paid hourly, like the pit boss and floor men did. Little Mickey would toss me a few bills after I pulled a shift, half of which I'd dutifully hand over to Gus. The boss would count it all carefully and make a note in his ledger, all the while puffing away on one of his Cubans.

Unfortunately, between paying off my marker and paying for the room at the Apache and the cab rides to work, there wasn't much left for good old Eddy's pocket.

Hey, don't get me wrong, I was alive and had three hots and a cot. Hard to beat that when I got a reminder of the alternative while looking out the window on the ride in every morning. It's just... I was dying to sink my teeth into some real cabbage. Something that would let me take a chunk out of my marker, take a step up in the world.

Instead, I'd spent the last handful of weeks watching *other* people live it up. It was exactly as boring as it sounded. The upswing was that it had given Little Mickey a chance to suss out a better use for my time. I had thought nothing about it at first, but according to him, I had a talent for spotting the cheats.

Don't ask me to count cards or explain how it's done. Math was *not* my game. Eyeballing a fella who *was* counting? That was easy. I could pick them out a good ten hands before the pit boss got wise. Same for the lowlifes who'd try to swap chips at craps or mark cards. I didn't know why it was so hard for the other guys to pick up on it. A cheater just came across obvious to me.

In the months since Mr. Greenbaum and Mr. Sedway had taken over the Flamingo, the joint had started jumping. Every weekend was booked solid almost a year out, which explained the new construction on a place that was barely a year old. They needed room for more tables, more slots, more money flowing into the Outfit's pockets.

A bigger crowd meant more cheats. We had teams of them coming in to work every angle you could think of. There were blockers who'd run interference with the pit boss or distract a player while their crony capped the bet. They'd do a few legit rounds before and after to cover up what they were doing. Like... like that jagoff over there.

I slowed my pace, then elbowed myself into a spot at the bar. From there, I could keep my eye on the craps tables without being obvious. Didn't want to spook my meal ticket. I got a juicy bonus when I pinched a cheat, much more than I'd get for just holding the carpet down.

Sure enough, the guy beside the croupier was laughing up a storm, the life of the party. With every punchline, he'd slap the shoulder of a Stetson-wearing Texan on his other side. While I watched, the Cheat leaned into the Texan's side to point out the generous helping of cleavage on display across the table as the lady in question scooped up her winnings.

While the Texan ogled the view, the Cheat slipped a

chip from the end of his mark's rack into his own. Slapping the Texan's back one last time, the Cheat emptied his drink, scooped up his chips, and made for the cage.

Before he'd gone ten steps, I gripped his elbow. "Sir, I want you to come with me right now." I pulled him toward the security door.

Mr. Cheat planted his heels and strained against my grasp. Greasy sweat popped up on his forehead as he stammered something about me having the wrong guy. I dug a finger into the nerve in his elbow to shut him up.

Alfie, one of the Flamingo's uniformed security—the legitimate kind—nodded as he opened the door for me. "Another one, Eddy?"

"Seems like there's a live one every day, these days."

Alfie took lead, and I shoved Mr. Cheat into the hallway, trapping him between us. I slapped the back of Mr. Cheat's head. "Every damn day, some smart guy thinks he can help himself."

"I can, uh, pay." His voice shook as much as the chip tray rattling in his clutches.

"Shaddup," Alfie and I both said at the same time.

Alfie unlocked the door to the waiting room, plucking the rack of chips from Mr. Cheat's hands while I shoved him inside. Alfie banged the rack on the table and pointed at the room's single chair. "Sit." He turned to me. "All yours, Eddy."

I stopped Alfie with a hand. "This chump had already hit a mark by the time I spotted him. Texas-looking guy. Big hat. Can't miss him." I eyeballed the rack. "Got taken for two hundred that I saw."

"I'll handle it." Alfie paused once more. "I think this is the guy who hit the Boulder Room the other day." His voice was low, never rising above a whisper. "Las Vegas's finest are overworked. He must've slipped through the cracks.

The boss wants repeat offenders handled 'internally' for the foreseeable future, got it?" With a last nod, he closed the door behind him. Now it was just me and Mr. Cheat.

"Internally" had become code for Little Mickey's crew over the last couple of weeks. What it meant: we had the freedom to do whatever we considered appropriate to, ahem, dissuade folks from plying their trade at the Flamingo or any other casino in town.

It *didn't* mean I could nix the poor SOB. That call wasn't mine to make. Though I was pretty sure I could handle it if they did make that call. I'd stamped my fair share of tickets in the Pacific and I slept fine. No sweat.

Probably.

Hell, I wasn't even supposed to do anything drastic enough to require a hospital stay. But then, these situations couldn't be handled with a light touch, either. The message had to be received loud and clear.

Mr. Cheat shrank back against the wood of the chair, pit stains already darkening his shirt. His fingers danced out a random beat on the tabletop.

"Pockets." I jabbed my finger down in front of him. "Now." His eyes rolled from me to the door and back. Shoulders slumped, he turned out a rumpled pack of smokes, a couple matchbooks, a set of keys, and half a pack of breath mints.

"No wallet? ID?" I asked.

He shook his head, sending sweat flying. "N-no."

I took a perch on the edge of the table and plucked the pack from the pile of his things. Tapping one out, I made like I was offering it to him, only to pull back when he reached for it. I lipped a smoke from the pack, tucking the rest in my pocket for later. "What's your name, Mac?" Once I'd puffed up a good cherry, I blew the smoke in his face.

The only answer I got was a few coughs.

I slammed my hand down on the table directly in front of him, and the sound echoed like a shot in the small room. His mints went airborne from the impact, landing in his lap.

"J-J-Johnathan." His voice cracked.

I rolled my hand in a "go-on" gesture.

"Johnathan Turrell."

I hopped off the edge of the table and leaned over him.

"I swear!" He flinched back. "That's my name. Johnathan Turrell."

I set the cigarette down on the edge of the table and crossed to the cabinet, which was the only other furniture in the room. I made a show of pulling out a ring of keys, flipping through them one by one, holding up the winner. "Ah-hah." I rummaged around, my body blocking Johnathan's view of the cabinet's interior.

"Oh God. Okay, okay, I'm sorry I was lifting! I won't do it again, I swear!" Johnathan's words tumbled over one another. "Look, I didn't even take that much! A hunnert bucks, tops! I didn't even take anything from you!" His voice was climbing in pitch as he tried to talk his way out of the fix he was in. "The casino, I mean. The Flamingo."

"This time." I'd found what I was looking for and swung the cabinet door shut. "But stealing from our guests is like stealing from us. You *do* know who I'm talking about when I say 'us,' don't you, Johnathan?"

Okay, I wasn't what you'd call "made" by any means, but Gus had given me the leeway to throw weight around on behalf of the management.

"Oh, fuck nonononono," John whined.

"Oh, yes." I showed him what I held in my hands.

A Kodak camera.

John's whine trailed off as his brows beetled. "What's... what's that for?"

I snapped my fingers for his attention. "Look at the birdie, John."

While Johnathan tried to catch up, I snapped a few. Once I had a variety of unflattering shots, I returned the camera to the cabinet and picked up my cigarette. I took a slow drag and held it. I hadn't been a big smoker before coming to Las Vegas, but when in Rome...

I blew out a cloud and flicked the butt at John. It bounced off his forehead as he flinched in the wrong direction. I said, "One of those photos is going up on the wall in the office right here. The rest we'll send to all of our good friends, all the *other* casinos in town. Do I have to spell it out? That your Las Vegas days are over?"

John's shoulders sagged. He shook his head. "No."

"Good. You're gone, John. Leave town no later than lunch tomorrow. Don't come back." I put some weight in my tone. "Ever."

Relief crashed over his face like a wave. Guess he'd been waiting for the other shoe to drop, the one that would put him in a pine box. Now there was light at the end of the tunnel. "Right, yes, you're right. My car's in the lot. You'll never see me again." He was definitely counting his lucky stars.

"Oh, by the way, John." I put on a friendlier tone. Almost buddy-buddy. "I saw you lift that cowpoke's chips myself. Smoothly done. Neither the pit boss or the croupier was wise to it."

John's mouth gaped open like a fish ready for the hook. He closed it with a little snap. His ego caught up and the corner of his mouth twitched into a sly smile. "Well."

I held up a hand. "I'm just recognizing the skill that went into that move. In this job, I've seen a lot of chumps fumble their lift. When someone puts in the time to get it right, I can tell."

"Yeah, it took a couple of years." His tone was cautious, hesitant.

"Well, it shows." I dusted my hands on my trouser legs and stuck one out. "Just wanted to say I know that kind of skill took effort, okay?"

John looked at my hand like I might have a snake in it. His grip, hesitant at first, firmed up when I merely shook his hand like an old friend. When he tried to take his hand back, my grip clamped down, grinding the bones of his fingers against each other.

The color drained from John's face. "*Owww.*" He dragged on my hand, his feet sliding across the concrete floor as he fought for traction.

I kept the pressure on. "Thing is, *John*, I know that a guy like you puts in all that time, all that practice, until he's an expert." I leaned in. "He's not just gonna stop. No matter what I say, no matter what we hold over your head." I used the table to stretch his arm out in front of him. "Even the photos wouldn't stop you. You'd just grow a beard or get a rubber nose. Something. You'd be back. To. Steal. From. Us." I increased the pressure of my grip with each word.

John's whine slid up an octave. He clutched his wrist with his free hand as his feet slithered across the floor, seeking purchase.

"The only real guarantee that a man with a skill will stop using it... is to take away the skill."

John tore his eyes from his trapped hand. His mouth worked, trying to get the words out while he stared at me in horror.

With my free hand, I got a grip around the base of his pinky finger.

"No, no, please." His pleading whisper rose in a whine.

I'd gotten better at this in the last month—plenty of

opportunities around here for practice. I'd stopped hesitating, stopped wincing in anticipation of the sound it made.

With an easy pull, I broke the trapped finger. The flesh around the break flushed a startling shade of maroon. John, sobbing now, heaved against my grip and nearly broke free. I braced a knee on the table and dragged him back to me. I gave his ring and middle fingers the same treatment. John sagged against the table, snot bubbling from his nose.

"Almost done, John. Only one more."

A muffled *pop* and his index finger joined its siblings. I took a moment to inspect my work. I didn't want the breaks to heal clean and put my efforts to waste, after all. Once I was satisfied, I let him go. He cradled his hand to his chest like a little bird.

I fished another smoke from John's pack. "Tomorrow, John, by noon. That should give you enough time to get your fingers set so you can drive out of town. Got it?"

John mumbled something through the snot dripping from his nose, followed by a sullen nod.

Alfie, or one of the other guards, would take over from here. They'd make sure he got to his car or a taxi without inconveniencing the other guests. Meanwhile, since I'd worked up an appetite, I aimed myself at the lounge.

Time for lunch.

Chapter Twelve
Now

My brain popped on, coming to life as if dawn had flipped my switch, as the last sliver of sun was swallowed by the Spring Mountains to the west. In my previous life, my first instinct would have been to pour myself a cup of mud. These days, coffee was little more than brown water, and even the aroma had lost its appeal. I *was* feeling a bit peckish for the red stuff, but it hadn't hit critical levels just yet. I could put it off until later, once my new consultant had a chance to show me her stuff. When the time came, there were a few numbers I could call.

Bright-eyed and bushy-tailed despite sleeping on the floor, I slipped the mattress home on the cheap motel bed. I did *not* rise to my feet like a plank being tilted on its edge. That's movie shit. Besides, I've tried. Doesn't work. Instead, I clambered to my feet like anyone else.

Xenia had planted herself across from me, cross-legged, on the room's only chair. I suppose she'd wanted to keep an eye peeled while I slept, trust still being thin on the ground. Instead of watching me, however, her eyes were glued to something in her lap. From the movement of her hands, I would have thought she was knitting. Except she was knitting with empty hands, without yarn or needles. Just waving her hands around. While I watched, she rotated the object of her focus: a pair of dark glasses. As she turned the frames around, I caught the barest glimmer of light on the wire. I blinked and, as I tuned in to that other spectrum, the room filled with streamers of otherworldly light.

Xenia reached out without looking and pinched a thread from a ribbon of textured green-but-not-green light that flowed from floor to ceiling beside her. Her brows creased and the tip of her tongue poked from the corner of her mouth as she dragged the filament down to the tangle of similar threads floating around the glasses.

"Is that magic? Are you casting a spell?" I asked, unable to keep the excitement from my voice.

Xenia jumped as if I'd shouted, *BOO!* Her eyes went wide as saucers. Terror twisted her face for an instant, vanishing as her spell unraveled before her. It was as if a flashbulb had gone off, flaring in the unseen spectrum of light. A *pop* that was at the same time deafening and utterly silent hit my ears. A wave of pressure washed over me, ruffling my hair. The eyeglasses dropped to the floor, trailing a streamer of bluish smoke.

"God *damn* it, Eddy! Don't *do* that!" Xenia cried, hands clutching the sides of her skull. "*Oowwww.*"

"Ah, shit. Sorry, uh, Xenia. Okay, lesson one. Don't interrupt wizards when they're doing wizard shit." I ticked an invisible check in the air with my finger.

"Ow." Her fingers made little circles at her temples. "No, the first lesson is don't call me a fucking wizard. Only posers who read too many children's books call us that." Her boots clunked against the floor as she sat up straight, the fingers of one hand steepled at her collar, and adopted a lofty tone. "The accepted term for a practitioner is 'magician.'" Then, her shoulders slumped and her feet kicked out

120

in front of her. "I'm glad it was only a minor crafting you interrupted. Otherwise, the blowback would've been a lot worse."

I winced.

"Well, I shouldn't be so focused on my work that I don't notice a vampire rising in the same room." Xenia chucked the twisted frames into the trash. "Good thing you hired me, 'cause you clearly don't know the first thing about... what'd you call it?" She waggled her fingers in the air, leaving little trails of light. "The hoodoo shit? Yeah, lesson two. Don't interrupt when I'm working, please. Magic is dangerous."

"Got it."

Xenia shoo'd me out of the way and began shoving her scattered belongings into her backpack. I took the hint and rescued my coat from the sorry excuse of a closet. "C'mon. I need breakfast, lunch, *and* dinner." She nailed me with a look, a lock of green flopping to obscure one eye. She flipped it back. "You're buying, right? Boss?"

I thought about how Rebecca had gotten her hooks into the Fortune's security in a handful of hours. Even more time had passed since then. "Well, there might be a hitch—"

Xenia snapped her fingers, hooking a thumb toward the outside.

"Who's the boss here?" I muttered. "Fine, a deal's a deal." I swept my arm out in a half bow. "After you. We just need to make a quick detour on the way."

———

BACK WHEN I'D first woken up dead, paranoia had ruled my nights. As a result, I'd used my "skills" to pull together a network of safe houses and hideaways. Places I could go to ground if it hit the fan, or just to wait out the daylight hours. I had alternate IDs, weapon and money caches, getaway cars, the works. Since I'd settled into the good life at the Fortune, I'd been slacking on all of that. I'd sold off the extra properties and cars, relying instead on my penthouse fortress.

Hey, it had worked out just fine until last night.

The ultimate proof that I'd gone soft hit me. I'd given the cab driver directions straight to the storage facility that housed my only remaining safe house. Now both the driver and Xenia knew where it was.

Mentally kicking myself, I let it slide. The driver didn't know me from Adam, and Xenia... well, trust had to start somewhere.

I'd used the drive from downtown to give her a rough sketch of what had set me dogging her heels last night and why I didn't think hitting the Strip to fill her tank was the best idea, the eternally watching eye-in-the-sky being my primary concern at this particular instant.

"Dude, not even a problem," Xenia said. "Okay, you losing your home is a problem, but the cameras. Pfft. No big." She flicked her fingers at me. "Go do your thing. I got this." She began rummaging in her pack.

While Xenia went to work in the back seat of the waiting cab, I hoofed it into my safe house. The storage facility wasn't much to look at, but then I'd chosen it specifically for its lack of charm. A fence composed of parallel, vertical iron bars sharpened to points secured the entry. Beyond that lay rows of low cinderblock buildings. Steel roll-ups granted entry to each of the units on the outer loop, with smaller doors for the cheaper ones in the interior.

A quick beep on my unit's keypad and I was inside my home away from home. I didn't want to dilly-dally. In and out. Reload my cash supplies, get a wallet with a clean identity and a burner.

While I was filling my pockets, I kept catching a whiff

of a spoiled, scorched odor. Lifting an arm, I confirmed that the source of the stench was me. Right, I'd gotten a little melty, a bit steamy, when the sun graced me with its gentle caress this morning.

There wasn't time for an actual shower—I'd had one installed in the double-sized storage unit when I'd set it up as a safe house—so I broke open a pack of camping wipes and gave myself a quick rubdown. I then swapped my ripe suit for a Zegna stashed in the line of wardrobes that served as a retirement home for my out-of-season duds. A pair of Lobbs for my feet and a Baume & Mercier to replace the watch I'd given Xenia, and good ol' Eddy Fry was ready to roll.

Any guilt about taking the time to make myself presentable went out the window when I saw Xenia was still hunched over her work. She'd barely noticed I'd been gone.

I signaled the cabbie to hit the road as I dropped into the back seat. Xenia handed me something as the cab lurched into motion. "Put these on."

I examined what she'd forked over. Plastic sunglasses, the kind promoters give out with energy drinks and tchotchkes on the street. Cheap Day-Glo *neon green* sunglasses. "Absolutely not." I tried to return her "gift," but she shoved my hand back.

"Put them on. They'll keep facial recognition systems from recognizing your..." She waved her hand around her face.

Oh, magic. "But they're so... so *green*. They'd go better with your hair."

"Hey. It's all I had after you interrupted and fried the good pair," Xenia said. "It's Vegas. No one gives a shit."

"I give a shit," I muttered. Fine. I slipped the repulsive

plastic shades onto my face. I waited for the magic to kick in, but I didn't feel anything other than shame.

"You won't feel it, but trust me"—she flicked a finger against the rings in her ear—"it works."

The Coliseum's Dionysian Feast Buffet had been pulling in rave reviews for years. Their spread featured cuisine from every continent in the world except Antarctica, or so they claimed.

When the cab dropped us off, Xenia had made a beeline for the first food court she'd seen. I put a stop to that line of thought right away.

If we were going to give her anti–face camera hoodoo a trial by fire by cruising the Strip a mere hop, skip, and jump from where Rebecca was lurking, then by God we going to do it *right*. Especially since I was footing the bill.

A healthy tip in the right hand landed us a booth in a discreet corner where she could give me the whole megillah in privacy.

Xenia sampled every station in the buffet, traveling around the culinary world and back. While she chowed down, I contented myself with a sniff at a glass of mid-range bourbon, pushing noodles around on my plate for appearance's sake.

"Do you miss it?" Her loaded chopsticks paused halfway to her mouth.

"Miss what?"

"Food. Eating." She chased the noodles with a marrow-smeared toast point.

"Oh. Believe it or not, I don't. Once I woke up that first night, it just wasn't important anymore," I said. "Sometimes I'll order a steak, rare as it comes. It's just not the same. Nothing tastes like anything, now. It's like the volume on my tongue got turned all the way down. I can eat it, but I can't taste it or live on it." I swirled the liquor around the bottom of my glass. "My sniffer works better than ever now, at least. Which is a plus *and* a minus, depending on the company." I let the whiskey's aroma percolate in my nose.

Sometime after her third trip to the chocolate fountain —where she'd scandalized the dessert chef by trying to dip a beef rib—Xenia leaned back against the bench seat, let fly a rib-cracking belch, and said, "Okay, where do you want to start? I'm still not sure what it is you actually want me to do." She dragged her mug of Joe close and took a swig.

"Hmm."

"Hmm?"

"Hmm," I said. "Well, ol' Eddy here is not as up to snuff on his so-called peer group as circumstances might lead ya to believe."

"No, really?"

"Oh, go on. I didn't plan any of this. I got into this gig by accident."

Xenia perked up. "Accident? How the hell do you become a blood-sucking monster—no offense—by accident?"

"Some taken, and it's a long goddamn story," I said. "I got in a jam and woke up on the slab at the morgue. Biggest surprise of my life. I'd figured myself a shoo-in for the pitchfork crowd after the life I'd led, not that I really thought about it all that much." I watched the lone cube melt into my drink. "Things've been hunky-dory since, until someone muscled in on my operation kicked and me out of my home."

"Okay, start there. You haven't said where home is. Something about a room at a casino?" Xenia eyed a leftover cupcake while she spoke. Decision made, she plucked at the paper.

"Oh, I own the Golden Fortune."

The cupcake landed with a *plop* in her lap. "No shit?" She rubbed at the frosting, smearing as much into the denim as she wiped off.

I nodded.

She tilted her head back, finger tapping her chin. "I am not charging you *nearly* enough. Okay, so who's gonna muscle you, muscle you out of..." Her skin blanched to an unhealthy hue. "Oh, *fuck* me. One of the vampire families is finally making a move on Las Vegas, aren't they?"

"Does 'House Harkness' mean anything to you?" I asked.

"God *damn* it, Eddy, Harkness is the great-grandpappy of American vampire clans." She shook her head, her green hair swinging with the movement. "Change of plans. I'll tell you whatever you need to know tonight. First thing, at dawn, you pay me for today, I get a ticket out of town, and I am gone-zo." She bit a nail. "I am not down for a vampire turf war, nuh-uh." Her eyes darted around the edges of the buffet.

I pinched the bridge of my nose. That would have to do, I guess. "Honestly, I was hoping you would stick around longer. School me on more of this crap."

"If it were another House, maybe Cabrillo from LA, I'd consider it. But House Harkness is the worst of the worst. At least here in the US."

"How so?"

"You gotta understand, Eddy. Vamps might treat humans like cattle. As food. But always at arm's length because human numbers would flatten them if the truth ever came out. So they focus their attention on the supernatural community, the Clandestine. I'll get to that in a minute," she added when I opened my mouth. "To get their jollies. Vampires might technically be part of it, but they consider themselves special. Above all others. The non-vampire supernaturals are beneath contempt, lacking the numbers or power to challenge them. In most cities, they're knocked around, abused for sure, but can live something close to a normal life as long as they toe the line." She smacked a fist into her palm. "Harkness, on the other hand, is an actual monster. To him and his house, the Clandestine is their personal pool of slave labor. New York, his Estate, has no underground, no community of supernaturals because they've all been enslaved, killed, or run off. As a magician, I'd be at the top of the 'enslave or kill' list. Sorry, dude, I can't hang around for that."

"Fine. I get it. If I wasn't so attached to the Fortune, I'd be hot on your heels on my way out of town."

I flagged down the waitress and asked for something with a lot of peat. The smell would calm my nerves even if the alcohol wouldn't. "Right, we're on the clock. I knew vampires were real." I pointed a thumb at myself. "Clearly. But if magic is real too, what else is? How much fairy-tale shit am I looking at? Is that the Clandestine thing you mentioned?"

"Yeah. It's pretty much everything you've heard of, to some degree," Xenia said. "Why do you think there are so many legends and myths?"

I let that sink in. "How come none of this is on the news? How do they"—I gestured at the diners scarfing all around us—"still think it's all just a bunch of fairy tales?"

She shook her head. "Do you advertise that you're a vampire?" She went on before I could answer. "Same deal for everyone else. No one wants the normies to know they exist. The Underground has stayed off the radar for centuries, any way it could." Xenia tapped a finger on the table. "Take magicians, for example. There is a... well, they call themselves a council, but they're more like a loose group of obsessive-compulsive geezers. Self-appointed. A bunch of self-aggrandizing Merlin wannabes who spend their time using magic to scrub out any mention or proof of *real* magic wherever it pops up. Stuff gets through, of course. But mostly, they've kept the real meat of it out of the public eye." She sighed. "It's not just magicians. Your folks do it too. They're just a lot messier about it." Xenia bared her teeth in a snarl. "Same with other underground communities. Fairies, kitsune, anyone who has power over the human mind. That handles most of the leaks. Anything else"—she tapped her phone where it rested on the table—"anything online is *super* easy to mess with. If it's in a computer, it's all just ones and zeroes. Energy states on a chip. Energy set to a purpose. Magic, at its simplest, is nothing more than energy put to a purpose."

"So you're saying there's an app for that?" I grinned as she gave me the finger. "So how did *you* learn magic, if all of it's hidden away?"

"Wasn't easy, believe me." She sank back into her seat. "Came at a cost, too." Xenia blinked hard a few times, then looked at me. "Why didn't your Sire teach you any of this?"

There's that word again. "Didn't have one. I'm a self-made man."

"That's not how it works, Eddy."

"I said it was a long story. The short version is, he killed me and I killed him." When a passing porter gave me a weird look, I made a mental note to leave a bigger tip.

Xenia was staring at me like I'd grown a second nose. "No one taught you anything, and you don't have a Sire or a House?" Xenia shook her head. "Dude, you're outclan. That makes you fair game for any vamp that wants to take a shot. You're lower than the cattle, as far as status goes." At my blank look, she clarified. *"We're* the cattle, Eddy. Us humans. The things you eat."

Xenia's head tilted in thought while her fingers drummed on the table. "Clear something up for me, boss. You said, and I quote, that you had 'ladies lined up to feed you.' Tell me right now. Are you killing women to feed yourself?" Her hand had slipped into her pocket while she spoke.

"No! Hell no." She tensed up as I leaned forward, but I didn't care. "Yes, I've killed," I snapped. "I've killed in service to my country. I've killed for the Outfit." My hand slapped down on the tabletop. "But Eddy Fuckin' Fry does not, I repeat, does *not* kill women. Or kids." I crossed my arms. "End of story." Guilt tugged at my guts, and I averted my eyes from the mirrored wall beside us. The past was the past.

Xenia was still wound up. "Fine. What about compulsion?"

"The what?"

Xenia pointed at her eyes. "Compulsion. The mind games you bloodsuckers can pull."

"Oh, that. Pfft." I buffed my nails on my coat and examined the shine. "I have never needed help with the ladies, and I *certainly* don't need to resort to *compulsion,*" I said with a sneer. "Every single one of them was a willing donor." I smiled. "Enthusiastic, even."

"Gross," Xenia said. "All right. Let me be clear. If I find out you've been lying about this, any of it, I will absolutely end your shit." She pulled the bottle of sunshine from her pocket and waggled it. "That's a promise."

"Fine, message received." I'd never been fond of ultimatums, but I needed her help right now more than I needed to nurse my ego. I pushed my outrage down and sipped my scotch. The smell hadn't done a thing to calm my nerves.

Neither would drinking it, but it gave me something to do with my hands. "Moving on. My vamp-pappy was supposed to learn me on all the finer points of being a blood-sucking monster? What have I missed?"

Xenia, apparently satisfied with my protestations of innocence, went on: "I don't have all the details. My source wasn't the most reliable and might have been trying to mislead me. But this is what I know." She sipped at her mug and took a breath. "I was told that the vamps are constantly collecting human followers. People who have connections, money, or power. Sometimes it's someone with a skill they want to exploit." Xenia's teeth clenched as she spoke. "Sometimes it's just a person so hot they want to preserve their looks. The vamp gets a crowd of followers, slaves, Renfields, whatever you want to call it. Someone to see to their interests during the day while providing an easy meal. Eventually, their master will turn them if they're deemed worthy of the 'gift.'

"Since this involves killing the servant, they're given a" —she made finger quotes—"proper burial. Coffin. Six feet under. The works. It's all done under the watchful eye of the top vamp of the family, mostly to keep the bodies out of morgues and funeral homes. I think embalming fucks with the vampification process. Maybe they just don't want death records. I don't know." Xenia ran her finger through some errant powdered sugar on a plate and looked at it for a moment. She wiped her finger clean with a napkin. "They spend the next day, the daylight hours, buried. Changing. You're more familiar with that part than I am."

"I don't remember it at all, just the bits on either side."

"Okay, so the Sire and his crew show up at sundown at the vamp-to-be's grave. Waiting for baby to pop out of the ground. When the poor bastard wakes up, they find themselves in an airtight box, six feet under. They're still weak from turning and will stay weak until they have their first blood. The new family doesn't dig them up. They're waiting to see if they're strong enough, worthy enough, to claw their way to the surface. It can take a new vamp hours before they emerge. If they do it at all." Xenia drained her coffee and held it for a passing porter to fill. "From what I hear, whatever makes it to the surface isn't too sane. The vamps have to corral the 'newborn' to keep it from going on a killing spree and making an inconvenient mess."

I dredged through what I recalled from all the movies I'd watched. Hey, it was research, okay? "What makes them straighten up and fly right? Does the mama vamp suckle her young on her own blood or what?" I asked.

"Hell no. Vamp blood is super toxic, even to other vamps. When a regular human ingests it, they die real quick. The only reason anyone would take a sip in the first place would be to become a vampire themselves. I'm not sure, but I think vamp blood could even kill another fang-head if they were dumb enough to drink it. They don't get shit from feeding off one another," Xenia said, appraising me over the rim of her mug. "You hoping for a power-up? You've been watching too many movies." Her eyes crinkled as she slurped. Then she set down the mug and cocked an eyebrow. "No Sire, right?" I shook my head. "So what kept you from, y'know, going berserk and getting staked right off the bat?" Her face paled. "Please tell me you didn't kill a bus full of nuns when you woke up."

I held up my hands. "No, nothing like that. I just woke up. Like normal. Kind of. I mean, I was also dealing with the shock of being alive." I rolled my glass between my hands. "When I got hungry, it was, well, it *was* bad. But not massacre bad." I set the glass down. "So how long does it take them to..." I groped for a word. "I dunno. Grow up? Become productive contributors to vamp society?"

Xenia rubbed one hand over her mouth. "It depends. Some never snap out of that blood fever. Those are revenants, and they get put down right away. Even older bloodsuckers are wary of them. Otherwise, if everything goes well, a vamp will come to their senses in five, maybe eight years."

I sat back. "I might have been out of sorts that first night," I said, "but I was at the tables playing blackjack by the next."

Xenia stared at me. "I hate to tell you this, Eddy, but that's fucking weird."

Chapter Thirteen

ONCE XENIA'S BOTTOMLESS STOMACH WAS AT LAST satisfied, we hit the bricks. Time to work on our respective next moves. I had to figure out how to get the Fortune back. Xenia needed a way out of town. I aimed us away from the Golden Fortune and the Beau Rivage.

"Once this is all over, why don't you look me up? I'll give you the grand tour, set you up with a suite at the Fortune. I'll even throw in some show tickets."

"Psshht. The Golden Fortune? That place is for old people. Not to mention the cultural appropriation."

"The what? Never mind. Then why were you working the slots there when I saw you?" I said. "I'll have you know we cater to a diverse crowd, thank you." We'd reached the Strip exit of the Coliseum, and I shoved the spinning door, splitting a gaggle of drink-toting party people. "Old people, my ass," I muttered.

Xenia dodged the spinning doors. "Eddy, I hate to tell you, but *you're* old people." Her grin said she didn't hate to tell me at all.

"You know, you're pretty cheeky for a dame who was

shaking in her boots the first time she saw big bad Eddy Fry."

"Dame? Cheeky? I rest my case," she said, flipping her hair out of her eyes. "What are you, like a hundred?"

"Don't be silly. I'm still in my prime! Barely fifty..." I stopped. Xenia moseyed a few steps along the walkway before she realized that I wasn't with her. I was running the numbers in my head. Had it really been that long? What the hell? "I guess you were pretty close to the mark," I admitted.

"Hey, dude. Eddy, don't worry about it," Xenia said. "Losing track of time is something vampires do. I think that's why there are so many stories of one being tricked into obsessively counting grains of rice or whatever."

I nodded. "I thought the rice thing was more for hopping vampires?"

Xenia raised an eyebrow.

"Movies. Anyhow, I've felt no particular urge to count anything obsessively. Except maybe my chips, and that's just good sense in this town."

Xenia walked backward for a few steps, the whole time giving me the hairy eyeball. "Okay, it might be rude to ask..."

"Shoot."

"Right. Well, from what Sensei told me, vampires mostly all have the same powers, capabilities. The compulsion, healing, near-immortality. That shit."

"I'm with you so far."

"But there are rumors that there's more than that. As a vampire ages, they gain power. Weird shit." She shrugged. "No one's really sure, and it's hard to confirm because any witnesses usually get eaten. What about you? You got anything else under the hood? Do you dissolve into mist? Turn into a bat?"

I laughed. "I can neither confirm nor deny that I've made an ass of myself trying that last one. Frank Langella made it look too easy. No, and I'm not just playing coy here. I don't have anything going on like that. Not that I've noticed, at least."

Xenia nodded, swinging her pack from one shoulder to the other. She leaned against the railing of the pedestrian bridge and fished out her phone. She snapped a few photos of the view. "I can't believe I have to leave Vegas already. I just got here."

"I took you for the jaded type. Immune to Sin City's charms."

"Eh."

"So what brought you to my burg? You don't strike me as a degenerate gambler."

"A show." She flipped the phone around and the screen filled with a shaky video of a blond lady screaming into a microphone. In the foreground, blurry fists pumped in and out of frame.

Pure noise assaulted my ears, and I winced. "Takes all kinds, I guess. I'm more of a Sinatra kind of guy."

Xenia stuck her tongue out and tucked the cacophony away. "Also, I needed to scare up some cash, and there ain't no better place to do that than"—she shook her hands around her face, jazz hands—"Vegas!"

"What, you use your hoodoo to scam the casinos?" I asked.

"Don't you?"

"Well, yeah."

"You thought you were the first person to get that idea? Sorry, Eddy, scamming the straights running Sin City is a longstanding tradition." She struck off toward the escalator descending into Diamond Cove, the next casino on this side of Las Vegas Boulevard. "Taking money from a casino is just good practice."

"Why haven't any of your hoodoo set, or the vamps, muscled in to take the town before now?"

"Tradition, really. Open city."

Back in the old days, when the Outfit ran Las Vegas, we'd considered it an "Open Town." With the East Coast, Chicago, and LA crews all angling for a piece of the pie, they'd fallen into an agreement that all of them could invest in the legal gambling paradise without feathers getting ruffled. Apparently, that arrangement had more ramifications than I'd suspected. "Yeah, I might know a thing or two about that."

"Well, the Clandestine," she stage-whispered, "abides by the same tradition. There's plenty to go around. No one wants to rock the boat. As a result, magicians have been using Las Vegas as *the* place to scrape up operating capital."

"Can't you folks just turn lead into gold or whatever?"

"Hah! No. Do you have any idea how hard transmutation is? All those protons and neutrons get testy when you give them orders. You get one *tiny* detail wrong and *bam*!" Xenia lifted her hands together in front of her, spreading them out as they rose. "Hiroshima, dude."

I wasn't sure if she was pulling my leg or not.

"Anyhow, it's become a rite of passage for the newbies. Everyone comes up with their own way to tip the scales without setting off alarms. But not too much, right? The IRS is worse than any vampire clan."

We made our way through the thinning street crowd, dodged drunks and the *thwip-thwip-thwip* of the card hawks. I'd been down this sidewalk hundreds of times before, but now... something about the crowd was giving me the heebies. I'd gone snooping behind enemy lines on Okinawa more than once and it had felt...

It had felt a lot like this.

It might be the thought of Rebecca out there, putting the whammy on who knows who. Any one of these folks could be dropping a dime on us and we'd never know it.

I stepped up my pace and tried to take my mind off how itchy the back of my neck had gotten. "Damn. Lansky would have shit himself inside out if he'd had any idea his cash was being poofed away like that. Heads would literally have rolled."

"Who?"

"Meyer Lansky. Used to own half of this town? Pretty big in Havana too?"

"Hold up. You were a mobster? Like 'offer you can't refuse' real gangster?" Xenia squeaked. I couldn't tell if it was excitement or outrage. A few of the passing vacationers turned their heads at her outburst. Even after all these years, any mention of the Mob would draw attention.

"Ixnay on the obstermay, will ya? The natives are getting restless." I picked up my pace, widening the gap between us and the prying ears. "*Was* a mobster. Past tense. I considered myself retired when I bought the farm. I'm my own man now, toots."

Xenia stopped. "You mind knocking off all that 'dame' and 'toots' stuff?"

"Sorry. Old habits." I spread my hands. "Anyhow. Bus, plane, or train?"

"What? Oh, right." Xenia's head tilted as she considered her options. "I hate flying, and the only train in Las Vegas is the monorail. I got here by bus, but a car would be more flexible, considering the situation. I'll get a car. Actually, *you're* going to get me a car. Consider it my final expense." She caught my look. "Nothing fancy. I want to stay under the radar. Stop complaining."

"Where will you go?"

"Someplace with no vampires. Which means avoiding any big cities. Magicians and bloodsuckers don't mix, for obvious reasons."

"Right," I said. "Wait, what reasons?"

Xenia gagged a bit as her expression turned dark. "Oh, it's nasty. People who do magic are basically irresistible to vampires. I think it's because we touch the primal forces of creation on the reg. We're saturated with it. Supposedly it's a vamp's favorite treat. Crack candy."

"Oh, *that's* what that is!" I slapped my forehead.

"Hold up, Drac. What *what* is?" Her hand was straying near the pocket, and her bottle, again.

No trust, I swear.

"Hey, keep it cool, sister." I held up my hands. "That's what drew my attention to you in the first place, when I stopped by for that chat. You had a... let's call it an aroma that I'd never picked up on before." I tapped my nose. "I got curious."

"Aroma, huh?"

"Ever been to that bun place at the mall? Like that, but more."

"Cinnabon?" She raised an arm for an investigative sniff. "It's just pit sweat to me. Ain't had a shower since before the show."

"Trust me, it's a doozy."

"So you *were* gonna feed on me, back in the casino. Dude, not cool."

"Cool your jets, I wasn't going to jump you. I wanted to find out what the deal with the aroma was, and then, if things worked out..." I waggled my eyebrows.

"Absolutely not going to happen."

"I'm crushed. My heart is in pieces. How could you possibly resist all of this?" I spread my arms and sashayed in a little circle.

Xenia rolled her eyes. "You're not exactly my type, Eddy."

"Oh, what is your type?"

Xenia lowered her head, staring from under her brows.

"Oh," I said. She kept staring. "Oooohhh! Got it."

"Whatever. But yeah. There's a reason magicians hole up in out-of-the-way places. Keeps us off the grid *and* the menu both." Her eyes dropped. "It doesn't always work. That's how..." She shook it off. "Speaking of out-of-the-way places, this has been real, boss. But I'm getting the fuck out of Dodge before the vampire turf war kicks off."

"I thought you were waiting for dawn?"

"Changed my mind. You helping me get a ride or what? You gotta know someone in town who can hook me up." Xenia marched off toward the casino's front, and I had to step on the gas to catch up.

To be honest, I was sorry to see her go. We'd barely scratched the surface of all that nonsense out there. Not to mention having someone with actual magic on hand would be a major bonus when the chips were down. But then, I wasn't going to force anyone to face the music with me, not when it wasn't their problem. Besides, I'd started to take a shine to the spunky little dame. Gal? Lady. I'd hate to see her take a shot meant for me.

"I might know where we can find some wheels. Let's get a cab."

———

THIS BEING LAS VEGAS, of *course* there was a twenty-four-hour car dealership. Desert Star Motors specialized in buying cars, vans, trucks, and motorcycles from the desperate.

An hour and a few thousand dollars lighter, Xenia

pulled out onto Desert Inn Road in a used Toyota something or other. It wasn't an American car, so I hadn't paid all
that much attention to the details while she'd haggled with
the man.

Xenia brought us to a halt by the curb outside my
storage lot. "Hah! *This* is your safe house, Eddy?" Xenia
craned her neck to take in the RIGHT SPOT STORAGE sign.
"No one would suspect that a big scary vampire was hiding
here. I'll give you that."

"I use it for storage most of the time, shockingly enough.
I haven't *needed* a safe house in years. Why are you
surprised, anyhow? We were just here."

"Busy casting, remember?" She flicked the sunglasses,
which were still puke green, where they rested on my nose.
Maybe I could talk her into doing her jazz on a decent pair
of shades? I think I had a sweet set of Masahiro Maruyama
shades in a drawer.

"Hey, Eddy." Xenia's voice was quiet. "Since we're
settling up, you should have this back." She unclipped the
Rolex on her wrist.

I stopped her with a hand on her arm. "No dice. It was
my down payment, fair and square. You keep it." I must be
going soft. "It really does go with your hair."

Xenia thought about it, then nodded. "Okay." She
snapped the clasp tight and rotated her wrist. The polished
face of the watch glinted in the streetlight's glare.

I twisted in the narrow passenger seat until I could face
my former consultant. "Guess it's time for you to go where
you're going and for me to go where I'm going. Thanks for
all the help, kid. Keep your head low, will ya?" I held out my
hand.

Xenia blinked a few times. Was that a hint of a tear in
her eye? The corner of her mouth quirked up. "Don't call
me a kid—" Her eyes flew wide. "EDDY!"

Pebbles of glass exploded through the interior of the car as the window behind me burst. A vise clamped itself to my shoulder. I found myself torn from the car, taking the door with me as I flew through the air.

Chapter Fourteen
Then

"Hey, Eddy!"

I turned back to my gal and got a snoot-full of snow for my trouble. Scraping the ice from my eyes, I saw Darla wind her arm, ready to let fly with round two.

I'd stopped by the Thunderbird to see her between shows, and she'd dragged me out to the edge of the lot. She'd wanted to take a gander at the blanket of white fluff that had coated the valley.

Yeah, snow in Las Vegas. I couldn't believe it either.

Darla and I had been a thing for about four months now. It was going swimmingly, if I did say so myself. We'd met when Little Mickey had arranged for a few of the show-girls at the 'bird to spend time with his crew. She must've taken a shine to me because *she* had called me a day or so later. We'd been an item ever since.

Don't ask me. I couldn't explain it either. Especially since I didn't have the scratch to show her the kind of time a gal like that deserved. Not yet.

Every time I got my hands on a bit of cash, I had to kick it up to Mr. Greenbaum, who would pass it along to Mr. Cohen. Now, math wasn't my strong point, but I knew I'd handed in over a grand by now. The thing killing me was the vig. Simply put, it was the interest on the "loan" I had with Mr. Cohen. Except Mr. Greenbaum and Mr. Sedway both had to get their beaks wet too. I could keep a little back from what I made on the job, show Darla a good time now and then. I had the proof of that in my coat pocket right now. Darla's birthday was next week, and I was going to surprise her with something special.

But I couldn't do too much of that, not if I wanted to keep the payments flowing to Mr. Cohen. Otherwise, *I'd* be the one sitting in that chair.

At this rate, I'd be on the hook for the rest of my damn life.

I ducked Darla's next snowball and scooped up my own wad of white stuff. I grinned and made like Dizzy, spinning my arm in a big showy wind-up.

"Don't you dare, Eddy, don't you dare," Darla said through a shower of giggles.

I kept winding, spinning my arm around and around. "Revenge!" My laughter ruined the threat.

"Eddy, my call time is in ten minutes! Don't you muss my hair! Don't you do it!"

"You should have thought of that before you beaned me!" I let fly with the weakest limp-wrist toss of my life. The snowball plopped into the ground at Darla's feet, to which she doubled over with a fit of the giggles. Before she recovered, I'd looped my hands about her waist to spin her toward me. Darla leaned in and slid her arms under my coat. We turned slowly, swaying to the music that floated across the Thunderbird's parking lot. Another flurry of white flakes drifted about, swirling in the rising wind. Darla shivered and snuggled in. "Should've worn your coat," I said into the top of her head.

She laughed. "Who's got a winter coat in Las Vegas?"

143

"Darla! Call in five!" Caroline, one of Darla's high-kicking coworkers, bellowed across the lot. Perfect timing, as ever.

Darla sighed into my chest and gave me one last squeeze. When she raised her head, her eyes were half closed. I took the hint and met her halfway. Her lips brushed mine, cold in the winter wind. I gave her my best shot at warming them up.

"Darla! Come *on*. You two can wash tonsils after the show! I need help with my hair!"

Darla pulled away with a small, sad smile. "Gotta go, baby. See you after the last curtain?"

"Unless Little Mickey's got something on tap, it's a date."

Darla stuck her lower lip out. "Okay." Darla knew how things worked around here and to not ask questions. She never had boo to say about what I did for a living, but I could tell she didn't like it.

Maybe once I'd cleared my marker, I'd look into something else, some other line of work. Maybe.

I watched her backside dash toward the light streaming from the backstage entrance. "Darla!" I yelled when she'd gone about halfway.

She turned. "Yeah, baby?"

"Next week. You. Me. Crosby?" I called, waving the tickets I'd spent so much on over my head.

"Eddy!" Darla squealed. She clapped her hands together and scurried back to me. Coming up on her tiptoes, she planted another kiss on my lips. I leaned in, hoping to make it last, but off she dashed.

Caroline and her damn hair.

———

As Mr. Lansky's car pulled away from the Flamingo, on its way to deliver the big boss to the new airport, I headed straight for the bar. I needed a drink, maybe three.

He'd flown all the way out from Havana this week to check up on the operation, not to mention collecting his cut of the profits. I hadn't known it when I'd first arrived in Vegas, but Lansky was one of the Flamingo's biggest investors right from the get-go. Not only that, he'd been in charge of overseeing the entire project on behalf of various Outfit investors. It was on his order that Gus and Moe got put in charge of the Flamingo after Bugsy's unexpected "retirement."

I'd tried to keep a low profile while he was in town. Little Mickey hadn't thought it would be a great idea to have someone like me—not officially "part of the family"—skulking around while he was doing business. That plan went out the window right from the start. Not only was Mr. Lansky aware of me, he'd wanted a few words. It wasn't long before he'd made it clear to everyone that he wanted me gone.

Little Mickey had stepped up, putting his own neck on the line on my behalf. Which, between you and me, had been a hell of a surprise. He said I was doing the work, paying down my marker, doing right by Mr. Greenbaum, Mr. Sedway, and Mr. Cohen. No complaints. He's also pointed out my "knack" for busting the cheats.

It had been that last bit that bought me time. Unfortunately, if Mr. Lansky didn't change his mind soon, my days in Las Vegas would be numbered. Not to mention my days breathing.

I'd knocked back my second shot and was waving for a third when a massive hand dropped onto my shoulder. The bartender paused, the bottle hovering above the shot glass.

"Eddy, Gus would like a word," Little Mickey said.

Just peachy.

I trailed him back to Mr. Greenbaum's office. I didn't know if this was the axe coming down or what, but it wasn't like I had any place to hide if it was. Little Mickey rapped a knuckle against the door and, at a muffled word from within, swung it wide. He tilted his head at the office and stepped back. When I stepped in, he stayed put, shutting the door behind me.

Mr. Greenbaum's comb-overed head bent over a piece of the ever-present paperwork littering his desk. His finger slid down the page as he jotted something on the form beside the one he was reading. Satisfied, he gathered the pages, tapping them even before dropping them into a drawer.

I fought the urge to cough. Or even breathe too loud.

Mr. Greenbaum flipped open the ever-present cigar box on his desk, rummaging his fingers across the selection as if it were a Rolodex. He slipped his choice into the waiting mouth of a silver cigar cutter and, pausing, caught my eye. While he held the stare, the cigar cutter went *snip*. Flipping open a box of wooden matches, he clamped the stogie in his teeth.

"Eddy Fry." He raised a match to his cigar.

I nodded.

Mr. Greenbaum shook out the match and pointed it at the chair waiting for me by his desk. "Sit."

I sat.

He puffed a smoke ring into the air between us. "Seems we have a little problem, Eddy."

Damn it. Lansky had given the order. The back of my neck sprouted a crop of goose bumps. I was good as dead.

After a thoughtful pull on his cigar, he went on. "Thing is, according to Little Mick, you've been, and I quote, 'an invaluable member' of his team."

"That does sounds like something he'd say, sir."

A chuckle escaped Mr. Greenbaum. "He has a vocabulary, that guy." He fished around in the stacks of papers until he produced an overloaded marble ashtray. "From what he tells me, not only have you been one of our more productive debt collectors"—he stressed the last two words —"but you've been extra helpful on the floor. Alfie backs him up, says you got an eye for plucking cheats out of the crowd." He tapped off his ash. "Says that the bums you've had a word with stay gone. Not one of those lowlifes has come back. Not to the Flamingo, or to any of the other joints in town." He leaned forward, eyes narrowing. "Think you're scary, Eddy? You a dangerous man?"

"Not really, sir." I tried not to break eye contact. "No."

A curl of smoke swirled between us.

"It's important," I went on, taking a chance, "that those lowlifes take the Flamingo, and the management"—I tilted my head toward Mr. Greenbaum—"seriously. *Very* seriously. I guess you could say I'm a man with... a man who can make a credible argument."

Mr. Greenbaum slapped the desk, causing a stack of papers to slide off and flutter to the floor. He ignored them. "Hah! I'm fucking with you, Eddy! Good answer, though, good one." He leaned back with another pull on his stogie. "Little Mickey has gone to bat for you since the day you arrived. God knows why. Some two-bit loser, a deadbeat who couldn't pay what he owed."

I winced.

"But for some reason, that big galoot was convinced you're worth the patience and whattayaknow? You've been bringing it in. Sure, you still owe on the principal of your marker, but you've been putting cash in my hand." A tiny nod, maybe acknowledging that his vig had been making my life hell. Maybe not. "But Meyer wants you gone."

That's it, I was fucked. "Mr. Green—"

He held up his hand, stogie wedged between his fingers. "Normally, Meyer gets what he wants. But this is your lucky day. I'm not willing to chuck you out with the trash just yet." He shook his head. "Not yet." He leaned way back, the chair creaking ominously. Blew smoke into the air over his head without getting a ring. "Ever since Bugsy passed, every two-bit hack with a typewriter thinks he's going to grab hisself a Pyu-litzer." He spat the word. "Digging up dirt on our operation. Going after Meyer or me. Won't let Moe alone, the man's health being what it is."

What the hell was he talking about? What did this have to do with Mr. Lansky ordering my ticket punched?

Mr. Greenbaum dug around in the mess of his desk until he produced a scrap of paper. Held it up in front of his eye. "Montgomery Carmichael. *This* bum thinks he's the next Doug Edwards. Word came down that he's pried up something on how we *allegedly*"—he rolled his eyes—"skim from the profits before the Revenue Man gets his cut."

Okay, that could be a problem. The skim accounted for the lion's share of the Outfit's illicit profits. Considering that the mastermind directly responsible for the shady accounting at the Flamingo, and several other casinos, had just casually brought it up, this either meant I was on my way to a dirt nap or...

"Monty has a source, some fucking *rat*," Greenbaum snarled. "Here in the Flamingo. Gotta be." A vein pulsed in his temple as he spoke. "He's got his *story* all typed up neat and clean, and he's looking to sell it to the highest bidder." He barked out a laugh. "As if our ears aren't in every newsroom this country has." He swung around in his chair. "So, Eddy, what do you think I should do about this fella?"

"Gotta send a message," I said without hesitation. "Can't have some jagoff airing our..." I almost paused, but

Mr. Greenbaum hadn't batted an eye. "Airing our dirty laundry for the world to see. Someone's gotta have a word with this guy. Get his story, get his papers, get him to cough up his source. Then, make an example of him before the *next* guy gets the bright idea they can just stick their nose into the Outfit's business."

Mr. Greenbaum slapped his hand down on the desk and jabbed his stogie at my face. "Attaboy. Little Mickey knew what he was talking about when he backed you up to Lansky." He stabbed the cigar out. "Get it done, Eddy."

"Me?"

"Get it done. Make sure you find out who this fucking rat is before you finalize the reporter. Get everything. Every paper, note, and receipt." He dragged another wooden match across his desk and touched it to the note bearing Carmichael's name. Tossed the burning scrap into the ashtray. "You need a piece? I can arrange some hardware if you need it."

I had that handled, thanks to the United States Army. I *may* have neglected to turn in a few things. "No. Got that covered."

Mr. Greenbaum nodded. "You get this done, Eddy." He flipped open the cigar box again and eyeballed the contents. "Get it done, and I'll consider your slate wiped clean. Debt paid." He spun the cigar box around. "Stogie?"

———

IF THERE's one thing that *really* annoys me, it's waiting.

Oh, I know I should've had that trained out of me by the Army. Guess what? It's still a pain in the ass to just sit around while someone takes their sweet time.

I thought about Darla. The whole time I'd been putting this job together, she'd been on my mind. It had cut into our

149

"social calendar," as she liked to put it. Since she was still showgirling at the Thunderbird and I'd been trying to track down this Monty character, it had been over a week since our last date.

We'd hit up the El Cortez, kicking up our heels until late, before she took me back to her place. Her roommate was out, home visiting family, so we'd had the room to ourselves. She'd been in a *very* good mood when I'd left the next morning. I nearly whistled, remembering that thing she'd done with her tongue...

Two *ding*s filled the stillness of the house. I glanced at the mantle clock. Two in the morning. I tilted my Timex until the dial caught light from the window; it was two minutes slow. I popped the crown up and nudged the minute hand to the correct time before returning my hand to the Colt 1911 resting on the chair arm beside me.

Montgomery was in his thirties. He'd come to Las Vegas after a scoring a minor scoop at some rag in Iowa. Whatever the story had been, it had paid well enough to buy him this house. It was the first one on his street to be completed, placing it right in the center of the recent development expanding across Las Vegas's east side. All the other houses for nearly a mile in every direction were empty. Some seemed to be ready for their new owners, others were bare wood frames. No neighbors, no witnesses.

Monty habitually would get home just before midnight. Tonight, though, I suppose he was living it up. He *was* expecting a major payday any day now, so I couldn't blame the fella. I only hoped that he staggered home instead of passing out at some dame's.

One more hour. Then I'd have to track the bum down. Again.

I had slouched in Monty's armchair, but the rolling crunch of gravel from outside made me sit up. The curtains of Montgomery Carmichael's living room were shut tight, so I couldn't see for sure if it was his car that had pulled up. My heart began knocking against the back of my breastbone. I took a deep breath and held it to calm my ticker.

No sweat, Eddy.

Drunken giggles floated in from outside as a car door slammed: a dame's laugh, not Monty's. I let out the breath I'd been holding as keys jingled by the front door. A muffled curse followed, then more giggles as they picked up the keys. The lock rattled.

Cold, greasy sweat slid across my forehead, I dragged the back of my sleeve against my skin to keep it out of my eyes. As the lock rattled, my heart thundered in my ears and I shoved down the memory of saltwater and cordite clamoring for my attention.

Last chance, Eddy.

I clicked off the Colt's safety.

Monty bumped the door open, using his ass, his hands plucking at the blouse of a dame who was likewise tugging at his belt. From the sequins on her tight skirt, I guessed she was a cocktail waitress he'd managed to sweet-talk into coming home with him.

Monty himself almost looked like he could be Frankie's brother if it hadn't been for that weak chin. Monty's gal could've been Darla's roommate's sister; they had the same poofy hair and long face. She made a sound halfway between a giggle and a husky growl when his hand slipped inside her blouse. His other hand fumbled behind her, searching for the wall switch.

I blinked in the sudden light.

"Monty!" The dame grabbed Monty's arms, trying to pull him around while she peered at me wide-eyed over his shoulder.

151

"Yeah, baby doll?" Monty murmured, his lips working her collar bone.

She hammered a hand against his back. "Someone's here, Monty!" Her voice rose to a squeak and her eyes showed white all the way around.

I shifted the Colt, thumbing the hammer back as I aimed the suppressor at the pair. The 1911 was an automatic, which meant you didn't *have* to do that, but the sound speaks louder than any word.

Monty froze, his hand in Baby Doll's brassiere. His head crept around until his wide eyes found me. A tiny whine escaped his throat. Just one.

"Close the door," I said. "Lock it."

Shuffling like they were contestants in a potato sack race, Monty and Baby Doll moved all the way into the house. Monty dislodged his hand to swing the door shut.

"Hands," I instructed, wiggling the Colt. Like guilty teens in the back of a movie theater pinned by the usher's flashlight, they jumped apart. Shoulders hunched, Baby Doll made an attempt at modesty, tugging her blouse closed before raising her hands. Monty's arms shot up like he was trying to catch a football pass.

"W-w-what do you want?" Monty said, jaw trembling. "I don't have much money." His eyes flitted around, from me to Baby Doll and back. Then, so quick I nearly missed it, they darted to the clock on the mantlepiece.

Interesting.

"Oh, don't worry. I'm not here for your money," I said.

Baby Doll's blouse gapped open again, and she dropped a hand to tug it closed. The gun jumped in my hand, the suppressor making more noise than I'd expected. A neat little hole appeared between Baby Doll's eyes, and red fanned out on the wall behind her. Her eyes crossed as she slumped to her knees before pitching over onto her face. Her poofy hairdo hid the ruin at the back of head.

Monty and I both stared at the body. I hadn't *meant* to blast the dame, hand to God. My heartbeat, which had calmed as the couple had entered the house, went into jackhammer double-time.

C'mon, Eddy. You weren't shy about stacking bodies back in Ormoc Bay, so why is this one giving you hives? Besides, Gus had been crystal clear about what needed to happen.

Monty's mouth worked, opening and closing without a sound. Unable to tear his eyes off Baby Doll's body, he began to tremble. A dark stain grew at the front of his trousers.

Fighting to keep my own shock under wraps, I stood. "Really, Monty?" My voice caught in my throat once before steadying. "You're pissing your britches already?" I waved the Colt at the couch. "Sit down."

Monty continued to stare at the body.

"I said sit *down*, Monty."

He flinched and tore his eyes away from Baby Doll to stare at me. Another little whine escaped from his throat. I raised my pistol until the suppressor lined up with his left eye. Both eyes rolled back and he crumpled to the floor, his form a mirror image to Baby Doll.

"Oh, for fuck's... *This* is the reporter brave enough to take on the Mob?" I said to the room. I bit back a sigh and slipped the Colt under my coat.

Turns out, it's *really* difficult to maneuver a body with wet pants up onto a couch, then tie him up with his own neckties, without getting piss on your hands. At least I was wearing gloves.

I slapped Monty across the cheek. "Wake up, asshole."

Nothing.

When I raised my hand to whack him again, Monty's head rolled back and a ragged snore gurgled from his chest.

I stomped off to the kitchen to rifle his cabinets until I found a bowl large enough for my needs. Into the container went ice from the icebox—I just love the modern conveniences—and water from the tap. All of which I dumped straight into Monty's snoring face.

He sputtered, water spraying from his nose and mouth like he was a breaching whale. "Muh-wuzzah-fuck, do you think you're—oh *shit!*"

"Monty, I have exactly two questions for you. They're very important," I said, as I crouched in front of him.

His lower lip quivered. "You're gonna kill me too, aren't you?" I could see the tears welling up in his baby blues, even through all the water on his face.

"I'll level with you. That won't be necessary if you answer my Two Important Questions." I tilted my head to one side. "Think you can handle that?"

"Uhh, okay?"

"Okey-dokey. Number one." I held up a finger. "Where is the manuscript for your article and your notes?"

Once again, his eyes slid to the side, toward the fireplace. Bingo.

"Um, it's not here," Monty said. "My editor—"

Ignoring him, I approached the fireplace. Centered on the mantle was a basic wooden clock, glass dome over the face, wide on the bottom. Rosewood, maybe. It was the only thing on display, no framed pictures, no bric-a-brac. The brickwork of the chimney rising behind the mantle had been painted white to match the room. Recently too, judging by the faint odor of turpentine tickling my nose.

Sliding the mantle clock to one side, I could see that the pair of bricks directly behind it protruded slightly more than their neighbors. Giving Monty a glance to make sure he wasn't going anywhere, I stashed the Colt under my coat.

There was just enough of an edge to the bricks to get a grip. The mortar around the pair was for show, not for securing the bricks, and wiggling the set back and forth caused them to slide free of their slot in the chimney.

The room's light didn't reach very far into the gap, but I could see paper hiding in the shadow. Dragging it out into the light, I examined my prize.

A thick manila folder, bound in string. Undoing the string revealed a stack of typewritten pages held together with brass brads. "THE ART OF THE SKIM BY MONTGOMERY CARMICHAEL" was emblazoned across the front page of the manuscript. The rest of the folder's contents consisted of a handful of notepads covered in an illegible scrawl.

Bingo.

I stuffed everything back into the folder and retied the string. "Very nice, Monty. Clever hiding spot." On a hunch, I jammed my hand into the mantle. The very tip of my finger brushed something round, and I had to stretch to get a grip on it. Out came a nice little roll of bills bound by a fat rubber band. I weighed it in my hand, giving it a toss before tucking it away in my pocket.

"Hey!" Monty blubbered, snot dribbling from his nose.

"Monty, Monty. I got your pee all over my hands when I was tying you up." I waggled my gloved fingers at him. "You owe me a new pair."

Monty's chin dropped onto his chest.

I dropped the folder onto the coffee table and crouched by Monty's leg. "That went so well. You're gonna have no trouble with my second question." Without waiting for a response, I grabbed him by the shoulder. "Who's your source, Monty?"

I could see the shakes roll through him. Starting from his lower lip, the trembles spread down through his shoulders until his whole body was quaking. "I-I can't," Monty forced through his chattering teeth. "I can't tell you." His eyes squeezed shut as his shoulders hunched around his ears.

"Monty, Monty. That's the wrong answer." I pulled the Colt free from my coat. I raised my eyebrow, waggling the pistol under his nose. Monty kept his eyes screwed tight, tears seeping from their corners. I shrugged and set the end of the suppressor to his kneecap.

"Nnno. No. I can't. I can't," Monty moaned.

I leaned away as I pulled the trigger. The Colt barked, and Monty shrieked like a train whistle. He leaned back into the couch like he was trying to get away from his own ruined knee, eyes rolling in their sockets. I stepped to one side to keep clear of the spreading pool of blood. I figured I had a minute, maybe two, before he bled out. Maybe more if I tied off his knee.

"Oh God, oh God," Monty groaned.

I snapped my fingers in his face until he focused on me. His breath was coming in big gulps that hitched in his chest. I made sure he was watching as I set the Colt against his other knee. Cupping my free hand behind my ear, I gave him a last warning. "I'm listening, Monty."

His eyelids fluttered as his head lolled against the couch cushion. Monty was starting to lose it. I tapped the Colt against his knee, hard. His head rolled back to me and he blinked.

My fingered tightened on the trigger.

"Okay! God, *I'll talk*," he gasped. "It was Wally!"

I blinked. "Wally?" I didn't know any Wallys.

Monty's breathing had grown ragged, and his eyes lost their focus. Shit. I didn't need Monty expiring just as I had the answer I needed. Grabbing a spare necktie from when I'd tied him up, I used it as a tourniquet to halt the blood loss. Once I was sure he wasn't about to drop dead, I slapped his cheek again. "Talk to me, Monty. Wally who? Tell me, and I'll get your knee fixed up."

"Wally," Monty slurred, eyes peeling open. "Wallace Marsh." His eyes drifted shut again.

I fished around the manila folder until I found his notebooks. I leafed through the mess of scribbles until I located four spots where he'd referred to a "W" or "WM." Monty had been straight with me. Mr. Greenbaum would know who this Wallace guy was. I jammed everything back into the folder and tucked it under my arm.

Monty wasn't looking so good. His skin had gone all gray and pasty. He stared at his ruined knee with half-lidded eyes. I think shock had set in.

"Well, Monty, it may have taken some convincing, but you came through. I believe you."

Monty's head lolled to one side, and his eyes slowly tracked over to me. A small sigh escaped his lips. "Oh thank God."

"Yup," I said and shot him in the heart. I put another one through his eye to make sure. I slipped the Colt back into its holster and stepped over the blood pooled around Monty's feet. I tried not to look at Baby Doll's body while I slipped out the door.

I had my ride stashed in a carport down the street, in one of the development's partially completed homes. Tossing the folder in the trunk with the Colt, I slid behind the wheel of the Ford. My stomach was see-sawing between nausea and growls from missing dinner.

Good thing you can get a steak twenty-four hours a day in this town.

Chapter Fifteen
Now

Flung from Xenia's car, I pinwheeled through the air until the iron fence surrounding the storage lot caught me. While the metal bars stopped my tumble, the insides of my head kept spinning. Whatever had attacked me definitely had some juice in its arm. Through the stars swimming in my vision, I got the impression of something huge and gray looming over the car. Its roar was gravelly and deep enough to set my teeth rattling.

I hung there, my feet clear of the ground. The impact with the fence had embedded me *into* the iron bars, deforming them around my battered frame. The positioning was just awkward enough to prevent me from getting traction, and my arms wouldn't bend the right way to unwedge myself.

As my head cleared, the big, gray thing swam into focus. I'd halfway expected to see Rebecca's henchman, Felix, coming at me. Or, considering the stuff Xenia had been filling my head with, maybe a wolfman straight out of a matinee. What I *hadn't* expected was a seven-foot tall great white shark stomping toward me on a pair of bodybuilder legs.

The hell was a *shark-man* doing in the middle of the desert?

Before I could follow that train of thought, Sharky got his mitt tangled in my shirt, clawed fingers digging furrows across my chest, and yanked me clear of the fence. I heard the bones in my left arm, all three of them, break as I came free of the twisted iron. Sharky turned on his heel and, with a grunt, heaved me straight into the side of Xenia's car. I caught hold of the open door frame with my good arm in time to stop my flight. My face halted inches from Xenia's, and she blinked at me while I worked on uncrossing my eyes.

"Urg?" It was all I could manage as Sharky's mitt clamped my ankle and tore me out of the car. My fingers slipped from the door frame and my noggin dented the curb when I landed. Sharky, maintaining his grip on my ankle, swung me overhead onto the roof of the car, crumpling it.

Ow.

Pebbled glass sprayed around me, and I *definitely* heard more bones snap, though if I could get Sharky to back off, they'd take care of themselves eventually. What I *really* wanted was the chance to get a few licks in myself. I'm no slouch in a fight, but who can throw a punch while being rag-dolled by Jaws?

Beneath me, I heard Xenia's breathing as she twisted in the car's compacted interior. Scrabbling turned to thudding as she hammered against the door. "Fuck." Her muffled voice was calm, but the tempo of her heart betrayed her panic. When Sharky had slammed me onto the roof, the impact had wedged the door in place. Xenia was trapped.

"Hey, if your beef is with me, big guy, just let the girl—"

Sharky's jaws opened wide in a roar, and I made out four rows of saw-edged teeth in there. Warm, salt-smelling spittle dotted my face. The massive wedge of a head tilted to bring one jet-black eye to bear on me. "*Bampira!*"

"Hey!" Xenia's voice came from under me. "Stop killing my client! He hasn't paid me yet!"

Aw, she does care.

It had been almost forty-eight hours since I'd last had a bite to eat, so my reserves weren't exactly where I'd have liked them to be. My bits were putting themselves back together, but not as quickly as they should have. Which was why I failed to dodge the double-handed hammer blow Sharky landed on my chest.

Below me, Xenia squeaked as the available space in the car halved. "Dammit! Stop!" I wasn't sure, but it sounded like she'd tumbled into the back seat. The wreck had been a two-door, so that had put her *farther* away from an exit.

Punctuating each blow with a grunt, Sharky began to hammer his fists against me. The steel of the car's frame groaned as I was slammed into it repeatedly.

If I didn't get myself clear, while giving me a beatdown, Sharky was going to crush the car with Xenia still inside.

Sharky's pummeling finally let up. His swings weren't coming as fast, and his breathing had taken on a ragged edge. Along each side of his neck, gills flared wide every time he dragged at the air. The flesh inside was dark red and layered.

I was thinking his endurance might not be so hot without saltwater flowing through those gills.

While he gasped, his wide head turned this way and that as he watched me. Finally, the angle was right and I got a clear view to both of Sharky's beady eyes. Perfect. I let loose with both barrels of the ol' eye whammy.

Nothing.

My power had just slid across those flat shark eyes

160

without finding anything it could get hold of. I couldn't get in his head.

Sharky's shoulders heaved and a wet gurgle came from his gills. The jagoff was *laughing* at me! "That won't work, *bampira*." The gravelly voice was labored, as if it took effort to push the words out. That liquid chuckle came again. "Great white not so easy to control."

So far, his movements had been on the slow side, ponderous even. Sharky had the sort of lumbering lurch one expected from a seven-foot slab of seafood. He'd been holding back, though. There was some speed in him, after all. The dark eyes rolled back, protected by pale inner lids, and his head surged forward. Razor teeth snapped shut where my head had been as I used my partially healed arms to haul myself off the roof of the car and onto the ground at his feet.

Sharky pressed his attack, stomping me with a clawed foot. With a sound like wet twigs cracking, my chest got a whole lot flatter than I liked, ribs snapping on both sides. With a grunt, he booted me into the side of Xenia's car once more. My spine creaked as it dented the side panel.

The massive wedge head came up, eyes rolling down from under their protective lids. His foot continued to grind me into the side of the car. Splinters of rib were creeping dangerously close to my heart. I didn't want to find out what would happen if they jabbed my ticker. I couldn't budge his foot, my hands batted against his massive ankle, and I lost the skin from my fingers as they slipped across the sandpaper-coarse surface. A shard of rib nicked my heart, and the feeling in my body, pain and all, flickered like a bad signal on a television.

Inside the crumpled car, Xenia took a deep breath and yelled, "Goddammit, *stop!*"

Sharky blinked once. "Wait. I was—"

A hissing *crack* sounded directly behind my head, followed by the *crunk* of metal against pavement. The section of car Sharky had me pinned to rocked against my back.

Sharky and I both craned our necks to take in the damage. The little import car had been split diagonally. Metal gleamed bright from the edge of the exposed frame. The far half rocked, tilting until it at last rolled back to expose the interior.

Upside down from my vantage point, Xenia rose from the car like some sort of heavy metal avenging angel. Silhouetted against the street lamp, her form sprouted a halo of spikes as the silvery studs of her leather jacket grew into two-inch points. Ripples ran through the leather, and the ends of the zipper shot together as if magnetized. As the zipper zipped upward, the material of the jacket pressed into form-fitting tightness around her torso. The collar inverted itself, pressing against her jawline and revealing a grid of overlapping steel plates that armored her neck.

"Wait." Sharky raised a conciliatory hand, and his weight shifted forward onto the foot still planted on my chest. The pressure sent more bone slivers on a journey toward my heart, and I let out a very un-Eddy-like squeal.

"I said"—a fingerless glove, every inch decorated by a dense network of lines, wrapped the hand Xenia raised—"*stop.*" With a sharp exhalation, she flicked the gloved hand toward the shark-man.

Something, visible only as a distortion of the air, flashed from her to Sharky with that same hissing *crack*. The line of force struck him high on the chest, and his skin split in a bright crimson line from pectoral to shoulder. Either she'd lowered the power of whatever that was, or Sharky was made of sterner stuff than a used car. Instead of coming apart into sushi, he only staggered back, blood

162

welling from the cut. His hand came up to touch the wound, and a clawed finger probed at the shallow laceration.

I don't need to breathe anymore, but I took the deepest breath I could in order to get my collapsed rib cage back into the right shape. A *snap-crackle-pop* signaled that my ribs had put themselves back where they were supposed to be. More or less. Grudgingly, the fragments began to sort themselves into shape.

"Why do you attack?" Sharky's head tilted, puzzlement clear on the wide face.

"I told you to stop!" Xenia said. "I warned you, man." Pebbles of car window glittered in the spray of her emerald hair. Threads of red marked her skin where the flying glass had scored her face. She took a deep breath, and her hand came up for another strike.

"No, *no!*" Sharky raised both hands, palms out. "I was just trying to protect you from..." The pointed nose tilted down until his eye caught me. The jet-black eye narrowed, and I swear that *he* was seeing red. "*Bampira!*" He raised his foot for another stomp.

Here we go again.

The skin on Sharky's side split along a two-foot length as Xenia let fly with her magic. As he flinched away from the wound, his foot slammed into the pavement beside my head instead of flattening it.

While he was staggered, I made my escape. Which, since most of me was still broken, ended up being a herky-jerky backward crawl across the pavement. Every time the big guy made a move to take a whack at yours truly, it was met with another of Xenia's whip-crack blows.

Apparently, Sharky had been talking straight when he said he wasn't here to hurt Xenia but to protect her. While she landed a flurry of strikes on him, he hadn't so much as taken a step in her direction. His arms were up, but only to protect his eyes as he backed away.

My hip popped back into its socket, and I was able to lever myself upright, mostly, by leaning on what was left of the hood of Xenia's ex-car. I shook my hands to get the feeling back before tapping the massive shoulder in front of me. "Hey, big guy."

"Eddy, no..." Xenia said.

As Sharky turned, I hauled off and landed the best right hook I could muster straight into the point of his snoot. Lights out, seven feet of man-shark thudded to the pavement at my feet.

Whataya know? Discovery Channel was right.

"Thanks for the distraction," I said. "Shark Week here had me on the ropes." I tried to straighten up, but something in my back was out of whack. The best I could manage right now was an awkward lean.

Xenia wiggled gloved fingers. "*Wind Razor.*"

"Awesome." My hip popped back out, and I crashed to the ground alongside Sharky.

Sharky had given me the biggest pounding I'd received in maybe ever, worse even than that bar fight back in... what? The eighties? My lower back made an unpleasant *thunk* as the bones of my spine tried to realign themselves. My stomach added its complaints to the mix, reminding me of how long it had been since my last meal. The breeze chose that moment to pick up, bringing Xenia's familiar smell of cinnamon and magic to my nose. My legs twitched against the gritty asphalt.

Xenia's scent was flush with fear and adrenaline from the fight, and my hunger made it clear that what I needed to get shipshape was *right there*. I squeezed my eyes shut and fought the hunger down. At least the injuries that made it so difficult to resist that siren scent also made it impossible to act on that need.

Shaking the glass from her hair, Xenia gave me a critical eye. "Not looking too good there, boss."

"Naw, I'm dandy. Cup of coffee and a smoke'll have me back on my feet in no time."

She snorted, blowing the lock of hair from in front of her eye. "Well, we can't have either of you two jokers lying on the street for the normies to trip over."

"Safe house is in there." I pointed my chin at the row of storage units behind the dented fence line. "You got anything in your bag of tricks that could hold him? He's not going to stay out forever, and the SOB's strong as I am."

Xenia raised one eyebrow.

"Maybe a teensy bit stronger," I admitted. "Definitely not in the mood for round two."

"Enough space in there for a seven-foot Child of Amanikabli?"

"Is that what he is?"

"Best guess I got," she said as she fished her arm back into the wreck of the car. Pack retrieved, she tucked her magic glove away inside. "C'mon, let's get you up." She crouched by my side, and her scent filled my head.

"No, don't—"

"You gonna bite me, boss?" She raised an eyebrow. "You gave your word I wasn't on the menu."

I forced my fangs to behave. "No."

"See? *No problemo.*" She snapped on a pair of latex gloves. Oh, right. She'd said my blood, vamp blood, was toxic. I was probably leaking from more than one spot. Better safe than sorry.

Careful not to jab me with any of her jacket's spikes, she got her arm under mine. With a grunt from each of us, she hauled me upright and we shuffled around to face the storage lot entrance.

"What about the big guy?"

"I see a cargo pallet over there," Xenia said. "I'll manage."

Chapter Sixteen

"I ASSUME, SINCE YOUR SAFE HOUSE IS HERE, THAT YOU have access to the cameras." Xenia jerked her thumb at the black plastic dome in the hallway as she shut the door to my safe house. Ever thoughtful, she'd returned the cargo pallet to its home at the front of the lot. "Have to scrub our friend here from the drives. I'm sure you don't want to end up on the evening news either."

Slumped in a chair, I nodded and winced at the jolt it sent through my head. The semi-concussion was fading, slowly, but it had caused me to miss how Xenia had levered the shark-man onto and off of the pallet. Something else from her backpack of tricks, likely. "No kidding. I'll have a chat with the night guard when I'm back on my feet. I'm sure we'll see eye-to-eye."

"Oh, har-de-har-har."

Rows of fluorescent tubes flickered to life, illuminating the garage-sized space. Originally set up as a room where I could wait out the daylight hours in style, now only half of the space still served that function.

Even so, it provided all the needs of a vampire on the run. A trunk, lock on the inside, for sleeping. Table, chairs, tasteful carpet, and a wardrobe stocked with plentiful—if out of style—clothing. A boxy slab of a safe contained a small arsenal of firearms, alternate identities, and cash in multiple currencies.

The other half of the space had been initially used to house a nondescript getaway vehicle. Now, the overflow from decades of impulse buying, keepsakes I couldn't bear to part with but didn't need, filled every spare inch. In the center of that cardboard chaos, in line with the wide roll-up door, sat the tarp-cloaked form of my pride and joy.

"Pack rat much, Eddy?" Xenia's head tilted to take in the mess. Slinging her pack underhand into one of the waiting chairs, she laid her armored jacket on the floor beside it. Rubbing her chin, she moseyed over to my collection to snoop.

"Can't blame a guy for keeping some knickknacks," I said. "Hey, sticky fingers, we need to get the big guy secured before he comes to."

"I'm looking, I'm looking," Xenia muttered as she prized a cardboard box open to peer inside. Lifting a Ferragamo that had gone out of season three presidents ago, she gave me a raised eyebrow before dropping it back where she'd found it. "You got anything useful in here?"

"I'm thinking." *Did* I have anything other than clothes in here? The safe was just guns, money, burners, and some paperwork left over from buying the Fortune. None of the furniture, hardwood though it might be, was heavy enough to pin down something that had nearly tied me into a pretzel.

Xenia slid a stack of boxes to one side and bent to peer under one corner of the tarp-shrouded form filling the center of the storage space. "No fuckin' way." Grabbing a double handful of cloth, she swept the tarp clear. Batting at the resulting cloud of dust, she stalked around my baby. "Eddy, is this—?"

"A 1959 Cadillac Eldorado Biarritz convertible, *with* a custom baby blue paint job," I said with just a little pride. I loved that car.

Why hadn't I driven it since... Damn, had it been over a decade?

Xenia whistled as she ran her hand along the winged tail fin. She tugged open the driver's door and leaned in to admire the interior.

"I bought that beauty the minute as I saw it on the showroom floor. Perfect timing. I'd had a big score, and the cash was burning a hole in my pocket. All that chrome was shining in the sun, pulled me in like a lure. Must have been destiny."

Xenia's head came up. "Sun? When did you buy her?"

I shrugged—my shoulders were working again, finally. "It was brand new, so... 1959?" With a little effort, I clambered out of the chair. My body had taken its sweet time, but things were finally coming together. Though I should probably avoid any more fights with the shark-men of the desert before I had a chance to fill my tank.

Xenia nodded. "Right, right. You're old." She gave me a nose-wrinkling grin before her brows came together, and she crossed her arms. "You were going to let me drive off in that beater when you had *this* fine lady just waiting around?"

"Hey, now—" I started.

Behind me, Sharky moaned, gills twitching.

"Shit," I said.

"Shit," Xenia agreed. "Come on, you must have *something* useful around here."

Inspiration struck. "Tool chest behind the Caddy. I think there's a tow chain in there."

Moving double-time, Xenia pitched another stack of boxes to the side and dragged the tool chest from its hiding place. Tow chain secured, she dashed back to where Sharky lay. "I got this. Stand back." Xenia sat on her heels.

Sharky moaned again, louder this time.

"Time's running out," I said.

"Dude, let me concentrate." Cracking her knuckles, she raised her hands before her, like a conductor just before the downbeat. Her eyes gained a half-visible incandescent ring about each iris as they darted around the room before settling on the length of chain once more. She nodded, and her fingers plucked at the air. The plucking became a weaving motion; beside her, the chain twitched.

I took a step back.

Brows knit, Xenia leaned toward the shark-man, tongue tip peeking at the corner of her mouth. As she added a wider, sweeping motion to her gestures, the chain slid across the carpet. Moving on its own, like a metal python, it slid up and over Sharky's chest. The sinuous movement continued until the chain had spiraled around the shark-man's torso to pin his arms to his sides.

Curiosity struck, and I opened my sight to see what Xenia was *really* doing.

As I'd expected, the room was full of the streamers and currents of magic's otherworldly color, but the usually random arrangement of the currents seemed to have taken on purpose. Gossamer filaments stretched between the writhing tow chain and Xenia. Hands enmeshed in a cat's-cradle of impossible color, she wove even more of the surrounding magic into the pattern animating the chain. The metal itself was nearly invisible for how dense the cage of glowing fibers interlocked with the links had become.

On a whim, I reached for the streamer of magic beside me. There was no resistance, no sensation at all. My fingers passed through the ribbon of light as if it were a figment of my imagination. "Why can't I touch it?" I barely realized that I'd spoken aloud.

Xenia spared me a glance, eyes flitting to me before returning to the task at hand. "Because you're dead, Eddy." Sorrow colored her voice. Gathering the skein of magic in her grip, she wiped sweat from her forehead with her free hand. "My body and spirit are still one."

Oh.

Xenia leaned forward, bringing her hands up to hover above Sharky's bound form. The ends of the chain rose, arcing over in an echo of her movement. Xenia clenched her fists, and the chain struck, ends rocketing into the floor. Punching through carpet and concrete, the links twined around the exposed rebar. With one last rattle, the binding around our captive pulled tight. Snug as a bug on my rug.

Her hands dropped from their conductor pose, and Xenia swayed. Slapping away my offered hand, she tottered upright and over to where her pack lay. A side compartment produced a bottle of water, the contents of which she chugged down without pausing for breath. She dropped herself into the waiting chair, boots kicking out as she slouched against the leather. "Did the best I could with the time I had. Pulled some extra strength into the steel too. That chain *should* hold him now." Making a frame with her fingers, she squinted at her handiwork. "Not too shabby for an extemporaneous working, if I do say so myself."

"Made it look easy," I said.

The corner of Xenia's lip twitched up.

While I hadn't just bent the laws of physics like a noodle, I *had* recently gone two rounds with the slab of muscle currently holding down the carpet. I still wasn't sure if I was entirely in one piece yet. I dragged the room's other chair around until I had a good view of our guest and

171

dropped my weary bones onto the padding. Stretching my leg out, I planted a heel in Sharky's side. "Hey. Big fella. Wake the fuck up."

"Eddy," Xenia said, "be nice."

"This jagoff wasn't too keen on being nice. He should be thanking his lucky stars I don't punch his card while he's out cold."

"He said he was trying to protect me." Her cheek dimpled. "Which is awfully nice of him, considering I don't have the slightest idea who the hell he is."

"Whuuu?" Sharky groaned. Beady black eyes blinked as he took in his predicament. When they landed on me, the muscle-bound body went rigid. He writhed, straining against the chain binding him to the floor. Clawed toes wiggled and his fingers tore at the carpet. "*No!*" Sharky bucked like a bronco, unable to break the magically augmented bonds that Xenia had wrapped around his body.

I gave him another thump with my heel. "Hey. Simmer down or I'll have her shrink that chain to half size." I clenched a fist. "Turn you into shark sushi."

Xenia shook her head, eyes wide. When the big guy's head swung her way, she put on a poor imitation of a tough expression.

"What? I don't..." Sharky grumbled. He didn't have eyebrows, but nevertheless he managed something like a frown. The point of his nose swung around and he bared approximately a million teeth at me. "Why are you helping the *bampira?*"

Xenia leaned forward, propping her elbows on her knees. "Mr. Fry and I have a business arrangement." She waited for the wedge of his snout to swing back her way. "Why were you trying to kill my client?"

Sharky's head, swiveled like a tennis fan's from Xenia to

me and back. His shoulders heaved against the chain, and a brittle crackling echoed from the floor beneath him.

The chain held.

As he accepted defeat, the massive shoulders sagged and the wide head thumped back onto the carpet. He spoke to the ceiling. "It was... okay when it was just one of you. Alone in your tower, leaving us be." His gills flared. "But now you bring friends, other *bampira,* and kill..." His chest heaved once more, bucking against the chain. The rebar in the floor groaned at the strain but held.

"Hold your damn horses, Mac," I said. "What do you mean, kill? Who got killed?" I didn't need to ask *who* had done the killing.

Xenia slid off her chair to kneel beside Sharky. "Can you tell me your name?" Her hand hovered above the shark-man for a moment before gently coming to rest on one wide shoulder. "You said you were going to save me?"

Sharky's eye swiveled to point at her. The wide jaw trembled.

"Came to see." The nose pointed at me. "Him. Confront him. Saw that he had you trapped in the car," Sharky mumbled.

"You thought he was going to feed on me?"

The massive head nodded.

"Aw, that's really nice." She patted the watermelon-sized bicep. "So what's your name, big guy?"

Black eyes squeezed shut. Gills fluttered as he drew in a gurgling breath. "B-Bruce."

"Hi, Bruce. I'm Xenia. It's very nice to meet you." She sat back on her heels. "Hey, would you like to change? It might be easier to talk, to have an actual conversation."

"Change?" I said. "What does he change into?"

Bruce raised his head, and the both of them stared at

me. Like I was supposed to know what was going on. I threw up my hands. "Okay, okay."

Bruce continued to glare at me with his little shark eyes. "Can't trust his kind."

"Eddy promises he won't hurt you if you don't attack again," Xenia said, her eyes not open to disagreement. "Okay? Eddy?"

"Sure," I said. "Whatever. As long as Brucie-boy keeps his teeth to himself."

"Your word, Eddy."

"All right, all right. I give you my word." I nodded at them both. "Truce."

Xenia patted Bruce's arm again. "What do you say?"

Bruce looked at her, then back to me. "Truce." He took a deep breath, gills fluttering, his chest straining against the chain. When he exhaled, his breath hissed between clenched saw teeth. As the air left him, his entire body seemed to deflate with it.

The pointed snout receded into a narrowing skull. His gray skin lost the pebbled texture as it darkened, shading from pale through tan until it took on an almost amber hue. Dark hair, showing streaks of gray, sprouted from his scalp and upper lip.

The wounds, the slices made by Xenia's *Wind Razor*, had scabbed up earlier while we'd worked to secure him. Now they shrank, knitting themselves closed until no trace remained.

Bruce's muscular form was evaporating, shrinking, and the chain binding him rattled as it shifted to maintain tension around his changing size.

With a final huff through his clenched, now entirely human teeth, Bruce took a regular breath. While a minute ago he'd been a seven-foot hulking mass of shark-meat, Bruce had become a slender, middle-aged man.

174

A very *naked* middle-aged man.

His eyes, still dark, had a lively glint that his shark eyes hadn't shared. A pencil mustache decorated his upper lip, and I wondered how the hair knew to grow back perfectly groomed like that.

Xenia snapped her fingers, and the chain fell from around Bruce's arms and chest.

Bruce shivered and wrapped narrow arms about his bony knees. Jumping to her feet, Xenia dashed across the room. Pulling a wool blanket from the mess of boxes, she draped it around Bruce's shoulders. He bunched one hand in the rough fabric at his throat and looked up at her gratefully.

Xenia offered her hand. "Hello, Bruce. Nice to meet you all over again."

Hesitating, Bruce took her hand. Leaning back, she helped him to his feet. When she gestured at the chair she'd vacated, he sat, carefully wrapping the blanket to preserve some dignity. "Hello, Miss Xenia. It's rather nice to meet you too." Bruce's voice, no longer deep and rumbling, held a trace of an accent. Familiar, but I couldn't put my finger on it.

"Eddy Fry." I waved a hand by my forehead in a lazy salute.

"Ah yes," Bruce said. "I know *of* you, Mr. Fry. But only by reputation."

"I have a reputation?" I was confused. "And here I thought I'd been keeping a low profile all this time. What's my reputation? With who?"

Bruce sighed and pulled the blanket tight. "It's been general knowledge in the community that a vampire had taken up residence on the Strip." He touched his nose, as if to verify it was in the right place. "We'd caught your scent on and off over the years. The tourists have been oblivious to your presence, of course, while we have done our best to avoid you." Bruce spoke with precise, clipped tones.

I guessed that a mouthful of big teeth plus the gills made speaking a bit of a chore.

"From the day we became aware of your presence, we were all concerned you'd come to us demanding tribute. In treasure and blood both." The narrow mustache curled in a sneer. "There was talk of preemptive action. Of finding your lair, dragging you out into the sun."

I shifted, finding the chair no longer comfortable.

Bruce shook his head. "You never showed yourself to the Underground. You never attacked, killed, or even spoke to any of us. We didn't even see evidence that you were killing your blood meals. No bodies, other than those Las Vegas creates on its own, had turned up. The community decided it was best to not rock the boat. To let sleeping dogs lie." He raised his nose in a sniff. "More the fools us."

Xenia propped her hip against the table at Bruce's side. "What changed? Why did you come after him now? Why alone?"

Bruce's shoulders quivered and his eyes shone under the fluorescent lights. "Mr. Fry's new associates came to the Underground tonight. Just after sundown." The trembles reached his voice. "Two of them. A woman and a giant of a man."

Xenia's face hardened, and she looked at me.

I shook my head. *Not my friends,* I mouthed.

"The woman did the talking. Demanding. We were now all of us subjects of House Weir, she declared." His eyes squeezed shut for a moment before he went on. "They told us to spread the word, to inform everyone that in two nights' time they would demand tribute... and an oath." A shudder shook the blanket wrapped about his shoulders. "I was there, having a drink with a friend." A fat tear swelled in one eye. "A c-close friend." Spilling over, the tear rolled down Bruce's cheek.

Xenia rested her hand on his shoulder; after a ragged breath, he laid his hand atop hers.

"Michael always had a quick temper. He never did like being pushed." Bruce gritted his teeth. "He yelled at her, this vampire woman. He made a scene. Called them oppressors." His lips pressed into a line. "Michael was always quite political."

A moment passed. Xenia asked, "What happened?"

"Michael and some others, I didn't know all of them, they stood together and demanded that she leave. Leave and never return." The tears spilled down his cheeks unchecked. "I was scared. I hung back. I've seen what the *bampira* were capable of, long ago." Another shuddering breath. "It all happened so fast. The big one. He knocked them all down. Alone. Even the others who should have been as strong as he was seemed weak by comparison. He fought five or six of them like they were children. The vampire woman, she... she said she was going to make an example." He squeezed his eyes shut, the flow of tears hardly slowing. "She beat Michael herself." His eyes opened, staring at but not seeing me. "I can still hear his bones breaking." Bruce's voice was distant, miserable.

Xenia rubbed a hand across his back. She glared at me, fury darkening her eyes, then looked away.

"I went to his side. I tried to change. To protect him. But the big one, it was so cold. I couldn't find my other self." Bruce shivered with the memory, pulling the blanket tight. "I should have shifted sooner, before it was too late."

Felix. That one was going to be a problem.

"Then they were gone. Left him there on the floor as if he was trash. I took him home to his family. He asked that of me. I don't know if they can help him, if he's even still

177

alive." His eyes focused on me. "That's when I came looking for you. I knew if I could get you away from the big one, I could get answers out of you. Why had you changed your mind, invited the other *bampira* into your domain? Then, I saw her in the car with you, and things got a bit out of hand." He grimaced. "A great white is quite focused on the hunt. Emotions are simpler, more direct. Before I knew what I was doing, I'd become my other self." He shrugged. "The rest, you know."

I rubbed my temples. "Okay, I am really, really sorry about your friend. But let's get one thing straight. I have *nothing* to do with that crew. That dame ain't my friend, and until a day ago I didn't even know there were any other vampires out there. Or wizards, or shark-men, or whatever the *fuck* that big guy is." I threw my hands up in the air. "Why would you assume I had anything to do with it? When I wasn't even there with them?"

Bruce looked puzzled. "But you are the vampire of note in Las Vegas, are you not? If that *bampira*"—he spat the word—"does not report to you, Mr. Fry, then to whom?"

I tried not to roll my eyes. "Vampire of note. Uh-huh. I don't think that argument is gonna fly with them. That dame, she's the ringleader of that circus, not me." At Bruce's look, I went on. "She's gunning for me the same way she's gunning for your people."

Bruce's jaw dropped.

I *thunk*ed my head against the chair's backrest and stared at the ceiling. A tension that had nothing to do with the recently broken bones pulled at my shoulders.

Even though I'd just learned that they existed, I would've thought a bunch of shark-people like Bruce could hold their own in a fight. Instead, Felix had bowled them over as easily as he'd done me.

Not the news I'd been hoping to hear.

WHILE I DUG into my supplies for something to replace the suit Bruce had ruined by introducing me to the roof of a car, Xenia hauled her spiky, armored jacket into her lap. Sweat popped out on her brow as she did something that caused one of the two-inch spikes to shrink into its former, flatter stud shape. Gradually, the jacket returned to the form it had held when I'd first met her. Bruce was fascinated by whatever she was doing with the metal and couldn't tear his eyes away.

Once I was presentable, I scrounged up an old Armani that I didn't mind parting with for Bruce. I had no idea where *his* duds were. Presumably scattered on the ground wherever it was he'd gone all toothy.

In human form, he was nearly the same height as I was, just with a lot less meat on his bones. The suit fit him well enough that it only made him look a *little* bit like a disco scarecrow.

Sartorial needs seen to, I filled them in on my side of the Rebecca situation. I didn't enjoy spilling my guts, but I had to face facts.

I needed a crew.

"The giant—you said his name was Felix?—was able to render you unconscious as handily as he did us?" Bruce asked a bit breathlessly.

"Well, I don't know about handily—"

"Fact is, this guy can one-punch a recently fed vamp," Xenia interrupted. "You said he took down Michael and *his* friends without breaking a sweat?"

Bruce nodded.

"I seriously can't think of anything with that kind of power." Xenia dragged a hand across her face. Dark circles had formed under her eyes. Either from stress or from the cost of all the magic she'd been slinging around, I couldn't tell.

"Some expert you turned out to be," I snapped.

"Hey, you hired me to teach you what *I* knew." Xenia's voice was strained. "This is *way* beyond the scope of what you hired me for. As you recall, I was on my way out of town before we got distracted." She smiled at Bruce and waved away his apologies. "No, you're fine. I was just hoping to keep my scent out of Rebecca's nose if I could. If she finds out there's a magician in town..."

"That reminds me. Gotta see about getting you a fresh set of wheels. Not *those*," I added as Xenia's head swung toward the Caddy.

"About that." She glanced at Bruce. "Change of plans. I can't see bailing on this. Not now."

"What happened to 'not being down for a vampire turf war'?" I made air quotes.

Xenia pinched the bridge of her nose. "Yeeaah. If it was just my neck on the line, I'd be halfway to Albuquerque by now. Car or no car. But it's not. It's not about me, or you, or even Bruce and Michael. Rebecca will claim this as her territory, and then she'll do to the hidden people of Las Vegas what vampires have done in almost every other city. What House Harkness did to New York."

Bruce looked away.

I had a pretty good guess where she was going with this. I nodded for her to continue.

"She'll compel obedience. Her victims won't just be slaves, they'll be joyfully, enthusiastically enslaved. She'll feed from them. Kill anyone who won't bend the knee or can't be made to serve, or even just for fun. For people in the supernatural community, it's still the Dark Ages. Feudalism's still going strong."

"Las Vegas, for many years, has been one of the very

few havens that the vampires have not claimed," Bruce added. "It's why so many of us have made our homes here. Free from vampire and human oppression." He buried his face in his hands.

"Yeah, I get it." I'd seen how "regular humans" treated people whose only difference was skin color. It didn't take much imagination to know how Joe Six-Pack would react to having a shark-man living next door. "You're sure you're up for this?" I asked Xenia. "I've been in turf wars before, back when I still had a heartbeat. They ain't pretty. I only made it by the skin of my teeth, and I was loaded for bear."

Mouth pressed into a line, Xenia nodded. "I can't leave. Not now."

Well, that tears it. I'd been giving serious consideration to just dusting off the Caddy and hitting the road. I hated to go, *really* hated the thought of leaving the Golden Fortune behind, but I'd come to the conclusion that I was outgunned. However, if some scrap of a teenager wasn't going to get while the getting was good, how the fuck could I? "I could draw her out," I said at last. "Get her alone and grease her. No more Rebecca, no more problems."

"Don't be so sure it'd be that easy," Xenia said. "We've got no idea how old she is, and believe me, that matters. If she's got more than a century of vamp time on the books, she'd probably wipe the floor with you."

Xenia wore a hole in the carpet with her pacing while I took that in.

Bruce lifted his head from his hands, "Mr. Fry, I hesitate to even ask, but in all honesty I am desperate and cannot see another option."

Xenia paused in her circuit across the floor, and I sat up in my chair. "Shoot."

"If what you say is true, then this Rebecca represents as much of a threat to your life and livelihood as she does to ours. Perhaps we might stand a better chance if we were to join forces." Bruce rose from his chair. "You said you were staying to help, didn't you, Miss Xenia?" He turned toward her.

"Just Xenia, and yes. I'd feel like a *complete* asshole if I bailed now and left a friend in trouble."

Bruce glanced at me and then back to her.

Placing her hand on his shoulder, she added gently, "You, silly."

Bruce smiled for the first time since he'd changed to his human form and patted her hand. "Thank you. *Thank you.* I don't wish to be rude, but would I be correct in assuming that you are a—"

"Magician, yes."

Bruce's smile grew wider.

"I don't mean to be the fly in the ointment," I said, "but a couple of shark-people, a clueless vampire, and Sabrina the Teenage Witch are hardly going to be a challenge for Felix. Not to mention anything else Rebecca has up her sleeve."

"I'm frickin' twenty," she muttered. "I've been a magician for six years."

Bruce cleared his throat. "And I'm afraid I'm the sole, ah, shark-person in Las Vegas, Mr. Fry."

I threw up my hands.

"But there will be plenty of others in the community who would swell our ranks, if we can get word out." Bruce glanced at Xenia. "Especially when they learn that we have a magician on our side."

Xenia flipped her hair out of her eye and tried not to look proud.

They'd lost me again. "Okay, someone needs to get me up to speed. Which, unless I'm mistaken, is what I'm paying the teenage *magician* to do. What community are we talking about if Bruce is the only shark guy in town?"

"The Hidden People," Bruce said.

"The Clandestine," Xenia said at nearly the same time. "Told you about them earlier?" she added.

"There's been a lot going on, if you ain't noticed. Slipped my mind. Okay, clue me in."

"The Clandestine, Hidden People, the Unseen—these are all accepted terms for the community of supernatural or otherwise nonhuman people who live in and among the human population. I don't just mean here, in Las Vegas. Everywhere. 'The Underground' just refers to whatever common place they gather at." She leaned a hip against the table. "A place for supernatural folks to be themselves without having to pretend to be what they're not. Some places, it's just a bar or club. In others, you'll find an entire city hidden within the human one. Take San Francisco, for example."

"So it's a clubhouse for monsters."

"Are *you* a monster, Mr. Fry?" asked Bruce.

"I mean..." To be honest, even with the fangs and the liquid diet, I still thought of myself as a regular Joe. "Sorry about that, Bruce. Didn't mean any offense."

Bruce's eyebrows shot up, and he nodded once.

I said, "Okay, Bruce, you said that's where Rebecca attacked your... Michael? That's where everyone was? This clubhouse?"

"At the Underground, yes." The smile was gone, but Bruce pushed on. "The powers that maintain the establishment in Las Vegas are apparently of low humor and actually named it 'The Underground.'" He shrugged.

"Okay, what say we go see this Underground Club? You can check on your folks, and my consultant and I can reconnoiter. Gather intelligence." It'd been ages since my last battle plan; I only hoped I could remember enough to put something together. "If we're lucky, we might even round up enough muscle to show Rebecca and her crew the door." I shoved myself out of the chair. "Xenia, what do you think?"

Xenia looked unconvinced. "Sure? It resembles a plan, I guess." She tugged her jacket on. "I haven't been to The Underground yet." She narrowed her eyes at me. "My plans got derailed, for some reason."

"Bruce, what do you say? Be our guide to"—I threw my arms wide—"*The Underground?*"

"I don't see why not," Bruce said.

"We're all gonna die," muttered Xenia.

I pretended not to hear that.

Chapter Seventeen
Then

USING MY SHOULDER, I PINNED THE PHONE BOOTH handset to my ear. I wasn't actually talking to anyone. It was just an excuse so I could keep an eye on this stretch of sidewalk without turning heads. I had a nickel ready to go anyway. If the mark pulled anything funny, it was my job to keep the crew up to date.

I gotta tell you that this fella, today's mark, was absolutely perfect. I'd gotten the tip from a lady working the cage at the Nugget, who I had a little thing going with.

To be honest, I had a "little thing" with a gal at almost every casino cage or front desk in town. It brought in quality intel for the crew, and it kept my mind off of the Darla Disaster.

I'd wined and dined that gal all over town, spending every penny on her that hadn't gone over to Gus. Then I found out Darla was schtupping two other guys. A regular gold digger she turned out to be. She broke my heart so bad, it was the closest I'd ever come to giving a dame the back of my hand.

As for the mark, Little Mickey and I had snooped

around, made some phone calls. This fella ticked off every box on Little Micky's list: Big win, but not big enough to hit the news. Cashed out, and didn't wire the moolah home. Alone, or with one other person *only*. Drove into town. Most importantly, *no* connections to anyone higher up the food chain.

That last one would be a killer if we messed it up.

Anyhow, I'd been tailing the mark all over Fremont to find out where he'd stashed his ride. Other than his car, I needed to make sure he didn't check into another hotel and feed his winnings right back into the house. That had ruined more than one job, believe me.

The mark finally put in an appearance, popping out of the chili joint next to the Pioneer Club where I'd last seen him. He let fly with a belch I could hear across the street and jammed a toothpick into the corner of his mouth. Fresh from a three-beer dinner, judging by the wobble in his step. I waited a five-count before hanging up and hitting the pavement at his heels.

Tailing a rube in Las Vegas can be a coin flip. You never know when something shiny'll catch their eye and drag them off course. Blink at the wrong time, and they're in the wind. Then, like today, there's the crowd.

A family of eight spilled onto the sidewalk, and I had to hop just to avoid kicking the stroller. The mark had vanished around the corner on First, and I needed to get my eye back on him before he had a chance to disappear.

My luck held. He was only a block away. I maintained that distance while he moseyed down the street, suitcase swinging by his side. I kept an eye on the street behind me, too. It's not too common, but sometimes another crew will step on you to get a mark. So far, so good.

Bingo. He'd chucked his bag into the back seat of an

older Ford. I kept walking, trying to seem as if I were nothing more than a fellow gambler looking for my car, until I was close enough to make out his plate number.

Step one, check.

I'd parked my ride all the way on the *other* side of Fremont, so I needed to leg it over there as fast as I could. On the way, I stepped into the phone booth I'd holed up in and rang Little Mickey. He would relay the plate number and vehicle description to the rest of the crew.

There were four routes a driver would take when leaving Vegas, and we had a pair of eyes on each one. Sure, you could just stake out 91 south to Los Angeles. But then you'd get a Mormon going home to Salt Lake, and you'd be out your score.

A tense five minutes passed before the phone rang. "It's 91 south. Go," Little Mickey said.

I had to swing wide, around Fremont and downtown, to pick up the guy Little Mickey had stuck on Route 95. Once he was in the car, I put the hammer down, southbound. The other two had their own car; we'd link up on the road. Now that we had a line on the mark's direction, the two teams would catch up and tail him until we were far outside city limits, deep in the desert.

We'd been tailing the mark for the better part of an hour. The sun was low, and around us a whole lot of nothing stretched as far as the eye could see. My old friends, the Grace brothers, pulled up alongside in their car. Ronnie waved over to me and pumped his fist, followed by a gesture that told me they were going to take lead.

The Grace brothers *always* wanted to take the lead.

"Here we go," I said to the guy riding shotgun. Clarence —I shit you not, that was his name—reached under the seat to pull out an Ithaca 37. Clarence was the freshest face in the group, and I didn't know him all that well. He'd shown up a month or so ago, and Little Mickey had said he was part of the crew. So he was on the crew. Nice guy, I guess, but he wasn't much of a talker.

Clarence grinned at me while he racked the shotgun.

In the other car, Donnie, the Grace behind the wheel, gunned it to pull past the Ford. Once he got *his* Ford into the lane ahead of the mark, he sped up as if he'd just been passing.

Then it was my turn to step on the gas. I pulled into the other lane and kept the speed until I drew even with the mark. At same time, Donnie tapped the brakes until his fender was inches from the mark's car.

Clarence leaned from his window, leveling the shotgun at the mark. "*PARK IT!*" Clarence shouted to be heard over the wind. Those were the first words out of his mouth since he'd gotten in the car.

The mark tried to make a run for it, but with the Grace brothers swerving to match his every move, he didn't have much luck. Eventually, he made the right call and pulled to the side of the highway. As his car rolled to a stop, Donnie backed his ride right up against the mark's grille while I boxed him in from behind.

Colt in hand, I sauntered over to the driver's window. The Grace brothers made themselves and their guns —Donnie really loved that tommy gun—visible while Clarence kept an eye out for any unwanted traffic.

I tapped my piece against the glass, and when the mark rolled the window down, I gave him my best movie cop impression. "Do you know why I pulled you over today, sir?" Off to the side, Clarence slapped his knee.

Hope had bloomed on the mark's face when he heard me, but the lack of a blue uniform and spinning red lights quashed that right away. "Dammit, I knew my luck wouldn't hold." The whine in his voice half covered the quaver of fear.

"Play along, and you'll be on your way home in no time." I waved the Colt. "Come on, Mac, shake a leg."

Once his suitcase had been transferred to the back seat of my car, we hit the road. I'd told the poor SOB to lie face down in his back seat and wait ten minutes. By then we'd be long gone. We weren't too worried about Las Vegas's finest figuring out which of the town's many, *many* goons had ripped this guy off if he should go squealing.

———

An hour later, we were marching into the clubhouse with the spoils of the day. Well, "clubhouse" might be too generous. We'd taken over a pair of rooms at the Park Lane Motel. I wouldn't have called it fancy, but it would do until we moved up in the world.

We'd had the motel furniture dragged out and replaced with some halfway decent chairs, a table, and a couch. Little Mickey even had himself a fine desk to run the crew from. Once we'd brought in our first score, he'd bought a state-of-the-art television set. With that massive sixteen-inch screen, it was the biggest TV I'd ever seen.

As we piled into the room, the frosty screen was displaying a familiar face. Moe Sedway, seated behind a cluster of microphones, appeared to be in a courthouse. He shared the room with a gaggle of senators who were grilling him about his stake in the Flamingo.

"Can you believe that Kefauver dragged Mr. Sedway in to rake him over the coals?" Little Mickey pronounced the senator's name "Cow-Fever."

On the tube, one senator was trying to pin our former boss down. "You don't get anything out of the Flamingo?" he was asking.

Moe's voice was bland. "I get my room. I get my board."

Beside me, Donnie Grace snorted.

Not satisfied with Moe's response, the senator went off on a righteous tear. "You say you knew Lucky Luciano? He is a moral pervert and the scum of the earth!"

Little Mickey chuckled as he tilted his hand back and forth. "The senator's a bit on the money with that one."

I would've watched the rest of Moe's testimony just for the laughs, but Little Mickey, I think, was looking to make sure no one in the room got called out by name. When the committee called some auto parts guy I'd never heard of to take the stand, Ronnie Grace clicked the set off. "Eddy, make with the goods, will ya?" he said. "Ain't got all day."

I wasn't about to let the mark's suitcase out of my sight. Since we arrived, I'd kept my hand tight on the handle. I slid the narrow case onto the table, knocking over a couple empties in the process, and popped the latches. With all eyes on me, I rooted among undershirts, trousers, and unmentionables until I turned up our prize. I upended a suspiciously heavy sock and shook it until it coughed a fat roll of bills into my waiting hand. I held that beautiful sight up for all to see before placing it in the center of the table.

Each member of the crew took a turn counting it up under the boss's watchful eye. He'd insisted that this was the only way to keep everyone honest.

The total take from this job, if you ignored the cheap watch in the suitcase, totaled just over ten large. Once we'd cut out a percentage for Gus—we were operating in his territory—Little Mickey came away with the lion's share. Being the boss had its privileges. The rest was a four-way split that put twelve hundred bucks and a cheap watch in my hand.

After that, we got down to the serious business of draining a few bottles of beer. It had been a good day. This was our first score after a dry month.

True to his word, once I'd handed over Monty's papers and the name of the rat, Gus had torn up my marker. He'd even called up Mr. Cohen back in Los Angeles and made sure everything was copacetic.

Unfortunately, he'd also cut me loose from the Flamingo. Lansky got what he wanted after all.

Without a source of folding money, a place to hang my hat, or a dame, I'd packed what little I had and hit the road for Los Angeles. I'd made it as far as the first hill that dropped the glitter and shine of Sin City out of the rearview mirror.

I'd been born in LA. Raised there. Pop had jumped out a window downtown when the crash hit. I'd buried Ma there. Except for my time in the Army and the last three years, I'd spent my whole life in Los Angeles.

But Vegas was my *home*. I spun that steering wheel around and high-tailed it back to Glitter Gulch.

Now, I spent most of my time at the clubhouse, waiting for the phone to ring. While most of those calls would bring in a tip on a road job, the boss had begun offering small loans. Nothing too large, just the sort of thing to get someone down on their luck back into the game. Anything larger than that got passed up to Moe and his deep pockets. And if someone thought they could miss a payment? Well, I was still the man for that particular job.

The other fellas in the crew had their own things on the side too. Donnie and Ronnie were running a couple of girls out of another motel, keeping it low rent to avoid stepping on anyone's toes.

Once he'd warmed up to us, Clarence had confessed that he might be "good with cards." Guy might look like some kind of professor, had a thing for bow ties even, but he was a regular card sharp. He was so smooth with palming cards, not even God could see him do it. Naturally, we'd started running a poker game once a week. We set it up in a suite at the Flamingo, which meant Gus took a piece off the top of the rake.

Little Mickey kept it all organized. The man had an eye for opportunity and the mind of an accountant hiding in that gorilla body. He kept us under the radar and out of trouble. It was only a matter of time before we had a *real* clubhouse to call our own.

That being said, our current arrangement had its own perks. The Park Lane had a liquor store right in the front. It was the work of a minute to use a bit of my share of the day's take to pick up a fine bottle of bourbon. Before the fellas had noticed I'd stepped out, I was back and pouring a round of shots for everyone, except Clarence, who was a teetotaler. I'd bought him a Coke.

"To a job well done, boys." I raised my glass high.

"Hear hear," Little Mickey said, clinking his drink with mine. "Keep this up, gentlemen, and we'll have our own casino in a year's time."

"I'll drink to that," Donnie cheered.

"Eddy, make sure you thank your little lady at the Nugget properly," Little Mickey said. "That was a good tip."

"Which one? You know Eddy's a *real* ladies' man. Got a gal in every neighborhood," quipped Donnie. "I hear he's even got a skirt over on the west side!"

"Yeah, yeah." Let them laugh. "A gentleman never tells."

"A gentleman!" Donnie barked. "*Clarence* is the gentleman around these parts."

At this, Clarence winked, tugging on his bow tie and tipping an imaginary hat.

"You just talk a good game, Eddy," Ronnie muttered into his glass. Guess he was still sore about me knocking him on his ass back when we'd first been introduced.

Chapter Eighteen
Now

Dawn was approaching, but with Bruce's assurance that it was "daylight safe" (the sun being an issue for more folks than just vampires, it seemed), the three of us piled into a cab for the journey over to this Underground joint. I hadn't really paid attention when he'd given the cabbie directions, so I was both surprised and let down when I saw the owl logo of our destination.

I said, "You're telling me the super-secret underground club for supernatural folks is in the *Hooters Casino*?" Even Xenia seemed taken aback.

Bruce waved us into the alley between the casino and the parking structure. Midway down the narrow access, the concrete walls sported a few nondescript steel doors. They looked like the sort of thing maintenance workers would use for electrical or water utility access. Nothing you'd look at twice.

Bruce approached a door that was identical in every way to the others save for a tiny emblem, a stylized flower in black and red, set at eye level. Unlocked, the door opened at his touch, and we followed him inside.

Instead of a duct-lined utility corridor, the door opened

on a well-decorated hallway. The floor was dark marble, shot through with veins of gold, topped with the proverbial red carpet. Crystal sconces with faux flaming torches provided an ambiance that blended invitation with mystery. At the end of the brief hallway sat a private elevator whose panel contained a single button, imprinted with an icon twin of the one on the outer door. When the car moved, it didn't surprise me to find we were heading down.

After a short ride, the elevator doors dinged open. Whatever I had expected from Las Vegas's supernatural hangout, a full-blown casino, teeming with tourists, hadn't been on the list.

To be honest, I should have expected it.

Bruce hung back as Xenia and I both gawked at the scenery. The Underground was full of the same clatter and jingle, the same muted roar of excited conversation, as any joint on the Strip. Rows of slot machines clamored for attention, tables crowded with party people testing their luck. The decor, though, ran in darker colors, and the light levels were lower than what you'd expect topside, but it was hardly what I'd call ominous. There was even a lounge complete with band, the singer of which was crooning about driving Cadillacs in their dreams. Exactly the type of fare you'd hear in my Lotus Lounge.

The crowd, though. That was something else entirely. At first glance, maybe you wouldn't notice anything unusual. Until you realized the guy over there and his gal had blue skin. Or that lady who had fins rippling down the length of her arms. Or the... I had no idea what even to call that. A walking shag carpet?

Xenia elbowed me in the ribs. "Not polite to stare, Eddy."

I tore my eyes away. "You're one to talk. Your head's been on a swivel since we walked in the joint."

"Just taking in the décor," she said, unconvincingly.

"This has been here the entire time?" I asked Bruce.

"Since the mid-fifties, yes." A hint of a smile peeked from under his pencil mustache. "The owner, or owners, move the entrance every year. It can always be found next to a casino, however. Sometimes a nightclub."

"Welcome to the Underground Las Vegas, Mr. Fry," an unfamiliar voice said.

I turned to see who here could possibly know my name. The speaker was an attractive woman in a conservatively cut Tahari suit. The clipboard in her hands, the flower logo pin on one lapel, and the crossed keys on the other marked her as part of the resort staff.

Even though I hadn't been listening for it, beside me, the quickening of Xenia's heartbeat came through clear as day. Apparently, she had a type.

"Shizue Takanashi," she said, extending a manicured hand. "I represent the management in the day-to-day matters here at the Underground."

"Japanese? I served in Okinawa back in the day. You wouldn't happen to know a—"

Xenia's hand gripped my elbow, and she raised a finger to the concierge. "We'll be just a moment." Once she'd dragged me back the way we'd come, she stared at me for a handful of elevated heartbeats. "Were you *seriously* about to ask her if she knew someone you met on the other side of the world nearly seventy years ago? Dude, that is..." She glanced over her shoulder, a hint of color rising in her cheeks.

"Hey, there was a Colonel Takanashi I had dealings with. Can't blame a guy for being curious."

She rolled her eyes. "Times have changed, you know. Assuming someone knows someone else of the same... well, it's pretty racist, you know? Look, you hired me to get you up to speed on the stuff you don't know—"

"Yeah, the woo-woo shit." I waved at the crowd of crazy-looking folks milling around. "This stuff. Not to rap my knuckles like a schoolmarm."

"Just tone it down." She glanced over her shoulder again. "As a favor to your favorite consultant?"

Ah-hah. "Say no more." Once we'd returned to where Bruce and the concierge waited, I cleared my throat. "Miss, ah, Ms. Takanashi. I apologize for any insensitivity on my part. It's something I'm working on."

"Thank you, Mr. Fry. No apology necessary. Accounting for cultural friction is a part of my—" Shizue began.

"'That geezer was bang out of order, 'ee was." A second voice, from somewhere behind Shizue, interrupted. "Oi'm gonna put one roight across 'is canistah."

Shizue's cheeks colored. Brushing a lock of hair into place behind her ear, she discreetly gave the back of her head a quick jab with one pointed nail.

"Cor! Awroit, awroit," the voice muttered.

"Mr. Fry, Ms. Findlay," Shizue continued, "on behalf of the management, please enjoy your stay at the Underground Las Vegas." She turned to Bruce. "You as well, Mr. Malihan. Management extends their deepest condolences to you and your companion for the earlier events."

Bruce went stiff. He nodded once, sharply.

"Did Rebecca and her pet gorilla get the same VIP greeting? Did you comp them the buffet after they knocked the other customers around?" I asked.

"Management was unsure of their intentions when the party in question arrived." Shizue's mouth turned down in a little moue. "Until they acted against our patrons, we extended them the same courtesy all our clientele receive. Their behavior was absolutely unacceptable, and although they departed before security could arrive to handle the situation, measures have been taken. Unfortunately—"

"Here it comes," I muttered.

"Management must remain, for the moment, neutral in matters that relate directly to vampire politics. While her subordinates are barred from the premises, Ms. Weir enjoys a certain... political *immunity* thanks to her patron and may enter as she pleases."

"Of course." I tried not to roll my eyes *too* much.

Her knuckles whitened around the edges of her clipboard, and she leaned toward me. In a hushed tone, she added, "Personally, I don't agree. I can't imagine that allowing that woman free rein over the people of Las Vegas will result in anything but a total disaster. Both for us and for"—she lifted her eyes to indicate the streets above us—"them." Shizue stepped back, one hand tugging her jacket into place. "Please enjoy your stay in the Underground." With a nod to each of us, she strode off, already flipping to the next page on her clipboard.

"Well, that was weird," I said.

"Eh, as far as weird goes, that barely tips the scales." Xenia craned her neck around. "Damn, If I'd known the Underground was this nice, I'd've come here first."

"You should've asked for her number."

Xenia goggled at me. "Are you joking?" Her laugh was nervous. "No way she'd..." She shook her head. "Anyhow, she's on the clock."

"So find out when she's off and buy her a drink. Life's short."

"Ironic, considering who's speaking," Bruce said.

"Bruce," I said, "big guy. Where do we start? Where do we look for the hitters in this joint?"

Bruce's eyes fell to the floor. "I should go see Michael. I haven't spoken to him since I ran off looking to..." He fell silent.

Xenia put her hand in front of me. "Hey, it's okay, we understand." She glanced at me. "Don't we, Eddy?"

I considered the situation. "Go on, take care of business."

"Do what you need to do. Eddy and I will explore, since it's our first time here." She put a hand on his shoulder and gave it a squeeze. "We can reconnect afterward. You can tell us how Michael is doing. Then we'll worry about finding people who will help."

"Thank you," Bruce said. "If Michael's family doesn't hate me too much for running away, I think they might help us locate those who are willing to take a stand against the vampires." Bruce glanced at me with me a small, sad smile. "The other vampires, that is."

"Go," Xenia said. "Call us when you can."

———

I KEPT my eyes peeled for trouble as we made our way through the hidden casino. Just because the concierge had said Rebecca's goons were barred from entry didn't mean they'd gotten the memo. My neck itched as we orbited the roulette tables.

Of the fracas Bruce had described, there was no sign. Either it had gone down in a different part of the Underground, or their clean-up crew was better than mine.

A pang of preemptive loss sliced through my gut, frosted with a sense of my own short-sightedness. How had I missed *all of this*? And it was all just going to go away if Rebecca got what she wanted.

Our casual tour and my thoughts were interrupted by

Xenia's stomach when it cut loose with a rumble audible *without* my special hearing.

"Need to find something to eat." She pressed a hand to her middle. "You know, we might find something here for you." Xenia glanced over her shoulder. "Something ethically sourced, even."

That idea hadn't even been on my radar. I'd had to "source" my own meals for so long it had never occurred to me that there could be other options. "You think so? That wouldn't be the worst idea. Bruce really did a number on me." My spine twinged its agreement.

As Nevada casinos go, the Underground was a bit on the small side. Closer to what you'd see in Reno, or Laughlin maybe. Geometric stonework featured heavily in the decor. A Mayan theme, or Aztec? I wondered if the Underground's designer was available. Could be time to retheme the Golden Fortune, assuming I ever got it back.

Or survived the next twenty-four hours.

As we passed a bank of elevators, I realized that my preoccupation with how everyone around us *looked* had run interference for how they were *acting*. Chiding myself for being slow on the uptake, I gave the crowd a second look.

Sure, folks were throwing the dice, yanking on the one-arms just like they'd be doing upstairs. But there was a wilder look in their eyes, fewer smiles than there should have been in this party crowd. The scents reaching my nose were heavy on the desperation, the despair. Of the usual excitement, the spikes of thrill and joy, there was hardly any to be found. Grimly determined to have fun no matter what, the Underground's clientele had all the signs of a party the night before the apocalypse.

If what Xenia and Bruce had told me was true, it probably was.

The itchy feeling on the back of my neck dug in its tiny claws. Expecting trouble, I scanned around for the source.

Maybe fifty feet down an aisle, by the spin-the-wheel, a fella stood like a rock in the current of the crowd. Elbow supported in one hand, the other cupping his chin so the fingers obscured the lower half of his face. His unblinking almond eyes, dark in the low light, and the prominent nose were all I could make out. The stranger's skin was dark, almost ochre, as if he spent all his time in the sun. His suit, a bespoke masterpiece in black linen, was complemented by a red silk shirt.

I watched him watch me, waiting for him to make the first move. "Any clue who that guy is?" I asked Xenia.

Xenia pulled away from the map kiosk she'd been examining. "Who?" If she'd picked up on the tension in the crowd, she was hiding it.

"That guy." I made to point out the stranger in the magnificent suit, but he was gone. "Never mind."

In our search for some place to eat, we took a pass on: the Iron Tiki Bar (those fruity drinks didn't appeal to either of us), the casino buffet (it wasn't open at this hour), and the sports bar (too full and too noisy for conversation). We settled on the lounge bar.

A waitress, looking very human and very bored, cruised over with menus as we sat ourselves at one of the small tables. "Anything with a pink plus sign next to it is safe for basic humans to eat, folks." She snapped her gum as she spoke. "Anything I can start the two of you out with?"

I didn't have a clue how to ask for "vampire chow." If I asked for blood, would the waitress think I was asking for *hers*? "Uhh," I said cleverly.

"Just get him the most expensive bourbon on the shelf," Xenia said without looking up from her menu. "Holy shit, you have Moxie! I'll have one of those."

"Youbetcha." As the waitress sashayed off, a long, narrow tail swished from underneath her black sequined skirt. Her tail ended in a barbed point with a bow, in matching black sequins, tied on just before the barb.

"So, what do you think she is?" I asked, leaning toward Xenia.

"Okay, I'm going to pass this on to you the way it was to me. *Generally*, you don't ask someone that sort of thing if you don't know them well. With humans, it can be rude. With some of the Clandestine, it can start a fight." A lock of hair slipped over her eye as she bent her head to look at the menu. Her finger tapped a section of the laminated page. "Here you go: hematophage specials."

I glanced down at my own menu. "Hemato-what?"

"Blood eaters. Vampires aren't the only group to have a specialized diet, ya know."

I gave the menu another look, curiosity piqued. The section in question was surrounded by a red dotted line. The red dots were tiny cartoon drops of blood. Cute. There wasn't much of a selection; Blood cake, blood sausage, and "ethically sourced" human blood.

"I'm not a hundred percent sure about this," I said, "but what the hay, right?"

The waitress returned with our drinks and left with our orders.

My consultant had ordered nearly everything on the menu that featured the pink cross, while I'd been predictable and asked for just the blood.

I was honestly curious to see how my meal would arrive. Would one of the waitstaff just mosey over and bare their wrist? Would they lead a junkie in a gimp suit to the table on a leash? I hoped neither. Drinking was just a bit too intimate for that sort of public scenario. Even a tiny sip would cause a... display. Let's leave it at that.

I needn't have worried. My meal arrived in a simple glass decanter with a cut-crystal shot glass beside it.

While Xenia dove into her triple-decker cheeseburger, I took a careful sniff of the decanter. Human blood, the real deal. The glass was even warm to my touch, body temperature. There was no whiff of anticoagulant, yet when I poured a measure of red into my glass, it flowed as smoothly as if it were straight from the vein.

My first sip was thick and coated my tongue in a familiar way. The flavor was rich, hearty, and reminded me of summer mornings. It went down smooth but lacked the fire I needed. "Damn."

"Whuff?" Xenia spoke through a mouthful of fried pickles.

"The blood. It's the real thing, all right. Tastes fine, but won't put fuel in my tank. I was kind of hoping this place" —I nodded at the establishment—"would have solved that problem."

Xenia raised an eyebrow while she went to work on her street taco platter.

"Ran into this problem years ago, back when I was trying to get my feet under me. I had the bright idea of raiding the blood bank. Perfect solution, right? Willing donors, no bodies to worry about. Convenient packaging, even." I poured myself another crimson shot. "The problem was, turns out that blood loses something when it's been out of the, ah, donor for more than a minute or two. It lacks a certain..." I flipped my hand in a circle as I reached for the right word. "Zing? Oomph? I can drink it. It tastes fine, and it stays down. It just doesn't do a damn thing for me."

"*Élan vital*," Xenia said. "The spark of life. Interesting. So are vamps feeding on the life force and the blood is just the medium of transfer?"

I shrugged.

"The accepted wisdom on the subject was that vampires preferred living sources out of cruelty and arrogance." Xenia's brows scrunched in thought. "I should be taking notes."

"Eddy? Eddy fucking Fry??" a gravelly voice interrupted. I swiveled my chair, ready to jump should things go sideways.

Chapter Nineteen

THE LOUNGE HAD A LOW WALL SEPARATING IT FROM the casino at large. Standing on the other side of that barrier was a skeleton. No skin. No hair. Empty eye sockets. A walking skeleton. Wearing an eye-searing Hawaiian shirt, real coconut buttons, Bermuda shorts cinched in tight above the pelvis, and red plastic flip-flops on the bony feet.

A skeleton on vacation.

"*Now* I've seen everything," I told Xenia before turning back to Bones. "Do I know you?"

"Oh, right. I've lost a little weight since the last time we saw each other," Bones said with a burst of clacking laughter.

Familiar laughter. The voice might be older, carrying a few decades of booze and cigarettes since I'd last heard it, and there was a weird tone from whatever let a skeleton talk. But I knew that voice. "Bobby? Holy shit, is that you?"

"In the flesh!" Bobby cackled. His fingers clacked against his ribs as he ran his hands down the front of the aloha shirt. "So to speak, hah-hah!" The eye sockets swung to Xenia. "Who's your lady, Sergeant? She got a friend?"

Xenia set down her soda, eyebrows knitting. "Watch it."

"Bobby's always had a shit sense of humor," I warned her before she blew him up. "Xenia, Bobby. Bobby, Xenia. The two of us were thick as thieves back in the war. We must've landed on every island in the Pacific while in the 77th." I tilted my head at Xenia. "She works for me in a..." I checked to see if she was cool with me spilling the beans. She nodded. "In a magical capacity."

"No shit?" Bobby took a step back. "Magician, eh? Can you trust her?" His finger made a hollow *thunk* as he tapped it against the dome of his skull. "Had some unsatisfactory experiences with magicians in the past."

"She's cool, Bobby. Saved my bacon."

"If you say so." Bobby offered his hand. "Nice to meet ya, toots."

Xenia hesitated before taking his hand. She shook it once. "Same."

I said, "Hey, pull up a chair. Ain't seen you in an age and a half."

Bobby obliged, hopping over the barrier, and dragged over a chair from the next table. "How long's it been, Eddy?" The bare skull tilted in thought. "Damn, it was that race, wasn't it?"

"Goddamned Barbara B!" we yelled in unison.

"Honest to Pete, I thought Dom had you rubbed out." Bobby's jovial voice turned somber. "I thought I'd gotten you killed with that stupid bet. You stormed off after giving me one hell of a shiner. Vanished right after that. None of the guys knew where you'd gone off to. It messed me up for a long time." He shook his skull. "Damn, but you are a sight! You ain't aged a day since! What's your secret?" Bobby leaned in, raising the back of his hand to the side of his mouth. "And where can I get some?" He head bobbled, and I realized he'd tried to wink one of his empty sockets.

"Oh, nothing special, really. I was minding my *p*'s and *q*'s and *bam,* I'm dead. Next day, I wake up looking like this, sporting a pair of these beauties." I smiled, pushing out my fangs so he could have a gander.

"Oh, *fuck.*" If he'd still had eyebrows, they would have reached the back of his head. "You're one of *them*? You're with the Houses now?" His chair tumbled over as he jumped to his feet.

"Hold your horses, Bobby." I held out my hands. "I'm with *me*. I got nothing to do with those jagoffs. Hell, that's part of the reason I've got Xenia here helping out."

Xenia nodded. "He's outclan. They'll kill him on sight or force an oath from him, just like they would with one of us."

Bobby's face darted between the two of us as he lowered himself back into his chair. "No shit? You're still yourself, Sergeant?"

"Are you still you, Private Bones?"

Bobby turned to Xenia. "Yep, that's the Sergeant. By his wise-ass you shall know him." He slapped his knee, nearly knocking the kneecap off. "You got some lousy timing, brother, coming to town the same day that Harkness witch decides she's taking over."

"Oh, I've been here, Bobby. Vegas is my home. That bad bet? My plan to pay it off landed me in Sin City. I liked the scene, so I put down some roots. Been here ever since. Frankly, Rebecca and her flunkies are here because of me."

Bobby propped his knobby elbow on the table. "Wait, that was you? *You're* the Vegas Vampire?"

Xenia laughed. "Oh, that's a keeper. Eddy Fry, Vegas Vampire."

Ignoring her, I pressed on. "So everybody here knew I was around, but no one took the time to drop in? Say, 'Hi,

Eddy, how's tricks? By the way, there's an entire world of crazy shit out there!'"

"I don't know what you've heard, but the bloodsuckers aren't exactly what you'd call popular," said Bobby.

"They do have a tendency to enslave or kill first, tear the answers for their questions from the quivering wreckage after," Xenia interjected. Her expression had grown dark, and she stared at her plate.

"We were all happy you were staying in your tower and not down here making waves. I'm sure your gal Friday knows the score," Bobby went on.

"I'm not his gal anything," Xenia muttered as she flicked half a fried pickle at Bobby. The greasy morsel bounced from his jawbone and tumbled through the collar of his florid shirt to vanish in his rib cage.

"Hey! Watch it!" Bobby jammed one hand under his own ribs as he fished around for the pickle. "It'll stain!"

Turning to me, Xenia added, "That's what Bruce was saying. If you recall, I wasn't exactly overjoyed to see you knocking at my door, either."

"Yeah, I'm getting the picture," I said. "Where've you been all these years, Bobby? How'd you end up looking like an extra in *Jason and the Argonauts*?"

"Okay, okay. I stayed in LA, right? After you vanished. Got myself a contractor's license and a wife—you remember Sofie? Had us some good years, business was jumping. That postwar boom kept the bills paid." He scratched his jawbone. "So one day this job comes in. Client wants a big-ass shed, custom design. A real beaut. He was *real* specific about materials, how the foundation needed to be laid out. Everything. Took almost a year to get it built. The permits alone took half that time." He shrugged. "I must've messed something up cause I get a call a week later. I figure I'm

208

going to get bitched at, maybe have to make good with a refund or some pro bono work. Smooth things out, he's happy, I'm happy. Everything copacetic, right?" He looked back and forth between Xenia and me. "Nope! He says my error, my 'shoddy workmanship' had cost him more than I could ever hope to repay him. Next thing I know, *boom!*" The silverware rattled as he slapped the table. "I end up like this!"

"Necromancer?" Xenia offered.

Bobby clicked a pair of finger guns at her. "Got it in one. Some ritual or whatever backfired, and he blamed me for it. Next thing I know, I'm on the world's worst diet plan." Bobby leaned in, voice eager. "Get this. Fucker didn't even kill me first. No sir. He binds my soul to my bones. Then he raises them, animated the skeleton right out of my living body." He made an explosive motion with both hands. "Imagine ripping a bundle of sticks through a bowl of Jell-O."

Xenia made a gagging sound.

"So this necro guy just goes and bones you for a simple mistake?" I asked.

"'Bones me.' Oh ho ho. Good one." Bobby tilted his skull. "Well, *maybe* the steel I used to reinforce the foundation didn't exactly meet the specifications he'd given me. *Perhaps* it wasn't the custom alloy blend he'd paid for. Where the hell do you even *find* selenium anyhow?"

"There's the Bobby I know," I said to Xenia.

"Yeah, yeah. Anyhow, as far as the family's concerned, I am *spectacularly* dead and I gotta stay out of sight. I didn't have anywhere else to go, so I end up hanging out in the graveyard for a few years with the other not-quite-dead folks before I got clued into the underground scene. I tell ya, that internet? Makes it a lot easier to make ends meet when you can't show your face at the mall. Now? I'm in Vegas full time." He tugged at his collar. "Well, until this vampire situation kicked off, that is. Those people are like the Mob on steroids. Once they get their hooks into a town, everyone on the hidden side, us undergrounders, we gotta bend the knee. Even if they're not biting your neck, they've got a boot on it."

"That's why we're here. The Underground, I mean." Xenia waved at the casino around us. "We're hoping to find more people who will stand up against House Harkness. If we can stop them before they bind too much of the civilian population, before she claims the city—"

Bobby held up a hand. "Let me stop you right there, little lady."

Xenia frowned but held her tongue.

"Okay, okay. You're talking a full-on war against the vampire Houses. The way I hear it, the last time anyone put up a proper fight, really dug in their heels to keep a vamp House from claiming a city they wanted? That battle went on so long and got so big it spilled over into the civilian, the human side of things." His eye sockets turned toward me. "The Great War, in case you was wondering."

"Bobby, we ain't asking you to go five rounds with Rebecca's pet monster. Just..." I thought for a moment. "If there's anyone you know that might want to live in a city without all the obligations and bullshit bowing to an outfit like a vampire House. You know, the way Las Vegas was? Just pass the word along. Have them look me up."

Bobby stared at me.

"It's not just about us, Bobby." Xenia's finger swung between Bobby and herself. "Look around you. It's like the last waltz on the *Titanic* around here."

Ah-hah, she *had* picked up on it.

"You think any of this is going to survive? The way it's been, I mean?" Xenia shook her head.

Bobby looked away, fingers rapping on the table. "I can maybe make a few phone calls. See if anyone is game for getting their face ripped off."

"Attaboy," I said.

Chapter Twenty
Then

"OH MAH GAWWD, EDDY! JUST LOOK AT THAT VIEW!" Rosie gushed for the hundredth time. "Look at it!" Juice sloshed from the mimosa clutched in her hand as she pressed her button nose against the glass.

Ever since the Sky Room had opened, Rosie had been begging me to take her. I hadn't exactly been putting it off. It's just that the crew, meaning me, had been extra busy lately. There hadn't been time for fancy meals and dancing, even if I had been seeing this gal for a while.

The Feds had, for the very first time, announced in advance the date for one of the atom bomb tests they'd been doing in the desert up north. The Desert Inn had jumped all over the chance, immediately announcing an "Atomic Breakfast" viewing of the event. Since the Sky Room, up on the third floor, was the highest restaurant in Las Vegas, it had booked up almost immediately. It was too good to miss. Not only would it get Rosie off my back about the Sky Room, I'd get to see the Feds blow something up with an atom bomb. So I spread some cabbage around until I prized up a pair of tickets to the event.

"Nothin' but the best for my best gal, that's right," I said to Rosie. A former showgirl, now she was working the front desk at one of the motels springing up on the edge of town. We'd been seeing each other since February, and if things went the same as they had with Margie, Lottie, and Annie, I could expect this to last until at least August before I got restless.

I watched Rosie's shapely rump shimmy under the cloth of her skirt and downed my breakfast scotch.

Maybe September.

While I considered changing up my next drink for one of those mimosas Rosie was putting away, I tugged at my belt. The goddamn cleaners had shrunk another pair of trousers on me. I made a mental note to have a few words with that fucker the next time I dropped off a suit.

The view from the Sky Room's floor-to-ceiling windows continued to hold Rosie's attention, which gave me a chance to check out the talent in the crowd. Some dames nearby had their hair up high, hair-sprayed into something that was supposed to resemble a mushroom cloud. I only knew what it was supposed to be because Rosie had wanted the same 'do for today. Too bad for her that Gigi, the hairdresser at the Flamingo who did 'em, had been booked up.

I winked at a gal whose white sweater was tight in all the right ways. I didn't get a wink back, but I'm pretty sure she smiled when she turned around.

"Eddy, you dog! Stop hitting on the other ladies!" Rosie, lower lip trembling, slapped my arm. Rosie tried to glare, but she just didn't have the temperament for it. Or the face. The worst those big brown eyes and baby doll face could pull off was a pout. "At least when we're together, okay, baby?"

"Sure thing, Rosie." I slipped my arm around her waist. "You know you're my best gal." I rattled the ice in my empty glass. "Another round?" We got two steps through the standing-room-only crowd before I pulled on her arm. "Holy shit! Is that Frankie?" I pushed up on my toes to catch a better glimpse. Rosie managed to jam her fluffy hair smack in my face while trying to get her own look at the crooner.

Sinatra had been a regular headlining at the Desert Inn since the day it opened. I'd made it to every show I could swing a ticket for. As far as I was concerned, he was the voice of Las Vegas, no contest. Of *course* he'd be up here for a momentous occasion such as this! However, the crowd had gotten so thick I could barely see the back of his head, much less get any closer to the living legend.

The speakers crackled to life, pulling our attention away from the singer. The establishment had placed TV sets around the room so the atomic-mad audience could hear Fred Henry while they watched the view, live, from the windows.

A tuxedo-clad fella, the manager was my guess, stepped up onto the stage in the corner, where normally a band would play for the room. He tapped the microphone in his hand and with a squeal of feedback, the speakers around the room came to life.

"Ladies and gentlemen, thank you for joining us this morning as we witness a truly historic and memorable event." He paused as a round of applause rippled through the crowd. "I hope you've had a wonderful time so far, and I would like to invite you all down to the casino floor afterward to celebrate."

Another man in a tux stepped up beside the manager to whisper in his ear. Nodding his thanks to the messenger, he raised the microphone again. "Ladies and gentlemen, it's time! It's time! Operation Charlie is about to begin!" He looked to the windows on the north wall, and everyone in the room followed suit. Around the dining room, the waitstaff had switched on all the TVs. A washed-out, grainy view of the Nevada desert filled each tube.

A hiss and a crackle sounded from the live feed that had been patched into the dining room's speakers. "Bombs away, bombs away," Fred Henry's voice announced. He counted the seconds, marking the time since they had released the bomb from the B-50 Superfortress flying high over the test site. As he reached twenty, a second voice joined him with the countdown until detonation.

"Five, four, three, two, one."

At zero, God's own flashbulb lit the sky above the mountains to the north. It only went on for a couple of seconds, but it dazzled my eyes like I'd stared at the sun. Even when it cleared, there was a dark spot right where the center of the flash had been. I squeezed my eyes shut and blinked hard a couple of times to clear it up.

In front of me, Rosie let out a whooping war cry and threw her hands into the air, mimosa flying from her glass. A cheer erupted as the crowd of revelers went wild, glasses clinking together and hats flying into the air. A man who'd been standing beside us at the window seized my hand; a wild grin stretched from ear to ear as he pumped my arm and slapped my shoulder.

"Hell of a thing," he bellowed. "Hell of a thing. God bless America."

"Well, there it is." The voice of Fred Henry came again from the speakers. "The first public demonstration and the biggest continental atomic detonation in the history of the world." A massive thump followed his words. "That, of course, was the shock wave," Henry explained.

Rosie threw her arms around my neck and hauled me down for a kiss. As she counted my molars for the second time, the floor beneath us heaved. The chandeliers swung as the windows rattled in their frames. The pane closest to us cracked from floor to ceiling with a sound like a gunshot. Gasps went up all around the room, punctuated by the crash of breaking glass at the bar.

There was a breathless pause from the audience before another cheer went up, this one even more raucous than the first. Here and there, party streamers snapped into the air.

Rosie pulled back, peering up at me through fluttering lashes. "My first shock wave kiss. Did the earth move for you too?"

"Baby, the earth moved for everyone in town." That lower lip trembled, threatening to push forward in a full pout. "But it *definitely* moved more for me." I added a wink for good measure.

Rosie smirked as she thumbed the lipstick from my mouth. "Damn right, baby."

"I'm gonna go scare up another round of drinks. Then we can go see if that's really Frankie," I said. "Maybe I can shake his hand."

Chapter Twenty-One
Now

WE SPENT THE NEXT HOUR, BOBBY AND I, JUST shooting the shit. Catching up on two lifetimes' worth of memories was a welcome distraction from Rebecca. He'd filled me in on how he'd gotten by since joining Team Undead. Turned out there were a lot of folks who can't show their face in human society for one reason or another and had a hankering for what they couldn't have. Bobby had himself a little empire facilitating the purchase of "human stuff," straight from the mall to the customer. That was, until internet shopping came along and yanked the rug out from under him. Amazon would deliver a package *anywhere*.

"No big deal," Bobby said. "Now I've got a podcast, *Bone's Eye View*. We talk about adapting to life on this side, for folks like us who started out human and ended up something else. Hundred thousand subs and climbing. Hey! You should be on as a guest! Assuming we don't all die horribly in the next forty-eight hours."

I told him I'd think about it. After I got Xenia to tell me what a podcast was.

For my part, I gave him a rough sketch of my time with

the Outfit, with Little Mickey's crew. Not too much detail, though. There were a lot of secrets that weren't mine to blab, even to an old friend. What I could tell him made his jaw drop, literally. Especially once I told him I owned the Golden Fortune.

"Okay, you two geezers might be immune to sleep, but this girl's gotta get some downtime if she wants to keep working the night shift. I'm getting a room. Y'all might want to consider coming up with a plan. You know, to handle the hostile vampire invasion? Lates." Hoisting her pack, she struck out for wherever this joint hid the front desk. She paused long enough to add, "I'll save the receipt."

"Say, Eddy." Bobby scratched at his jawbone. "You ain't still sore at me for getting you tangled up with Dominic back then, are ya?"

I gave that some serious consideration. "You know, to be honest, I *was* pissed at you for a long damn time. If you'd shown your face in those first few years, I'd proba-bly've landed you in the hospital. Somewhere along the line, though"—I looked at the bare skull waiting on my answer and tried to see the shape of my old friend's face in the curve of bone—"I think I just forgot about the whole thing. Now? Fuck, Bobby, I'm just glad to see someone from the old days. Bitch of a thing, I'm sure you know, living this long. Everyone ends up in a pine box except for you." Another sobering thought popped into my head. "You have any clue how long you'll be like that?"

"Not a bit," Bobby said. "The SOB that did this to me wasn't exactly forthcoming with the details. Once the curse kicked in, I couldn't get within a mile of his place to ask." He smacked a fist into a bony palm. "Got more than one question for that fucker, too."

"Tell you what, brother. If this all shakes out in our

favor, I'll put in a word with Xenia. See if she can do something about that curse."

Bobby's jawbone hung open. "You'd do that? Damn, Eddy, I didn't even think to ask her myself!" He turned the bones of his hands in front of his face. "Do you think she could do it? Get me back into some flesh and blood?" He looked away. "I'd even take the other option, if that was the only one left on the table."

"Dunno, but I'll ask."

Before we could get any more maudlin, my burner interrupted me. The buzz from my pocket brought everything I'd been trying to keep from thinking about crashing back in. And other than Xenia, there was only one person who had this number.

Kurt.

I wasn't sure I wanted to take the call. What if he wasn't himself? Had Rebecca gotten into *his* head last night too? Damn it, what *was* his schedule? Had he even been on the clock yesterday? Okay, I was reasonably sure he'd been home last night, which meant there was a solid chance he hadn't been press-ganged with Franklin and the others.

The sun was up. The odds were good that Rebecca was in her box at the Beau Rivage. With any luck, Felix, whatever he was, had an allergy to daylight too. "Morning, Kurt, what's up?"

"Boss! Eddy, any chance you can fill me in on what the hopping *fuck* is going on at the Fortune?" Kurt's rough voice snarled into my ear. "I just got here, and before I can even clock in, I hear that 'Elwood' has kicked you out into the street!" His voice lowered to a hoarse whisper. "I thought *you* were Elwood?"

"Yeah, Kurt, buddy. We got problems."

"No *shit*."

"Look, I don't want to get into details over the phone.

The most I can say is there's a hostile takeover in progress. Emphasis on the hostile. Look, you need to get out of the Fortune and pronto. Franklin and the others aren't exactly in their right minds, if you catch my drift."

"What? Oh. *Oh*. Right, shit. You know what? I feel a flu coming on. Time to use all that sick leave I've accrued." I'd been hearing the familiar jingle of the Fortune's entry parlor behind Kurt's voice. Now the hiss of street traffic rose in the background as he presumably walked himself off the premises.

"Good call. You should avoid Leandro and the other department heads too. They're all in on it."

"Oh crap, what the hell? Leandro too? Okay, we should meet up. You need to get me up to speed, ASAP."

Meet? Where the hell could I meet Kurt in the middle of the day? How would I even get there? I didn't think a guy like him would be welcome in this Underground place. Besides, I wanted to keep an ace up my sleeve. Putting my hand over the phone, I turned to Bobby. "Hey, this joint have more than one exit topside?"

Bobby's thumb popped up. "Yeah, talk to the concierge. They can get you an exit pretty much anywhere on the Strip."

I stared. Anywhere? Oh, right. Magic. "Great." Back to Kurt. "I got a spot. Coffee counter at the Tortuga Bay. You know the one, next to the big waterfall with the animatronic mascot?"

"Got it. See you there." Kurt hung up.

"That sounded intense," Bobby said. "Good news or bad?"

"Not sure. That was a new, old friend. Head of security at the Golden Fortune."

Bobby whistled, somehow. "Damn, Eddy, I'm still wrapping my noggin around the fact that you own a whole *casino.*" He tapped a finger on the table. "We win this shit, you gotta hook me up."

"Hmmm, I'll think about it," I said with a wink. "Gotta fly. Make those calls, will ya?"

"Will do." He pulled a phone from his pocket, along with a little rubber doohickey. The rubber bit slipped over his index finger bone and he started poking at the screen. I dropped some bills on the table to cover the tab and hit the road.

———

WHEN I FINALLY LOCATED THE concierge desk—this place was even more of a maze than your average casino—it was no surprise at all to see a familiar face waiting there.

"How may I help you, Mr. Fry?" Shizue was entirely too chipper, or maybe I was just too jumpy.

"Any chance you can help me get someplace? I need to get to the Tortuga Bay, right in the middle, away from the doors and *especially* away from that fuckin' skylight."

Her cheeks dimpled. "Of course I can. Express Destination Exits are available to members of our Black Orchid Loyalty Club who maintain a Gold Level membership."

"I shoulda known." I rubbed my forehead. "Fine. Sign me up."

In the end, it took most of the cash in my pocket to book two rooms, one each for me and my "associate," for fourteen days apiece. That done, the concierge fussed around behind the counter until she produced a shiny black card embossed with the Underground's flower emblem. She nodded toward the elevator doors behind me. "Use this in the card reader. The system will take you where you're going."

"You're a peach."

Yes, I tipped her. I'm no bum.

Once in I was in the elevator, I slipped the black card into the reader above the bank of floor buttons. No sooner had the edge of the card entered the slot than some mechanism sucked it right out of my fingers. A sloppy, moist, crunching sound emerged from within. The topmost button in the panel lit with a soft *ding*, and the doors slid shut on the Underground.

When they opened again, it was to reveal a space hardly deep enough for me to exit the elevator car. Once I'd pressed myself flat against the wall opposite, I felt the car's doors slide shut across my backside. A moment later, the pressure on my rump eased and I could turn around.

The elevator was gone.

The space vacated by the magic elevator was now filled with "wet floor" placards and cleaning equipment. I was in a supply closet. Easing the door open, I pressed my eye to the crack.

The waterfall centerpiece of the Tortuga Bay resort splashed cheerfully on the other side of a stretch of tropical-themed carpet. An animatronic turtle implored anyone who would listen to "sample the delights" at the Bay. Shizue had landed me exactly where I'd asked.

I slipped out the door, closing it behind me before anyone noticed my trespass. The door I'd emerged from was one of a set of three, a red-and-black flower logo inscribed at eye level on mine. As I watched, the emblem faded into the painted metal. A second later, all three doors were identical.

Something occurred to me then, and I felt like an idiot. Keeping my face turned toward the wall, I fished around in my pockets but came up empty. That's when I remembered I'd lost Xenia's magic sunglasses. Bruce had knocked them clean off my face when he'd ambushed me, and I'd forgotten to ask her to gin up a replacement.

I'd just have to chance it.

The coffee counter lay just around the curving faux volcanic rock structure of the waterfall. The whole setup was comfortably far from any entrance, not to mention the lobby skylight.

I recognized Kurt's cheap suit and buzz cut long before he made my approach. I hung back, peering over an outcropping of fake stone to make sure nothing looked hinky. If Rebecca had already gotten into Kurt's head, this would be a trap.

That's how *I'd* do it.

I watched Kurt order himself a coffee, taking it over to one of the stools at the counter. He checked out the passing crowd, then returned his attention to the flatscreen over the counter. A news story, something about an "unprecedented archeological find" in the Atlantic. The big announcement was about the follow-up expedition. Some movie director, the guy who'd shot that flick about that shipwreck, had been hired to film the expedition.

I had to take the chance that Kurt's brains remained unscrambled. Bracing for a fight, the pressure of a million unseen eyes on my back, I crossed the last couple of feet to Kurt. "Thanks for coming."

He jumped, and coffee sloshed over his hand. "Boss! Damn, you made it." His eyes narrowed. "How'd you manage that with the sun out? Where have you been?"

I ticked off my fingers one at a time. "Good to see you, too. Got new friends with interesting connections. Conferring with those same friends." Even though it meant I wouldn't be able to see trouble coming, I planted my back to the passing crowd. The better to hide my face from any prying eyes.

"Okay," Kurt said, "I guess. What the hell is going on? How the hell is 'Uncle Elwood' in town giving orders if you're out here, and why are you persona non grata at the Fortune?" He frowned. "Is this another batch of operators? Like we had last week?"

"Worse. Someone's gotten to the upper management and the key staff, convinced them that Elwood is back and giving orders." I tapped a finger beside my eye. "The same way I make convincing arguments, if you catch my drift."

"Oh, damn." Kurt's gruff voice was faint. "Wait, you mean there's more than one of you? How many we talking?" He looked worried, like *really* worried, but he wasn't running yet.

"Well, there's only one Eddy Fry," I said with a smirk. "But yeah, another one like me. Turns out there's an entire organization of them out there. Every city's got its own bloodsucker running the joint. From what little I've learned since this went down, they pretty much run the whole world. Pulling the strings from way, way behind the scenes. One of 'em decided now was a good time to finally make a move on Las Vegas."

Kurt sipped at his java while that sank in. "That is not the sort of news I wanted to hear today."

"No shit. Here's the deal. The only one actually in town, that I know of, is a dame by the name of Rebecca. About yay high, black hair, curves for days. Dresses like a movie star. You see her, you run. No questions asked. She gets her claws in you, she'll scramble your brains six ways from Sunday. Just like Franklin and the others."

Kurt nodded. "I'll keep my eyes peeled."

"Kurt! My man!"

I froze. I'd been too focused on Kurt, forgotten to watch my six. While I tried to keep my shoulders from hunching, I pretended to sip from Kurt's coffee cup.

"James?" Kurt half slid from his stool and slapped hands

with the man in the uniform of Tortuga Bay security. "How's tricks?"

"Oh, you know how it is. Fight Night coming up in two weeks. See you there?"

Kurt seemed to weigh his options. "No promises." His eyes flitted to me. "Got a lot on my plate."

"Hear that! Scuttlebutt is the parent company got acquired, might be facing some layoffs in the near future. Pay cuts for sure."

"Ah shit." Kurt did a bad job of acting surprised. "You going to be okay?"

"As long as they don't fuck up my 401(k) too much, I guess so. What about your boss, he looking?"

Again, Kurt's eyes slid my way. *Lousy fuckin' poker face there, brother.*

"Not sure. I can always ask. Might be some changes headed my way, too."

"Well, if you hear anything, shoot me a text, 'kay?" James tipped his cap to me and ambled after his partner.

"Say hello to Molly for me, will you?" Kurt called, getting a wave in response.

Glad that I didn't sweat anymore, I forced a few things to unclench. "Woof. Okay, I'm gonna level with you, Kurt. Now would be a good time for early retirement. I can get you cash, enough to set you up nice and comfy." I forced a laugh. "You should get a boat. Go sail around the world, do some deep-sea fishing. I don't think there'll be too many of these bozos out on the high seas. Be a change of pace after all these years in the desert."

Kurt paled. "Oh, hell no. I got enough of the ocean when I was in the fuckin' Navy. Dry land for me all the way. I don't even like seafood." His face turned thoughtful. "Might take you up on the offer, though. I've always wanted to visit Rio."

He shook his head. "Who am I kidding? Okay, there's only this one"—he mouthed the word *vampire*—"in town running this show, right? I could get a team together. Put our own set of operators on the job. Wax this bitch while the sun's hot."

"You saw how well that went for the group that went after me," I said. "And I didn't even know they were coming. Rebecca is going to know I'm gunning for her. She'll be ready and waiting for it. Plus she has... well, I don't know what he is, but he put my ass on the ground, no sweat. I don't know what else she's got up her sleeve, but any contractors you send in'll get flattened."

"We're screwed, then."

"Not entirely. Those new friends I mentioned? Well, they're not run-of-the-mill folks."

Kurt sputtered into his coffee. "More like you?"

"Not exactly. Turns out the world is bigger, a lot bigger, than either of us knew."

Kurt leaned in. "What, like werewolves and shit?"

"Maybe? Not in this bunch, though. I don't have all the details yet, but I'm getting the picture that all that fairy-tale stuff has more than a grain of truth in it." Call it an abundance of caution, but I didn't feel like Kurt needed to know about Xenia or Bruce right then. "How much of an idiot am I, Kurt? I end up this way and not once did I ask myself if there were any more of me out there. Turns out the answer is lots. Everywhere, in every city. Just living separately, apart from regular folks."

"No offense, boss, but you never struck me as being the curious type. At least not about anything that wasn't wearing a bra and a skirt."

I laughed. "Got me pegged all right, buddy." I forced myself to stop fidgeting around with my hands. I should've gotten my own cup of coffee just so I'd have something to hold. "The bad news for these fairy-tale folks is, if Rebecca gets her claws into this town, they're the ones that get it the worst of it. That being said, there's a good chance having that looming over them will motivate a few to stand their ground. With any luck, I'll be able to line up my own crew of 'special' operators."

Kurt rubbed his chin. "Good luck with that, boss. I hope you know what you're doing."

"Think about retirement, okay?"

"Will do. Where will you hole up until you get this special crew of yours put together? That secret casino?"

"Maybe," I said. "Rebecca's been throwing her weight around there too, so it might not be the best spot for me to lay my head. I got a couple of safe houses leftover from the old days. I'll probably use one of them. Look, Kurt, you've been working for me. What? Twelve years now? Fourteen?"

Kurt's mouth was a tense line. "About that, yes."

"I just wanted to tell you thanks. For everything."

Kurt stared. "Is this you firing me, boss?"

"No, no. I just wanted you to know now, in case things go south."

"Chh." He scoffed. "Is the great Eddy Fry going soft on me?"

"Oh fuck you, Kurt," I laughed.

"Uh-huh. Well, okay. You're welcome. I guess. I'm going home and maybe pack a bag. Put some thought into that retirement idea of yours." He shoved off from the counter. "But you need me, you need anything, you call." He patted the phone clipped to his belt. "Got it?"

"Got it. Go. Take care of yourself. Give me a day, and I'll get you a nice severance package to see you off."

Kurt nodded. "Get some rest, Eddy. You're looking a little rough around the edges." He tilted his head. "You know, I don't think I've ever seen you look this tired or pale."

"Gee, thanks."

He waved and vanished into the crowd.

Of course, it was only then I realized I'd missed something.

I didn't have a way back into the Underground. The sun was still up. No way I could stick my nose outside without burning it off. Plus, if Kurt had, knowingly or not, led Rebecca's goons to me, then I'd be leading them back to the Underground. To Xenia.

I had about three hours before the sun went down and I could move freely. I needed to kill time and make sure I wasn't being shadowed. So I did the only thing I could think of.

I went to the resort theater to watch a movie.

Chapter Twenty-Two

I'VE HAD A LOVE-HATE RELATIONSHIP WITH WAR FLICKS. On the one hand, I've lived that shit. Once was enough. On the other, passing time watching a ragtag crew of soldiers steal art back from the fuckin' Nazis wasn't the worst way to kill an afternoon. Plus, sitting in the back row meant I could keep my eye on the crowd and the exits.

Once the sun was safely down, I took a winding route to shake any tails I couldn't see back to the only entrance to the Underground I knew of.

Rapping a knuckle on the door to Xenia's room got me the familiar sting of magical wards. "It's me," I called out, shaking my hand and cursing myself for not checking first.

The door cracked open an inch and a bloodshot eye peered through the gap. Apparently satisfied, she disengaged the chain and stepped aside for me to enter.

I nudged the door shut with my shoe. "You hear anything from Bruce?"

"I slept fine. Thanks for asking." Xenia planted her hands in the small of her back and leaned, wincing at the crack. Retrieving her phone from the bedside table, she dropped herself into a chair. "Nope, nothing yet."

"Damn it."

"Eddy, it's only been half a day," she said. "I'm worried too, but it's going to take a minute. We can't force these people to fight for us. They have to want to fight, for themselves." Hooking open the mini-fridge beside her, she fished out a can. Glancing at the price on the shelf, she winced. "Daaayum, fifteen bucks for a Coke? Glad you're paying, boss." Grinning, she popped the tab. "So, your buddy on board?" she asked after a thoughtful slurp.

"Yeah, he's in. I don't know exactly what he can bring to the table, but every bit counts." I looked at the room's miniature coffee pot with longing. For the first time in years, I missed caffeine. Between healing from Bruce's misplaced beating and pulling an all-dayer, I was running on empty. If it weren't for the fact that I *can't* sleep once the sun is down, I'd be taking a nap right now. A proper meal would help, a lot, but to get myself back to normal, I *really* needed some rack time. "It better not take *too* long. I don't think we have a lot of time before Rebecca owns this town."

"How so?" Xenia polished off her can and reached for another.

"When we had our little parley, she told me she 'claimed' this city and demanded I hand over ownership of the Fortune. The way she said it sounded to me like she already had most of her pieces in place. In my experience, when an Outfit moves in and is talking about 'owning Vegas,' what they really mean is the casinos, the Strip. *Maybe* a golf course or two. Nobody ever gave a shit who was in the mayor's chair when I was with a crew. All the power and money in this town comes from the casinos. Own them, and you own the city."

"Okay."

"Big difference is, for the last twenty years and change, when you talk about who owns Las Vegas, you're talking about a bunch of gaming corporations. Those companies are bigger than this town, and most own properties all over the world, anywhere casino gambling is legal. Rebecca has all the same skills I do." I tapped my temple. "But even if I could whammy a boardroom full of suits all at once, I don't think I could set up a takeover of *one* multinational, much less a dozen of 'em. I wouldn't have thought Rebecca could have pulled that off on her own either. So why would she be gunning for me like this unless she already had all the other resorts in the bag?"

"Easy," Xenia said. "She wouldn't have done it on her own. She has all of her Sire's resources to do it with. Vampires are the oldest of old money, Eddy. Pretty sure if you looked behind the curtain at most of the big players, you'll find blood money pulling the strings. It can't have been too hard to arrange some asset transfers to whatever holding companies Harkness uses."

"So her sugar daddy's buying up all the casinos for her and she's installed her own patsy in *my* baby. I think it's safe to assume that if she doesn't own *everything* by now, she will in a day, maybe two." I pinched the bridge of my nose. "What's her next move?"

"Fuck if I know."

"What exactly am I paying you for again?"

"I'm a magician, not a psychic."

Anger bubbled over then, mostly at myself for letting Rebecca dominate the battlefield until now. "*Fuck* this waiting shit," I said. "Here's what we're gonna do. We're taking the fight to her. Rebecca had this weaselly little guy doggin' her heels. Human, I think, so he's probably one of her daylight operators. Marcus."

Xenia nodded.

"We're gonna put the feelers out, get a sense of what they're doing *right now*. Either he's with her, and we wait until daylight, or he's on his own, and we nab the little SOB."

"What, by myself?" Xenia looked uneasy.

"You're a big girl. You fought Bruce to a halt, didn't you? Hell, we get Bruce to help!"

"Okay, we grab this guy. Then what?"

"We all got our particular skills"—I tapped my temple again—"so we put them to use. Get him talking. Find the weak spot in Rebecca's big plan and blow it sky—"

From my pocket came the *bzzz-bzzz* of my burner. I was in such a hurry to get at it I nearly sent the little slab of plastic straight into the trash. "About goddamned time," I told Bobby. Flipping the phone to speaker mode so Xenia could add her two cents, I set it on the bed between us.

"*Sor-ree*, Sarge." Bobby's bony voice rattled out of the speaker. "I've been burning up the lines all day, tryin' to make something happen."

Xenia, levering herself upright, began snatching her belongings from where they'd fallen—they were scattered like a bomb had gone off—and stuffing them into her pack.

"At least tell me you got *something*," I said. "Someone has to want a piece of the action around here."

"I'm not going to lie to you, brother, it ain't ideal. Most of this crowd are either running for the hills or digging a hole and pulling it in after themselves. There's a few contenders, but nothing for sure just yet."

"What about all the folks I saw down here in the Underground? Some of those Joes looked like they'd go toe-to-toe with King Kong and walk away smiling."

"Eddy, Eddy. The lion's share of that crowd are *tourists*." A note of frustration entered Bobby's tone. "Why would they put their ass on the line for us? Especially since most of 'em would have to explain them-selves to their personal vamp-in-charge as soon as they got

232

home. Not everyone around here is a free agent, ya know?"

"I'm getting the picture. Damn it."

"So, Eddy, I'm coming around to the line of thought that you should maybe do option B." The sound of finger bones scratching jaw bone came through the speaker.

"Yeah?" I perked up. About time Bobby had something to contribute.

"You might want to go ahead and trade that gal you got in your pocket for a seat at the table. A magician'll pull a decent price in vamp circles. Might even be enough they'll overlook your lack of, hah, affiliation."

Xenia froze. "What the *fuck!*"

"I'm on speaker phone, aren't I?"

"Shit, Xenia, there's no chance I'd do something like—" I started.

"That's what this was all about?" Snatching up her leather jacket, she jammed her arms inside. One hand shot into a pocket and emerged wrapped in a familiar glove.

"Hey, babe, sorry. I didn't know—" Bobby began.

Air hissed between clenched teeth and her hand shot forward. The burner phone jumped into the air, sparks crackling from the exposed guts of the device as it split in two. In the same instant, the bedcovers and the mattress below parted along an invisible line of force.

I held up my hands. "Calm down, at least let me—"

Emerald hair spilled forward over eyes gone wide as Xenia hunched her shoulders. Hyperventilating, she scrambled backward, knocking her chair over in her haste to put her back against the wall. The line of her jaw quivered, and the hand with *Wind Razor* came up for another strike.

I froze.

"No, no, no, not again. Not again." Xenia's words tumbled over one another in a babble. Eyes clenched, she

233

ground the heel of her hand against the shaved side of her head. Her eyes popped open, white showing all around. I knew then that she wasn't exactly seeing me anymore.

I knew that look, that panic. I'd seen it in the eyes of the soldiers around me, on the beach. Felt it myself when the man next to me dropped, felled by a Japanese sniper.

Shit, what had this kid seen?

I squatted on my heels, held out one hand. "Hey." I kept my voice low, tried not to flinch as another invisible blade whip-cracked past my shoulder. "It's okay." I put as much strength into my voice as I dared. "I am *not* going to hand you over as bargaining chip. Rebecca is not going to get her fangs into you." While I talked, I rose up out of the squat and took slow, shuffling steps across the carpet.

Trembling enough to rattle the studs of her jacket, Xenia blinked out of her reverie for a moment. Seeing how close I was, her hand came up again. I had to risk moving faster than human-normal. I didn't want to hurt her, but I didn't want her to take my head off, either. I caught her gloved hand in mine, then her other as it went for a tab riveted to her collar, which I suspected was the trigger for her jacket's spiky alter ego. "Xenia," I said again. "Do you understand what I'm saying? Can you hear me?"

Tears spilled over her cheeks as her eyes finally met mine. I could have whammied her right then, told her to calm down, but it wouldn't have been right. There'd be no trust to be had after that. Besides, I didn't think something like this could be fixed with brute force.

Her fingers gripped mine with a strength that surprised me. "I... I can't... I don't..." She closed her eyes and shook her head again. Her chin slumped to her chest and a pained whine slipped out.

"It helps to talk about it," I said, giving her advice I wish

234

I'd gotten all those years ago. "I know it doesn't *seem* like it right now, but it does."

Another tremor ran through her, and after a moment, she nodded. "I was... taking classes? Training? My aunt set it up when she found out about..."

"That you could do magic? Teach you to use it?"

"Yeah." She swallowed. "He was awesome. Like something out of a comic book, or a movie. But it was slow. I was slow."

I waited as she choked back another sob.

"Then, there was another one. Another magician. I couldn't believe it, in my town? *And* he thought I had potential too? Wanted me to be *his* apprentice. He showed me how to do other stuff, magic that Sensei wouldn't, couldn't teach me himself." A steady drizzle of tears pattered into the carpet from her lowered head. "I was rude, the way kids are. Said stuff I'd give anything to take back."

I had a bad feeling about where this was headed.

"Then my new teacher's *patron*"—she spat the word—"showed up."

"A vampire."

"Yeah." A ragged breath. "He was going to hand me over, as a gift, to his master."

Ah shit.

"Sensei stopped him. They fought. Sensei Shouga kicked his ass up and down." The grief in her voice couldn't hide the pride and awe she had for him. "The vampire killed him for it. Drained him while I was forced to watch." Her hands tightened on mine. "He got me with his eyes. Then he just... left. Said he'd be back when I'd 'ripened.' Once I could move again, I went looking for my *new teacher*." Contempt thickened her voice. "And because he was still weak from the fight with Sensei, I killed him."

"Attagirl," I murmured.

Releasing her grip on my hands, she leaned forward until the top of her head bumped my chest. Quiet sobs followed. I lifted a hand, unsure of whether I should, before awkwardly patting her on the back.

I wasn't sure how long we stayed that way; Xenia crouched with her head against my chest, my arm not quite around her. Eventually, a knock at the door broke the moment. Xenia went stiff and her heartbeat edged back up to panic levels.

I patted her back again, having picked up a familiar scent—and an unfamiliar one—outside. "Hey, no worries. It's just Bruce."

Nodding as the tension, most of it anyway, left her shoulders, Xenia levered herself to her feet. This time, she didn't refuse the helping hand. "I'm just gonna... I'll be in the bathroom." Rubbing her eyes, she shut herself away into the room's luxurious facilities.

Careful of her wards, which didn't extend to the inside doorknob, I swung the door open. Bruce, arm in arm with a man I didn't recognize, gave a start when he saw me instead of Xenia. "She's in the can," I said. "Who's your friend?"

The stranger in question disengaged his arm from Bruce's and thrust his hand forward. "Michael, and *you* must be the mysterious 'Vegas Vampire' we've been tiptoeing around all these years. Nice of you to descend from your ivory tower at last." The twinkle in his eyes took the sting out of his words, and I decided not to take offense. Besides, he was right.

I took the offered hand. "Eddy Fry. I *own* that ivory tower, by the way, assuming Rebecca hasn't fucked that up."

A shadow crossed Michael's face at the mention of the vampire that had beaten him near to death. A beating that he showed no sign of, other than the cane in his other hand. He must have sussed out what I was thinking because the cheerful smile returned. "My Nan has a way of patching folks up, so long as they're still breathing when they're brought to her. Absolutely thrilling to finally meet the man that Bruce has been bending my ear about. He's says you're of a mind to help us?" He winked. "I assure you that our cause is just." Throughout this exchange, Bruce had hovered, face alternating between concern and a smile that threatened to split his head in half.

Stepping aside so the pair could enter the room, I shook my head. "At this point, we're all in this boat together. The more paddles we get, the less chance we'll sink."

"'We must, indeed, all hang together or, most assuredly, we shall all hang separately.' Isn't that what your famous Yank said?" Michael lowered himself into one of the waiting chairs with a wince. Not back to one hundred percent, despite his Nan's skills, it seemed.

"Um, yes." I'd heard that quote before, but I couldn't place it. I'd skipped a lot of schooling back in my younger days. "Something like that."

"Bruce!" Xenia came bursting out of the bathroom, face and hair damp. She'd slathered a layer of heavy metal eyeliner on, but it didn't completely cover the raw redness from her crying. Surprising everyone, she grabbed the slender man up in a bear hug. "I'm so glad you're back!" Releasing him, she stepped back and eyeballed his companion. "Michael?"

"Sharp as a tack, this one," Michael said to Bruce. Hopping to his feet, he proffered his hand. "You must be Xenia, Bruce's magician friend."

"I must." A bit of strength worked its way into her voice as she shook his hand. "We have a plan," she said as Bruce opened his mouth.

Bruce and Michael shared a look. "You better fill us in," Michael said.

Chapter Twenty-Three
Then

THE SETTING SUN FLASHING FROM THE RIVIERA'S NEW tower half blinded me just as I underhanded my car keys to the kid at the valet stand. The keys went wide, and I got myself a good laugh as he dove to make the catch. Good thing he missed my fender with that tumble or I'd have put a shoe up his ass.

I took in the Riv's new lobby, which had been renovated when the tower had gone up. Gus had definitely been working his magic on this joint since he'd come out of "retirement." I was hoping there was some cabbage left over for yours truly. I'd had some lean days lately.

The crew had run into a streak of bad luck not too long ago. While we'd shifted our focus to other sources of income, we'd never completely stopped doing highway jobs. So when we got a tip on practically the juiciest mark ever, we dropped what we were doing and went after it. Fella had won but *big* at the tables and was a total nobody. No connections at all. There'd be no heat from upstairs when we took this guy for everything he'd won.

I didn't know if that jagoff fancied himself a vigilante or what, but no sooner than we got this guy off the road, it all went south on us. Total shitshow. Both of the Grace brothers went down in a hail of bullets. Never had a chance. Somehow, Clarence and I made it out by the skin of our teeth.

That was the last I saw of Clarence. As soon as we got back to the clubhouse, he hit the road. I still couldn't decide if I was steamed he did a runner or jealous that he made the smart call and left town for good.

The final straw came a month ago. I'd been out on the town, showin' a new dame the sights. When I got back to the clubhouse, Little Mickey was face-down on the carpet, throat open from ear to ear. From the look on his face, he'd never seen it comin'.

Out of that entire crew, *he* was the only one worth a damn. I was gonna miss that guy.

I'd been giving some serious consideration to following Clarence's example and hitting the road myself when Gus had looked me up. To say I was surprised to hear from Gus after all this time... well, that'd be a hell of an under-statement.

It's not that we were on the outs. It was just that old Gus had made a truly heroic effort to retire from the busi-ness. He'd gone so far as to move himself and his missus down to Phoenix. He'd been having a ball, I was sure of it, since he'd turned down an offer from the Outfit to come back and oversee operations at the Strip's latest, the Riviera.

The way I heard it, after the fact, was that his refusal had gone over like a lead balloon. The Outfit had sent Gus a counteroffer in the form of his sister-in-law turning up smothered in her own bed. Gus was back on board the very next day. He'd taken the job at the Riv, splitting his time between the office and his home in Phoenix.

He'd called to see if I was open to an opportunity that might come my way. Not having anything better to do, and needing the green, I'd said yes. Which is why I was heaving myself up onto a stool at the Riviera's theater bar.

Before I could signal the bartender for a drink, a shortish fella, hair gleaming with a double handful of pomade, took the stool beside me. "Eddy Fry?" He stared at me with all the brotherly love of a dead fish.

"Got it in one," I told him.

I'd never met this guy before, not in person, but I'd seen him around. Knew him by reputation. Marshall "Johnny Shoes" Caifano was one of the LA Outfit's made men, a serious hitter. I flagged down the barkeep and ordered us a round. "What can I do for you, Mr. Caifano?"

"Call me Johnny," Caifano said, picking up his glass. The kid behind the bar did a double take when he saw Johnny's face and found someplace else to be posthaste. "Gus tells me you do good work. Might be a notch or two on your own belt, if you catch my meaning."

"I might have done a thing or two for Mr. Greenbaum. Moe too, when he was still with us, God rest his soul." It's always good to play up the piousness when you're dealing with an Italian. "Ran with Little Mickey's crew until recently. Never heard anyone complaining."

The crowd in the bar, here to see some piano guy —Liver-something—made their way into the theater next door. Before long, we had the run of the joint. I saluted Johnny with my glass and we knocked 'em back. Reluctantly, the barkeep swung by to top us off. "So what can someone like me do for you, Mr. Caif— Johnny?"

He nodded. "Might have a job, if you think you can handle it."

If *he* was asking, then the Outfit was asking. That meant I had as much choice about taking this job as Gus had coming back from retirement.

"Of course," I said. "If you don't mind, I might have one question—"

"Why I'm asking you and not one of my guys?" He dragged a sleeve across his mouth and tapped his glass against the bar. Once our glasses were full and the kid had fucked off, he went on. "Sure, I got my go-to guys. Shooters, drivers, you name it." He tossed back his shot. "Hell, the *paisan* I wanted for the job is off banging his new *gumad* in Miami." He aimed a finger at my eye. "So when Tony tells me to do this thing, I think 'Hey! Who's gonna watch my back?' So I ask Gus who he's got that's worth a shit. Who ain't gonna be a big pussy about doin' the work."

I tipped the shot glass back and rolled scotch over my tongue while I thought. "And he says me."

"He says, 'Eddy Fry.' Lucky you gets the job."

"Lucky me." As long as this wasn't a setup, the job being to put two in the back of my head, this would be a step up for me. Doing work with Johnny Shoes would put my name into the ears of some well-connected people. It would also keep me out of the clink; Johnny had, allegedly, whacked a truckload of folks, and not once had the Feds been able to get any of it to stick. "What's the job?"

Cocking his head to one side, he said, "You got a full tank of gas?"

————

"Take a right," Johnny said as he tilted his map to catch the light from the passing street lamps.

Spinning the wheel, I guided my Cadillac around the corner, smooth as a boat on a lake. "Let me guess, this job's got something to do with Gus?"

The sun had just dipped below the hills to the west; the drive south from Las Vegas had taken most of the day. The whole time, Johnny had talked my ear off. Booze, women, you name it. There'd been an extra helping from him when he'd gone off on "that NASA bullshit," as he'd put it. I didn't have the nerve to ask him if he preferred the Russkies winning the space race.

He'd talked about nearly everything, it seemed, except the job that had planted him next to me for this drive. Any time I tried to bring it up, he'd give me the stink-eye until I changed the subject. Sometime past Kingman, I'd stopped asking about it.

"Right on the money." Johnny folded his map and set it between us. "The bosses want him out, for good. Gone." He rubbed the side of his nose with his thumb. "I went to Gus last week, told him I'd buy out his shares of the Riv. Then he could finally retire to Arizona like he wanted. Done and done. Even though we'd had to convince him to come back to work on the Riv, he'd started off doing the job the right way. Like a fuckin' magician with that skim. The money's flowing in like a river. For that, Tony was gonna let him keep his dignity and let him retire." He slapped the armrest at his side. "Now? Now he gets to be a message."

I nodded. I'd heard the rumors too. Gus had been slipping up. Which was something of a shock to me. For as long as I'd known Gus, he'd been neatly slipping the Outfit's cut out of the casino take before it ever hit the official ledger. That skim off the legal gambling made the Outfit more money than the wire, girls, or pills, ever had. Not that they'd given *those* up, no sir.

Gus hadn't stopped doing the work; he was still doing his magic with the ledger. The problem was his behavior while he was in town to do that work. While he'd always had a thing for girls on the side (who didn't?), he'd let it get out of hand. Then there was his newfound love for a needle in his arm. Well, he'd gotten sloppy. He'd overstepped the bounds to pay for his habits.

Everyone knew that the guy who ran the books for the skim dipped his own beak in. Perk of the job. The Outfit just expected that skim off the skim to be reasonable.

Considering they'd sent Johnny Shoes, Gus had passed "reasonable" a *long* time ago.

Johnny stretched his arm across the bench seat to punch me in the shoulder. "You ain't gonna have a problem with that, are you?" His eyes failed to reflect the friendly tone in his voice. "I hear you and Gus go way back."

"Naw." I thought about the extra time it had taken to pay off my marker thanks to Gus "handling" my payments. "Business is business." I might miss the old bastard, but I wasn't going to miss him *that* much.

"Right answer. Pull up there, by those palms."

I parked the Caddy where Johnny had instructed and checked out our target. Half a block ahead lay a corner lot ringed by a low fence. In the center of the neatly trimmed lawn sat what I assumed was the Greenbaum residence. The blueish glow of a TV set flickered through a window. From where I'd parked, we could approach the homestead from the rear. "What's the plan?" I'd heard that my current partner had a thing for shotguns and dynamite. "I have a heater in the trunk."

Rapping his knuckles on the dash, Johnny said, "This one needs to be up close and personal. That's the word straight from the horse's mouth." He twisted on the bench seat until he could look me in the eye. "Tony tells me, 'Don't blow his head off. I want everyone to see the look on his face!' Also, we got some respectable families in the neighborhood we don't want picking up a phone." His fingers walked in the air between us. "In and out, nice and quiet.

We get this done. We go home and sink our teeth into a nice pair of steaks, *capiche?*"

I nodded.

Biting my lip as Johnny scraped the bottom of his door on the curb (I'd check the paint later), I hauled myself out onto the street, keeping my eyes peeled for traffic while Johnny scouted ahead. Once I was sure there were no prying eyes in the neighboring windows, I followed him through the little gate in the Greenbaums' fence.

We kept our heads low while we hustled across the width of the lawn until we were out of the kitchen window's line of sight. Johnny had his hand on the side door when I glimpsed someone I didn't recognize inside. Bess, Gus's wife, was chatting with another woman in the kitchen.

Shit.

"We got an extra guest at the party," I hissed.

"Shit. This way."

I followed him into a narrow gap between the garage wall and a hedge. We edged in sideways until the tight-packed leaves of the hedge blocked us from view.

We'd been holed up for maybe five minutes when Johnny tapped out a smoke. He didn't offer and I didn't ask. I just hoped no one saw the ember while he got his fix.

"I'll be back in a jiff, dear." Bess's voice drifted to our hideaway, and the two of us flattened ourselves against the wall. I crept to the other end of the garage in time to see Bess back her car out, the other lady beside her.

After I gave Johnny the all-clear, we rounded the garage, heading for the side door. There was no resistance as I applied pressure to the knob, the door opening without so much as a squeak. Inside was a short hallway that looked to end in the living room. Immediately to the left lay the kitchen, where the rattle of ice in a glass halted me in my tracks. Maintaining pressure on the doorknob to keep the bolt retracted, I eased the door shut as a burst of studio laugher echoed down the hallway. Pressing my ear to the door, I followed the thump of Gus's footsteps as he left the kitchen. "Damn it, what'd I miss?" he muttered to himself. I gave it a second before opening a gap to peer through.

All clear.

Johnny shoved by me, knocking the door out of my grip. I lunged and caught it before it could thump the wall and announce our presence. Rolling my eyes when Johnny wouldn't see it, I quietly shut the door behind me.

When I caught up with him, Johnny was pulling a plastic bag from the trash over his hand in a makeshift glove. He seized a lengthy knife from the counter with his protected hand.

Following his lead, I scanned the kitchen for a weapon of my own. Judging by the mess scattered across the countertops, Gus had been in the middle of preparing dinner when he'd stepped away to see what he'd missed on the tube.

Unfortunately for me, Johnny seemed to have grabbed the only visible knife. I didn't want to take forever searching drawers and rattling about, so I grabbed a bottle from the wine rack over the icebox.

My partner glared across the kitchen at me, holding up the knife in his hand. I tossed the bottle into the air and caught it by the neck. It'd do.

With a shake of his head, Johnny turned to find Gus. It wasn't much of a search. The blare of "Hi ho Steverino!" came from two doors down the hallway, followed by the bray of Gus's laughter. Doubled over and slapping his knee, Gus had his back to the door as the two of us joined him in the bedroom. I couldn't say why, but as soon as I saw the back of his balding head, I threw myself at the older man, bottle raised. I nearly clobbered Johnny in the face as I swung at Gus.

I'd expected the glass to burst on impact, to spray both of us with merlot. Instead, a heavy thud traveled up my arm as the curve of the glass met the curve of his skull.

Stumbling from the impact, Gus staggered toward the bed. His knees bounced from the edge of the mattress, and he wobbled but didn't go down. "What the fuckin' fuck?" His eyes rolled as he tried to focus on me.

Whunk. A second blow laid him out, sending Gus sprawling across the bedspread. Drool streamed from the corner of his mouth and one eye, the pupil expanded wide enough to swallow the iris, lined up with me. "Eddy?"

Johnny shouldered me aside. "Get him all the way onto the bed," he ordered. Stepping to the other side of the room, I got my hands under Gus's arms and hauled him to the center of the bed. Johnny clambered onto my former boss to finish the job.

I'd thought Johnny was just gonna stick Gus a few times and was surprised when leaned in to saw the kitchen knife into Gus's throat. Half in a panic, I shoved a couple of pillows over his face, just in time to block the spray. "Give me a heads-up next time, will ya?"

"A heads-up!" Johnny's giggle was enough to set my teeth on edge. He gave the knife a last pass through the ruin beneath the pillows. Pulling one cushion aside to make sure the job was done, I winced. I could see spine showing through the yawning void in Gus's neck.

Message sent.

"Have you started the steaks yet, dear?" Bess called from the kitchen.

Johnny and I stared at each other over Gus's body. Decision made, he nodded. I retrieved the wine bottle from the bed, and the two of us walked out to greet Mrs. Greenbaum.

LATER, while watching the red spiral down the kitchen drain as I washed my hands, I took in the spread Gus had left waiting on the counter. A fat pair of sirloins, heavily dusted with salt and pepper, were resting on a tray beside a cast iron pan. Sniffing the air, I leaned over to take a gander at the oven. Sure enough, our host had left us a pair of foil-wrapped spuds baking away inside. "Hey, Johnny?"

"What?" he called down the hallway. He had a lot more blood to wash off than I had.

"You still in the mood for a steak?"

Chapter Twenty-Four
Now

Xenia and I outlined the plan, such as it was, to Bruce and Michael. While Bruce was hesitant, unsure, Michael was fired up, all in on the idea.

"Yes, I remember the chap. Slunk around while that Weir woman gave me the thrashing of my life." He waved off Bruce's hand. "I daresay it will be far less of a bother to waylay this villain during daylight hours."

"But I won't—" I began.

"Chill," Xenia said. "If he's Rebecca's close servant, or even her Second, he won't be far from her side while the sun's down. Which also means he's the one she'll have put the most trust in to do her daylight dirty work." She shook her head. "Since the whole plan is to get him *away* from the ice dude..."

"Fine." I hated being cut out of my own plan, but if anyone could handle a weasel like Marcus, she could. Not to mention having Bruce's muscles and Michael's... whatever at her side. I nodded for Michael to go on.

"I have a few friends who work downtown. If he's been poking around the bureaucracy on his mistress's behalf, they'll know."

"If he's left anything with them, anything he's touched more than a little, I can use that to track his ass." Xenia was jittery, unable to sit still. She punched one hand into the other. "Then we *kick* his ass."

"Woah there." I held up a hand. "We need him in one piece if we're gonna get him spilling his guts. No *Wind Razor*ing the Weasel."

"Yeah, yeah." Xenia tucked her magical weapon-glove into a pocket. "Okay. We track him down, nab him, and—"

"Bring him to me. Then I put the whammy on him. Crack him wide open. But *only* if you can do it safely. You so much as catch a hint that Felix is near, beat it."

Bruce and Michael, having experienced the giant's unnatural winter themselves, nodded in agreement. I held Xenia's eye until she, at last, nodded.

———

WHILE THE TRIO got some shut-eye to be ready for the day's hunt, I headed for the concierge to arrange an exit.

Because the plan required daylight to cut out Rebecca and, I hoped, Felix, it meant I had to stay on the sidelines myself, so I'd given Xenia the code to my safe house. Once they'd nabbed the Weasel, they could bring him directly to me for "interrogating." I'd also given her a few pointers on how best to wake me from my daylight snoozing.

A bellhop, scales coating every visible inch, attempted to pardon his way past me. I glared at the guy, a kid really, as he leaned against an overloaded luggage cart. Dual eyelids blinked back, unimpressed.

Realizing I was taking my frustration out on a kid who didn't deserve that, I stepped clear of the aisle. As he strained the cart back into motion, two more just like it fell into line. Looking around, I saw that bodies packed the casino's aisles around me as everyone headed toward what I guessed was the main exit.

Either this was the usual Sunday rush to the airport, or news of the impending vampire takeover of Las Vegas had hit the Clandestine News Network.

Seeing the crowd, I thought about taking that other option.

I could run. Find a small town, somewhere *way* off the grid. Live a simpler life, just like my folks had before I came along. Then again, from what Xenia had said, the vamps had their claws in everywhere. Chances were good they'd just track me down and stake me no matter where I went.

While I flipped some mental coins, the itchy feeling on the back of my neck, ever present since I'd fled the Fortune, kicked into overdrive. Someone *definitely* had me in their sights. One of Rebecca's goons? Felix? Playing it casual, hands in my pockets, I turned to search out the source of the itch.

Behind me, more tourists beating a retreat. No Teutonic giant loomed at my back, ready to turn me into an ice cube. Instead, an impossibly wide-eyed—cat?—gazed at me from the arms of a woman wrapped in a lacy shawl. Silver bangles woven into the woman's hair chimed as she turned her head, whispering into the tufted ear of the creature cradled in her arms. "Outside face, *s'il vous plaît*, Babette." The freaky cat-thing, its eyes never leaving mine, twisted in the woman's arms. Smooth skin swallowed the fur as bones realigned themselves. The enormous dark eyes shrank and lightened, moving closer together until the face of an eight-year-old girl gazed at me. She blinked once and raised her small hand. Short fingers wiggled *au revoir* at me.

Suddenly, the word "freaky" didn't sit so well anymore. Everyone here, those milling about with suitcase in hand or working whatever job in the casino, all of them wondering if the blade would come down before they could leave. They were all... people. Just people.

"Face it, Eddy," I muttered as I dragged a hand over my face. "You're not built for the small-town life." Fine. Next step: get to the concierge, have a word with Shizue.

Turning to go, I nearly tripped over a fella. He'd planted himself right in my personal space. Once I'd opened up a gap between us, a jolt of recognition hit me.

It was the guy, the oddball who'd watched Xenia and me when we'd first arrived at the Underground. As before, his fingers covered his mouth, elbow propped in the opposite hand. An aroma—bright, vegetal, and blended with the arid bite of sunbaked earth—hit my nose. This close, I could see the heavy links of multiple gold chains glittering from the open neck of his ochre silk shirt.

"Help you with something?" I hoped he wasn't about to throw down right here in the middle of all these families.

"A moment of your time, Señor Fry," he said, hand coming away from his mouth at last.

"Why not?" He hadn't gone for my throat, yet. Maybe he was one of the folks who'd gotten their ass kicked with Michael, or part of Bobby's crowd. "What's on your mind?"

His arm swept out in a wide arc, light dancing from gemstone-encrusted fingers, and he marched off. He led me, not so much walking as strutting with the assumption I had followed, to a tiny lounge set away from the bustle of the casino core. Thumbing his coat button open, he swept himself into one of a pair of chairs flanking a low table. He crossed one ankle over his knee, the thin arc of visible sock above his leather shoe a match for the crimson of his shirt.

I took the seat opposite him, more envious of the quality of his socks than the liquid grace of his movements. The lounge, secluded as it was from the crowd, was as quiet a space as I'd ever experienced in a casino.

251

"I know you, Señor Fry," he said, breaking the hush at last. "Or rather, I know *of* you." The bejeweled hands folded themselves over his raised knee as he tilted his head. Long earrings, flat teardrops in mother-of-pearl, swung from under the sweep of obsidian hair.

"Oh, you do?" I waved at the surrounding resort. "Lot of that going around these days. Everyone down here, out there too, knows about the famous 'Vegas Vampire.' Makes me feel a bit the fool that it took me this long to find out about them in return."

"You had merely to step from your tower of ivory for more than the span of a brief shopping *excursión* to learn the truth of the world, Señor Fry. Eddy. May I call you Eddy?"

"Knock yourself out."

"In any case, I believe we share a certain unpleasant new acquaintance, recently arrived to our city."

"Rebecca."

"Just so." The dark eyes blinked in assent. "Should it come to pass that her aims are realized, neither of us will have a home in this city. Nor would it remain the city we have long enjoyed."

"Got that right." Wood creaked, and I forced my hand to relax before I snapped the armrest off.

"It is possible, however unlikely it may be, that the future this creature desires to build within this valley is one in which I might continue some semblance of my current endeavors. It is more believable to assume that would not be the case. The change inflicted in her name would doubtless destroy the very flower she seeks to possess."

"What do you expect me to do about it? My people at the Fortune are all twisted around her dainty little finger, and she's got a... *Felix* to keep me from getting in there and *un*twisting them." I shrugged. "Not to mention her sugar

252

daddy buying up the town and handing it to her, tied up with a little bow. If it was just the two of us, me and her, I'd forget my rule about hitting dames and wipe the floor with her."

Throwing his head back, the man sitting across from me cut loose with a musical laugh. He didn't hold back at all; his entire body shook with merriment, and it was a moment before he spoke again. "Oh, Eddy. If only you truly knew. That one is so much more than she appears. She is very much older than you." With a flick of one hand, he cleared an errant hair from his forehead. "You do understand the role age plays in the strength of your kind, do you not? Or what that might make her capable of?"

"No, but I'm getting the idea."

The man nodded. "Indulge me a bit more if you would."

"Shoot." At this point, what did I have to lose?

"After you died, why did you choose to remain in Las Vegas? There was no longer anything that tied you to this place. Why not travel the world? With your newfound power, surely nothing would have been beyond your grasp."

I thought about it. "It felt right. There might have been nothing keeping me here, but there was nothing to pull me someplace else, either." Of course, I *couldn't* have left. If I'd stepped into another vamp's turf, they would've waxed me before I knew what was happening. But then, I hadn't known that when I'd decided to stay.

The man leaned forward, hands steepled in front of him.

I went on: "What can I say? This is my home. I wasn't going to run off and start a new life someplace else just because I'd died. That's why I'm not about to run off now. Just because I'm up against impossible odds? A man fights for what's his. Even if it's a losing battle."

The man folded his hands on top of his knee once more, peering at me through half-lidded eyes.

"All right, I opened up. My Ma would be proud," I said. "What's your deal? What do you care about why I'm gonna get my ass kicked?"

"It is no simple thing. Until now, I have enjoyed a Las Vegas without the petty rule of any vampire lordling. That time, for better or worse, is at an end. From now on, Las Vegas will have its vampire." His lip curled. "I would rather it be the *koyotl* who loves this city as I do than the *koyotl* who would see it ground to dust in her quest for an excess of power."

"You're talkin' like you won't be in the fight with the rest of us. We could use you on Team Eddy. A clueless vamp, a sharp dresser, a magic-slinger, and a shark-man. Who could stand in our way?"

He barked out another laugh. "Indeed, we would be unstoppable. But alas, I cannot stand by your side when you stride into battle."

"The hell are you talking about?"

He held up a hand. "There are... complications. Long before this city was built, I suffered a defeat. As a result, I was bound to the rock and stone by powers beyond my ability to overcome. I may invite you and all these"—he waved his hand at the crowd passing outside the calm of the lounge—"into my home, but I cannot join you above."

"You're kidding me. What a bunch of bull."

He inclined his head. "Absolutely, it is bullshit. Yet here I am, burdened by rules not of my making." His eyes sparkled in the dim lounge, and his sudden smile was a devious thing. As he tilted his head, the smile became generous, joyful, ecstatic, all of these and none. "While I cannot directly interfere in these matters with my own hand, this is, after all, Las Vegas. It would not be unusual for the house to tilt the odds in its favor. A thumb on the scale. A word, perhaps, in the ear of a cousin who yet roams free as the wind. Such a thing would have to be earned, of course."

"I'm listening."

"A wager."

"Hah! Now you're talking." I rubbed my hands. "What've you got in mind? Poker? Baccarat? Pool?"

"Oh, I am a simple creature, Eddy. Let us have a simple game to match. A guessing game. A single round."

"And the stakes?"

His hand slipped beneath his lapel, emerging with a knife lightly gripped between his fingers. As he rotated the black blade, reflections danced along the scalloped edges. With great care, he set it between us, the volcanic glass making a tiny *tick* against the tabletop. "It has been a very, very long time since I've received a new suit."

I swallowed. Best not to lose.

"Fine. Let's do this. What am I guessing?"

He slid to the edge of his chair, hands on his knees. The light dancing in his eyes caught mine, and I froze. Gone was the polished gentleman in the bespoke suit. In his place sat a statue hewn from black glass. Heavy crimson crossed his face and chest in wide stripes, the fingermarks of the artist still visible in the swaths of paint. A headdress of feathers bloomed in emerald, scarlet, and topaz above the statue's head. The lounge chair was gone, too. It was now a throne sculpted from a single block of rough stone. Fresh flowers were piled at his feet, higher at his sides and spilling over the throne's back.

I blinked, and he was a man once again.

He said, "I wager you cannot guess my name."

Son of a *bitch*. My stomach lurched as if I'd been gut-punched by one of the Grace brothers. How in the tapdancing hell was I supposed to have a clue what this guy's name was? Xenia, if she wasn't sacked out at the moment, might have had a shot of guessing the answer. I was as good as skinned.

"I just met you, Mac." I braced for the worst. "Let's get this over w—"

The clap of his hands stopped me. He brought his hands together with another *crack*, and once again, slow applause. His lips twisted in a knowing smirk. "I was not sure you had it in you, Eddy. Well done."

"The hell are you talking about? I didn't even guess..." Wait. Thumb on the scale. "Hah, shit."

Mac raised a hand as he relaxed into the cushion of his chair. From behind the lounge's tiny bar—which I hadn't noticed until then—hustled a cocktail waitress, loaded tray balanced atop one hand. The server arranged the contents of her tray on the table where the knife had rested. She departed after offering my host a deep bow.

Still reeling, unsure if I'd actually won or if I'd just been outplayed, I leaned in to read the label on the bottle. Fuenteseca 21 years. *100% de Agave Azul*. The good stuff. Beside the bottle sat two simple earthenware cups.

Cracking the wax seal, Mac splashed a generous slug into each cup. "I did not think you would care for *pulque*," he said with a wink. "When you least expect it, Eddy Fry." He raised his drink.

I suppose I could live with that. "Cheers." Clunking my cup against his, I tossed the *añejo* back. Fire tore across my tongue, searing every surface in my mouth. Gasping drew air in, and the fire expanded into butterscotch and oak. Coconut and spices I couldn't name tingled on my tongue as saliva gushed across my palate. I worked my tongue, pressing it to the roof of my mouth as I tried to prize every flavor from the only thing other than blood I'd tasted in nearly fifty years. The room swam, water filling my eyes, not entirely from the burn of alcohol. "I..." My voice cracked. "I haven't had anything like that since..." I knuckled my eye, at a loss for words.

One shoulder rising in a graceful shrug, Mac sipped at his own cup. Eyes dancing, he plucked the bottle from the table. Eager for more, I thrust my cup forward. "*Salud.*" This time I sipped my tequila, intent on savoring every drop.

When I felt like I could speak without sounding like a giddy fool, I said, "You know, there's something I've wanted to ask since we first met."

Mac's cup paused halfway to his lips. "And what would that be?"

"Who *is* your tailor?"

Throwing his head back, Mac rocked with laughter.

Chapter Twenty-Five
Then

"EDDY FRY, YOU SON OF A BITCH."

I spun around, ready to plant my fist in someone's mug.

"Hey, woah, lower the guns." The fella headed my way had one of those Italian names I could never remember, so I'd taken to calling him Jake.

"Heya, Jake. What's the good news?" He'd been over at the Riviera doing this and that back when I'd done that job with Johnny.

"You know how it is. Life in paradise. You lookin' to get on this crew, too?"

I'd been knocking around Vegas with nothing to keep me busy, or flush, for a couple months now. While the scratch Johnny had handed me had paid for some good times with some agreeable ladies, it hadn't gone much further than that. Which meant it was time to get back in the game. The jagoff currently in charge at the Riv didn't know which end of his dick he pissed from, which was why I was hanging around the dusty showroom of Burke's Furniture, wishing I had a drink in my hand.

"Pull up a chair, Jake." I took my own advice. "I been waiting on these guys all morning."

No sooner did Jake's ass hit the couch than the door in back swung open. A beefy guy with a flat cap perched on his blocky head stepped out. "Jacopo, that you? Get your ass back here!"

You gotta be shitting me. "Hey, what about me?"

"What about you?" Flat Cap said. "Boss'll see you when he's ready."

"Sorry, Eddy, you know how it is." Jake and Flat Cap started slapping each other's shoulders like they was old pals as the door swung shut behind them.

Fine.

Ignoring the sign forbidding it, I propped my heels on the coffee table and pulled out my flask. Might only be cheap bourbon, but it'd do the trick.

"You're up, chief," Flat Cap called out from the back of the room.

"About damn time."

Flat Cap led the way through a sizable but mostly empty warehouse. To one side was a flight of stairs, which we took. Positioned at the top was an office with an over-view of the floor below.

An older guy, as beefy as Flat Cap but going soft around the edges, was waiting for us. He had on a vest, no jacket, and had a watch chain jumping between the pockets. He even had sleeve garters, just like Pop used to wear. The old guy sat at a wide wooden desk—complete with one of those leather things on the top—that filled half the room. It must be easy to fill your office with high-quality, serious-looking furniture when you're operating a furnishing store as your front. He even had a fancy leather chair to sit in while he stared at me.

I glanced around, but there was no chair for me on this side of the massive desk. The room's only other feature was a slot machine, still shiny from the factory, with its front panel swung open to expose the mechanical guts.

While I was checking out the fella's office, he'd continued to stare at me, blinking maybe once. So I stared back.

Okay, I was never any good at staring contests. I said, "I hear you're looking for a guy with my experience."

"Did you?" When the old guy finally spoke, it was in a flat, nearly emotionless voice. "I asked about you, Edward. My friends in Chicago were of mixed opinion." His eyes flicked to the phone on his desk. Guess that's why the wait had taken so damn long.

"Hey, if it's about that thing in the Riviera showroom—"

"I wasn't finished. I was told that you were a reliable worker even though you weren't formally part of their, or any other, organization. That you had done some work for them more recently that had left quite the favorable impression." He blinked slowly. "Until the incident at the Riviera. One of my friends is of the opinion that an insult like that should be dealt with harshly."

I fought the urge to tug at my collar. "Look, I went back to apologize, but that dame had already vamoosed."

"Regardless, Edward. You've come to me with your hat in hand, asking for work. All of this must be taken into consideration. What we do here has consequences for many people. Am I hiring the trustworthy, reliable Edward Fry? Or the drunken fool?"

I took a step toward the desk, fists clenched. I forced my mitts to relax and took a breath. "Hey, good ol' Eddy Fry gets the job done." I kept my voice light. "Everyone knows that."

"That remains to be seen. Do have any mechanical experience?"

I blinked. "Ah, no? I can change a tire if I have to." What did this grease monkey shit have to do with anything?

"Pity. Jacopo demonstrated an acceptable level of skill." He nodded at the slot machine beside me. "I had been hoping to double my mechanical team today."

———

BOSS BURKE WOUND up sticking me with the pickup and delivery crew. Which meant picking up a batch of one-armed bandits from around Vegas and then dropping them off again when Jake's guys were done with them.

Turned out old Harold here, Boss Burke, had been cutting deals with the shops and bars that filled every off-Strip nook and cranny in this town. Any place you could rest an elbow, and some where you couldn't, had a bandit to soak up the spare change.

The State Gaming Commission inspected and certified each and every one of those machines. Once the suits were gone, we'd make our little modifications. Then those slots would only pay out a jackpot if you were wise to the trick. Burke paid each of the shopkeeps a bit of the take so they'd keep their yaps shut.

Sweet deal, right? Maybe if you were Harold Fuckin' Burke, it was. *He* didn't have to schlep two tons of one-arms around every day on the promise of some chump change!

If it wasn't loading a damn slot into the truck, it was lugging a canvas sack of coins. I could have eased my load, made those sacks lighter before they got back to Burke's Furniture Showroom. If it wasn't for Simon, AKA Flat Cap, breathing down my neck on every run.

After a couple months of that bull, I was just about ready to throw in the towel. But before I could make the call to leap one way or the other, I heard from Simon that the boss wanted a word.

Upstairs, Burke, hands clasped behind his back, was gazing out his window at the bustling warehouse floor. These days, they'd crammed the space with end-to-end workbenches, tool racks, and rows of slot machines waiting for Jake's tender mercies.

"Edward."

I'd tried to tell him my name was Eddy, just Eddy, but he never listened.

"I hear you've been tugging at the reins of late."

"Ah, nothing like that, boss. Just thinking we should do more with all this manpower, ya know? Lot more ways for us to be pulling in the cabbage in this town."

"Ways for *you* to pull it in, you mean."

"Well..."

"As a matter of fact, I agree with you."

"What?" I couldn't help it. My jaw was hanging. "I mean, you do? Boss?"

"The slots were only ever the beginning. A means to an end, Edward. For me *and* my people. It was a niche that had been overlooked, and now we're seeing competition beginning to encroach. It's time we secured our territory, expanded and diversified our income."

"Now you're talking. I'm guessing there's some jagoffs you want me to have a word with?"

"That is correct." Burke pulled a slip of paper from one of the desk's many drawers. "This is a list of the business that have handed the take from their slot machines"—his fist clenched around the list as his voice lost its monotone for the first time since I'd met him—"the ones *I* selected for modification, to our new rivals." He smoothed the paper on his desk, then thrust it at me. "See that they remember who that money belongs to."

I took the list. "You got it, boss." I paused halfway out the office door. "You want anyone should be permanently reminded?"

Burke's hand made a lazy wave as he turned to the window. "Not at this time, no. Just be thorough, Edward."

Chapter Twenty-Six
Now

I left the Underground through the men's room at the gas station a block from my storage unit safe house.

I had planned to find a quick bite to eat, but after killing that whole bottle with Mac, I no longer felt like I was about to keel over. Don't get me wrong, it wasn't the same as a proper meal, not even close; the tequila had only worn the sharp edge off my hunger. But I felt the better plan was to get some shut-eye first. The blackout oblivion I experienced at sunrise wasn't *exactly* like grabbing forty winks had been back in my breathing days, but it was still a required part of the regimen if I wanted to stay functional. So while I was still hungry, it was exhaustion that had me wobbling during the walk up the block.

Or maybe that was the tequila.

I was happy to see that Xenia's wrecked car was gone, either towed or stolen. One less thing to draw attention to my hideaway. The only evidence remaining from my encounter with Bruce was scattered glittering pebbles of glass and a massive dent in the fence. Any blood I'd left behind would have evaporated as soon as the sunrise had touched the stain.

Inside, my floor was still a wreck from where Xenia had tied Bruce down. There wasn't much I could do about the exposed rebar, but I could sweep up the dust and bits of concrete scattered about.

Once I'd tidied up as much as I could, there wasn't much time to kill before dawn put my lights out. Just enough for a wardrobe change. Sure, I'd be a couple of decades out of style, but I was past caring. I put the fold-away shower to use, then slipped into an ancient Armani from the back of my wardrobe.

Now that I no longer smelled like a vampire hobo, I was ready for a day's rest. I passed on my sleeping trunk. Waking up in tight quarters reminded me too much of the berths I'd had to share while they'd shipped my unit around the Pacific. Besides, I hated all those movies clichés, like sleeping in a coffin. Or on dirt. I didn't do that, and I *certainly* knew how to use a napkin after eating. Hissing was right out.

I opted for the inflatable mattress. It wasn't the fanciest place to rest my head, but it would be better than the floor while I waited for the sun.

While I set about connecting the pump, my foot sent something skittering across the floor: a tiny lapel pin depicting a leaping unicorn with a rainbow shooting from under its tail. It could only have come from Xenia's gear.

With a smile, I tucked the little pin away. It would be safe with my cuff links until Xenia came by with the crew later—with Marcus in tow, assuming things went to plan.

From another box, I retrieved the last of my burner phones and powered it on. I added Xenia from memory and keyed in a message so she'd have the new number.

Dawn was pressing on me from the outside. In a moment, the sun would crest the mountains to the east and I'd be able to sleep. Finally. A day's shut-eye was just the ticket to clear my head. Ahead of me was a big night of monkey wrenching *all* of Rebecca's plans.

The air mattress squeaked under me as I shifted around, trying to make myself comfortable. Not that it would matter in a moment.

Dawn.

I was gone.

Chapter Twenty-Seven
Then

You'd think that after all these years, people would know who ran this town. But no, there was always gonna be some jagoff who thought they'd be the one to make a stand. Tell us where we could do business.

The boss had saddled me with one of the new guys, told me to take him along while I did the rounds. Kid was still wet behind the years, I tell ya. The neighborhood we were collecting from today wasn't the richest or the classiest street in Vegas. Just a handful of mom 'n' pop shops a mile and change from downtown.

It stuck in my craw that Burke was still settling for these rinky-dink neighborhoods. Okay, so the big boys owned Fremont and the Strip, but that didn't mean there weren't juicy pickings to be found next door. As long as you weren't stepping on their feet, the Outfits didn't care who you shook down as long as they got their beak wet.

The rigged slots were still raking it in, but that scam wasn't one you could scale up too fast. The Gaming Commission couldn't wait to come down like the hand of God on anyone they could find, and nobody wanted that kind of heat.

It wasn't like Burke hadn't been expanding the business. The cash from the slots got us slinging go-go pills for the night shift crowd, a bit of shylocking, and running protection on a couple of streets.

Which was what me and the new guy were up to at the moment.

New Guy was some goof from Philly; I thought he was Burke's cousin's kid or something. I didn't really care. Fella was a narrow slice of nothing without the muscle to throw a paper airplane, much less a punch, if you wanted my opinion. But then, you try telling the boss no when he says, "Take him along," I dare ya. So I took him along.

First things first, though. Breakfast.

"You don't think it's a bit early for that kind of thing?" New Guy whined in my ear.

I ignored him long enough to finish my scotch and flag down a refill. "The hell you on about, Mac? You don't like breakfast?"

"Eddy, it's almost eleven! Burke wanted us to finish collection over an hour ago."

"So I'm not a morning person. Sue me." Now that I was fortified for a day lugging a whiny kid around town, I figured it was time to hit the road. I waved two fingers by my brow at the guy who'd been pouring and left a couple bills for his trouble.

Outside, I ran a hand along the rear fin of my Caddy. I'd paid cash for that baby as soon as they'd rolled it onto the showroom floor, and not a day went by that I didn't feel like a fuckin' prince when I was behind the wheel. "Watch the curb when you open the door, or I'll rip your balls off." I smiled to let New Guy know I was serious.

Every tourist seemed to think today was the day to cut me off with their horns blaring, but I got us through traffic in good time anyway. I got a good laugh out of New Guy at least. There were a couple moments when I thought he'd leap right out of the car, the pussy. Some folks can't handle the passenger seat. He'd just have to get used to it. If he thought I was going to let him get behind *this* wheel, he had another thing coming.

"Eddy! *Watch out!*" The New Guy had some lungs on him, right in my fuckin' ear! I took my eye off the skirts on the corner long enough to see what had him in such a tizzy. Just another jagoff walking in the middle of my street. I laid the horn on thick and hauled the wheel over enough to ruffle his shirt instead of running him down like he deserved. "Outta the street, you bum!" I yelled before telling New Guy to look for someplace to park.

To his credit, once he unclenched himself, New Guy found me a primo spot at the end of the block. The minute the car had stopped rolling, he was out like a shot.

He was going to have to wait on me, though. The *one* problem I'd had with the Caddy were the springs in the driver's seat. They were fine when driving around, but as soon as I needed to get out of the car, it was like hauling myself out of a pit. I swear, if I'd been sold a bum seat, that salesguy was going to get a few choice words from me and the tire iron. I had to crack my back as soon as I had gotten myself upright. Bum springs, for sure.

I let Junior lead the way to our first stop. Of the twelve of so little shops on this street, Burke had us collecting payments from all but the payday loan place. That one was also ours.

"Simple stuff, once you get the hang of it. Everyone knows the drill. It's easy money. I come by once a week, show the flag. You get the stink-eye from anyone, they get a reminder of what they're paying for. Stuff gets broken. That always wises 'em up, gets that register drawer open quick."

"Yeah, Eddy. I know how it works."

"Hey!" I jabbed a finger at the little fucker. "Watch your tone. I was doing this when you were still hanging from your momma's tit." Some broad with a stroller looked at me like she wanted to start something. "What?" She hurried away with her rug rat. "That's what I thought."

"Take it down a notch, okay?"

"Yeah, whatever." I waved him off and shoved open the door to our first stop. A little bell jangled above my head as I entered Lucky Clean Laundry. This joint, like most laundry places, was run by an old Chinaman. When he saw who was coming, he jumped off his stool and damn near shoved his wife into the back room. By the time I got to him, he was standing at the counter, back ramrod straight, with his hands folded behind him.

"Good morning Mr., uh, Nug, uh..." New Guy had a little notebook in his hand, and his eyes crossed as he tried to read the old-timer's name.

"Nguyen." His eyes flitted between the New Guy and me.

"Whatever. You know what day it is," I said, ignoring the look from New Guy.

"I am not paying," Mr. Nguyen stated each word firmly. "No more. We can't afford to stay open. Not when we're paying for the electricity, the city, and you leeches. No more." He sent a defiant glare my way.

"Issat so?" I said. Beside me, New Guy snapped his notebook closed, tucking it into his back pocket. "On our very first stop, too. You're up, greenhorn."

New Guy took his time moseying around the area in front of the laundry's counter. Passing a rack of doodads, he hooked it with a finger. The clatter of the wire rack bouncing off the linoleum was loud in the small space, but nothing on that rack had been fragile enough to smash when it hit the ground.

"Oops." He wasn't even able to make it *look* like a threat, the way he was avoiding the old fart's glare.

I rolled my eyes. Amateur.

As New Guy paused by the counter, Mr. Nguyen never broke eye contact, continuing to glare straight at New Guy. New Guy gave him a "what can ya do" shrug and booted his foot through the wood-paneled front of the counter.

A gasp came from the old lady, who was still hiding somewhere in the back. Mr. Nguyen's jaw worked, his lips trembling as he clenched his teeth.

New Guy worked his way down the counter, leaving a trail of holes, until he reached the flip-top. Raising it, he wandered into the back where Mrs. Nguyen and, presumably, all the laundry equipment were hiding out.

The smash and tinkle of glass breaking echoed through the shop, and the harsh smell of chemicals followed close on its heels. As New Guy wandered back into view, he cupped his hands around his mouth. The flare of a lighter lit his face, and he took a deep drag from his cig. The lighter, still lit, dangled from his hand as he looked over his shoulder. "Say. That stuff ain't flammable, is it? Could be dangerous." The lighter snapped shut with a flick of his wrist.

Mr. Nguyen's eyes scrunched shut as sweat rolled freely down his balding dome. From the rear depths of the laundry came the sound of muffled sobs.

As much fun as this was, I had eleven stops to go on this parade, and lunchtime was getting close. So I ambled over to the counter and reached around to the cash register. I slapped buttons until the drawer sprung open with a happy *cha-ching*. "Looks like you've got plenty, old man. I don't want to hear any more bull about not being able to afford us." I helped myself to a stack of greenbacks.

Mr. Nguyen closed his hand around my wrist. "No." I

could feel the tremble in his grip, but when I met his eyes, his face was calm.

"Best be removing that hand, old-timer. Before something else gets broken."

"I. Said. No."

I smiled. "Have it your way." Dropping the cash, I wrenched my hand free of the old man's weak grip. All he had for hair was a thin half donut around the back of his skull. I got a few wispy strands wrapped in my mitt and bounced his coconut off the countertop. Then once more for good measure.

I let him go. I had to shake my hand to get his hair offa my fingers, and he left a red streak behind as his face slid across the counter. There was a shriek, and Mrs. Nguyen came dashing out of the back in time to catch her husband before his head hit the floor.

"You killed him! You killed my husband!" She sank to the floor, the old man's head cradled in her lap. Her hand hovered, trembling, above the ruin of his nose before stroking his forehead. A bubble of blood formed at Mr. Nguyen's flattened nostril as he groaned.

"Eddy," New Guy began.

"Just take the cash." I waved him off. "I'll handle this." If the missus wanted some, I'd be happy to deliver.

"They got the message, Eddy. Enough," New Guy insisted.

I spun on him. "It's enough when I *say* it's enough. You got that? Huh?"

New Guy stepped back, his open hands held up in front of him. "Okay, okay. Jesus." He shook his head as he stepped over to the register and began fishing bills from the drawer.

I followed him around the counter, and Mrs. Nguyen

pulled her husband up against her, hunching to shield him with her body. "No!" she shrieked. "Please, someone help! He's going to kill him!"

"Oh shut up, will ya? Tired of your whining." I hauled my foot back to take a shot at the old lady.

"Eddy!"

"*What!*" If showing him the ropes meant showing him when to keep his yap shut, then so be it.

"We got an audience." New Guy hooked a thumb toward the front of the laundry. People had started smushing their faces against the glass, hands shading their eyes as they peered inside. I guess the old lady's voice had carried. While I watched back, two heavyweight blue-collar types joined the growing throng of looky-loos.

A siren wailed in the distance.

"Well, now you've gone and done it." When I glanced to New Guy, he patted a pocket. Payment collected. "Okay, rookie. Time to go."

———

"What have I told you, Edward?" Burke wasn't happy, but his monotone voice wasn't showing it. The lines at the corners of his mouth did. They got deeper and more prominent as he chewed me out.

"Stay out of the spotlight," I said.

"Stay out of the spotlight. And what did you do today?"

"Hey, the geezer needed his attitude adjusted. Thought he could get out of paying up. You want me to just walk away, let the rest of the street get ideas?"

"Use some common sense, Edward," Burke said. "No, we do not let a mark welsh on a payment. However, violence is to be applied judiciously. For instance, direct it toward a heartier member of the family. Putting an elderly man in the hospital is not conducive to business. Law enforcement becoming involved over such a trivial amount is also counter to our interests." He slapped one square hand onto the desk blotter with some force. "Now, more payoffs will have to be made, more favors offered, until the heat dies down. The heat that *you* caused."

"Sounds like the cost of doing business to me, boss."

Beside me New Guy slapped one hand against his forehead.

"Oh, does it?" Burke's voice actually went up a notch. "Since when do you make the business decisions in this organization, Edward?"

I'd been thinking for a while that it was high time I had a crew of my own. After all, I'd been doing this as long as Burke had. What made him so all-fired special? Burke would get his soon enough, so I kept that kind of thinking to myself.

For now.

"Sorry, boss. Won't happen again."

"No, it won't. Oscar, next week, that route is your responsibility." Burke tilted his head a fraction. "The laundry gets a pass until Mr. Nguyen is out of the hospital."

"What if they still play the rebel when he does? The old fool was stubborn as a mule," I said.

"If his recalcitrance continues, then I"—Burke's eyes locked on mine with an icy glare—"and *only* I will allow a more permanent lesson to be taught." He placed his hand on the stack of bills that New Guy (Oscar, I guess) had set on his desk. "Dead business owners can't pay. But rebellious ones don't pay either. It's about striking a balance, Edward."

"Yeah." I clenched my fist in my pocket while I smiled for Burke. "Okay."

"For now, go help with the trucks. Consider it penance."

In my pocket, fingernails bit into my palm. Working the trucks paid jack compared to collections.

"Something on your mind, Edward?"

"No." I stomped out the office door. *"Boss."*

Chapter Twenty-Eight
Now

Normally, once I'd conked out for the day, I'd be literally dead to the world until the sun went down. There were no dreams, no actual sense of being "asleep" while I was out cold. There was only the thinnest sense of time passing, an instinctual awareness of the sun's position in the sky.

Occasionally, such as when the hit team had shown up a week ago, Kurt had tried to rouse me from my sleep. He'd had to burn me with a silver Franklin half dollar that he'd started carrying for the purpose before I'd wake up. Once I was down for the day, I'd only snap out of it for an undeath-threatening emergency.

An emergency like having the cinder block wall of my safe house blown open by a breaching charge.

I snapped awake as cinder block shrapnel bombarded the room. The punctured air mattress, popping like a massive party balloon, dumped my ass onto the concrete floor.

The entrance doors to my safe house faced to the west, which was why I'd picked it out of the options available to me. I'd thought that might buy a few moments in the event of a panicked dawn entry. I should have chosen one of the middle units in the lot; then, I'd have another storage room at my back instead of an alley.

The new entrance to my safe house faced directly into the midmorning sun. Whoever had blown the wall had picked the perfect time because the sun had a direct line of sight over the nearby buildings and straight into my shelter. Rays of golden light cut through the smoke and the dust to smack me dead in my face.

It hurt.

It hurt like *hell*.

Arching as if I'd touched a live wire, my back spasmed from the sudden agony. My hands and face felt like someone had applied a giant blowtorch to them. In the corner of my vision, I could see my skin had flushed a fevered scarlet. Blisters seethed across the backs of my hands, bursting to expose the raw flesh inside. My suit was no protection from the direct light of the sun either. Needles of molten iron burrowed into every inch of me hit by the light.

As I writhed, tangled in the shreds of ruined air mattress, my only thought was to reach the safety of my sleeping trunk. The five feet of floor between me and the refuge might have been the width of the Sahara for all the progress I could make. The flesh sloughing from my blistered hands was too slick. I couldn't find purchase on the thin carpet flooring.

A shadow fell across me. With the full might of the sun's fury bearing down on the room, something as insignificant as a person's shadow offered exactly no relief. It did, however, shade my scalded eyes enough for me to see three others join the backlit form.

Three of the black-on-searing-white figures were blocky, indistinct, and wavering. The fourth, though. I'd recognize that squared-off crew cut anywhere. One way or another, Rebecca had gotten to him.

"Kurt," I tried to say, except with my lips and tongue swollen and bubbling, what came out was closer to "Glurp!"

"You're not looking too good there, boss." Kurt knelt by my head.

I was doing my best, trying to push through the pain, to grab Kurt by the throat. If I'd taken the time to find a meal before I'd sacked out, I might have had the strength to snap his fuckin' neck. Instead, since I hadn't had a drop in nearly forty-eight hours, the best I could manage was a limp swipe.

Turning to one of his backlit accomplices, he said, "Better do it now." Rising to his feet with a grunt, Kurt stepped to the side as the shortest of his three companions approached.

My hands slid across the floor, flesh peeling away to expose tendon and bone, and my vision took on a foggy, blurred aspect that suggested that my corneas had joined the blister party. Even through this distortion, I recognized the bulbous weapon being aimed at my chest. I'd last seen it when I'd zoomed into the security feed while watching a hit team invade my home. The too-wide mouth of the barrel was a void save for a glint of silver.

A pneumatic *chuff* sounded as a two-foot length of wood slammed into my rib cage. The burn of the silver point barely registered against a background of the sun's fire.

I'd expected this to be lights out for Eddy. Instead, my struggles ended in one last spasm. I flopped onto my back like a puppet whose strings had been cut. Being pinioned by the sun had made it nearly impossible to move thanks to the agony ripping through my flesh, but this... this was worse. Even as the sun continued to wreak its havoc on my body, I was unable to so much as twitch a muscle. Even the frenzied convulsions had stopped. The wooden stake impaling my heart had severed the connection between me and my body. A distant part of me marveled. That lump of muscle had been quiet, unbeating since the moment of my death, yet there must still be a purpose for it in this second life if a bit of wood switched me off like this. Bullets hadn't, so why wood? And why had it just paralyzed me instead of chucking me from this immortal coil? Maybe that's why all the old tales said you needed to stake *and* behead the vampire to end it once and for all.

I supposed the beheading would come next.

I was unable to turn my eyes, but impressions of movement flickered in the edge of my vision. The pressure of hands gripping my ankles and armpits seeped through the waves of agony wracking my body. Gagging sounds came from the silhouette gripping my shoulders.

That was fair. I wouldn't want to touch me right now either.

I was hoisted like a sack of potatoes and slung onto something thick and rubbery. The sun had broiled my eyeballs to the point of blindness, but my ears still worked. A heavy zipper went *vurrrp* and darkness, glorious darkness, closed around me. The flamethrower torment of the sun's rays cut off, leaving in its wake the bone-deep ache of traumatized flesh. The stake in my chest burned with a throbbing pain that mocked the memory of my heartbeat.

The body bag they had loaded me into rose off the floor, and I swayed as they carried me from my safe house. There was a clatter of rubble, followed by the sound of a vehicle's rolling door. With surprising delicacy—worried about dislodging the stake paralyzing me, I suppose—they loaded me into the van. The floor tilted to one side, then the other as doors slammed shut all around me. Sirens became audible over the sound of the van's engine, and the vehicle lurched into motion.

I was pretty sure I knew where we were headed.

With the body bag protecting my vulnerable flesh from the fury of the sun, paralyzed by the stake rammed through my ticker, unable to so much as wink an eye, I did the only thing I was still able to do.

I let the darkness take me.

Chapter Twenty-Nine
Then

"Can you believe the nerve of that guy?" I muttered while eyeballing the slab of prime rib overlapping my plate. Deciding I'd start at the herbed crust, I tucked the cloth napkin into my collar.

"Who's that?" Doris flicked her eyes toward me while she added a dab of mint jelly to her lamb.

"Business." I stuffed the hunk of beef into my mouth. "Forget I said anything."

Knowing better than to ask about my work, Doris returned her attention to her plate.

While the prime rib lived up to the joint's reputation, I was still disappointed. I'd taken my gal to the Golden Steer, hoping that seeing Old Blue Eyes would cheer me up and take my mind off the fact that Jake, that asshole, had had the nerve to talk back to me in front of the crew this morning.

Frankie had become a regular at the steakhouse over the last year, coming in for dinner and drinks several times a week. When I'd heard that, I'd gone right over, Doris in tow, hoping that we could get a seat with a view of my favorite crooner. Only when we'd gotten there, it turned out he'd bought out the whole house. We'd gotten in tonight, but Frankie was nowhere to be seen, dammit.

"Say, Eddy."

"Yeah, doll?"

Doris slathered her potato with whipped butter. "I picked up some brochures. You know, for our trip?" She sighed. "I'm just *dying* to see Cabo."

"Aw, jeez, Doris, not this again. I told ya. Second I get a solid payout, we're on. Until then..." I sawed at the thick stripe of fat running through the prime rib's center.

A whine crept into Doris's voice. "Eddy. You keep *saying* that. 'Too busy right now. Gotta get the simoleons for it.' You're just making excuses." Her lower lip jutted out.

"Look, doll, cash flow is a little tight right now." I took a swig from the cocktail glass next to my plate and winced. The waiter had recommended something called a sidecar. I hated it. The sugared rim was making my teeth hurt. But I wasn't going to waste booze I'd paid for. "We'll go in the spring. Scout's honor."

"Sure thing, Eddy. Whatever you say." Her shoulders slumped as she pushed her plate away.

Did everyone think they could give me the business today? "Yeah, that's right." I rapped my knuckles against the tabletop. The silverware jumped. "Whatever I say."

Doris hunched her shoulders and glanced away. I caught the edge of something mumbled under her breath.

Heat rose around my collar. "What was that?"

Lip trembling, Doris turned to face me. "I said, this isn't fun anymore, Eddy."

"Oh, it's not, is it?" Prime rib juice speckled the table-cloth as I jabbed my fork at her. "Is this joint not good enough for you? Do you not get tickets in your hand so you can see all the shows with your girlfriends? Is that rock around your neck not sparkly enough for you? What about all the cash I give you to blow on twenty-one?" I stabbed at the slice of beef waiting on the plate, and the fork hit the china hard enough to skip out of my hand. Tumbling, the fork snapped the stem of my cocktail glass and sent glass and booze sloshing across my plate. "Just look at what you did!" My lip curled. "You worthless bi—"

"*SHUT UP!*" Doris shrieked. "You shut your mouth! You don't get to talk to me like that. In a nice restaurant even, in front of all these nice people!" As she spoke, the quaver in her voice gained a firmness that I didn't care for.

"Lower your damn voice, woman. You're making a scene."

"*I'm* making a scene? I am?" Her hand flew to her chest. "Oh, dear me! Am I embarrassing the big bad gangster?"

Heads everywhere were turning, everyone twisting their necks to catch the show. One busboy popped out of the kitchen door only to reverse course when he saw the source of the fuss.

"You keep your mouth shut about that, or so help me—"

"What? You'll what?" Doris snapped. "Hit me? Again? Do you have *any* idea how much foundation I've gone through since we started seeing each other?" The fingers of one hand brushed her cheek.

Tablecloth bunched in my grip as my hand curled into a fist all on its own.

Lips pressed together in a narrow line, Doris placed each of her hands with great care on the edge of the table. Her eyes glittered in the dining room's amber light as she stood. Retrieving her clutch from the back of the chair, she held it before her, gripping it with both hands as if it were a shield. "Eddy. I don't want to see you anymore." She dragged in a shuddering breath. "We're through."

Someone in the back of the dining room shouted, "Woo!"

I shoved myself to my feet, and my chair toppled over behind me. Tearing my napkin from my collar, I threw it to the floor. Another busboy started forward, likely to retrieve it, but an older waiter stopped him with a hand and a knowing shake of his head.

"Oh, is that right? We're through?" I said through a snarl. "Get in the car. We'll finish talking about this back at my place."

"I'm not going with you. I'll get my own ride."

Crimson tinged the edges of my vision as I stomped around the table. She held her ground, only lifting her clutch higher in her trembling hands. She raised her head to meet my glare, defiance shining in her eyes.

"You want to be quits? We're quits. But I'm taking that rock back." I snatched at the pendant hanging around her neck. That stupid thing had cost more than I liked. No way was I gonna leave it with her.

"Don't you touch me!" Doris batted my hand away.

My pulse thudded in my ears, growing until its roar drowned out the gossipy chatter of the room. No one hit Eddy Fry, no one. *Especially* not a fuckin' skirt. I'd teach her a proper lesson.

When I tried to swing, a hand caught my wrist.

"That's enough, Eddy."

I spun, intent on flattening the sonofabitch who had the balls to lay hands on me.

Simon, Burke's second-in-command, stared at me over my raised arm. For the first time since I'd first laid eyes on him, he wasn't wearing that stupid flat cap.

His grip tightened, and I couldn't stop him from forcing my arm down. His free hand came to a rest on my shoulder, and he leaned in. "What's the boss going to say when he hears one of his enforcers beat up a *woman* in front of an audience?" His voice was low, pitched for me only. "Do you think he would appreciate that kind of attention? Is this the sort of reputation he wants for his organization?"

"She—"

"Don't care. It doesn't matter. You have a beef with your old lady, you handle it *in private*. Got it?" The hand on my wrist clenched, and I couldn't stop myself from wincing.

I fought against the grip he had on my shoulder and arm, but the younger guy had caught me off guard. He'd pinned me but good. Otherwise, I would have easily flattened that jagoff. "Fine," I forced out through clenched teeth.

Releasing my wrist, Simon slid a friendly arm around my shoulders. Raising his voice, he addressed the dining room, "Apologies to everyone, from me and my friend here. He had a little more to drink than he could handle, that's all. I'll get him back to his place safe and sound, put a pot of coffee in him. Meanwhile, how about a round of drinks for the house? My treat." He waved one of the hovering waiters over as a cheer went up around the room.

I looked back to where Doris had been standing.

She was gone.

Chapter Thirty
Now

For the first time in I didn't know how long, I didn't just pop awake. Instead, it was a miserable slog from oblivion to consciousness. Like Sunday morning after a night with the boys, head pounding with Satan's own hangover.

Only worse.

Every inch of me, even the skin covered by my suit, was a raw nerve. The brush of coolness against my throbbing face told me two things: they had decanted me from the body bag, and I was some place with air conditioning. The red-hot poker of agony inside my ribs told me that the stake was still in place.

Well, that and not being able to move at all.

Wherever this was, it was dark. Which was confusing. Ever since waking up dead, I'd been able to see in any darkness, even without the slightest hint of light. Now, though, nada.

The first notes of panic began to burrow through the cotton and glue clogging my thoughts. If it weren't for the stake transfixing my heart, I'd have thrashed like a fish on a hook.

An ungentle hand twisted its fingers in my hair and dragged my head upright. Based on the dry-ice burn where the fingers pressed into my scalp, Felix was doing the grabbing.

Rebecca's voice floated out of the darkness before me. "Has our guest awakened yet?" A rustle of cloth. "Goodness, Mr. Fry. The state of you. You simply *must* take more interest in your health, to say nothing of your appearance." The *tut-tut* that followed was full of cruel humor.

The length of wood snagged in my ticker moved. Lightning bolts of agony sizzled from the point of contact as the dowel slid. It might have only been a couple of feet, but as it grated against my ribs, it might have been two miles long.

Even though I didn't need to breathe, I gasped like a drowning man the instant the silver tip cleared my chest. Air, ice cold from either the air conditioning or Felix's proximity, flooded into my abused chest. The cool air in my lungs was *amazing* after the inferno of the sun's attention, but a spasm of wet coughs cut my enjoyment. Lumps of something I didn't care to identify tore loose, and I doubled over, heaving until my throat was clear. When the spasms finally subsided, Felix renewed his grip on me, placing a hand on each of my shoulders.

The only thing that came out when I tried to speak was a whistling gurgle.

Rebecca's voice purred beside me. I'd been too busy with the coughing to follow her movement. "Marcus, bring me one of the volunteers."

A door opened nearby, and I realized I had been alone with Rebecca and Felix until that moment. Neither of those two registered to my senses as more than a voice, a grip, the sound of movement. Dull and distantly perceived. However, once that door opened, the awareness of people, many more people, slammed into me. The presence entering the room had something Rebecca and Felix didn't.

Living blood.

I wasn't able to see, could barely hear, but my nose locked on to that scent of blood. Flowing, pulsing, waiting just below the skin, that blood was a siren call.

I'd been so well fed for so long, from a supply so eager and willing to donate, that I'd all but forgotten what *true* hunger was. This was worse than anything I'd felt in my living years, beyond even the deprivations of my childhood. My fangs burst from my gumline, the needle points gouging my already ravaged lips. Raw, animal *need* coursed through me, and if it weren't for Felix pinning me to the chair, I would have thrown myself at the source of that smell, heedless of any damage I might cause.

"Patience, Edward, patience," Rebecca's syrupy voice admonished. "Darling, over here if you please." The shuffling of feet on the carpet came near. The smell of blood grew, and I felt the warmth of their life against my skin. *So close.*

Hand tangled in my hair, Felix wrenched at my head. With my neck strained near to the breaking point, my jaw gaped wide.

A tiny, wet *snap* sounded from above my waiting mouth. The blood scent, maddeningly close, became a flood. The first droplet hit my tongue, and its heat seared a path down my throat. Another followed, and then a trickle. I strained, trying with all my might to lock my mouth to the source as the blood's warmth wicked into my battered body. The icy grip tangled in my hair and its matching lock on my shoulder were all that kept me from drinking my fill. From drinking *everything* that warm body had to offer.

"Not too much now," Rebecca said as the trickle thinned. A moment later, it cut off entirely, and an animal whine escaped my throat. I snapped at the air for *more*. In my gut, the blood's fire thinned to nothing as my sun-ruined body fought over the paltry sip of the fuel it needed to repair itself.

With a moist *squick,* my eyelids split from the congealed mass of tissue they had become. I blinked in the sudden light. Bits of jellied flesh still clung to the ruin of my face, partially obscuring my sight.

While that meager sip hadn't been enough to set me right, it had cleared some of the cotton from my head, and I got a handle on the hunger still screaming in my core. As Felix released his grip on my head, I glanced down to see how bad the damage was.

The Armani was a goner, absolutely unsalvageable. I wouldn't have sent this rag to my worst enemy's dry cleaner. Fluids I couldn't name, and didn't care to, had soaked through nearly every square inch of the Italian wool.

My hands, when I raised them, were half-melted candlesticks. Gobbets of liquified flesh had frozen in drips along each finger. The bits that were still where they should be were pale, thinned to the point of translucency. I could see tendons and veins beneath the waxy skin.

"Welcome back, Mr. Fry." Rebecca stood in front of my chair, wrapped by yet another knockout bit of attire. This one clung to her every curve, the dusky crimson enhancing her figure with its velvety sheen. Arranged in a graceful pile, the mass of midnight curls on her head spilled across one eye. Diamonds winked from the arc of her bare ear.

Beside her was a young man, his dazed and dreamy face barely out of his teen years. The backward ball cap on his head and the T-shirt declaring him a "Federal Boobie Inspector" marked him as a college kid on his first trip to Sin City. Rebecca clung to his side, arm looped in his, and he gazed at her with adoring eyes. One of his hands absentmindedly gripped his wrist to stanch the wound that Rebecca had used to feed me.

I hawked goo from my half-healed mouth until I could make myself understood. "All right. I'm patched up enough to talk. That's what you needed him for, right?" I grimaced at the stubborn gurgle in my throat. "Make him forget all this and cut him loose. He's donated enough for one day."

Rebecca's arms wound around the frat kid, and a stupid smile crossed his face as she pulled him close. Between his obvious lack of panic at seeing my fucked-up self, much less bleeding into my mouth, I knew she'd already put the whammy on this kid. He'd step off the Orbital Casino's tower without a second thought if she told him to.

As if to reward his service with a kiss, Rebecca cupped his face between her palms and drew him closer. With a final, gloating look for me, Rebecca bared her fangs and tore the kid's throat open.

I screamed, struggling against Felix's mitts, but I just didn't have the strength to break his grip. Or any strength at all, really.

The poor sonofabitch kept that look of dopey bliss the whole time Rebecca drained him. Before long, his strength faded and she had to hold him upright, supporting him as if he weighed no more than a child. It was only at the very end, as the last bit of color left his skin, as his lips shaded a dull blue, that panic at last surged into his eyes. His mouth gaped for a scream that never came, only the rattle of his final breath leaving.

The kid crumpled to the floor, discarded like an empty gum wrapper. Without sparing him a glace, Rebecca dabbed a silk hankie at the excess red gathered at the corner of her Kewpie doll lips. An effortless kick from one stiletto-heeled shoe sent the corpse tumbling across the floor into a carpeted recess. A conversation pit.

My conversation pit.

Confusion warred with rage as I craned my neck. Over my shoulder, behind Felix, the Las Vegas Strip blazed at me through the arc of my living room windows. Gone was the entertainment console with its massive flatscreen TV. Gone as well were my coffee table and all the framed prints and photos from the walls.

Rebecca, that bitch, had moved into my home, and she was *redecorating*!

"Not feeling so high and mighty now, are you, Eddy?"

Sure enough, the Golden Fortune's head of security and my *former* friend was grinning at me from the suite's entry. Looking like a wet dog next to Rebecca's bespoke finery, he sauntered in to join the party. With him were the Three Stooges, the hit team that had invaded my home.

As the mercenaries took up parade rest positions by the wall, Kurt paused in his saunter when he caught sight of the corpse lying in the conversation pit. An uneasy look crossed his face, and he tore his eyes away from the body.

"I kept my end of the deal, ma'am. One Eddy Fry, aka Elwood Friese, signed sealed, and delivered." He shot a glance at the three goons waiting by the wall. "I still say I could have handled the pickup without these guys. But *goddamn* the look on your face was satisfying when that wall blew open."

"Kurt, buddy, this ain't you. C'mon, brother, you know what I can do. You've seen it with your own eyes. Get me outta here, and I'll get her fishhooks out of your head, pronto."

Kurt stared at me, a chuckle rising to his lips. Gales of laughter tore through him, and he doubled over to slap his knee. Behind him, Team Leader and the other two goons joined him in having a laugh, and even Rebecca's cheek gained a dimple.

"Someone want to let me in on the joke?" I said as soon as there was a pause in the laugh-in.

Kurt sneered, "Eddy, *brother*. Rebecca didn't have to look me in the eye to get me on her team. I fucking *volunteered*."

I spent a little time, I wasn't sure how much, blinking my gummy eyes while I tried to process what Kurt had said.

"Friend, brother, buddy," Kurt went on. "You keep calling me that. But have you ever treated me like a friend?" He jabbed a finger at me. "*No!* Nearly twenty goddamn years you had me running errands, looking out for you, being your lackey. And for what?" He threw up his hands. "A regular paycheck? A 401(k)?" He shook his head. "How about this? Can you honestly tell me you never used that mind control trick on me? Not once?"

I tried, but I couldn't meet his eyes.

"That's what I fucking thought. Meanwhile, I have to watch you living like a playboy, clubbing every night, banging any chick you want. Not *once* did you ever ask if I wanted to come to the party." His laugh was a tiny thing, bitter and dry.

"You didn't listen to me, not really. It was always about you." Spittle flecked my cheeks as he pushed his face close to mine. "I kept it up, though. Did the work, watched your back. Why? Because I figured one day, you make it up to me, reward my loyalty."

Oh no.

"I figured the day would come when you'd say, 'Kurt, buddy, come on in! The water's fine!' And you'd make me like you. Young again. Powerful. Rich." His lip twisted in a snarl. "But that day *never* came."

"Ah shit. Kurt, man. I'm sorry." When I tried to lean forward, Felix slammed my back against the chair.

"Save it. Once I saw that someone connected enough to

292

wipe that face-rec database had sent operators after you, I knew your days were numbered." Kurt turned to look at Rebecca. "So I made a deal. Serve House Weir. Deliver you to her." He swallowed. "And she would bring me into the family."

Behind him, Mr. Shotgun elbowed Number Two and made a show of rolling his eyes. His partner's sides shook as he fought to keep from laughing out loud.

"Face it, Eddy. I was nothing but a servant to you. At least House Weir will reward my service."

When Kurt had said "House Weir" again, Felix's mitts clenched until my collarbones creaked.

"You shall be rewarded handsomely, my new pet," Rebecca purred. "You have indeed kept your promise in bringing me what I desire." Her head turned, and for the first time I noticed Marcus leaning against my bar as if he'd been there the whole time.

Someone needed to slap a bell on that sneaky fucker.

"You did well bringing him to me, Marcus."

"I live to serve, my lady."

"Yeah, that's great, kudos all around. But could we skip to the part where you explain why I'm still kicking? Seems like you got everything all wrapped up. Everyone downstairs thinks Elwood's in residence to give the orders. I'm persona non grata in my own home, and all the local Clandestine are on the ropes, worried sick about Big Bad Rebecca coming to blow their houses down." I scratched at an itch, stopping when the patch of skin slid loose. "Could have just let the sun finish the job once the A-Team over there blew my wall open."

"Oh, but what fun would that have been?" Rebecca glided across the floor to stand in front of me. "Seeing an enemy brought low brings me so much joy."

"Enemy? Lady, I barely know you. I mean, sure,

stealing my home was a dick move, but it's not as if you and I have history."

Crimson flooded the whites of her eyes. "Anyone standing between me and what I desire is my enemy, nothing less." Her lips curved in a smile that failed to reach her eyes. "There is also this. You have something that I desire. Something I require in order to complete my collection."

"And that is?"

"I have had majority shares and ownership of every other casino on the Las Vegas Strip transferred to my control. Every casino save one."

Again, Felix's grip tensed painfully on my shoulders.

"The Golden Fortune."

"Exactly so."

"So what?" I said. "You already have the staff dancing to your tune. I'm sure one of your patsies, probably Shifty Eyes over there"—I jerked my chin at Marcus, which got a smirk in return—"has been parading around as my alter ego Elwood in order to sign all the paychecks."

"But of course." Rebecca gave a little wave of her hand. "It would be no effort to keep that charade going indefinitely if I cared to spend the time doing so." Her eyes narrowed. "But I do *not* care to, Edward. Plus, there is the additional fact that the Golden Fortune is unique in Las Vegas."

"Damn straight." I didn't bother to keep the pride from my voice.

"It is the last casino on the Las Vegas Strip that is still independently owned. No tiresome corporate middlemen, no shareholders, no layers diluting my authority. My commands will come from my own lips, and they will be *heeded*, Mr. Fry." Her eyes bored into mine. "I do not wish to wait for my prize to wend its way through the slow, mortal legal system after the death of the current owner has been arranged."

"Ya know, for someone who's got a decent shot of living forever, you're not very patient, are you?"

"No, Edward, I am not." She flicked her fingers, and Marcus slunk over from his perch at the bar.

"The owner's shares of the Golden Fortune, where are they?" Marcus asked. "They're not here in this room or in the casino vault. As far as I've been able to determine, none of your aliases maintain accounts or deposits at any bank other than the ones listed in the casino books. The shares are nowhere to be found."

That explained Mr. Shotgun and company's little home invasion.

"Rutger's search of your safe house also failed to turn up anything other than old clothing and an old car." He made a face.

Sometimes the best way to keep a poker face is having that face melted off by the sun. "Can't help ya, chief. No clue what you're talking about."

Marcus took a step forward, halting only at a twitch of Rebecca's finger.

"We won't waste any more time attempting to squeeze blood from this stone." She smiled at her own joke as she stepped even closer. Since Rebecca was a bit of a short stack and I was stuck in the chair, this put our heads at the same level. Her lips brushed my ear as she leaned in, and when she spoke her breath was hot with the life she'd stolen.

"I will achieve everything I desire without your help, Mr. Fry. The Golden Fortune will be mine despite your recalcitrance. It only requires time. Time that, as you pointed out, I have so very much of." In the corner of my vision, fangs flashed in her smile. "And you have so very little." Her voice became a whisper; even my hearing had trouble picking up her words. I doubted anyone else here could catch what she was saying. "With few scions surviving the Gift, and so very few of the Blood remaining, it is an obscenity that one such as yourself rose as a peer. I nearly regret having to end your miserable existence, Outclan. If only you had been more receptive to my offer. You would have known *true* power in serving me. But I have met many men like you, Mr. Fry, and experience informs me that no offer nor threat would bind you to my service."

She stood, the movement abrupt, like a bad edit in a film.

"And now I have grown bored with you, Edward." She turned to Kurt. "What say you, my new pet? How shall we dispose of your erstwhile employer?"

Kurt's eyes darted between us. "Oh, really?" He rubbed his chin. "Well, it looked like he was having tons of fun when we dropped in on him this morning. Why don't we help him get that tan?"

Rebecca clapped her hands in a flutter, like a little girl. "Delightful! See that it is done. I have a city to rule." Her attention returned to me, and as she extended her hand, Marcus laid a familiar shaft of silver-tipped wood across her palm. "Good-bye, Edward. You were barely adequate entertainment."

I didn't even get a last word out before she rammed the stake through the half-healed wound in my chest. The wood might as well have been iron, white-hot from a forge, from how it seared through me. Any screams I had were stuck with me in my head as the telephone line to my body was cut. Again.

Fortunately, I didn't have to put up with the agony transfixing my rib cage for long before I blacked out.

Chapter Thirty-One

RUTGER, THE MERCENARY I'D DUBBED "TEAM LEADER," had his team lug my body bag down to the loading dock. There, they dumped me into the trunk of Kurt's old Buick. The jostling of the stake in my chest was enough to rouse me from my temporary coma.

"Mistress Weir has instructed us to allow you to finish the Outclan on your own, Mr. Sullivan." My hearing was still good enough to follow Rutger's voice through both body bag and trunk lid. "If you want, we can come along to make sure everything—"

"No, there's no need for that." Kurt's voice. "He and I have some history. I'll take care of this myself."

"This is a test, Kurt. *Everything* is a test. Mistress Weir does not tolerate failure from those in her service, no matter how tiny the error."

"No, she does not." A gruffer voice. Mr. Shotgun, I thought. "You *sure* you don't want backup? Even messed up like that, he'd be more than a match for a regular dude like you if that stake comes out. Just remember, the stake in the heart paralyzes him, but he can still see and hear everything we're saying."

"Nah. I got it covered. Stick stays in, he stays dead."
Kurt thumped his hand against the trunk lid. "Hear that,
boss? They're worried I can't handle a clueless twat like
you." Another thump. "Enjoy the ride."

———

DELIRIOUS WITH PAIN AND HUNGER, my mind drifted in
and out of consciousness. I lost track of time, lost track of
the turns and stops Kurt made on the drive. I didn't know if
he was taking me north or south, east or west.

After an indeterminate time, the ride got bumpy. *Really*
bumpy. Every time I bounced from the trunk liner, I had a
moment of hope that the impact would knock the stake out
of me. No dice. Rebecca had wedged that sucker in my ribs,
but good.

The crunch of the tires on gravel halted at last, signaling
our arrival at whatever funhouse destination Kurt had in
mind. The car swayed under my back as Kurt's weight came
up off the springs, and I followed him with my ears as his
footsteps crunched their way back to the trunk. I caught the
jingle of car keys as he swung them around his finger on
their way to his pocket. On top of that, the jagoff was
whistling.

"Mornin', sunshine." Kurt's voice came through more
clearly as he opened the trunk. His florid face swam into
view as he hauled on the body bag's zipper. "Aw, cat got
your tongue?"

*Hilarious, Kurt. If you'd shown me this side of you back
in the day, I might have hung out with you like you wanted.*
Maybe.

Resuming his whistle, he got a hand on my ankles and
dragged me over the rim of the Buick's trunk. Overhead, the

desert sky was cloudless and shading purple with the promise of dawn. My head lolled to the side as it hit the ground—Kurt was just going to drag me around, I guessed—and I got my first glimpse of where he'd taken me.

Even with my vision limited to where my head aimed, I could tell we were in a shallow wash. Dun-colored soil and gravel rose in a gentle slope dotted with the occasional bit of scrub brush. Here and there, a larger rock thrust from the parched earth, the leavings of Nevada's infrequent but torrential rains.

Once Kurt had dragged me to whatever spot he'd chosen for my last hurrah, he dropped my ankles and set about arranging me to his satisfaction. He even propped my head up on a rock so I could see down the length of my body, down the wash he'd driven up, all the way to the mountains in the distance.

How thoughtful.

He made another trip to his car, returning with an armload of what, at first glance, looked exactly like giant nails. Nails with fins near the pointed ends and a loop just under the flattened heads. Tent stakes? A mallet swung from his free hand as he swaggered back to me.

I couldn't do anything but watch from the corner of my eye as Kurt hauled my arm out straight and, pinning my hand with his foot, laid the point of the first tent stake against my forearm. The pain, as he hammered the stake through my arm and into the soil, was a distant cousin to the molten agony in my heart. It wasn't even enough to distract me from the first pale light in the east.

As he stapled each of my limbs in succession to the desert floor, the wind picked up—a herald of dawn's approach that blew a handful of grit into my eyes.

Once Kurt had me completely nailed down, he stepped

back to admire his handiwork. He stroked his chin for a moment and then snapped his fingers. Kneeling by my feet, he tugged off my Ferragamos and my socks. It surprised me that his pettiness didn't go as far as pantsing me. The SOB even snapped himself a few keepsakes with his phone.

Unbelievable.

"Well, boss," Kurt said. "I'd say it's been fun, but fuck that noise. You were an arrogant playboy piece of shit, and absolutely no one is going to miss you." He cupped a hand behind one ear. "No last words? All right then."

When he clambered back behind the wheel of his Buick, I thought at first he was going to drive off and leave me to my fate. Instead, once he'd backed the car farther down the wash, he made himself comfortable as we waited for dawn's first light.

All the hard work of dragging me across the ground and hammering the tent stakes must have tuckered the old guy out. Because it wasn't long at all before a buzz saw drone floated from the open window of the Buick.

Having to listen to that fucker snore really put the cherry on the shit sundae of the last minutes of my extended life. Stuck with Kurt's snore and my own thoughts as my only company, I found myself rehashing every mistake I'd ever made. If I was being honest with myself— hey, never too late, right?—Kurt was right. No one would miss me. Any friend or acquaintance from my old life was long dead or, in Bobby's case, just as much of a selfish ass as I was. I might have been living it up, but I'd never connected with people. I'd always kept anyone I'd spent more than five minutes with at arm's length so they wouldn't learn the truth about what I'd become. I found myself missing Darla, wondering where she'd ended up, if she'd ever found whatever it was she was looking for.

The spot Kurt had chosen sloped down toward the east,

and the way he'd laid me out was just perfect to take in the view. The false dawn was already lending a hint of contrast to the sky behind the mountains, and the stars were losing their battle of visibility. A prickle of heat rash on my exposed skin told me there was maybe a minute left until things got spicy.

As a golden halo grew around the distant peaks, the wind, which had been gusting out of the east in advance of the rising sun, began to really pick up steam. Gusting in surges now, it veered off course until it was blowing ninety degrees from its original source.

Larger bits of windborne grit rattled against the Buick, and as the tempo increased, Kurt's droning snore ended with an explosive sneeze. "What the fuck?" Rolling out of the driver's seat, he jogged over to me, hand raised to shield his eyes. Satisfied I hadn't somehow freed myself, he turned his gaze to the north. "Mother*fucker!*" Kurt spun, retreating to the steel-and-glass shelter of the Buick. The rising wind fought him for the car door until he at last pulled it shut.

I was more concerned with the fingernail clipping of the sun that had crested the mountains. My melted-and-reformed skin, already sore from the brightening sky, erupted in fiery torment as the first direct rays hit me.

Every inch of my exposed skin spat out streamers of vapor as the sunlight went to work on me. Every passing moment brought the sun higher in the sky, brought more light to bear on my body. Now that I was fully in the sun's light, my clothing was no protection. Every inch of me boiled and seethed under the assault of daylight.

Even half blinded by the dawn, I could make out Kurt's face pressed to the glass of the Buick's windshield. Instead of the gloating smile I'd expected, his face was creased with worry. He kept turning to the north, watching something outside the limited range of my sight.

My skin boiled away, baring the tendons and veins below. Streams of vanilla- and cherry-colored gloop ran into the dirt as my muscles began to come apart. There, the slime boiled away before the thirsty earth could drink it down.

Relief was an unexpected shock. As darkness closed around me, I thought, for just an instant, that'd I'd finally bought it. However, with the darkness came about five million bits of grit and gravel, all of which smacked into my raw, exposed flesh. Understanding bloomed then, and I knew what Kurt had been so riled up about.

Dust storm.

The sizzle and pop of my cooking flesh faded, replaced by the howl of the wind. The sun did its best to punch through the storm and finish the job, but every time a thread of light reached for me, the wind would surge the gap shut.

A pile of debris began to build on my windward side. I didn't know if it would be lucky or not to get buried by the freak storm. Enough dirt would protect me from the daylight, sure. But I'd still be pinned down, trapped until someone came along and dug me out. I could be stuck here for years. Decades, even.

Part of me would rather the sun finished the job.

Kurt's blocky silhouette stumbled out of the cyclone of dust swirling through the wash. He'd knotted a handkerchief over the lower half of his face to keep the dust out of his lungs, but his hacking suggested it wasn't up to the job.

"You can't even die right!" Kurt tried to bellow over the wind. "I really wanted to see those fireworks, Eddy!" He staggered to one side, battered by a series of extra-strength gusts. Head down, Kurt forced his way closer, a standard-issue Army entrenching tool gripped in his hands. Bracing his back against the wind, he flipped the spade end over and twisted the locking ring. Eyes wide despite the gale-force wind, Kurt raised his makeshift weapon over his head.

If I'd been able to close my eyes, I would have. But then I wouldn't have seen Kurt fumble the spade as a bit of debris nailed him in the eye. Or the massive shape that loomed in the swirl of dust behind him.

Chapter Thirty-Two
Then

A WILD GUST OF WIND TORE THE BACK DOOR OF Burke's Furniture from my hand, slamming it into the warehouse wall. The impact added to the hangover chorus line that was currently kicking the hell out of my brain.

"Yo, Eddy," Jake called from his seat at the card table set to the side of the working floor. "You're here earlier than usual. What gives?"

"Boss called. Got any clue what's on his mind?"

Jake shrugged and looked at the other guys sitting at the table. All of them suddenly got real interested in the cards clutched in their hands.

That's how it's gonna be, huh?

"There any coffee left?" I grumbled. If this had been a real furniture shop, there'd be a gal to take care of all the little stuff like that. But no, the boss left all that to us working stiffs.

"Eddy!" Simon yelled from the door at the top of the staircase. "Boss wants you up here five minutes ago."

I dragged a hand over my face, struggling to get that hangover under control. "Lemme grab a cup of Joe. I'll be right up."

"Now!" Simon's yell was a knife in my ears.

"Yeah, yeah, I'm coming." Time to find out what had crawled up the boss's ass and started biting.

I found Burke hunched over his desk with one of those little magnifying tubes wedged into his eye. His hand angled the green shade of his desk lamp to light the open back of a pocket watch resting on his desk blotter.

I cleared my throat. "You wanted to see me, boss?"

Burke held up one finger and tweezed at something too small for my bleary eyes to see inside the watch. I did my best not to tap my foot while waiting for him to finish whatever the hell he was doing.

The snap of the watch cover brought my attention back to Burke. He caught the eyepiece as it dropped from his eye and set it beside the watch. "Edward."

"Yeah, boss."

"Do I truly have to explain to you how poorly it reflects on me when one of my men gets blackout drunk, makes an ass of himself, and starts a fight in not one, but two, bars on Fremont Street?" The boss delivered this in his usual monotone.

"Hey, boss, look. I got carried away, absolutely. Just living it up, you know? I'll get my head out of the bottle, stay away from the bars."

"Edward, you have been 'living it up' the entire time I have known you. While I agree that the spoils of our work are to be enjoyed and that life is to be lived, there is a limit. Excesses that impact the operation or reputation of this organization are to be avoided. Wouldn't you agree?"

The stiletto heels of the Hangover Chorus Line picked up the tempo in my skull. "Sure, yeah. I got it. I'll dry out and keep it cool. Boss."

The creak of Burke's hardwood chair stabbed my

eardrums when he leaned back. He *had* to be doing that on purpose.

"The only reason that you are not a pile of bones bleaching in the desert sun right now is because you have, on average, delivered to this organization more hard value than trouble." Burke's eyebrows knit together. "However, you are perilously close to tipping that balance out of your favor. There is also the matter of your attire. I expect my men to maintain their appearance."

A flush of red at the edge of my vision joined the thudding in my brain. Rat fuck didn't know what he was talking about. So what if I liked a drink now and then? This was Las Vegas! Everyone liked to tie one on! And what was wrong with my appearance? It wasn't my fault the cleaners had shrunk my shirt. Again.

I was thinking it was high time this organization had a change of management. Hell, I'd been thinking it for a while. I was long past due to make some moves.

Plucking a pen from the black-glass-and-brass ornament at the top of his blotter, Burke dashed off a line or two on a scrap of paper. "This will be your final opportunity to recover some measure of my esteem, Edward." He slid the note across the desk. "This individual has recently purchased three businesses in our territory. These businesses had been key sources of revenue in that neighborhood. All three have subsequently ceased making their contributions without so much as a by-your-leave. Nor has this individual responded to, or made, any attempts to communicate. Needless to say, that is simply unacceptable."

"Hell yeah, boss, I got it." I swiped the note from the desk. On it was a name, Dufresne, and an address.

"To ensure that there are no misunderstandings, on either this individual's part or yours, Simon will accompany you." Burke steepled his hands on the desk in front of him.

I spun on my heel to face Simon, which was a bad idea. Everything inside my head kept going when I stopped, and it took some deep breathing to avoid puking. Simon's lip twisted as he waved two fingers by the brim of his flat cap.

I turned back to Burke, moving with more care this time. "Aw, c'mon, boss. I don't need a babysitter. I've been on the job longer than Simon's been chasing skirts."

Burke's hand brushed from his temple past his ear, even though every hair was already perfectly in place. "Come now, Edward. Like you, he will represent my interests. If one messenger is good, two will be better. Don't you agree, Simon?"

"Sure thing, boss," Simon said from beside me. He did something with his fingers, and a six-inch stiletto flashed into his hand. Light glinted from the blade as it spun around his fingers. With another gesture, the blade vanished back up his sleeve.

Simon was definitely on the list with Burke.

"Fine." I headed for the door and Simon fell into step beside me. "We'll take my car," I snapped at him.

This was gonna be a long damn day.

———

THE ELDORADO'S tires chirped against the pavement as I steered us into the lot on Bridger. Simon, prying his fingers out of their death grip on the door handle, gave me the evil eye. Fella didn't like being the passenger, that was for sure. The entire way over it had been, "Slow down, Eddy. Look out for that dog, Eddy. That was a nun, Eddy!"

Fuck him. If he didn't like the way I drove, he could take the bus next time.

I ran my hand down the Caddy's tail fin on my way to the trunk, giving the twin rocket flames of the brake lights a pat for good luck. From the stash in the trunk, I fished out a leather sap loaded with lead shot. I had my Colt slung in a shoulder holster, but I was in the mood to use some of the other toys. Making sure Simon's eyes were on the street, I grabbed my rainy day bottle from the kit.

"Don't."

I nearly bashed my head on the trunk lid as I jumped. The jagoff had snuck up on me like the rat he was. "Well, you were the one who ixnayed a stop for coffee. I gotta turn the volume down on this hangover *somehow*." I looked him right in the eye as I took a pull from the bottle. "Let's go."

———

EXECUTIVE ENTERTAINMENT ENTERPRISES occupied a ground-floor office in what looked like a converted storefront. The kind of place I'd never look at twice. Even the name didn't stand out. Do you know how many businesses in Las Vegas have "Entertainment" in their name?

I gave the door a shove and bounced off. Locked. Cupping my hands to the tinted glass gave me a view of your basic reception desk. Phone, pens, potted plant, and a slowly rotating chair.

Someone was home.

I thumped the door with the heel of my hand. "Hey! Open up!" Simon knew the drill and turned to keep an eye on the street. I gave the door another whack with the flat of my hand. "We got executives who need entertaining!" I shouted through the mail slot. Peering through the glass again, I plastered on my friendliest smile. Look, we're harmless.

"We're closed." The muffled voice came from the door at the rear of the office.

"On a nice day like this? In the middle of the week? Be

serious." I cocked my leg like I was going to kick a field goal into the door.

"Fine! Hold your horses." From the door in the back came a sight to behold. Fella was tall, but with the way he hunched over, his head wasn't any higher than mine. The cheap suit hanging from his skinny frame made him look like a kid playing in Daddy's clothes. A shock of straw-colored hair stood upright from his head and only enhanced his scarecrow look. A pair of deep-set, sly eyes flitted between me and Simon as he reached the door. "What do you want?" His voice was reedy and thin, like he wasn't getting enough air.

"Told ya. We represent some executives who require entertainment."

"I think there's been some misunderstanding," Scarecrow said. "We're not open for business yet."

"Ah shucks, that's a real pain. Well, if that's how it is, you mind if I use your phone? I gotta tell my boss it's a no-go. Save me the drive back to the office."

"Use the phone booth." Scarecrow pointed past my shoulder.

"Can't. Some kid yanked the cable out. Saw it on the walk over." I pulled a roll of bills from my pocket and made like I was going to peel one off. "Look, I'll make it worth your while. Get yourself lunch on my dime."

Scarecrow's pale tongue ran across his cracked lips as he stared at the cash. "Okay, one phone call. Make it quick."

As soon as the dead bolt *thunk*ed open, I shouldered my way in, Simon close on my heels. Once the both of us were inside, he shot the dead bolt home.

"Hey." Scarecrow's voice climbed into a whine. Close up, he had a smell, like sour milk and onions. He fidgeted with his tie, yanking at it like it was too tight.

"All right, Mac, take a seat." I pointed at a chair by the

reception desk. While Scarecrow arranged his gangly frame into it, I took a perch on the corner of the desk. Simon remained at the front door, arms crossed and blocking the view from the outside. Scarecrow's head bobbled back and forth as he tried to keep us both in view.

"Okay, here's how it is. You've gone and bought some businesses recently. Grocer, a bar, whatever. What you didn't know was that they came with..." I rubbed my chin, looking for the right word. The hangover was still clogging up the works.

"An obligation," Simon offered from the door.

I snapped my fingers. "Exactly. An obligation. See, around here our organization makes sure all you small-business types are looked after. I'm sure you can understand that, a smart fella like you." I leaned an elbow on my knee. "This service we provide isn't free though. There's a membership fee. That's where your obligation comes in. When you bought those businesses, you failed to maintain your good standing with us. You missed your dues. You can see how that puts those stores, and you, in danger."

Simon chuckled. "Why, practically anything could happen."

Scarecrow had begun to shake while I was giving him the straight dope. I'd just figured he was an even bigger coward than he looked, and then he gasped, and that turned into giggles. He slapped at his knee with a wide hand.

Laughing? The fucker was *laughing* at me?

"The fuck is so funny?" I flicked a finger against his forehead.

Scarecrow was still rocking in his chair, wiping at his eyes with his sleeve. He forced the words out through gales of laughter. "I thought... I thought you were tourists! But you're not, are you? You're the M-m-mob!" Another fit of giggles bent him over.

Simon raised an eyebrow and twirled a finger next to his head.

"A tourist, or a neighbor, I'd have to send them away. But lucky me—you're going to be *much* more fun!"

"Are you on dope or what, Mac? Been smoking them happy cigarettes?" Sniffing for the telltale scent of reefer, all I got was Scarecrow's rank BO. "Fuck this noise." I grabbed him by the lapels of his baggy suit and hauled him to his feet.

Air whooshed from his lungs when I planted my fist in his gut, but as soon as he'd pulled in his next breath, more giggles came tumbling out.

Simon took a step, but I shook my head. This was my party. "How fun is this, smart guy?" I held him at arm's length and bopped him in the snoot with a straight jab. The cartilage of his nose gave way with the second hit and blood drizzled from both nostrils. He teetered in my grip, and I gave him another wallop in the gut before turning him loose.

As Scarecrow, still giggling, prodded his nose, I snagged the handkerchief from his coat pocket and used it to clean my knuckles. He dragged his hand across his face, smearing blood over both his mouth and palm.

Before I could tell Simon it was his turn to have some fun, Scarecrow's pale tongue popped out and... he started lapping at the stain covering his hand.

"Okay, that is beyond nasty." Simon had a hand over his mouth. His eyes were wide as saucers as he watched the display.

I shook my head, forced myself to remember we had a job to do. "Okay, enough with the freak show. We can be out of your hair right now as long as you cough up what you owe."

Scarecrow's tongue vanished into his mouth, and a

nasty smile shone through the red on his face. A damp smear trailed his hand as he wiped it against the leg of his trousers. "Oh, is that what this is about? Money? We have plenty of money." His reedy voice was getting on my last nerve. "I'd have to get it from the safe..."

Safe? I liked the sound of that. "Fine. Why don't you open up that safe for us, and we'll let you know how much you owe. Then we can get out of your hair."

"It's in the back."

Chapter Thirty-Three

I SHOVED SCARECROW AHEAD OF ME AS WE TROUPED into the rear of the triple-E offices. Instead of finding the usual bits and bobs—boss's office, storage, the can—there was only a narrow hallway extending at a right angle to the back door. The door from the front room entered the hall at its left end. It stretched to the right before ending in two doors, one of which would lead us to the *real* back room of this joint.

To the safe.

The weird zigzag was getting my nerves riled up, so I pushed past Scarecrow to take point. Behind me, Simon clamped his hand on the guy's shoulder to keep him from trying anything funny.

The first door led to a tiny bathroom. A toilet, a sink, and a narrow shower stall were the only things showing in the light of the naked lightbulb dangling from the ceiling. The remaining door opened on a rectangle of darkness. I had no clue what kind of business Executive Entertainment Enterprises actually did, but I it looked like they needed a big darkroom to do it with. "Simon, you got a light?"

He shook his head. "Quit smoking last month."

"Those things'll kill you," Scarecrow singsonged.

"Shut it." A pool of light extended from the doorway a short distance into the room. I couldn't make out any details of whatever lay in that darkness, so I ran my hand along the wall. No light switch on either side.

"Charles. You know quite well that customers are not allowed in the back."

The voice that came floating out of the darkness was layered in a thick, nearly musical accent. I flinched as dozens of icy little feet ran up the back of my neck. What kind of freak sits around in a pitch-black room?

"My apologies, Mas... Monsieur Dufresne. These gentlemen claim we owe their social club some sort of fee." The giggles had stopped, and now his voice was hushed, almost reverent.

"Indeed."

I said, "All right, Mac. Cut the comedy, or you'll get the same lesson we gave your buddy here."

"Is that so?"

I blinked in the sudden brightness as the lights snapped on. Hand raised against the glare, I searched for the owner of the voice.

The room filled the rest of the building's space, all the way to the rear. A swatch of fresh brickwork sat where the back door should have been, meaning the only way in or out was through the door behind me. The room was half filled with a collection of antique luggage, steamer trunks, and other out-of-date travel gear. One wall held a row of cabinets—wardrobes maybe? Smack in the center of the room sat an enormous, elegant, four-poster bed. The source of the room's light hung above the bed and was, of all things, a crystal chandelier.

Beside the bed, a hand resting on one of the pillars, was a man of medium height. He was thin, but not as thin as

Charles the Scarecrow. Light from the chandelier gleamed from golden hair that swept from his brow to the back of his head, where the edge of a sapphire ribbon peeked.

He was wearing the fanciest suit I'd ever seen. I couldn't even begin to guess where you'd get that sort of thing in this town. Like Charles, his complexion was pale. But unlike Charles, whose skin was sickly and pallid, this fella coulda been carved out of a block of marble. It was difficult to pin down his age. His sculpted features were free of any visible line. He could have been anything from twenty-five to fifty.

I took a step forward. "Like I was telling Charley here..."

"*Oui*, I have heard every word. You are here to extort money from honest business owners and shopkeepers under threat of violence and vandalism." When this guy, this Frenchie, spoke, only his mouth moved. The rest of him stayed ramrod straight and stiff, much like the statue he resembled. His too-large eyes didn't blink once.

"Then why didn't you come out to say bon-jer while we were talking with your friend?" I cuffed the back of Charley's head; he didn't make a sound. "The truth is, both of you are in for a world of hurt if one of ya don't cough up the lettuce."

"We're not so bad, long as you stay on our good side," Simon chimed in. "Couple Gs would cover what you owe, no problem."

I produced the sap from a pocket. "Or you can watch while we teach your pal a more convincing lesson. Before we teach you one."

One eyebrow, so blond it was nearly invisible against the alabaster skin, drifted upward. His head tilted ever so slightly.

"So, Charley, I don't see this safe you were talking about." I turned to Scarecrow. "Help a fella out, why don't

315

you? Or we can do an experiment. See if you can walk without knees. *Capiche?*" I slapped the blackjack against my palm.

"Charles," the Frog said. "*Tu as ma permission, tu peux mettre fin à ta comédie.*"

"Yes, Master." Charley's voice took on an even more manic edge.

Screw *this*.

Aiming to knock the attitude out of the Frog's lackey, I took a swing at Charley's head with the blackjack. But instead of a satisfying *thunk,* a hand clamped to my wrist before I made contact. Stronger than I'd given him credit for, Charley bent my wrist. The sap clattered to the floor, and he kicked it away.

His ragged fingernails dug furrows in my skin as I wrenched myself free and skipped back a few steps. I actually did a double take as Charley stopped hunching over, standing straight for the first time.

The sonofabitch was *tall*. Six-five, six-six at least.

Charley knew how to fight, too. He ducked and weaved around every jab, every swing I took at him. Dancing like Jersey Joe, he circled around me, and before I knew it fireworks were going off behind my eyes. He'd landed a solid jab, right through my defense, to my cheekbone. He hadn't broken anything, but he'd rung my bell pretty good.

Out of the corner of my eye, I saw the Frog's lip twitch in a tiny smile.

Simon, who'd been taking his sweet time, finally got his head in the game. The next time Charley danced away from my punch, Simon slipped an arm around his neck. Before Charley could react, Simon had him wound up with a solid headlock.

"Oh, you want to play too, Mr. Gangster?" Charley's voice rang out in a childish singsong. "Okay, let's play."

Charley's feet shuffled around, his hands sliding along Simon's arm.

I'd hardly blinked before Simon was over Charley's shoulder, in the air and coming at me. Unable to dodge, I was slammed into the wall by his flight, and the two of us landed in a heap.

"Sonofabitch knows karate!" I said, dazed.

"*I can see that!*"

Charley's giggle bounced around the room. Slow claps sounded from beside the bed as the Frenchman applauded his employee's performance.

Back on our feet, Simon and I spread out to flank Charley. Instead of waiting for us to come to him, Charley dashed at Simon. Weaving around his guard, Charley landed a rapid-fire one-two-three flurry of blows. Simon staggered back, hands at his throat.

While Charley was attacking Simon, I went after Charley, hoping to get a few shots of my own in. Before I'd closed the range, Charley spun on his heel, and I got a Florsheim to the jaw.

Seeing stars, wobbling but not down, I threw a feint with my right. When his block came up, I lunged in with a head-butt. His nose, already broken, pulped against my forehead, and he fell back squealing. Blood gushed from his ruined schnoz, and both hands came up to stanch the flow.

As Simon staggered over to me, Charley bellowed. Blood and snot spraying from his face, he threw his arms wide and charged. I brought my dukes up, but Simon stepped into the charge. His hands, held low at his sides, flexed.

Charley might have had us both beat in the height department, but Simon outweighed him by at good sixty pounds. Still, Charley caught him up in a bear hug and hauled him off the ground as if he weighed no more than a child.

Charley froze then, his eyes stretching wide. Simon slipped from Charley's limp arms and staggered away from the madman. Blood bloomed through the fabric of Charley's shirt, leaking around the hilt of the stiletto Simon had planted there. His bulging eyes stared at Simon while his jaw flexed in silence. He swayed as he turned to face the Frog. "Master?" He sounded for all the world like a frightened child.

He managed a single step toward his master before collapsing in a heap.

"Go, Simon!" I pumped my fist.

Simon tossed his remaining knife from hand to hand. He only wobbled a bit as he took up a knife-fighting stance.

"*Pitié.*" The Frog, his hand held at arm's length, examined his nails. "I had such high hopes for Charles. No matter. Servants are easy to acquire."

"About the only thing you're gonna acquire now is a hole out in the fuckin' desert," Simon said with a growl.

Rolling his shoulders in an odd, liquid motion, the Frog beckoned to Simon with one hand. "As you wish, *Messieurs.* Time to die."

"Fuck that." I tugged my Colt free of its holster. My head was still ringing from Charley's bullshit, so I missed the headshot. The other two slammed home center of mass.

The Frog didn't budge an inch. There were two fresh holes in his shirt, but no blood leaked from them. "*Impoli.*" He brushed a hand across his ruined shirt.

"Got this. A vest won't stop a blade." Simon tossed his Smatchet knife, switching his underhand grip for an overhand. He took one step forward.

With a sharp *pop,* Simon's head vanished from his neck.

A faint puff of air brushed my face as blood geysered from the stump of his neck.

The room *tilted,* and Okinawan mud was sucking at my boots. Around me, my squad, my friends, were going down in droves. Japanese artillery raised gouts of mud as it sent us running for cover. *Goddammit, where was that counter-battery fire?* The man in front of me, a kid really, went down screaming. Desperately clutching the stumps of his legs, both severed at the knees, he tried to stem the flood gushing from the wounds. The taste of hot iron and pennies flooded my mouth.

Simon's head thumped to the floor, and I snapped back to the present. The knife falling from his limp hand clattered away. The flow from the severed neck slowed as his knees buckled. I watched as Simon's body landed beside Charley's. Nearby, Simon's head had stopped rolling, the faced aimed at me. There was no pain in his expression, only surprise.

Me too, bud. Me too.

During all of this, the Frog hadn't moved a muscle. Only the swirl of his coat settling betrayed any connection with what had happened to Simon's head. A tiny smirk twitched his lips. "I am afraid it is only you and your *petite association* who will be learning the lessons today."

"Oh, fuck you." I braced the Colt and emptied the rest of the magazine into him. Two more bloodless holes popped into existence on the front of his shirt. The rest of my shots, save one, went wide. The final round tore into the side of the Frenchman's graceful neck. I dropped the magazine and patted my pockets for the next.

Oh. Right. I'd gone for the bourbon in the trunk instead of loading my pockets. *Stupid, Eddy.*

I heard that *pop* again, and in the same instant, the Frog was in my face. He'd crossed the room in less time than it took me to blink. I raised my gun, even though it was empty, and he batted it from my hand with a force that broke a bone in my forearm, the wet snap reaching my ears before I felt the pain.

While I was gasping, one of his hands grabbed my shirt, and my feet left the ground. I dangled at arm's length, held aloft as if I weighed less than a sheet of paper.

Cupping my cheek with his free hand, the Frenchman looked nearly sympathetic. *"Ne vous sentez pas aussi mal, monsieur. Vous n'aviez tout simplement aucune idée de ce à quoi vous aviez affaire."* He turned his head to present the wound I'd made.

The .45 slug had torn through the curve of his neck, leaving a trench that would have bled anyone else out in a matter of seconds. This wound, however, only leaked a trickle of thin, gray-pink fluid. The exposed flesh of his neck was the gray of dead meat. The trickle of fluids trailed off and, as I stared in horror, the edges of the wound twitched. Like a candle melting in reverse, the trench in the Frog's neck filled in. When the skin sealed itself closed, it was smooth, featureless. As if I'd never shot him.

I was going to die.

"Fear not, you shall not go to waste."

I shivered as his icy hand caressed my cheek.

Shit, I was gonna die weird.

The hand on my cheek slid around to grip the back of my neck as he pulled me into a close embrace. I couldn't break that grip no matter how much I struggled. I threw everything I had, but it was like fighting a brick wall.

The hand on my neck forced my head hard over to one side. His face was close and he leaned in, as if to kiss me. Instead, his mouth yawned wide, filling my vision. Two of his top teeth, the canines, moved. Flowing in the same liquid manner as the flesh of his neck, those teeth grew until they were three times their original length. His jaw flexed, the joints crackling in my ear, to clear the length of those razor points. The whole time he was showing me the trick with his teeth, he hadn't taken a breath. He wasn't breathing at all.

He struck, fast as a viper. Twin lines of fire bloomed along the side of my throat as those fangs opened me from front to back. The needle points, red hot to my exposed flesh, sank in as he closed his mouth around the wound.

The room spun around me as he began to drink. He gulped down my blood in big swallows, the way I'd down a beer on a hot summer day. I shoved at his arms, his chest, but the strength was draining out of me. Draining away with the blood being pulled from the hole in my neck. Tiny sounds of pleasure bubbled up from *his* throat as he drank.

Scarlet rippled around the edges of my vision before a worrying haze pushed it away. Too late. The fire of anger wasn't enough to burn away the growing shock. *Come the fuck on,* I thought, *this is not how Momma Fry raised her boy.* Taken out by a goddamn Hollywood vampire. A *French* vampire!

I might check out in the next few seconds, but I'd be *damned* if I was going to go without leaving an impression.

Dufresne's slender neck was right in front of my eyes, so I did the only thing I could think of. The only thing I could do with my remaining strength. I sank *my* teeth into *his* fucking throat.

Dufresne pushed me away, fangs tearing through my skin as he roared. I held on, gnawing at him with my blunt little teeth like he was a baby back rib. There was a sound like ripping cabbage, and my teeth broke through his skin. His thin blood tasted of sewage and bile. I fought the urge to gag, biting down with the last of my strength. As my teeth sank into his neck muscle, he roared again. The scream was so loud that my eardrum popped from the over-pressure.

He shoved, tearing me from his neck, and a chunk of him went with me. I landed hard, right next to Simon's headless body. My noggin bounced off the floor and stars danced across my sight. I wasn't sure, but I think I'd swallowed some Frog.

"*Comment osez-vous, espèce d'idiot!*" Dufresne screamed.

My head still spinning from its collision with the floorboards—or maybe the blood loss, it was hard to tell at this point—I couldn't think of a comeback.

Dufresne stomped toward me as my hands slid across the carpet, grasping. He landed a kick in my side that snapped a rib and sent me sliding. A wet crunch followed the second kick, and my legs went numb. I slapped my hand against the floor, sending desperate prayers to anyone who might be listening that I'd remembered correctly.

Pale hands twisted in my coat as Dufresne hauled me into the air before him. My ribs creaked in his grip as the blood drizzling from my neck pattered to the floor below my dangling feet.

Dufresne's face filled my vision, his eyes ebony pits in twin seas of blood. His jaw stretched even wider, a shark's mouth of saw-edged points yawning wide. He really wanted me to see it coming this time because this lunge at my throat was slower than the first.

Numb below the waist, I wouldn't have been able to pull this off if it weren't for his grip on my chest to give me leverage. I swung my arm around, sweeping the knife that Simon had dropped in an arc that intersected Dufresne's neck.

I must have cut something he needed to swallow with, because those shark teeth halted an inch from my throat. As with the earlier wound, the gash I'd made began to knit up before my eyes. It would be gone in seconds.

Fingers cold, I knew this was my last chance before the knife slipped from my hand. I used everything I had left in the tank to swing the blade at his neck once more, this time aiming for his spine.

The double-sided point of the blade slammed through the vampire's neck and, with more luck than I'd ever deserved, carved straight into the joint between his vertebrae. The blade continued, grating against cartilage and bone, until the point popped clear of the skin on the far side of his neck.

I sent a small prayer of thanks to Simon for keeping his blades sharp.

Dufresne froze mid-lunge, his jagged teeth hovering over my neck. Tremors shot through him, and my ribs shattered as his hands spasmed. I slipped from his grasp, and it took all my will to maintain my grip on the Smatchet knife buried in his spine. My weight dragged the blade through his neck as I fell, opening it from the spinal cord forward.

I lost the knife, the handle skittering from nerveless fingers as I hit the floor. My head was heavy, but even with half of my neck open to the air, I kept Dufresne in view. I was terrified that the gap in his throat would close up like his other wounds.

Dufresne, his arms poised in the air as if he were still holding me aloft, took a step forward. The movement caused his head to fall to the side, resting for a moment on his shoulder before some remaining fragment of bone in his spine gave way with a brittle snap.

His shoulders slumped, arms falling to his sides. As his head lolled on the strip of flesh connecting it to his neck, he pitched over backward. When he struck the ground, that fragile strip parted and his head tumbled across the floor. I lost sight of it as it rolled under his fancy fucking bed.

I relaxed, sagging onto my back to stare at the stains on the plastered ceiling. I wondered if someone had heard the shots. Someone had to have heard his screams, at least. Help had to be on the way, right? I tried to call out, to yell for help, just in case, but the best I could manage was a gurgle.

Oh. Right. Massive hole in my throat where the vampire had bitten me. The light from the chandelier seemed a lot dimmer than when we'd arrived. At least my ribs weren't hurting so much now. I thought maybe I should apply some pressure to my neck, but between the broken ribs and my legs not working, I just didn't have the what it took to raise my hand. Maybe if I rested for a bit, I'd get my strength back. Then I could hold it together, at least until help arrived.

Yeah. Just gonna close my eyes for a minute.

Chapter Thirty-Four
Now

KURT SQUINCHED HIS EYES AGAINST THE TORRENT OF wind-borne grit and shifted his grip on the spade. Planting a foot to either side of my half-melted torso, he raised his arms high with the clear intent to drive the blade of the entrenching tool directly through my neck.

Lights out, Eddy.

Behind him, the towering shadow resolved itself into the familiar wedge-head of Bruce's hybrid shark form. Wide swaths of silvery duct tape had been applied to each side of the wide neck, protecting his gills from the dust storm.

Eyes rolled back until only white remained, Bruce swung his head from side to side. Some sort of shark sixth sense? I wasn't up to date on my great white anatomy lessons enough to know *how* Bruce was doing it, but he zeroed right in on Kurt.

Closing the gap between them in three long strides, he backhanded Kurt just as my former employee swung the spade for the coup de grace. Kurt went flying off past the edge of my fixed line of sight.

I'd never been happier to see a shark.

*Okay, big guy, just yank out these stakes and get me...
where the* fuck *are you going?*

Instead of freeing me, Bruce had tacked off course, heading after Kurt. Ah, crap. Overly focused on the hunt, he'd said about his shark-self, back when we'd first talked. Kurt's panicked, "No-no-no-no-no," reached my ears as Bruce vanished.

Fan-tastic.

"*Bruce!*"

Distantly, over the wind, I caught Xenia's voice. Keeping her T-shirt tugged up over her nose and mouth as a makeshift mask, the young magician stumbled out of the storm's fury. She took a few steps in pursuit of Bruce, then, raising her arm as if she was checking the time, she turned toward the wash where I lay.

Arm raised to shield her eyes, leaning into the wind, Xenia made her way closer. It was obvious when she finally caught sight of yours truly. Turning to one side, she dragged the neck of her shirt away from her face and hoorked her cookies into the dirt.

I knew I didn't look so hot at the moment, but still...

"Ugh, Eddy. You're more gloop than man," Xenia, said, wiping her mouth with the edge of her shirt as she dropped to her knees by my side.

Overhead, the dust storm seemed to hesitate, pause in its blowing, as if it had been waiting for this moment. The gusts resumed, but the enthusiasm was gone.

Xenia had better work fast. I didn't think we had much time.

Gunshots cracked out of the storm, followed by Bruce's furious roar. "Big mistake, dude." Xenia's head came up. "Bruce! Wait!" she called out. "Damn it. I could've used a hand here." She examined the stakes nailing me to the desert floor.

With a nod to herself, she wrapped her hands around the bit of steel protruding from my left wrist. Then she planted her feet and heaved.

No dice. It didn't budge so much as an inch. Kurt had planted the damn things in but good.

Cursing under her breath, she half crawled around to my leg and had a go at that stake. A flare of distant pain accompanied the movement as the earth, possibly loosened by the runoff from my melting flesh, gave way and the stake tore loose. With a cry, Xenia tumbled over backward as she lost her grip.

While she threaded the rod out of the hole in my leg, I couldn't help but notice the dust cloud overhead had begun to thin. Patches, here and there, shone brighter as the sun did its best to punch through and finish the job.

The remaining stakes, like the one in my left arm, were stuck fast. No matter how she'd heaved and ho'd, Xenia was unable to budge them. Frustration to match mine etched itself on her dust-stained face as she strained to dislodge even one more.

If she would just pull the stake from my heart, I'd tell her to get a rock and bash me to jelly where the tent stakes were. I'd heal from that once I got something to eat. Maybe.

Instead, Xenia sat back on her heels and raised her hands. Magic? Shaking her head, she moved her hands into a different pose. Again, she didn't seem able to muster whatever she needed in order to whisk the steel out of the ground.

"Okay, boss, you're gonna have to help me rescue you," she muttered. Without a warning, she yanked the stake from my heart.

Pain, all the agony that had been held at bay by the circuit breaker of the wood in my heart, slammed through me, and my back arched off the ground as my muscles spasmed out of my control. My eyes clenched shut and the heel of my free leg hammered against the ground, a drum-beat of pain.

I clamped down on the sensation, on all the signals my ruined body was sending about the damage the sun had done. Later. There was no *time* for this. No time to wallow in this misery.

At last, I was able to open my eyes, clouded as they were, and rolled my head toward Xenia. The goo in my throat meant the best I could force out was a congested bubble of greeting.

"Hey yourself." Twin tracks of moisture cut through the dust on her cheeks. "Eddy, I can't get these things out of you by myself. I'm going to need your help. You got any of that super strength left?"

I rolled my eyes. If there was one thing I had plenty of, it was muscle. The sun hadn't had a chance to get all of me, not yet.

Planting my head against the ground, using the stakes through my left arm and right leg as leverage, I gave my right arm the old heave-ho. The top of the stake had a wide loop of steel welded on, a cable tie-on, that Kurt had hammered down right over one of the bones of my forearm. Try as I might, I could not get enough clearance to slip free of the blockage. Same for my left arm and my pinned leg.

Maybe I'd spoken too soon.

Collapsing, the strength all but drained from me, I shook my head. "Glrmp," was the best I could manage.

"Shit." Glancing at the thinning dust clouds overhead, she began to dig in her pockets. "I didn't want to do this. I mean, I *really* didn't want to do this." She rocked back on her heels. "But I can't get you loose, and our muscle has run off in hot pursuit."

Wait, did she mean... Oh *hell* no. "Nnug!" I forced out,

which Xenia ignored. Flicking open the tiny penknife she'd produced, she made a short slice into the meat at the base of her thumb. The wind whipped away the spice of her blood's scent, but not quickly enough to keep my mouth from watering.

Turning my head away, I clenched my lips at tightly as I could. I would *not* let her do this.

"You told me you didn't kill when feeding, so I'm trusting that you know when to stop, Eddy." Reaching around my head, she jammed her hand against my lips.

I *tried*, oh how I tried to keep those first drops out of my mouth.

Fire bloomed across the ruin of my tongue and... I couldn't stop myself any longer. Every fiber of my ruined body screamed at me to *drink, goddammit, drink!*

I drank.

I knew that if I wasn't careful, if I lost control for an instant, I'd draw on the tiny wound. Pull the blood out of her veins faster than her heart could pump it. She'd be dead in less than a minute.

So I fought each sip, resisted every swallow. Struggled to only take the minimum, until I could push her away.

The fire of Xenia's blood raged in my stomach, like the opposite of heartburn. It spread out, diffusing into my body, and everywhere it went, my flesh began to put itself right.

A gasp from Xenia had my eyes, now clear of their sun-baked cataracts, popping open. A flush of color had crept up her neck and into her cheeks. Her lips twisted. and I realized that she was... ah, *feeling* things. I'd been hoping that I needed to get my fangs under someone's skin for that particular effect to kick in, but it seemed just feeding was all it took.

Enough was enough. I twisted my head around to disengage from Xenia's hand. But no matter how I turned my head, she maintained the contact. Eyes clenched shut, she went so far as to lean her weight into me, jamming the palm of her hand into my mouth. Her blood continued to flow steadily over my tongue while my traitor body drank.

A flicker at the edge of my vision caught my attention. Something with pearlescent scales and long teeth. Fangs, but not a vampire's, something more... reptilian. I shivered as a forked tongue slid up my—her neck. Another image, a nightmare in black marble shot through with flecks of silver, writhed out of Xenia's memories into my mind. An older woman in a tie-dye kaftan, her face alight with a warm smile.

Shit. I shoved Xenia's memories away. We were running out of time. Xenia was running out of blood.

Twisting my shoulders, I *heaved* on my arm, the one Xenia wasn't kneeling on, and was rewarded with the crunch of earth giving way. Right arm free, careful of the steel bar still impaling my flesh, I took hold of Xenia's wrist. Just as I pulled her hand away, breaking contact, numbers flickered through my consciousness. The concierge—Shizue's phone number? *Go, Xenia.*

I shoved on her arm, sending Xenia tumbling into the dirt. Her lip, too pale for my comfort, pushed out into a pout.

Freeing myself from the rest of the stakes was even easier than the first as the blood she'd fed me fueled my healing body. By the time I staggered to my feet, most of my skin had grown back. Or felt like it had, at any rate.

The wind, which had lost its rattling howl at some point —I'd been distracted by the blood in my mouth—stopped entirely. The desert around us began to brighten as the dust clouds overhead thinned.

Xenia blinked up at me. "Eddy? When did you get here?"

"That's enough blood donations for you, lady." My newly regrown skin had begun to sting. I hated for all of this to go to waste, but unless there was shelter nearby, I was soggy toast. And from the look of her, Xenia needed medical attention soon or she'd be joining me.

Kurt's car, wheels half buried in grit, was waiting by the edge of the wash he'd staked me out in. Unfortunately, he'd taken the keys with him when he'd run off into the desert, Bruce hot on his heels.

As more of the swirling dust precipitated from the air, I caught sight of a familiar finned silhouette beyond Kurt's car. Seems my consultant had helped herself. Not that I was in any position to object. Hell, the old beauty was a sight for sore eyes.

Steam hissed from my skin as the thinning dust let more of the sun's fury through. There was no more time.

Crouching, I scooped Xenia up in my arms. "Hold on to your butt, X." I leaned her head against my shoulder and found a keyring, my keyring, in the first pocket I checked. "Been a while since I've done this."

Making sure to support Xenia's neck, I put the pedal down. For the first time in ages, I moved at the top speed my condition made me capable of. With a *pop* of displaced air, I crossed the distance to the Eldorado in one of Xenia's heartbeats—I was trying, and failing, not to worry about how weak they sounded—and set her in the passenger seat. As the sun fully broke through, I flung myself into the Caddy's spacious trunk and slammed the lid shut.

The only thing missing was an umpire to yell, "*Safe!*"

———

EVEN THOUGH IT seemed like a small eternity of listening to Xenia's heart laboring to beat, it wasn't long before I made out the *crunch-crunch-crunch* of heavy footsteps approaching.

"Fry? Zee?" Bruce's basso profundo voice called out.

"Brucie!" Xenia's quizzical voice was followed by a fit of giggles. Still loopy from her donation, she was in no condition to drive.

"Oh no." Bruce's voice had already shifted to the higher pitch of his human form. Moments later, the V-8 engine roared to life. "What happened to Mr. Fry?" Bruce asked from the driver's seat.

I gave the metal above me a couple thumps. "In the trunk, Shark Week!"

As the Caddy began to make its way toward the highway, I let the pressure of the daytime hours put me under.

Chapter Thirty-Five
Then

IT WAS A SOLID MINUTE BEFORE REALIZATION STRUCK. I was awake! The total darkness hadn't helped; there was no difference in having my eyes open or closed. When I brought my hand up to wave it in front of my face, I found that the source of the darkness was a layer of something black and yielding above me. I pushed it away from my face, but it would only move so far before coming up short.

Wait.

There wasn't any hole in the heavy fabric or any light source I could make out, yet I could clearly see my hand, and when I looked for it, the zipper running down the length of the fabric above me. How the hell was I seeing *anything*?

When I let my head sag back to the surface I lay on, it gave off a hollow *bong*. A metal table? Realization slammed into me. I knew what this was.

I was in a body bag.

Everything came crashing back to me then. The Scarecrow, Charles. The gout of blood as Simon's head flew from his shoulders. Dufresne's teeth in my throat. Killing Dufresne.

Dying.

I had died.

Then how the hopscotching *fuck* was I awake? I fumbled at the zipper. I wanted out of this fucking bag. The pull tab was on the outside, though. Of course. How many dead men had ever needed to unzip their own body bags? Clutching at the rubberized fabric just pushed it away. The material was too thick, the surface too slippery for my fingers to get a grip on it.

Panic got its hooks into me. The table I lay on rumbled like a drum as my heels hammered against the sheet metal and I punched and kicked at my flexible prison.

Sudden light flooded the bag. Long rents opened in the fabric, and I thrust an arm through to the outside. Able to find a grip at last, I peeled myself out of that goddamn bag.

As my head cleared the fabric, I winced, throwing an arm across my face. Everything was too damned bright. What I could see of the room appeared washed out, like an overexposed photo. I tried to rub my eyes, but something jabbed my face. Blinking in the too-bright light, I examined my hand.

Daggers of white bone, each nearly two inches long, had burst from the ends of my fingers. The split skin at the base of the claws was gray, dead. Before I'd had more than a brief look at them, the claws shrank. Like icicles in the Nevada sun, the blades melted back beneath my skin, which flowed together as if I'd never had claws in the first place.

I'd think about that later.

Above me was a bland institutional ceiling. Only half of the fluorescent fixtures were lit, yet the room was brighter than the noonday sun.

That wasn't all my tender eyes were seeing. Bands of crystalline colors unlike any I'd ever seen filled the air above me, flowed in and around each other in ribbons of light.

334

Turning my head to follow one such streamer—what color was that, silver-orange?—I found that the light show extended through the entire room.

Kicking off the shreds of the body bag, I swung my legs around and sat up. I peered through the distraction of the light ribbons, which were getting easier to ignore as time went on, and took stock of my whereabouts.

I was in a morgue. Sitting on a gurney.

My gurney was one of a quartet, each with its own occupied body bag. The one beside me had a paper tag stuck to it with a bit of tape. JOHN DOE #1 scrawled on the line for a name.

Hand trembling only a little, I jabbed the shape inside the bag.

Nothing. No movement.

When I ran the zipper down, a wizened face, the skin thin as parchment and flaking from the bone underneath, came into view. Only when I saw the ragged gap in the neck, where the coroner had placed the head more or less where it was supposed to sit above the body, clued me in to the face that I was looking at Dufresne's body. Odds were good that the other two bags contained the remains of Charles and Simon.

The moment I slid from the gurney, my trousers hit the floor and I nearly face-planted into the crumbling corpse. I hopped on one foot until I got myself untangled enough to hoist my belt up to where it should be. The waistband had been, if anything, snug when I'd put them on this morning. Now there was room for two of me in here. Cinching the belt as tight as it would go, I examined the rest of my clothing. The same went for my coat and shirt. Everything hung from me like a tent. Since when did morgues swap out their customer's clothes?

No. Dried blood crusted the cloth everywhere I looked.

335

This was the suit I'd put on when I'd gone to see Burke this morning, the suit I had... died in.

Seemingly on their own, my hands flew to my neck, and I felt around the side where Dufresne had torn into me, fingers probing for the wound. Gone. The skin was smooth and unbroken. Taut, without even a hint of stubble. The extra bit of chin I'd been trying not to think about when I shaved seemed to be gone as well.

I needed a mirror.

A glance around the morgue revealed tables, sinks, cabinets, a wall of refrigerator-style square doors. No mirrors.

Belt cinched in one hand, I squeezed through the cluster of gurneys and made my way over to the double doors that, presumably, led to the rest of the facility. A peek through the scuffed plastic window in one door revealed an empty hallway, several closed doors, and a second hallway intersection about twenty feet away.

I took a final glance back at the cluster of bodies waiting for their ultimate destinations. *Sorry, Simon. You might have been a dick, but you deserved to go out better than that.*

The light in the corridor was even brighter than the morgue had been, and I squinted in the overload. No moisture came to offer relief to my burning eyes, though.

I needed a men's room. Those had mirrors, right?

Footsteps echoed from the cross-corridor ahead. A single set; just a poor sap stuck with the night shift, no doubt. I pressed my back to the wall. With any luck, the night watchman, or whoever, would go right on by without turning their head.

No dice. A youngish fellow in a white lab coat, eyes glued to the clipboard in his hand, swung around the corner. Clearly he hadn't been expecting to run into anyone else at this hour, much less someone in a baggy, blood-covered suit, which made his scream completely under-standable.

I held up my free hand while I tried to look as harmless as possible. "Woah there, buddy. Thereth been thome kind of mithtake. Thatth all."

The fuck was wrong with my teeth?

The orderly screamed again and threw his clipboard at my face. Tripping over his own feet, he fell on his ass. While he scrabbled backward across the linoleum, I poked a finger into my mouth.

My fingertip stopped when it encountered something sharp. Probing around to the other side revealed a second needle point.

"Aw thit." I'd caught a bad case of vampire from that fucking Frenchman, hadn't I? Just wonderful. Fine. I'd deal with *that* later. Right now, there was a guy wetting his pants that I had to attend to.

"Letth— Let's try this again, okay?" It was getting easier to talk around the extra helping of teeth. "Look, I'm not gonna hurt you. To tell the truth, I'm just as confused as you are about all of this. Honestly, I have no fucking clue what's going... Hey, are you listening to me?"

Too busy hyperventilating to focus, the orderly had continued to scooch his rear across the floor until he'd backed into a wall. His eyes, showing white all around, never left my face.

I snapped my fingers. "Hey!" His eyes flicked from the fangs in my mouth to my eyes. Something in my head surged forward, sliding along our linked gaze, until it connected with the man cowering before me. The sensation was greasy, unpleasant.

The orderly's struggle to get away from me slowed, then stopped. He sat, back against the wall, face placid. Best of all, he stopped screaming.

"Hey, fella. You hear me?"

"Yes." The orderly's voice was calm.

"Great." Now what? I needed a plan. "You got a change of clothes around here? A locker room or something?"

———

FIFTEEN MINUTES LATER, having swapped my bloody mess for Alton's—the orderly—street clothes, I slipped out of the city morgue's fire exit. I'd even retrieved my wallet and keys when Alton, who was feeling *very* cooperative, led me to where the coroner kept their customers' personal effects.

The ease with which I'd made the poor bastard obey me didn't sit right. A day ago, I would have gone on a bender of self-indulgence. Now, it seemed off. Nagged at me. Every one of my nerves was raw, oversensitive. Maybe that was all there was to it.

The plan was to get my car back. As long as it hadn't been towed, I was confident I could handle a couple of parking tickets.

The sight of the sky unfolding over my head stopped me in my tracks. Last night, the sky had been nothing more than a handful of glitter tossed on black velvet. Now, though...

There was no end to it. Leaning my head back to take it all in, I got lost in the sea of rich purples and blues that receded from my eyes to infinity. Hung in that endless abyss, the stars were glittering gemstones in such an endless variety of sizes and colors that my head spun with it. Filaments of vapor threaded their way between them, adding layers of texture to the void.

I had to force my eyes away from the enthralling vision above me before I was lost to it forever.

The city around me, lit only by a handful of streetlights and the stars, was noon-bright to my new eyes. Even the shadows held no secrets back from my vision.

According to the clock in the morgue's locker room, it was nearly one in the morning. Everything I knew about vampires I'd learned in a matinee, and all of it suggested that daylight was a bad idea. I had time, but once I'd retrieved the Caddy, shelter would be my number one priority.

I made it maybe two blocks before my stomach started ringing the dinner bell. More accurately, my guts were howling. A monster cramp doubled me over, and I stumbled against the wall of the storefront beside me. Another contraction set my head spinning. The hunger clawing at my guts had skipped past "pangs" and straight to "rabid tiger."

Footsteps pattered to a halt nearby. "Hey, buddy, everything okay?" The footsteps, hesitant, brought the source of the voice closer. "You're not looking too good, man. Hah, yeah. This town'll do that to you."

I fell to my knees as another spasm wracked my core. Without the strength to even lift my head, I watched as the sidewalk blurred and wavered. My new eyes were already failing me.

It seemed like my new lease on life was ending already. Maybe the vampire bug I'd caught from Dufresne hadn't taken? Well, at least I'd used my extra time wisely by spending it on a tour of the city morgue. It'd be familiar ground when they wheeled me back in.

A pair of battered shoes stepped into my line of sight. "Damn, buddy, you look half-dead already." A pause. "Guess you won't be needing this anymore." He slipped the wallet from my back pocket.

I was as surprised as the other guy when my hand shot

out and snagged the thief's wrist. His skin burned fever hot against my palm.

"Ow! Damn, not so tight, man. Here, take it back. No hard feel—what the *fuck*?"

Hand over hand, I hauled on his arm to drag him down to my level. His tug against my grip became a frenzied struggle once he caught sight of my open mouth.

My gums throbbed around the base of my fangs, matching the tempo of the would-be thief's hammering pulse. To my eyes, his neck was a road map. Every vein, every artery, every capillary visible through skin clear as cellophane. My attention fixed on the thick, pulsing vessel running from jaw to collarbone.

His flesh, when I bit down, offered no resistance. His blood, when it splashed across my tongue, was fire itself. As it flowed into me, it burned away the torment of hunger.

I drank.

———

WHEN I CAME to my senses, the thief, the man I'd fed on, was dead at my feet. Blue tinged his narrow lips, and his hollow cheeks were pallid.

Clammy fingers of guilt slithered through me to clutch at my heart. This poor sonofabitch had only been after a couple bucks, and as strong as I was now, I could have just taken my wallet back. Instead, I'd *killed* him for it. This guilt, this remorse—I'd felt nothing like it since that first beach in '41.

Warring with the guilt was the fact that I felt *amazing*. It was as if I'd had a meal of the best steak, the finest whiskey, and a roll in the hay with a knockout. I hadn't felt revved up like this since my teen years, and maybe not even then.

All I'd had to do to feel this good was kill a guy whose only crime, so far as I knew, was to lift my wallet.

My hands were trembling like leaves as I lifted the body of the man, my victim, up into my arms. I set him by the door I'd used to exit the morgue, uselessly trying to make the corpse comfortable where it leaned against the concrete wall. With a mumbled apology, I got the fuck out of there.

A block later, I stumbled to a halt as I caught my reflection. A watch repair shop's window, dark at this hour, gave me my first look at my new appearance.

The man staring back at me was almost a stranger. The last twenty years and change were gone, erased from my face. Gone as well were the jowls and the heavy frown lines. Even the tiny shrapnel scar I'd received on Okinawa had been erased. I'd lost weight too, but I'd figured that part out when my trousers had hit the floor earlier.

I'd expected my skin to be deathly pale, like the corpse that I was. Instead, it was healthy, flush with stolen blood.

Movement in the reflection sent me spinning to face whoever was creeping up on me. As far as I could see in each direction, the street was empty. I was the only one here.

Turning back to the glass, intent on examining my youthful face, I jumped back. A shadowed form stood by my side. I looked around again, but the figure existed only in the reflection. As I watched, its face emerged from shadow.

It was the thief, the man I'd killed minutes earlier.

He didn't move, or speak. His expression was as blank as it had been when I'd left him at the morgue. He just... stood there, gazing at me with dead eyes. I turned my head, hoping he would just go away, but when I returned to my reflection, he was there, watching me.

Another shade emerged from the shadows behind my reflection. Then another.

Dufresne stared at me, and at his side was the man I'd killed for Burke. Next were the Greenbaums, Gus and Bess. Monty and his date. I tore my eyes from the glass as the reflection began to fill with Japanese soldiers.

I'd go find my Cadillac. Find somewhere I could safely spend the daylight hours.

Then I'd figure all of this out.

Then I'd figure out how to keep from adding anyone else to my reflection.

Chapter Thirty-Six
Now

WHEN I CAME TO, I WAS IN DARKNESS. WHEN I TURNED my head, black plastic crackled against my nose. *Here we go again!* The next chump I saw would get a face full of vampire claws. Just to be sure, I did a little inventory of my current state of being.

Being staked and sun-blasted to the edge of actual for-real death had drained me to where I couldn't put up much of a fight. What little blood I'd gotten when Rebecca had bled that poor college sap hadn't helped me much at all.

Now, though, I felt... fine? It seemed like my fingers and toes were all still with me. As I thought about it, I realized I felt more normal than I'd expected. Not a hundred percent, but a lot closer than I should have been after healing up from my stake-and-bake excursion. Especially given how little I'd been able to take from Xenia without endangering her life.

The only explanation was something she'd mentioned earlier: that magicians were highly prized for their blood by vampires. Something about the quality of their blood. Now I understood why. In my normal liquid meals, the blood was a fire in my belly. Xenia's, by comparison, had been a thunderbolt.

Pressing against the plastic, I searched for a release or a zipper. There had to be one somewhere.

Bruce's voice, taut with worry, came from nearby. "He's awake. Eddy, it's us. No cause for alarm."

"Care to lend a hand?" Whatever they'd stuck me in, they'd wrapped it tighter than a burrito.

The crinkle of plastic was my only warning before my cocoon was yanked away and I tumbled across a dusty coverlet.

"Blackout tarps from the gardening center," Bruce offered as he rolled up the stiff plastic. "It was the only thing I could find that was completely opaque."

I'd come to rest on one of a pair of queen beds, in what looked to me like a midrange motel room. Xenia occupied the other bed, propped up on a nest of pillows. An IV drip ran from her arm to a hanging bag of saline. The crumpled carcasses of fallen snack foods covered her bed. Pork rinds, Devil Dogs, and two pints of ice cream had all fallen prey to the magician's appetite.

The slaughter didn't end there. As I watched, Xenia skinned back the wrapper of a triple-decker bacon burger. A bag overflowing with fries, paper smeared with ketchup, waited by her leg.

"Welcome back," Xenia said around a mouthful of burger. Her hand, when she shot me a thumbs-up, sported a gauze wrap over the spot where she'd cut herself to save me.

"Thanks." Sliding to the edge of the bed, I winced at the nasty squelching sound emerging from my still-moist trousers. "How the *hell* did you two manage to find me?"

"Oh, no big deal, really." Xenia's airy tone was offset by the smear of burger grease on her chin. She raised her arm and shook her wrist to rattle my former Rolex. "Tracking magic. Better than GPS."

"Ah. Well, if it's that good, why'd you wait until *after* sunrise?" I waved off her outraged comeback. "Then there's the little matter of you breaching our agreement."

"Excuse me?" Xenia, eyes ringed in dark bruises, goggled at me.

"As I recall, feeding me was specifically exempted from your consulting services." I let the phony businessman act drop. "You really didn't have to go that far, X. I might have—"

"Oh, shut the fuck up. None of this works without you. Besides, I owed you one for saving me from the big, bad shark-man." She winked at Bruce and got a chuckle in return. "Anyhow, you stopped yourself when I was in full-on fang fever. Guess I put my trust in the right bloodsucking fiend."

"Strictly speaking, you rescued *me* from the big, bad—"

"If the both of you are finished..." Bruce couldn't keep the smile from his face as he mock-glared at Xenia.

Something else tickled my brain then. "Since Marcus was present for my interrogation, I'm going to guess you folks weren't able to track him down."

"Nope." She dredged a mitt full of fries in ketchup and wedged the lot into her mouth. "Operation Weasel was a complete bust. We need another plan."

"To be fair," Bruce added, "it was a narrow chance to start with."

"Shit." Maybe we could sneak into the Fortune, hot-wire my window shutters and fry Rebecca's ass come noon. I should have thought of that earlier.

Xenia's nose wrinkled. Looking me over head-to-toe, she said, "Might I recommend the shower? You are *really* ripe, my dude."

Behind her, Bruce nodded in agreement. Nodded with a great deal of enthusiasm, actually.

"Fine." When I hopped to my feet, a rain of gritty sludge pattered to the floor around my feet. They might have a point. "Anyone get me a change of clothes during my siesta?"

Bruce pointed out a bundle folded on the side table.

A thought struck me, and I paused halfway into the bathroom. "Hey, either of you know what happened to Kurt? Mid-fifties, about six foot, gray crew cut, cheap suit? Last time I saw him, he was about to chop my head off with a shovel."

"Don't ask me," Xenia said. "I was loopy from blood loss."

Bruce found something on the ceiling incredibly fascinating, and his face flushed bright red. "I don't think he'll be a bother to anyone, now," he mumbled.

Offering Bruce a little salute, I vanished into the bathroom for my much-needed shower.

Once I'd closed the door between myself and the other two, I leaned against the sink. The laminate of the counter cracked in my grip as I lost my battle with the shakes. I'd been holding them at bay since awakening, and now they took over. The memory of the last twelve hours laid into me like Jersey Joe.

———

WHEN I EMERGED—DE-GOOPED and back in control of my nerves—I'd donned the off-the-rack but acceptable suit they'd found for me. Xenia and Bruce were knocking heads over something.

"No way, Bruce. I'm going." Xenia batted Bruce's hands away as she tried to pull the IV from her arm.

"Miss Xenia, please. It can take weeks before your blood count is normal again. Especially after losing so much." Bruce was trying to keep her in the bed, prevent her from removing the needle, and keep the IV stand from toppling—and failing at all three tasks.

"Go where?" I asked as I knotted my tie by feel.

The smell of Xenia's blood nudged my nostrils as she finally slipped the needle from her arm. Hand clapped over the tiny wound, she stared through the muss of her hair at the shark-man.

Throwing up his hands, Bruce retrieved a roll of tape and a gauze pad from the kit on the table and set about wrapping her up. "Michael called," he said to me as he worked. "Rebecca has announced that all prominent Clandestine families in Las Vegas are to swear fealty to her tonight. Right now, in fact." Tears gleamed in his eyes when he looked up. "Michael and his friends are on their way right now to stop her before she can claim the city. He's going to get himself killed."

I'd wondered where Bruce's partner had gotten off to. "Shit. Where are they?" I held a hand up. "Wait. Don't tell me. She's holding her shindig at the Golden Fortune."

Bruce nodded.

Xenia slid to the edge of the bed, waving off Bruce's helpful hand. Her skin had lost the deathly pallor from this morning, but she was still much paler than she'd been when I'd first met her.

"Hey now, partner. Are you even able to"—I made a throwing motion—"you know, cast spells in your condition?"

Xenia's glare was undercut as her legs gave way the instant she tried to stand. Eyes clenched shut, she pressed both hands to her forehead. "Fuck," she whispered. "Someone hand me my pack, please."

From the depths of her backpack, she produced a brightly wrapped bar of trail mix. When I peeked with my second sight, the bar's glow was brighter than a freshly cracked glow-stick. Seeing my look, Xenia waggled her prize. "Power bar." Unwrapped, it was a compressed mass of granola, nuts, and chocolate chips, all gleaming with magical potential. "This'll keep me going full tilt." She added the wrapper to the pile on the bed. "At least for a few hours. Then, assuming we survive, I'm gonna sleep for a week."

She downed the power bar in three bites; the effect was immediate. Arms running with goose bumps, her pale skin flushing with color. The dark circles around her eyes faded, and she hopped off the bed. The tired slog of her heartbeat picked up, becoming a tap dance that threatened to leap right out of her chest and dance around the room. "Holy *crap*. This shit might be addictive."

Snatching up her jacket and swinging it on in one movement, Xenia nearly ran Bruce down on her way to the door. "Let's get a move on, guys!" Pausing with her hand on the knob, the metal rattling in her grip, she turned back to the room. "Think you'll be able to face them this time?" she asked Bruce, her voice gentle.

"After our adventure in the desert, I believe so. I won't let Michael down again."

Xenia caught the older man up in a tight embrace. After a moment, he returned the hug. When they were done, Xenia glanced my way.

"Hey, I'm good," I said, holding up my hands. "We gonna kick ass now or what?"

Rolling her eyes, Xenia crossed to me, hand extended. "Ready to go, boss?"

When I took her hand, her grip was feverishly hot. "Damn straight, partner."

Her eyes lit up, and she yanked me in, her arms going around me. "I'm a hugger. Deal with it. Partner."

I patted her back with a sigh. It was going to be a long night.

Chapter Thirty-Seven

THERE WAS BARELY ENOUGH TIME ON THE DRIVE OVER for the condition of my Eldorado to sink in. I decided I could worry about what Xenia had done to my car, all that stripped paint and chipped glass, later.

If there was a later.

Michael had called again, from the lobby of the Golden Fortune, to tell us that Rebecca's little ceremony had begun. The supernaturally inclined residents of Las Vegas were arriving in droves.

I wasn't sure what he'd meant when he said she would "claim fealty" from them, but the twist in my gut told me it wouldn't be anything nice. If the way vampires ran things was anything similar to how the Outfit used to do it, it would be an offer no one would be allowed to refuse.

Before he'd rung off, Michael had told us he'd be waiting with the others in the lower level of the Fortune's parking garage, by the employee entrance.

"Not everyone can pass as human," Bruce was explaining as I wound us down the garage's concrete spiral, "so they borrowed one of those minibuses with the tinted windows for the drive over."

"They took a *party bus*?" Xenia shrieked. "Shit, we should have gotten one too!" For the entire duration of the drive from the motel to the Fortune, Xenia hadn't stopped moving, or speaking, once. Bouncing from one side of the Caddy's back seat to the other, I'd almost put the top back up out of concern she would vibrate right out of the car. "Boss! Boss! Eddy! Next time we do this—party bus!"

"Saved by the bell," I muttered as the bus in question swung into view ahead. Michael waved with enthusiasm when he spotted us.

Michael was decked out in a three-piece tweed suit, complete with bow tie. A golden watch chain looped from pocket to pocket across his vest. He held his walking stick in one hand and with the other tapped a bowler hat into place on his head to complete the ensemble.

"Damn, Eddy, Michael's a bigger fashion plate than you are." Xenia shouted as she stood in the back seat of the convertible, waving one arm overhead. "Hey, Michael!"

Not bothering to park the land boat, I pulled to a stop behind the bus. It was *my* damn casino, after all.

Michael slapped the side of the bus, and the doors folded open. Springs groaning, the party bus/troop transport disgorged as motley a crew as I'd ever seen. A baker's dozen of men, women, and nondeterminate types milled about, eventually forming a rough circle around Xenia, Bruce, and me. There were a ton of spines, jagged teeth, scales, and other things in view. Three of Michael's crew took this trend to the extreme, landing them very much in the non–human-passing club.

Bruce and Michael shared an embrace and a lengthy kiss. I gave them a minute. There might not be another chance for them after this.

Michael then swung into introductions. "Everyone here knows who you are, Eddy. You know Bruce, of course. Most of these fine people, however, would prefer to remain as anonymous as possible, for obvious reasons. Karl and Skårgund, though, don't mind you knowing their names."

Two members of the ragtag bunch nodded. One was six feet of scaled, bone-blade–studded muscle. The other, four feet nothing and the shortest of the crew, was a rotund mass of green skin sporting ears so long and pointy they touched above the dome of the bald head. I had no idea which name belonged to which one.

"Eddy, this is everyone I could find who was willing to put themselves at risk for the cause." Michael's expression sobered. "Not everyone in the community is a fighter, after all."

One of the women, whose only visible signs of being nonhuman were the leaves twined in her hair, raised a hand. Nodding at the man beside her, she said, "Bobby said you were looking for folks who wanted to keep Vegas the way it was." She glanced at her companion, who shrugged. "He said he would've come along for the ride, but he didn't think he was welcome."

Xenia muttered something I pretended not to hear.

I realized that every eye in the group was now aimed my way. Was I supposed to say something?

"Hey," I started, then shook my head. What could I say? I wasn't any better than Rebecca in their eyes.

Xenia dug her elbow into my ribs.

"Right. Like the man in the hat said, you all know me. At least by reputation."

That got some nods, and a muttered "Vegas vampire."

"I don't know a lick about any of you, other than you're here. Maybe it's because you and yours were personally threatened by Weir or her crew. Maybe it's because you're tight with Michael, and he asked. Maybe you just like a good scrap." At that, the little green guy smiled, his lips peeling back all the way to his ears, exposing dozens of tiny needle teeth. "Doesn't matter. You're here. You showed up. Thank you.

"If you're wondering why I'm out here with you and not in there with the other vampires, well. This place"—I tapped my foot against the concrete of the garage—"is my home. Not just Las Vegas, the Golden Fortune. This is my *home*. I built her from the ground up. This Rebecca broad took her from me, and I want her back." I looked around at the group, making eye contact where I could. No one looked away, the brave fools. Not that I was inclined to try anything with that contact. The old eye whammy would only be a strike against me. "If you know of me, like Michael said, you know I've kept to myself. Not once did I pull the kind of shit this bitch is planning to get up to. Hell, until the other night, I had no clue any of you even existed."

There were some uneasy nods after that as Michael's crew looked back and forth among each other.

I was starting to feel like I was running for office. "I can't promise things will go back to how they were before she shook the boat. But ain't none of us here going to have anything at all if we don't kick Rebecca's ass right out of Vegas."

Well, I hadn't expected them to cheer and throw hats into the air, but it would have been better than the quiet glares I got.

Xenia leaned over, one hand shading her mouth, and stage-whispered, "Don't take it personally, Eddy."

I rolled my eyes. "Fine. Fuck it. Let's go kill this bitch."

Michael, who'd been leaning against Bruce, spun his walking stick around the fingers of one hand. "You heard the man. Game faces on, people." The blue of his irises expanded, the color deepening until it swallowed his eyes and they became opalescent orbs.

Growls reverberated from the walls of the garage as the crew prepared for battle. Joints cracked and flexed into new arrangements, claws and fangs sprouted, and several drew weapons that crackled with power. The leaf-haired woman's skin turned dark, taking on the texture of bark. Her companion's skin lightened as it took on the appearance of granite.

Beside me, in the space of a heartbeat, Bruce swelled into his shark-man self. Carefully lacing his webbed fingers, he cracked enormous knuckles.

Michael thrust the silver knob of his walking stick into the air. "Tallyho!" he shouted. Grasping one of Bruce's giant hands in his, he strode forward, dragging the titanic shark-man along with him. "I've always wanted to say that!" he added gleefully.

———

THE SERVICE CORRIDORS of the Golden Fortune were quiet, eerily so, devoid of the usual hustle and bustle vital to an operating resort. Even on a weeknight, these halls should be a hive of activity. It seemed that Rebecca was still concerned about keeping the "normal" staff out of the supernatural loop. At least it meant that I wouldn't have to whammy any of my staff who witnessed my crew as we made our way deeper into the Fortune's inner workings.

Before long, we caught up with the tail end of a line of folks who were, if anything, more varied than my crew. Not just in appearance, but in age. I'd been expecting it, but the number of scared kids clinging to equally terrified parents hit hard.

More delicately than I would have guessed, Shark-Bruce excused his way past the civilians clogging the narrow corridor as Xenia, yours truly, and the rest followed

354

in his wake. Judging by how many we had to squeeze by, Rebecca's demonstration in the Underground had scared the Clandestine community shitless enough for them to show up for this farce.

It wasn't long before it was clear where the line was leading us. To be honest, I wasn't surprised. There was only one venue the Golden Fortune boasted that would suit Rebecca's massive ego.

The Cirque Diabolique Theater.

The line of "supplicants" entered the theater through a side door used by the cast during performance. Around us rose the familiar half circle of theater seating with its signature gold-on-crimson embroidery.

The line we'd passed must have had two, maybe three hundred people waiting to be let into the theater. The number of folks already seated inside was three times that.

Everywhere I looked, their faces blazed with fearful, anxious expressions. Mothers cowered with their children, wrapping them in their arms, hoping to shield them from what was to come. The sound of weeping reached my ears from every direction.

The crowd in the front rows, however, was different. Heads bowed low, every arm raised in reverence and worship. In that crowd, every arm I could see bore a pair of tiny wounds.

The main stage of the Cirque Diabolique Theater had been configured to bring up the *Trono del Diavolo* set. This split the wooden stage floor down the middle, and each half retracted to allow the circular arena to rise on hydraulic rams. The arena was a stylized depiction of Hell itself, stage-dressed with actual rock and soil recovered from the Fortune's plot when we'd broken ground to build the theater.

The *Trono*, assembled out of stone hewn from a local

quarry, loomed upstage center. Perched upon the very edge of the stone seat was the want-to-be Queen of Las Vegas herself, Rebecca Weir.

Predictably, Rebecca was decked to the nines in a satiny number that wouldn't have looked out of place on Rita Hayworth. Matching velvet gloves clung to her arms, all the way to mid-bicep. The spotlight shot sparks from the diamonds at her ears, neckline, and both wrists.

The trio flanking the throne was mostly familiar. To her right loomed Felix and the weasel Marcus. On her left was a man I'd never seen before, but just as when I'd first laid eyes on Rebecca, I knew him for what he was.

Vampire.

This newest addition to Rebecca's entourage was a tall drink of water, with fiery hair slicked into tight waves above eyes so green they practically glowed under the spotlight's illumination. Like Rebecca, his wardrobe was entirely bespoke.

Despite myself, I beginning to feel seriously under-dressed in my department store finery.

Rebecca's mercenaries, Rutger and his team, had traded in their tactical gear for something a little more domesti-cated. Their identical black suits gave them the appearance of fancy waiters, albeit waiters with shoulder holsters and coiled plastic earpieces. Hanging at each of their collars was a curved metal plate, filigreed in gold. Like the waitstaff they resembled, Rutger and his men were ushering individ-uals and small groups across the narrow bridge that connected the stage with the audience.

The latest of these was a pair of young men who clung to each other in visible terror as they crossed the bridge. When they reached Rebecca's perch, Mr. Shotgun encour-aged them, with the help of his boot, to kneel before their conqueror.

Leaning close, Rebecca appeared to share a few quiet words with the pair, making extended eye contact with each in turn. I could feel her power even across the width of the theater. She wasn't content with a sworn oath from her new subjects. She was getting up in their heads.

Hesitation fading, both offered an arm to their new queen, who nipped delicately at each wrist. Again, there was that ripple of power. Feeding must do something to the compulsion, I realized. Extend it, make it permanent even. If this was something I could do as well, or if it was exclusive to her, I had no idea.

The two young men, fresh converts to Rebecca's cause, backed away from the throne, bowing and scraping as they went. When they turned to find seats in the front rows, the dreamy smiles plastered across their faces gave me the creeps.

Next up for the Weir treatment was a family of four, two adults and two children. The youngest, barely able to walk on her own, wailed in terror. Her mother, tears in her eyes, hoisted her up on one hip as she tried to calm the tyke.

I'd seen enough.

Pitching my voice in the hope it would carry across the cavernous theater, I called out, "Getting a little ahead of yourself, aren't we, Rebecca?" My voice boomed out as if I'd used the stage audio system, something else I hadn't realized I was capable of. I was more or less successful in keeping the surprise off my face.

Rebecca's head snapped up, and the ebon pits of her eyes met mine over the heads of the family kneeling before her. "Edward, I'm delighted that you decided to attend." Her voice matched mine in carrying power. "Do you intend to pledge yourself to me after all?" At a tiny shoo-shoo motion of her fingers, Rutger and his men hustled the waiting family away from the throne.

With Bruce on one side, Xenia on the other, and Michael and the rest at my back, we outnumbered Rebecca's entourage nearly three to one. "Not on your life." I led my people across the narrow bridge to the stage and, as my shoes crunched on the gritty soil, my team spread out into an arc behind me.

I really hoped they would be enough.

"I'm going to make you a one-time offer, Weir. You and the goon squad pack your shit and vamoose. Your Las Vegas days are over. You're gone, Rebecca. Leave town tonight. Don't come back. Ever."

Rebecca's lilting laugh drifted across the arena. "Big bad Edward Fry. If I don't take your offer, what then?" She leaned against the stone slab at her back. "Are you going to have me—what is that delightful expression—'rubbed out'?"

"You wouldn't be the first person, and I'm being generous with that word, that I've planted in the desert. Every single one of you"—I met the eyes of each of the men flanking her seat—"will get the same." I spread my arms. "Your choice."

Marcus, Felix, and the as-yet unnamed vampire all seemed less than impressed with my offer. Felix was his usual bored, mountainous self, while Marcus had actually started filing his goddamn nails. The mystery vampire hadn't twitched so much as a hair since we'd arrived. He might as well have been carved from marble for all the expression he showed. Rutger's team had the grace to look like they thought about it, for a second or two at least.

Switching her gaze for the first time to the people I'd arrived with, Rebecca tittered. "Oh, Edward. Do you truly believe this... *rabble* will make the slightest bit of difference?" She leaned her chin against her fingers, and one sculpted eyebrow rose a bare fraction of an inch. "Why, is that a *magician* you have by your side? What a lovely gift. I will *very* much enjoy drinking her."

Beside me, Xenia bristled. Literally. Her arms snapped into a fighting stance as her leathers went all heavy metal. Stage light gleamed from the rows of silver spikes as they erupted. The armored collar fastened itself around her neck, and Xenia tugged *Wind Razor* into place over her hand.

The hair on my neck prickled as the tension level of my crew spiked. Everyone was on edge, focused on Rebecca and her stooges, ready to throw down.

Behind *them*, the audience rows that had already been bound by blood and will stood in unison. Puppets on the same string.

Rebecca had made her choice.

I threw myself across the arena, charging straight for Rebecca, hoping that everyone in my crew would be on the same page. Thankfully, they were. All around me, the air filled with growls, shrieks, and roars as they sounded their war cries.

Realizing that shit was about to get bloody, panic broke out among the audience members who hadn't yet sworn to Rebecca.

I wasn't moving at my top speed since I didn't want to leave my people behind or my back open. As a unit, we crossed the transplanted soil of the arena.

We made it about halfway before Rebecca made her move. She lifted a single finger from the arm of the throne. "Felix." Boredom dripped from the word.

I slid to a halt as the giant stepped forward, placing himself between me and his mistress. His skin had gone gray, acquiring the texture of wind-burnt leather, and his shock of blond hair paled to a wintery white. Incandescent blue sparks gleamed in the depth of his empty eye sockets as his lips pulled back in a rictus around blackened, broken teeth.

I made it a single step closer before all the warmth Xenia's blood had lent me was bludgeoned from my body by a wall of arctic cold. Gasps and cries sounded from my back, telling me I wasn't the only one affected. I hoped that *one* of those folks had the juice to push through Felix's winter hoodoo. I would have turned my head to look, but I didn't have the energy to remain standing, much less take a gander.

Just like the last time I'd faced Felix and his ice cube schtick, a cold unlike any I'd felt since I was alive clawed at me. The unnatural winter sucked the strength from my bones, and I fought to stay on my feet. A fight I was losing.

Xenia stumbled into the corner of my vision, thick crystals of ice clogging the spikes of her jacket. She managed two more steps before pitching face-first into the dirt. Her fingers, where they scrabbled for purchase, were windburned as if she'd spent the day at the North Pole without gloves.

I thudded into the dirt at her side as I lost my own battle with Felix's cold front. I was just able to turn my head in time to see Michael and the rest topple around me.

We'd lost before we'd even gotten the first punch in.

Chapter Thirty-Eight

A CLAWED FOOT THUMPED INTO THE STAGE BY MY nose. Bruce, straining as if he were walking directly into the gale of a blizzard, clomped toward Felix's icy form. "Great whites," he said, the strain clear in his basso profundo, "*like* the cold." His eyes rolled back for protection as he closed with his foe.

"Bruce, hell yeah," I managed to wheeze. If he could take out the giant, we'd have our shot.

Blurred by the ice crusting my eyelashes, I could just make out Rebecca above me. The corner of her mouth curved with a cruel smile as she watched her pet monster step forward to meet the shark-man. Four rows of saw-edged teeth glinted into view as Bruce stretched his jaws wide.

If we were lucky, he'd just bite the bastard's head off. I hoped it wouldn't give him food poisoning.

Felix brought one massive ham of a fist up over his head. Just as Bruce's claws snagged in his shirt, Felix brought the fist down in a tremendous hammer blow. He struck the wide head directly between the eyes, and Bruce collapsed at the giant's feet, motionless.

"Shit." My voice was a bare squeak.

"*This* was your plan, Edward?" Every one of Rebecca's words dripped with contempt. "A fool's brigade, charging into valorous battle while hopelessly outmatched?" She clucked her tongue. "I didn't expect much from you, and yet somehow I am still disappointed."

"Eddy," Xenia groaned from beside me. Her voice was weak, nearly inaudible.

Barely able to heave my head over, I could see that her hands were entirely blue with the cold. Her nose wasn't far behind. Hypothermia and frostbite would set in soon.

"Ch-ch-challenge." She forced the words through the chattering of her jaw. "D-duel."

"What?" I couldn't shiver anymore, but then I also barely had enough juice in the tank to speak.

"Single com-mm-bat." Xenia's eyes fluttered shut. Only her heartbeat told me she clung to life. But she didn't have long.

What the hell. It's not like I had a better idea. "Rebecca!" I forced the word out, then had to pause, gather my strength. How did they do it in those swashbuckler movies? "I challenge you. To a duel." My voice was a hoarse whisper, so faint it was possible that Rebecca was the only one there who could hear me at all. "Single combat."

The wintry assault ended, gone as if someone had flipped a switch. I took a moment to enjoy the cold's absence before I attempted to stand.

Xenia had regained most of her normal color, the blue having vanished with the unnatural cold. Her fingertips, though, still looked iffy. Her eyes twitched under their lids, but she didn't wake.

"Felix? My pet, why have you not put an end to this annoyance?" Rebecca sounded peeved.

The freeze-dried giant turned his head. "A challenge has been issued, Mistress." His voice was ice calving from a glacier. "Master Harkness has bound me to uphold the law."

A single line appeared between Rebecca's perfect eyebrows. "You do not dictate the law to me, Felix." Her voice was as cold as Felix's attack had been. "I am master here. You shall do as I command."

Felix turned his massive form. A single step brought him close to Rebecca's stone perch. "I serve the Master of House Harkness. He has merely lent me to you. A gift from your Sire. To aid you in doing *his* bidding." The pits of his eyes met Rebecca's red-and-black gaze. "Do not test me." Frost scrawled across the stone arm of the chair, halting a hair's breadth from Rebecca's fingertip.

Their standoff bought me enough time to check on my people. From the looks of it, Bruce was down for the count, as was nearly everyone else. Michael and the leafy woman had managed to get themselves up and were checking the rest for signs of life. A groan from Xenia told me she was still hanging on.

"So be it." Rebecca's voice rose to fill the theater once more. "Edward Fry, I accept your challenge. Single combat." She rose from the stone chair. "Alexander, Marcus. Clear the floor."

Worry shoved the boredom from that weasel Marcus's face as he slunk behind the tall vampire—Alexander—to the edge of the arena. While Marcus looked longingly toward the exit, Alexander assumed a casual parade rest beside the bridge to the audience. Meeting my eyes, he allowed the corner of his mouth to quirk up ever so slightly. His nod told me that, should I somehow best Rebecca in this duel, his challenge would come next.

One problem at a time, Eddy.

Michael slung Bruce's thick arm across his shoulders and, showing more strength than his narrow body seemed capable of, helped the titanic form of his lover limp from the stage.

"You got this, boss," Xenia said as she pushed herself upright.

I wasn't convinced. "Yeah, sure."

Tossing me a casual salute, she helped Skårgund and Karl get the rest of my people off the stage. I turned to Felix.

"All right, Frosty, you're the ref. What's the play here? Do I get a sword or what?"

The twin sparks of sapphire in his leathery face turned to me. "You fight to the death. If you wished to fight with a sword, you should have held a sword in your hand when you issued your challenge. You may only use what was in your possession when you issued the challenge. None may offer aid now, until one or both of you fall." A gust of cold blew against my face. "Upon pain of destruction."

"Got it." I shot a pair of finger-guns at Felix. "Thanks, big guy," I said with more confidence than I felt.

Shaking his slab of a head, Felix tromped to the rough center of the stage. Eyes on me, he aimed his finger to a point at stage front. Turning to Rebecca, he indicated a spot just before the throne. Rolling her eyes, she took a single step into her assigned position.

"Ed-dy, Ed-dy, Ed-dy!" Xenia chanted from the cheap seats. Her cheer petered off as the audience failed to match her enthusiasm. "Jerks," she muttered, and crossed her arms.

Lack of enthusiasm or no, none of the poor bastards who'd been waiting to have their brains scrambled into obedience seemed willing to use this chance to make a break for it, perhaps due to a fear of being tracked down afterward. Or they really wanted to see me get my ass kicked.

With a shrug, I turned back to the challenge. I shot Felix a nod.

Felix returned it. He trudged from the center of the stage's earthen arena to stand beside Alexander. "Begin."

I braced myself for the inevitable attack, expecting that Rebecca would cross the space between us in the blink of an eye. Instead, only her laughter reached me across the width of the arena.

It was a quiet laugh, at first. Her voice, an otherwise lovely mezzo-soprano, tickled the back of my neck as she chuckled. As the volume grew, so did the cruelty of her tone. As her laughter reached the thunderous volume she'd used to project her voice across the theater, she spread her arms wide, palms outward, and her curved fingers each sprouted a wicked three-inch blade of bone.

Hey, two could play that game. Hands raised, I grew my own set of claws. As my fingertips split around the lengthening bone, I allowed my eyes to change into a match for Rebecca's own black-in-red gaze.

Still laughing, Rebecca's arms rose further still. Standing as she was on the edge of the throne's spotlight, her shadow was a sharp black void across the stone chair behind her. I couldn't hide my surprise as the straight lines of her shadow moved. In an instant, the edges of that darkness were roiling and snapping like a flag in a hurricane. As the ebon curtain swelled beyond its original limits, swallowing the throne and the stage behind it in darkness, Rebecca gave us all a little curtsey and stepped backward into her own shadow.

I danced away as the edge of Rebecca's weird shadowthing surged across the arena. Dodging the wrong way caused *my* shadow to fall across the writhing dark. Starless night swelled around me as Rebecca's shadow used mine as a conduit, blotting out all light and visibility.

Grit crunched beneath my shoe. I was still in the theater. Still on solid ground. But even my super vampire sight could not punch through this unnatural darkness.

At some point, I wasn't sure when, Rebecca had stopped laughing. *Shit, where was she?* Was this shadow bullshit muffling her steps, or was she just a better sneak than I was? I didn't hear any footsteps other than my own. I couldn't get a lock on the would-be vampire queen.

Pain striped the back of my shoulders as she raked me with her claws. I spun, the air hissing as I slashed at the space she'd passed through not even a second earlier, but she was gone.

A paper cut, no deeper than a hair's breadth, traced itself into the flesh of my cheek. I flinched but held my ground. She would expect me to dodge *into* her next strike.

After what I hoped was a random enough pause, I crouched. Not so much as a single grain of sand crunched beneath my shoe as I duck-walked six paces to my left, then four forward. I spun, lashing out with both hands, hoping to catch Rebecca off guard. The very tip of one claw brushed the flare of her dress.

"Too slow, Edward." Rebecca's frigid breath blew into my ear.

With an air-cracking *pop,* I dodged as far as I could across the stage. The edge of this shadow shit had to be somewhere. A second *pop* echoed mine, and four daggers lanced into my bicep, twisting before tearing free in a *crack* of displaced air.

I slapped my hand over the wound as my arm dangled at my side. The laceration twitched against my palm as the flesh began to close. I'd heal, but my reserves weren't as deep as Rebecca's would be. How many poor bastards had she drained to prepare for tonight? Too many by far.

A line of fire traced itself across the back of my hand. Another paper cut from Rebecca's claw.

She could *see* me, I realized. This shadow-stuff might be impenetrable to me, but it was *hers*. No doubt it was bright as day for her. I'd been dancing to her tune while she played me like a fiddle.

Or something like that.

A slash across both of my calves sent me tumbling. Rolling across the stage, I heard the *crunch* of her claws slamming repeatedly into the dirt as she came after me. Once my ankles worked again, I kicked myself upright, pretending to fumble the landing, my arms windmilling for balance. A non-heartbeat later, I thrust with all my strength into the space at my side.

The very tips of my claws snagged in the soft flesh of Rebecca's arm as she spun away. "A hit. My stars, Edward. It certainly took you long enough. Let's see if you're capable of another."

I had a hunch Rebecca was the sort who liked to play with her prey, to drag the pain out. But I didn't know how much longer I had before she tired of the game.

Not long, it turned out. Razors cut four lines across the back of my neck and I dodged away, moving at my top speed. The air, thick as molasses as it flowed around me, collapsed in my wake with a drawn-out *zzzzaaarp* as my reflexes accelerated to match.

I ran right where Rebecca had aimed me. My own speed drove both of her claw-hands deep into my gut. Bone blades slashed through my entrails as she tunneled for my heart. Gagging on the sensation, I fought to pull myself off of her claws.

Rebecca's face faded into visibility, inches from my own, as she peeled her darkness back just so I could watch her gloat. Her claws clicked against the inside of my ribs, and the tip of her nose brushed mine as she drew me closer into this obscenely intimate embrace. Her Kewpie doll lips pursed into a moue. "Disappointing, Edward. I had hoped you'd present more of a challenge." Her fangs flashed at the corners of her smile.

She tore her hands free of my guts, eviscerating me, and I retched. I tried to hold my middle together as I staggered backward, the bright scarlet of Xenia's blood blending with my own thin, grayish fluids as they splashed from my severed stomach into the dirt. I was losing the battle to keep my insides inside. As the blood gushed from my stomach, my ability to heal the damage went with it. My legs gave way, and I crashed to my hands and knees.

I suppose Rebecca felt that the game was over because the absolute darkness of her shadow whipped away. In seconds, it collapsed in upon itself, becoming her regular, spotlight-thrown shadow once more.

Gore-coated to the elbows, her pretty gloves ruined, Rebecca strutted around me. Raising a claw, she briefly held it before her face. Her nose wrinkled with disgust. I guess there was too much of *me* and not enough *magician* on her claws for her taste. Her arm snapped in an arc that sent blood spattering across the arena sand.

She raised her eyes to the audience, to the doomed Clandestine of Las Vegas, to my crew. To my new friends, Xenia and Bruce.

"So falls your champion. Your so-called Vegas Vampire." A brief titter escaped her lips. "Let this be the end of your recalcitrance, my children." She gazed up into the ranked seats rising above us. "You will, all of you, serve me or die." Her voice was a lash, and the crowd shrank in their seats from the force of it.

I'd stopped bleeding, mostly, but my guts were still half out of me. To be honest, getting staked through the heart had been more fun than this. I levered myself up on one elbow. Maybe I could try one last... Wait. What was Xenia doing with her eyes?

From her seat beside the de-sharked Bruce, Xenia was making faces. Eyes wide, she was bobbing her head at me. Seeing that she'd finally caught my attention, she rolled her eyes and waggled her eyebrows. Why mock me *now*? I rolled to the other elbow to see if Felix had anything to say. As I did, something in my coat pocket thumped against my arm.

I glanced over to make sure that Rebecca was still gloating, lording it over the crowd. Something about killing one in ten to make a point. I levered myself up until I was sitting on my heels.

Gradually, hoping nothing would rattle, I eased a hand into the pocket. My fingers brushed something with rounded edges, its surface cool and metallic to my touch.

I glanced to Felix, and his ice-pit eyes met mine. His habitually bored expression gave me nothing.

As Rebecca at last returned her attention to me, my hand closed around the prize in my pocket. "No more games, Edward." Her clawed hand rose at her side. "Time to add your head to my collection."

As Rebecca sped toward me, vampire-fast, I tore my hand from my pocket. My thumb slid across the surface of the metal-clad bottle I'd found, searching for the clasp I knew to be there. As Rebecca's claws drew close to my neck, the tiny door sprang open at last, propelled on a tide of something faster than vampire speed.

Daylight.

The spear of pure sunlight lanced outward from the

exposed glass of the bottle Xenia had slipped into my pocket, vaporizing the flesh of my thumb as it went.

A summer day's worth of light slammed into Rebecca's torso, punching into her and halting her in her tracks. Pale flesh boiled to vapor in an instant, the lance of daylight carving a track through skin and muscle. Exposed bone withered under the onslaught of the captured sunlight.

Damaged by the release of light and slick with my blood, my fingers nearly lost their grip on Xenia's bottle. Rebecca's emerald eye burst in its exposed socket as the beam of daylight skewed across her baby doll face before guttering out. Her shriek was a teakettle whistle from her exposed larynx as she toppled backward into the dirt of the stage.

The glass in its pewter cladding went dark, the magic spent. I dropped the bottle of daylight onto the stage beside me.

I half expected Rebecca to launch herself at me then, but she was hurt. Maybe even more than I was. I crawled across the dirt and stone of the arena floor until I reached her side.

Propping myself up on one arm, I could actually see the dirt floor through her ribs. The daylight had carved away everything from her right breast upward, leaving a trench of exposed skull in her once-beautiful face. Her remaining eye rolled in its socket as she tried to bat me away with her working arm.

She'd wanted my head? I was going to take hers, and it wouldn't be the first I'd taken.

"My name isn't Edward," I wheezed. "Ma named me Eddy. E. D. D. Y. She couldn't spell for shit, bless her heart, but that's the name she gave me."

My fangs carved matching grooves in my lower lip as I spoke. Arm raised, claws out, I was ready to strike her head from her shoulders when Rebecca coughed. Her blood, thin and brackish, spattered across my face.

Into my mouth.

She must have seen the look on my face. Her expression, already twisted with fear, grew horrified. "No," she gasped.

Without understanding why, unable to stop myself, I tore into the undamaged side of her neck. The flawless skin offered no resistance and her vampire blood—diseased and toxic to me, Xenia had said—spilled into my mouth.

I drank.

Rebecca's feet drummed against the packed earth of the stage as I inhaled her blood. Vileness coated my tongue. She tasted of corruption and sewage, but I gulped it down nonetheless. When her blood hit my ruined stomach, instead of poisoning me, instead of tearing away what little strength I had, it bloomed in an explosion of power that almost flung me across the theater. I hooked my arm around Rebecca's neck, drawing her tight against me as I continued to drink.

The flesh of my gut flared, the wound knitting itself shut in a flash. The fire in my stomach shot out tendrils, burning down every vein and artery into my limbs. Everywhere that fire went, strength followed. In seconds, I was whole again, my head clear of the fog that had followed the blood loss.

I drank more.

Sheep roamed grassy, windswept terrain. Low hills rolling toward a distant forest. Father was cross that I'd lost an ewe. A lordly man stood at the gates of a manor house, yelling at Father. Soldiers. The hold of a ship. Mass at Trinity church in Manhattan. Pain. Loss. More pain. A child, lost at birth. A beautiful man, his hand extended as his emerald eyes flashed in the night. Twin daggers in my neck. Drinking from a cut in the beautiful man's hand.

371

Agony from my gut, worse than the labor pains had been. Waking to darkness. Fighting through the dirt and wood and stone until my hands broke free into the night sky. *Hunger*. Drinking my fill from the willing and unwilling alike. Standing in witness as an elder scion of my Master claimed territory with blood and power. Decades flowing one after another until one year was the same as any other. New York thrust towers of glass and steel into the night. The glow of Las Vegas seen from the window of a private jet. A man, his face handsome enough despite the sneer twisting his lip.

His face.

My face.

I tore my fangs from Rebecca's neck. The unburnt half of her face had lost its youthful fullness. Now the skin was slack, translucent. Pushing myself to my feet, I watched as Rebecca's flesh slid from her bones. Time, ever ravenous, held at bay no longer.

When I turned to look, Felix was his usual icy crag of indifference. Beside him, Marcus, his eyes darting about for an escape, seemed ready to piss himself.

Alexander, the other vampire, had lost his veneer of cool. His eyes, once bored and arrogant, had something new lurking in their depths. Something he was clearly unused to feeling.

Fear.

Pitching my voice so that only his ears would catch it, I taunted him, "Whataya say, Alex? Still up for the next round?"

With a *crack* of displaced air, the vampire disappeared. Pussy.

Thanks to the memories I'd stolen from Rebecca, I knew what I had to do next. I made my way across the arena to the pool of blood where Rebecca had eviscerated me. *My* blood.

I used my fangs to drag a trench through the meat at the base of my thumb and, before it could seal itself shut, thrust my hand into the coagulating pool of my un-life's essence. I shoved my power into that blood-soaked dirt, that soil dug from the ground of Las Vegas. The earth of what had become, by life, by death, and by my own choice, my native soil. I used this power and blood to claim the city, my territory.

From Frenchman Mountain to Red Rock Canyon, from Arden to Grass Peaks, the valley was *mine*.

Distantly, I became aware of a point traveling south-bound on Koval Lane, speeding towards the airport. I felt Alexander stumble as his power was torn from him by my claim on the land he now trespassed on.

He was no threat to me now. I let him board his charter jet and depart for home. Wherever that was.

I clapped dust and blood-soaked dirt from my hands as I rose from my crouch.

From the sidelines, Felix rumbled, "Victor. Eddy Fry." His skin had regained its human guise. Watery, pale eyes met mine. "We'll be in touch, Eddy."

He clapped a massive hand on Marcus's shoulder, guiding the smaller man toward the backstage exit. His other hand beckoned to Rutger and his men. As the mercenary trio doubled-timed after the giant, I searched for my friends in the audience.

Michael had given Bruce his tweed coat, and the two of them leaned against each other, relief clear on their faces. Beside them was Xenia; her face was washed in exhaustion but *extremely* smug. Catching my eye, she tossed a thumbs-up in my direction and propped her booted feet on the railing in front of her.

Around her, my crew, who'd chosen for whatever reason to walk into battle with me, had finally stopped looking at me like I'd been tracked in on the bottom of a shoe. Only the short guy with the tall ears—I *think* that was Karl—looked disappointed about being denied a chance to get his licks in.

The rest of the theater's occupants, the Clandestine of Las Vegas, seemed to hold their breath. The poor bastards whom Rebecca had brain-scrambled before we'd arrived were free. I knew that the bond she'd forced on them had died with her. Dazed, they looked around as if they'd just woken from a bad dream. Which they had, more or less.

The others, every parent and child, the individuals, the friends and strangers who had all come here against their will, under threat of violence and death—all of those eyes were on me. Waiting for my next move. Dreading the words yet to come from my mouth. Fearing what came next, now that I'd claimed the city.

I scratched the side of my nose while I considered my options. It was more than six hours before dawn, not that it mattered. Las Vegas never sleeps.

"What are you all moping about for?" I asked them, speaking so all could hear. I hooked my thumb over my shoulder at where Rebecca's bones were crumbling into the dirt. "The bitch is dead. Las Vegas is safe. None of you owe me a thing." I turned, as if to exit via the rear of the stage, then paused for effect.

"Everything's on the house today. Food, drink, whatever. For everyone. Ice cream for the kiddos. Knock yourselves out. Y'all've been through enough. Head to the Underground if you can't eat up here. Put it on my tab. The management knows I'm good for it." I sauntered past the *Trono del Diavolo* into the darkness backstage.

Behind me, someone (I just *knew* it was Xenia) started

clapping. A ragged cheer went up. As the applause spread, I slipped past the row of performers' dressing rooms. Passing a wardrobe mirror, I chanced a look.

For once, it was my face alone that gazed back at me from the glass.

Epilogue
One Week Later

THE ELEVATOR DOORS DINGED OPEN TO REVEAL NOT THE hallway to my private office at the Fortune but a dimly lit and rather familiar lounge.

The same low table with its matching chairs lay before me as I stepped from my casino into the Underground, and waiting in one of those chairs was a familiar face.

"Mac," I said. "Had a feeling I'd been seeing you sometime soon." I thumbed the button of my coat loose and dropped into the chair opposite my new acquaintance.

Mac smiled. Today's wardrobe choice was a riot of color, I observed with only the slightest twinge of envy. The rich silk of his coat incorporated the emerald, scarlet, and topaz hues of the headdress I'd seen when he'd allowed me a glimpse behind the curtain.

My host raised one jewel-encrusted hand. "A drink?" Behind him, the same cocktail server as before hustled out from behind the bar.

"Why not?" How could I say no? My mouth watered in anticipation.

Tequila was poured. Cups were raised. We toasted each

other's health and absent friends. For the first time, I saw something other than amusement in Mac's eyes.

If my suspicions about Mac, where he'd come from, and who (or rather, *what*) he was were correct, then he'd lost a lot more than I ever had. I let him have a moment or two for his memories.

"You have allowed the Hidden Ones of Las Vegas to return to their lives, untouched by your power," he said at last.

I leaned back in the chair and gazed out into his establishment as a couple pushing a stroller containing an *exceptionally* hirsute infant passed the lounge. "Yeah, well, I never thought of myself as the kingly type." I sipped at the excellent tequila. If I wasn't careful, I'd get a taste for this stuff. "I just wanted the Fortune back, y'know? Get my home, live my life." I waved at the passing tourists. "I figure that's what they want, too. Why rock the boat?"

"No matter how one steadies their vessel, there will always be another wave," Mac said over the rim of his cup.

I laughed. "Ain't that the truth. Well, it won't be coming from me. Not if I can help it." I set my cup on the little tray. "Oh, before I forget, thanks for the assist."

"How could I turn away so many hungry mouths? Properly celebrating such an occasion is not done lightly, even here in this city of celebrations."

"Right. I meant the other thing," I said, leveling a finger at him.

"I'm sure I have no idea of what you speak." Merriment danced in Mac's eyes.

"Uh-huh. Took me a bit, but once Xenia and I compared notes, it was pretty clear that your 'cousin' saved my bacon out in the desert with that oh-so-conveniently-timed dust storm."

"If you insist," Mac said, pouring the last of the bottle.

"Well, I owe you one." I raised my cup in salute.

Mac inhaled sharply. "My friend, you should exercise caution when uttering those words to one such as myself." He leaned into his chair, the sudden tension leaving his shoulders. "One never knows where it could lead."

I shrugged. "I'll take my chances."

I declined his offer to open a second bottle, which seemed to please Mac in some personal way. There was a mountain of paperwork waiting for me back in my office, and I wanted to keep my head clear. The faster I got that crap out of the way, the faster I could get back to business as usual.

With tip of my imaginary hat to Mac, I made for the service door at the rear of the lounge. As I suspected, it landed me right back in my office. The jangle of the Underground Casino and Resort, Las Vegas, cut off with a click as the door shut behind me.

In front of me awaited another stack of paperwork from Michael.

Franklin, my former general manager, hadn't responded well to the roughshod way Rebecca had rewired his coconut. Her control over him, and everyone else in the Golden Fortune's staff she'd whammied, had been broken when I'd killed her. However, the false memories and impulses she'd implanted didn't leave him completely, and they'd conflicted with his *real* thoughts and memories. The resulting breakdown hadn't been pretty. His old lady had taken him home to St. Louis to be with family. We'd had some friction, Franklin and I, but I'd valued the work he'd put in for me and the Fortune over the last twenty years. He got the platinum retirement, courtesy of dear departed Great-Uncle Elwood. Full pension, extra medical coverage, the works. I hoped things would work out for him.

That had left me with a gaping hole in my organization,

which I promptly filled with Michael. After all, the fella had organized a resistance movement in less than forty-eight hours; I was sure he could handle a Vegas resort.

Sure, this had ruffled some feathers among those in the staff who thought *they'd* be up for the post. Since I was feeling generous (and more than a little guilty for what Rebecca had done to them), I smoothed over any hard feelings with raises all around.

I owned a casino in the most gamble-happy city in the world. I could afford it.

I'd offered Bruce a spot at the Fortune as well. After all, I needed a new head of security too. However, he'd been quite adamant that he was *not* the man for that particular job. He was nearing tenure in his position at UNLV in their Department of World Languages and Cultures, and that would be just fine for *him*, thank you very much.

Last I heard, he and Michael were planning to shack up together. Good for them.

With one last longing look at my office door, and the city of entertainment beyond, I dropped into the chair at my desk.

I had work to do.

———

Xenia dropped in while I was still up to my tits in paperwork. I'd carved my way through perhaps a third of the mountain that had been sitting in my in-box.

True to her word, she'd slept the better part of a week once the effects of her "power bar" had worn off. I'd let her kick around in the empty suite next to mine, the sheik owner having existed only on paper.

Even after a week of rest, the aftereffects of the blood donation followed by a flash freeze were still visible on her face. If those dark circles under her eyes didn't clear up, someone might mistake her for one of my kind.

I let her stew while I tackled the endless flood of paper that accompanied the ownership and operation of a casino resort hotel.

Multiple casino resort hotels now.

Before he'd fled in the waiting charter jet, a very cowed Marcus had begged for an "audience." I'd been concerned when Felix had tagged along until he'd revealed that his purpose was merely to assure that Marcus would comply with the "Law."

I was still learning about all that rigamarole, but apparently if you challenge, and subsequently defeat, another vampire in an official duel, you get their shit.

All their shit.

On the run-up to making herself queen, Rebecca had pulled strings all over the place. Since she'd been theoretically operating in her Master's name, that Harkness guy, this had resulted in her gaining majority ownership of every casino, resort, hotel, golf course, and convenience store in the greater Las Vegas area. Exactly as she'd bragged to me. And since apparently too much was never enough, this grab-bag of properties included miscellaneous other assets around the country, mostly luxury hotels, as well as casinos in Atlantic City and Macao.

Marcus had announced, with the paperwork to back it up, that these properties now belonged to me. Mine, free and clear. Lock, stock, and barrel.

One of the lingering "fuck-yous" Rebecca had left in her wake had been to file a Notice of Death on Great-Uncle Elwood. That whole identity was toast now. Lucky for me, she'd missed the contingency plan I had hidden in the reams of paperwork.

No-good Great-Nephew Eddy Fry had inherited the

Golden Fortune from his favorite great-uncle, much to the disgust of Leandro and a few others on the staff. The owner's shares, which Rutger had failed to find when he'd gone back to search my safe house, had somehow turned up in the trunk of my Eldorado. With those in hand, I was able to claim my "inheritance."

Fuck 'em if they don't like it.

"Feet off the desk," I said halfheartedly as Xenia propped her Docs against the mahogany.

She ignored my demand. "How's the royal life treating you, oh Vampire King of Vegas?"

I bounced a wad of paper off the shaved side of her head. Xenia made a show of batting it away long after it had rolled under the desk.

"This is way beyond the wildest bounds of any shit I wanted, you know that?" I cradled my head in my hands. "I don't get headaches anymore, but this shit is giving me a headache." Using my foot. I dragged over the office bar cart and pulled the stopper from the tallest of the decanters. Hovering the bottle over a second glass, I raised my eyebrow to Xenia, who shook her head. "More for me." I inhaled the rich vapor of the top-shelf scotch. "Anyhow, I'm getting rid of it all."

"Everything? All the casinos and shit?"

"All the casinos and shit. Except my baby." I patted the desk. "I'm keeping the Fortune, natch. There's no shortage of takers. Some Japanese conglomerate wants Fremont Street. Everything else is getting tossed into a holding company and buried under as many shells as I can manage. Some of these properties are smack-dab in the middle of other vampire estates, and the last thing I need right now is another turf war." I took a delicate sip from my glass. Might as well be water. Ah, well. "Besides, the thought of having to visit New Jersey is giving me hives."

That got a laugh from her.

"All right, maybe I'm keeping just one or two little things."

"Just a couple?"

"Nothing too extravagant." Beneath the desk, my shadow shivered, the edge rippling as if the carpet were stormy seas. "What's got you up this late?" I asked. With the threat neutralized, Xenia had gone back to a daylight schedule as part of her rest and recovery. It was pushing three in the morning at the moment, way past the magician's prescribed bedtime.

"It wasn't easy, but I found the guy."

"What guy?" I glanced up from yet another sheet of paper demanding my attention.

"The cab driver? You wanted to make things right after you forced him to haul your ass all over town." Her nose wrinkled. "Looking for me, as I recall. Anyhow, I gave him the envelope."

"Oh, right. Good job, partner." I'd stuffed an envelope with what I figured a Vegas cabbie made in a good year, along with a bunch of comps for the Fortune's eateries. It was a only a little thing, but it'd been nagging at me.

"Got Dolores back from the shop, too." Xenia leaned her head back on the padded leather chair. "She's as cherry as the day I borrowed her." She spun my keys around her finger and let fly, sending them on a jangling arc to my desk.

"Dolores?"

"Your '59 Eldorado? You never named her, and a grand old lady like that deserves a proper name." She peered at me over the metal-shod toes of her boots.

I leaned back, glass in hand. Rolled the name around in my head. "Dolores. I like it." I raised my glass. "To Dolores, whose spacious booty has saved my own ass on more than one occasion." At Xenia's look, I added, "Story for another time."

"Mm-hmm." Xenia's eyelids drifted low.

Smiling to myself, I slid another stack of forms across the blotter. I busied myself for a few minutes, initialing here, signing there. Eventually, I felt her eyes on me. I said, "You're leaving."

"Yeah."

I set the pen down. "You're gonna break Bruce's heart. Fella's gone over for you in a big way."

Xenia blinked as her eyes got a bit shiny. "He'll get over it. Besides, it's not forever." Her boots clunked against the carpet as she sat up. "It's just..." Her voice drifted off. "There's stuff I have to do. Someone... I have to see. It's time to get moving."

"Oh?" I fought to keep my tone light. "How do you know that?"

Leaning one palm flat on my desk, she winked. "Oh, a little bird told me," she said, adding, "The bastard," under her breath.

Someday, I'd have to get the story behind that and our little visitation in her motel off Fremont.

She hooked my keyring and dragged it across the desk. "I'm taking Dolores, if you don't mind."

"You don't say. Big ol' surprise, that." Stepping around the desk, I stuck my hand out. "Door's always open, X."

Flipping the lock of hair from her eye, Xenia gripped my hand. "I know."

I tugged on her hand, bringing her in close, and wrapped my arms around her. "I'm a hugger." The words caught in my throat. "Deal with it."

Afterword

Ack, where to start? Or rather, how to end?

A few years ago, I was in the process of clawing myself from one of the deepest pits I've ever been in. On the spur of the moment, I took a day trip to, where else, Las Vegas. Arrive on the earliest flight into town, leave on the last one out.

I'd just *devoured* a muffuletta at Magnolia's Veranda, in the Four Queens on Fremont, and I found myself wandering around the blocks outside of the "Experience" for the first time. In my previous visits, I'd stayed on Fremont because what's out there? Parking lots? Bah!

Lo and behold, I stumbled across The Mob Museum.

A funny thing about that museum. It's housed in the old Nevada Federal Court building and contains the courtroom where, on November 15, 1950, Senator Estes Kefauver landed in Las Vegas to drag suspected members of organized crime... organizations up in front of his Senate Committee. The Mob Museum has restored the courtroom to its 1950 appearance, and you can see the stand where Moe Sedway complained about his indigestion.

What can I say, inspiration struck.

I'd spent a lot of time in Sin City in the past, going so far as to spend a couple months motel-hopping while between jobs. I have a soft spot for the town, so it seemed the perfect playground for a gangster-turned-vampire.

I knew I wanted the story to take place in modern-day Las Vegas, but there was *so much* history that Eddy would have lived through long before he ever woke up dead. I got to reading up on my favorite sleazy town.

As I said above, Moe Sedway was a real individual. In fact, most of the named gangsters outside of Little Mickey's crew were real people, although I have taken some liberties with their personalities and actions. I hope their next of kin don't regard me too unkindly for those choices.

In fact, while Eddy's Las Vegas is clearly not *our* Las Vegas, its history is a near match for ours. The events Eddy participates in, or witnesses, in his human days all occurred in *our* history.

Yes, even that massive snowstorm in January 1949 actually happened. The Greenbaum murders are still unsolved, although Mr. Caifano is still considered the most likely suspect.

It took me nearly a decade to get all the ideas out of my head and bash them around until they made sense. I wish it hadn't taken that long, but frankly I needed the time to figure out what I was doing.

So, here we are.

If this wasn't enough for you, if you find yourself wanting more... good! Seriously though, if this was your jam and you want more please consider signing up for my email list at russellisler.com/newsletter. You'll get a free e-book, a deleted scene from *All In* which answers the question "How *did* Xenia find Eddy out in the desert?" You'll also find out when the next book is coming out, as well as other fun stuff.

Oh, the next book? Yes, there will be one!

Russell Isler - May 6, 2023

Acknowledgments

First of all, thank *you* for coming along with Eddy, Xenia, and myself on this adventure. They've been living rent-free in my head for (checks calendar, winces) many years now. For most of that time, they've been near-constantly clamoring for my attention. I hope you had as much fun reading their tale as I did writing it.

Thanks to Paul Wilson, my best friend lo these many years. He's stuck with me through some of the worst times of my life—for which I am eternally grateful—and I've *tried* to include him for the best times just to balance the scales. Thanks, dude.

Thanks to Duane Matthews, whose friendship has also been an invaluable boon. Never one to mince words, he's kept me honest, even when it wasn't necessarily warranted. Also, while Duane may not have served in the same branch or in the same conflict, he was a great help with advice on Eddy's likely mind-set and attitudes following his service in the Pacific.

Merci beaucoup to Antoine Petitgerard for his translation services, which lent M. Dufresne's dialogue a certain *je ne sais quoi.*

Nimitstlasojkamati to Polokotsin of r/Nahuatl for helping me find an appropriately rude word in one of Mac's native tongues.

Thanks to Jessica O'Toole for her analysis of the manuscript. Set me straight on a few sticky points, she did!

Thanks to Astrud Aguirre for giving me her feedback

on an early draft. Hearing your thoughts on the good and bad combined with your passion for the book recharged my writing batteries when I needed it.

Thanks to Renate Rowland for being an early reader. Your enthusiastic feedback as an avid reader of vampire fiction was invaluable in helping me make this the best book it could be.

Thank you to my editor, Kelly Cozy of Bookside Manner, for catching all the little things that slipped through my typing fingers.

Thanks to my cover designer at Damonza.com, who blew me out of the water with their work!

Thanks to both The Mob Museum: National Museum of Organized Crime & Law Enforcement and to the blog VintageLasVegas.com for giving me a look at the Good/Bad Old Days with an unflinching eye.

And, of course, thank you to Mom and Dad for putting up with my BS lo these many years.

If you enjoyed this book, please consider leaving an honest review on your favorite store. I would be ever so grateful!

Thank You!

CPSIA information can be obtained
at www.ICGtesting.com
Printed in the USA
LVHW040820300623
750655LV00008B/11